Romantic Suspense

Danger. Passion. Drama.

Colton's Deadly Trap
Patricia Sargeant

The Twin's Bodyguard
Veronica Forand

MILLS & BOON

Patricia Sargent is acknowledged as the author of this work
COLTON'S DEADLY TRAP
© 2025 by Harlequin Enterprises ULC
Philippine Copyright 2025
Australian Copyright 2025
New Zealand Copyright 2025

First Published 2025
First Australian Paperback Edition 2025
ISBN 978 1 038 94056 8

THE TWIN'S BODYGUARD
© 2025 by Deborah Evens
Philippine Copyright 2025
Australian Copyright 2025
New Zealand Copyright 2025

First Published 2025
First Australian Paperback Edition 2025
ISBN 978 1 038 94056 8

This is a work of fiction. Names, characters, places, and incidents are either the
product of the author's imagination or are used fictitiously, and any resemblance to
actual persons, living or dead, business establishments, events, or locales is entirely
coincidental.

MIX
Paper | Supporting
responsible forestry
FSC® C001695

Published by
Harlequin Mills & Boon
An imprint of Harlequin Enterprises (Australia) Pty Limited
(ABN 47 001 180 918), a subsidiary of HarperCollins
Publishers Australia Pty Limited
(ABN 36 009 913 517)
Level 19, 201 Elizabeth Street
SYDNEY NSW 2000 AUSTRALIA

Cover art used by arrangement with Harlequin Books S.A.. All rights reserved.

Printed and bound in Australia by McPherson's Printing Group

Colton's Deadly Trap
Patricia Sargent

MILLS & BOON

Nationally bestselling author **Patricia Sargeant** was drawn to write romance because she believes love is the greatest motivation. Her romantic suspense novels put ordinary people in extraordinary situations to have them find the "hero inside." Her work has been reviewed in national publications such as *Publishers Weekly*, *USA TODAY*, *Kirkus Reviews*, *Suspense Magazine*, *Mystery Scene Magazine*, *Library Journal* and *RT Book Reviews*. For more information about Patricia and her work, visit patriciasargeant.com.

Books by Patricia Sargeant

Harlequin Romantic Suspense

The Coltons of Arizona

Colton's Deadly Trap

The Touré Security Group

Down to the Wire
Her Private Security Detail
Second-Chance Bodyguard

Visit the Author Profile page at millsandboon.com.au.

Dear Reader,

I'm so glad you've joined me for the second book in The Coltons of Arizona series. This is Max and Alexis's romance.

One of the many reasons I love reading and writing romantic suspense is that the stories bring together two powerful emotions, love and fear. When you combine these emotions, you realize that by holding on to one—love—you can conquer the other—fear. Love gives you the courage to face any fear. It's like the saying goes, "Love conquers all."

I especially enjoy putting ordinary characters in extraordinary situations and forcing them to discover whether they're up for the challenge. Max and Alexis don't have law enforcement or military experience. When faced with danger, all they have to fall back on are their wits and each other.

Will that be enough to survive the danger ahead of them? Read on to find out.

I hope you enjoy Max and Alexis's story, and the rest of The Coltons of Arizona series.

Warm regards,

Patricia Sargeant

To My Dream Team:

My sister, Bernadette, for giving me the dream.

My husband, Michael, for supporting the dream.

My brother Richard for believing in the dream.

My brother Gideon for encouraging the dream.

And to Mom and Dad, always with love.

Chapter One

"Excuse me. I'm sorry." Maxwell Powell III stepped back from Mariposa Resort & Spa's reservations desk late Friday afternoon. He pulled his ringing cell phone from the front right pocket of his pale gray Dockers and held it aloft. "This might be my family."

The young clerk on the other side of the counter wore a name tag that read Clarissa. She inclined her head with a smile.

Max took another step back as he looked at his screen. The caller wasn't a relative. "Sarah? Is something wrong?"

Sarah Harris was his administrative assistant for *Cooking for Friends*, his streaming channel show. She was the first person he'd ever hired who wasn't connected to one of his two restaurants. Why was she calling him? He'd told her—and his agent—that he would be on vacation for six weeks. In fact, this trip had been his agent's idea after his New York apartment had been broken into the second time.

"Max, I'm so glad I caught you." Sarah's voice was breathy with relief. "I know you're leaving for vacation today."

"I'm checking into the resort now." He glanced back at Clarissa. She was welcoming another guest. He was relieved the clerk wasn't waiting for him but still uncomfortable with the personal call. Max turned his back to the reservations desk and stepped farther away. "Is there something I can help you with?"

"No, nothing's wrong. Well, actually something's wrong. I'm calling to let you know I'm in Arizona. I'm staying with relatives in Sedona for a while."

Sedona? Surprise rooted Max in place. Sarah was here? "I hadn't realized you had family in Arizona."

He didn't want to tell Sarah that, coincidentally, he also was in Sedona. One of his motivations for coming to the resort was to get away from everything and everyone who could distract him from creating the new recipes for his cookbook. Sorry, family. The other reason was to catch up with his college buddy Adam Colton, whom he hadn't seen in person for years. Adam co-owned Mariposa with two of his younger siblings, Laura and Joshua.

"You didn't know about my relatives here because I haven't told many people. But I'm comfortable telling you." Sarah's soft laugh carried across their connection, which wasn't as far as he'd hoped. "I needed to get away from New York for a while. Luckily, my relatives invited me to stay with them. I wanted you to know where I am in case you needed my help for anything like your book or your show. Whatever."

"Thank you for telling me." Max was already shifting his thoughts back to checking into his bungalow, assuring his family he'd arrived safely and taking a nap, although not necessarily in that order. "I'd better—"

"I'm getting a divorce." Sarah's announcement was stark and startling.

"I'm so sorry, Sarah." In a dark, dusty corner of his mind, Max remembered Sarah had told him she and her husband had been childhood sweethearts.

Sarah's sigh was nervous and unsettled. "Thank you, Max. I really need the time away to deal with…all of it. I guess I should have seen it coming. Steve's very jealous of you."

He stiffened. "Of me? Why?"

"He's convinced we're having an affair." Sarah's giggle seemed inappropriate.

"What?" Max glanced around as he lowered his voice. "Why would he think that?"

He had never, nor would he ever, pursue a woman who was

in a relationship. That went double for married women. He had too much respect for the institution of marriage. He hoped to join it one day soon.

"Because of all those late nights we worked together at the studio." She sighed. "He *really* lost it when you bought me that bracelet."

"Did you tell him I'd bought bracelets as Christmas presents for *all* the women on the show?" He'd bought tie pins for his male employees. His younger sister, Melanie, designed jewelry. The gifts were a way to support her craft without seeming like he was humoring her and show appreciation for his team. They worked hard, put in long hours and did great work without ever complaining.

Max heard traffic noises on Sarah's end of the line, passing cars, squealing brakes and screaming horns. He imagined his young, redheaded assistant behind the wheel of a rental car. He hoped she was paying attention to the traffic.

Sarah made a rude noise. "He should've known better. He should've trusted me. Instead, he accused me of being unfaithful and threatened me with divorce. I called his bluff and told him *I'd* file for it myself."

Translation: no, Sarah hadn't told her husband there was nothing personal between them. Now somewhere out there was a very jealous man who was convinced Max had been sleeping with this wife. Max rubbed the frown lines forming between his eyebrows. Terrific.

"Sarah, I agree your husband should've trusted you, but I wish you'd told him the truth."

Sarah grunted. "If he could think so little of me, he doesn't deserve the truth."

Jeez.

He didn't like the idea of people believing he was the kind of person who'd sleep with a married woman. However, it wouldn't be wise to set the record straight with Steve himself. In fact, that would be stupid.

Just let it go.

Max closed his eyes, battling fatigue and exasperation. "Sarah—"

She interrupted. "Now I just need some time away to deal with the fact that my marriage is over. Steve and I were only married for seven years but we'd been together since I was fifteen. I'm about to be single for the first time in seventeen years."

Max was torn. On the one hand, he didn't want to tell Sarah he was in Sedona. He'd looked forward to taking a break from the show and everything related to it so he could focus on his book. On the other hand, she sounded like she needed someone to talk with.

He unclenched his teeth. "Sarah, I'm in Sedona also—"

"Really?" Her voice rose several octaves. "Where in Sedona?"

"I'm pretty tired right now. After I get some rest, I'll call you and we can set a date to catch up. I've got to go. I'll call you."

"I'd really like that, Max." Her sigh sounded like gratitude. "Thank you."

Max ended the call—and immediately started second-guessing himself. He and Sarah weren't friends. They were colleagues. She worked for him. He shouldn't blur the lines between their personal and professional relationships, especially since her husband suspected they already had. But it sounded like she needed support. He couldn't turn his back on her. With a mental shrug, Max returned his cell to his front pants pocket. He'd done the right thing.

Returning to the reservation desk, Max gave Clarissa an apologetic look. "I'm sorry. It was a colleague."

Clarissa gave him a bright smile. "No explanations necessary, Mr. Powell. It won't take long to get you checked in."

She was right. Within minutes, Clarissa was handing him the keys to his bungalow and a map of the property.

"And, finally, Mr. Powell, there's a package for you." Clarissa handed Max a square box roughly the size of a personal double-layer birthday cake.

"I wasn't expecting anything." He automatically accepted the parcel. It was as light as a dinner plate. A wide, plain white label listed his name, sent in care of Mariposa Resort & Spa with its physical address. There was no return address or post-mark. "Do you know who sent it?"

Max's mind was still mushy from the morning's eight-hour flight from New York City's LaGuardia Airport to Flagstaff Pulliam Airport with a layover in Dallas. Pulliam was the nearest airport to the resort. And then there was the helicopter trip that carried him to Mariposa. The two-hour time difference wasn't helping, either.

"I'm afraid I don't know the sender's identity." Clarissa's bright smile faded. A puzzled frown marred her smooth white brow. "The Mailroom staff received it and asked Reservations to give it to you when you arrived."

"Thank you." Max turned the box over to examine it from all sides.

It was wrapped in nondescript brown paper and secured with large pieces of transparent tape. But who was the sender? His family, his parents and two sisters, were the only people who knew where he was. Had one—or perhaps all—of them sent him a surprise for his vacation? Why wouldn't they have included their return address? Unless that was part of the surprise. What was the surprise for? It wasn't his birthday, and they'd already celebrated his book contract and wrapping the first season of his show. He was impatient to see what was in the box.

"Of course, Mr. Powell." Clarissa's smile returned, sweeping the frown from her round features. "I'll ask Aaron to help you with your suitcases."

He set the package on the counter and stifled a yawn behind his fist. Those sleepless nights were catching up with him, too. The stress of waiting to learn whether his show would have a second season, pitching his first-ever cookbook and having his home broken into multiple times had given him temporary insomnia. Max was looking forward to hiding in the resort's kitchen and experimenting with new recipes.

"The two-hour time difference can hit you hard." The rich, warm female voice flowed over Max like the soft, warm waters of a healing spa. He caught the faint scent of wildflowers before he turned to the speaker.

Max was face-to-face with one of the most beautiful women he'd ever seen. His heart stopped. His breath caught. Time stood still. Everything around them—sounds, sights and smells—faded into the background. She was the only thing he was conscious of.

Long-lidded hazel brown eyes sparkled up at him from a warm brown diamond-shaped face. She'd swept thick raven tresses into a bun at the nape of her neck, emphasizing her high cheekbones. Full, heart-shaped lips curved and parted to display perfect white teeth. Two-inch nude pumps boosted her average height to his chin. Her dark bronze blazer dress silhouetted her trim, athletic build and highlighted the gold undertones of her skin.

Suddenly wide awake, Max smiled in anticipation of a light flirtation with an attractive woman. And then he saw her name tag: Alexis Reed, Senior Concierge. The lovely lady wasn't flirting; she was welcoming him to the resort. And he recognized her name. *Thank you, Adam.*

She offered him her right hand. "Mr. Powell, welcome to Mariposa Resort & Spa. I'm Alexis Reed. I look forward to assisting you during your stay."

Max wrapped his long fingers around her much smaller, much softer ones. A current of awareness shot up his arm. Alexis didn't seem affected by it. Was this another symptom of sleep deprivation? He hadn't been able to get comfortable on the flight over. He was looking forward to taking a nap before meeting Adam for dinner.

"Thank you." Max couldn't believe his good fortune. "It's a pleasure to meet you, Ms. Reed. Adam mentioned you. Please call me Max."

Alexis inclined her head as she reclaimed her hand. "Thank you, Max. And I'm Alexis." She glanced behind her as a young man stationed a large scarlet-cloth-and-silver-metal baggage cart beside his suitcases. "I'll accompany you and Aaron to your bungalow."

Aaron tossed a friendly grin toward Alexis as he started loading the cart. Max's cheeks heated with embarrassment as the wiry young man stacked his three large dark gray cloth suitcases on the conveyor.

"Thanks, Aaron." Max returned the porter's smile as he searched for a way to justify having so much luggage. "I'm known for packing light for vacations, just a small suitcase or maybe a small suitcase and a knapsack." He adjusted his navy-blue-and-silver knapsack on his left shoulder and tucked his surprise package in the crook of his left arm. "But I'm staying at the resort for quite a while."

Alexis's captivating eyes were unreadable as she waited for him to stumble through his defense. "Adam said you'd be with us for six weeks."

There was no judgment in her tone. She turned to lead him to the parking lot at the back of the building. Aaron brought up the rear.

"That's right." Max's shoulder muscles relaxed. "Hence the uncharacteristic number of suitcases."

Alexis's nonverbal hum left him uncertain. She held the door open for him, Aaron and his luggage before leading him to a Mariposa Resort & Spa-branded minivan. It was pale yellow, drawing from the resort's pale-yellow-and-burnt-umber butterfly logo. Max sat beside her on the rear seat, setting the box on his lap and his knapsack between his feet. Aaron loaded his three suitcases into the cargo space in back before climbing in behind the vehicle's steering wheel. As they pulled away from the parking space, Max took in the view.

Sedona had fewer than ten thousand residents. The cozy desert town was dotted with diverse pines and cacti, and ringed by sheer canyon walls and majestic red rock buttes. Mariposa Resort & Spa sat on twenty-four acres along a ridge that backed up to Red Rock State Park. Adam and his siblings had assumed operation of the resort almost ten years ago, shortly after he and Max had graduated from New York University. The three Coltons had turned the property into an ultra-exclusive luxury resort with a five-star restaurant and private bungalows. According to reviews, their wealthy guests were happy to pay for the complete privacy—there weren't any cameras on the property—and tight security the resort offered.

A variety of cacti, grasses and wildflowers featured in the landscaping following the paths that wound throughout the resort. The public buildings and guest bungalows were contemporary structures with clean lines and large tinted windows. Their red-orange facades blended with the red-orange earth and stark, impressive mountains that rose all around them. Max's tension eased as his eyes followed the lines of the mountain ridge up to the cerulean blue sky dotted with whiffs of white clouds. Stunning.

"The resort is beautiful." This was Max's first trip to his friend's property. Why hadn't he visited sooner? Oh, right. Work.

"Yes, it is." Alexis's voice was quiet pride. "I've lived in this area all my life. The views never get old."

Max's eyes were drawn to her. She seemed serene and happy as she stared into the distance toward the soaring mountains. "Do you have family here?"

Her eyes widened with surprise. She must not have expected the personal question. "Yes. My mother."

The ride to the bungalow assigned to him was over far too soon. He could have spent hours looking at Alexis and getting to know her. But he'd have to be more aware of the woman and the vibes he was sending out. The one question he'd managed to ask during the drive may have been a little stalkerish. All work and no play had rusted out whatever skills in flirtation he may have once had.

They'd stopped in front of a bungalow that must have the best view in the resort. He needed to get Adam something great for his birthday. Max got out of the van, extending his hand to help Alexis step out after him. There it was again, that pulse of electricity that warmed his arm and jolted his heart when she touched him. She slipped free of his hold and stood beside him.

"Wow." All Max could do was stare at the bungalow.

Similar to the other buildings, the bungalow's red-orange stucco facade blended almost seamlessly with the soil in front of them and the mountains in the distance, making it appear to be part of the landscape rather than an addition to it. The foliage highlighting its perimeter was subtle and alluring. Max wasn't a botanist, but he recognized some of the plants, including the bouquets of warm gold brittlebush, deep blue desert chia, brilliant yellow desert marigolds, hedgehog cacti, prickly pears and, of course, saguaro, the cactus plant that appeared in every Western he'd ever seen.

Alexis tossed him a smile. Her eyes sparkled with pleasure. "Let's show you your home for the next six weeks."

She led him up the paved walkway. Max gripped his knapsack in his left hand and balanced the mystery box in the crook of his right arm. Aaron followed behind, wheeling two of Max's suitcases.

Alexis opened the door and stepped aside so he could enter his accommodations first. The bungalow was bright, open and spacious. The last remnants of his tension drained away. The natural light pouring in through the sliding glass doors to the balcony drew him across the room. The threshold framed the view of the mountain ridge just beyond his bungalow. Max dropped his knapsack beside one of the bamboo chairs.

"I'm glad I arrived early enough to appreciate this scene." Max turned, shifting the package to his left palm. He surveyed the room. It was comfortably cool. "I've stayed at several high-end resorts. This one puts them all to shame. Those Colton siblings know how to impress."

"I'm pleased you think so." Alexis stood near the center of the room. She looked good in it.

The bungalow's decor was minimalistic and tasteful. Both the floor and ceiling were made from bamboo. The off-white walls were bare, which was good. Max wasn't a fan of the generic paintings resorts usually displayed in their rooms. Instead, Mariposa let its surroundings, visible through the large windows, satisfy their guests' need for beauty. Vases of vibrant desert wildflowers were placed around the sitting area, providing color and adding a soft, clean fragrance to the air.

Aaron pulled his suitcases through a door to Max's left, probably the bedroom. He reemerged, sending Max another quick, polite smile. Although still professional, his expression warmed when he and Alexis exchanged looks. Alexis gave the younger man an approving nod.

Max drew his eyes from her and set the box on a chair beside the glass doors. He ran his hand over the chair's smooth bamboo back before wandering the bungalow. The bathroom was across from the bedroom. The spacious area included a burnt-umber-and-white-marble tub and frosted-glass shower.

Alexis gestured toward the glass doors. "There's a small golf cart parked behind your bungalow that you can use to get around the resort."

Max returned to the doors, angling his body to see the side of the patio past the hot tub. The vehicle was a two-seat white cart with the Mariposa butterfly logo. "That's convenient."

Another quick glance around his immediate surroundings confirmed his suspicion. There weren't any electronics in his room: clocks, radios, TVs. Luckily, he'd brought his laptop. He wasn't about to miss March Madness, the National Collegiate Athletic Association's basketball championship series. He could stream the games on his computer. He had a watch to keep track of time. As for music, he was still rebuilding his playlist, which he'd stored on his older cell phone. That device had been stolen during the second break-in two weeks ago.

Aaron returned with Max's final suitcase. He pulled it into the bedroom, then returned to the sitting area. "I'll wait for you at the van, Alexis."

Max started unwrapping the package he'd received from the reception desk. It gave him something to do with his hands. At the moment, he was more restless than curious. He would see Alexis again. She was going to help him purchase the fresh ingredients he'd need for his cookbook recipes. But for today, he wanted a little more time with her.

"Thanks, Aaron." Alexis waited for the porter to leave before continuing to enumerate the resort's features. "The paths back to L Building, which is our main building, and S Building, which houses our spa and gym, as well as our hiking trails and other amenities, are all marked."

She highlighted the resort's offerings, including horseback riding, swimming pools and fine dining at Annabeth, the resort's five-star restaurant, which was named for Adam's mother. Its menu included a champagne breakfast that sounded very tempting. Max set down the half-opened box and strolled the sitting area again. He focused more on Alexis's voice than her words. The warm, husky notes were at the same time soothing and stirring. It brought to mind images of champagne, canapés, cozy fireplaces and rumpled sheets.

Max had experienced an instant interest in attractive women before. But he'd never felt such a strong, immediate connection. It was a restless need to be near her, to learn everything about her. Did she feel this way, too? How would she react if he asked her to spend time outside of work with him?

"If I can." Alexis's words startled him.

He turned to her. She stood in the center of the sitting area. Her patient eyes were fixed on him as she waited for him to respond.

"Excuse me?" For a split second, Max was afraid he'd spoken his private musings out loud.

Alexis's polite smile remained in place. "I said I'd be happy to answer any question you may have about the resort at this time, if I can."

Max sent her a self-conscious grin. "Oh. No, I don't have any questions right now. Thank you."

Good grief. How did he recover from this embarrassment? He found himself back beside the chair on which he'd left the package. He picked it up.

"All right, but if you think of anything, please don't hesitate to ask. Anyone at Mariposa would be happy to assist you."

Max's hands stilled on the box as he shifted his attention to Alexis. "Thank you. I don't know whether I'll have a lot of time to take advantage of all the resort's offerings. I have a lot of work to do."

"I thought this was at least partly a vacation." There was humor in her voice.

"I'm sure I'll have some downtime." He responded with a slow smile. "But it's more of a busman's holiday."

Alexis took a step toward him. "Would you like to discuss that now? Laura asked me to acquire the ingredients you'll need for your recipes."

"That's right and I appreciate your willingness to help me."

His discomfort eased as he thought about the adventure of creating new dishes. "I'm adding a Southwestern twist to several of my dishes that I want to include in my book."

Her smile brightened into a grin. "Congratulations. It's all very impressive, your restaurants, your show and now your cookbook."

"Thank you." His eyes roamed her face, taking in her delicate features and the sparkles in her eyes. "I'll need fresh, high-quality ingredients, spices, fruits, vegetables, fish and poultries."

"You're in luck." Once again, Max heard the pride in her voice. "We have an excellent farmers market not far from the resort. It's open Sundays and Mondays from seven a.m. to noon. They have great fruits, vegetables, juices and condiments. They've also recently started selling poultry. I'll have to go to a separate market for fish, though, if you'd like me to pick that up for you."

Max shook his head. "I'll be coming with you."

He felt a surge of happiness at the thought of spending that time alone with her. Based on the surprise she quickly masked, Alexis didn't have the same reaction.

She lifted her palms. "There's no need for you to take the time and trouble to come with me. I'm happy to do the shopping for you." She lowered her hands. "You can just make a list of everything you'll need, and we can add those items to your final billing."

Max considered her professional demeanor. Her expression was calm and friendly, but he sensed she really didn't want him to do the shopping with her. Why not? A never-before-recognized imp of contrariness prompted him to dig in his heels.

"Well, you mentioned the market opens at seven a.m. That's pretty early." He spoke slowly as though he was considering his options. "And I'm not much of a morning person." Max saw the light of relief in her eyes. "However, this is really important to me, so I'll make the effort. In fact, we should get there before the market opens to make sure we get the best, freshest picks. After all, a great meal starts with great ingredients."

Alexis spread her arms. "I realize you're the expert, but I assure you, I'm capable of grocery shopping for you."

"*Grocery* shopping?" Max's eyes widened with surprise and disbelief. This time, his reaction wasn't feigned. "This isn't *grocery* shopping. It's much more than that. The produce has to be fresh and unblemished. The poultry and fish cuts have to be lean and perfect. I'm very particular. It would be best if I came with you."

Alexis considered him. Max sensed her sizing him up and going over his explanation. "Of course, Max. You're the expert and the guest."

Victory! He did a mental fist bump.

And, bonus, Max finally got the box open. His smile vanished. His body froze. His mind went blank. Inside the box were the two items that had been stolen from his condo during the break-ins: his old cell phone on which he'd saved his playlist and his deodorant. There was also a note, "Enjoy your stay at Mariposa Resort & Spa."

"Max?" Alexis's hand was warm against his bare forearm. She'd moved to stand beside him without his noticing. "Is something wrong?"

He raised his eyes to hers. "I'm being stalked."

Chapter Two

Alexis didn't need to hear another word. She urged Max onto the chair behind him before hurrying out to the van. She went to the driver's side, where Aaron was waiting for her behind the wheel. "We have an urgent situation. Could you please meet Roland in the L's lobby? I'll let him know you're on the way."

Aaron started the engine. His face was creased with concern, but he recognized this wasn't the time for questions. "Sure thing."

Alexis watched the young man speed away as she tapped Roland's number into her cell.

The director of security answered before the first ring ended. "Alexis, what can I do for you?"

Like her, Roland didn't believe in small talk. One of the many things she appreciated about him. "We have a situation at 11." She referenced Max's bungalow. "A suspicious package was delivered to the guest. Aaron's on his way to the L. Could you meet him in the lobby?"

"On my way." He ended the call.

Alexis returned to Max, leaving his front door open in anticipation of Aaron and Roland's arrival. He'd stood from the chair and put the box on the small bamboo end table beside it. He stood with his back to the room, staring out the rear glass doors.

His arms were crossed. Alexis took this moment to do what she'd wanted to do since they'd met: admire his appearance.

In her mind's eye, she pictured his dreamy, deep-set eyes in chiseled, sienna features. They were the color of milk chocolate and reflected a quick, sharp wit. A deep dimple had creased his right cheek each time he'd teased her with his sexy grin.

Her eyes traveled from his close-cropped, dark brown hair to the casual rust-colored shirt that stretched across his broad shoulders. The short sleeves hugged his biceps. For a chef, he was built like an amateur athlete. Runner? Swimmer? Cyclist? Perhaps all the above. He was tall, at least a couple of inches above six feet. Warm brown slacks covered long legs and exceptional glutes.

He turned toward her suddenly as though he'd sensed her presence.

Alexis's eyes leaped to his. Her cheeks burned. "Aaron's getting Roland Hargreaves, our director of security. You should give him as much information as you can about your suspicions regarding this package." She forced herself to stop babbling.

"Thank you. It caught me off guard." His baritone carried a hint of New York City. It made her hungry to hear more.

"That's understandable." Alexis turned to the mini-fridge hidden in the credenza in the dining area. She selected one of the twelve-ounce bottles of water and offered it to him. His long sienna fingers brushed hers as he took it. His warmth spread up her arm.

"Thank you." He spoke softly.

"Afternoon, Alexis." Roland's gruff voice came from behind her.

She turned to find him just inside Max's bungalow. Alexis didn't want to think about the speed with which Aaron had driven to return to the bungalow so quickly—but she was grateful.

A former Oklahoma State University football linebacker, Roland made Aaron seem even slighter. He was a capable and comforting figure in his security director's uniform: cider-brown suit, white shirt and burnt-umber tie. The Mariposa

Resort & Spa logo was embroidered on his jacket's upper-left breast pocket with the word "Security" underneath.

"That was fast. Thank you, Aaron." Alexis gestured from Roland to Max. "Roland Hargreaves, director of security, this is Max Powell III. He's just arrived." She pointed to the box on the small table near the rear glass doors. "That package was waiting for him. It had been shipped to his attention, care of the resort. I haven't touched anything. We've been waiting for you."

Roland stepped forward, offering Max his large right hand. "Mr. Powell, welcome to Mariposa Resort & Spa. I'm sorry your arrival has been marred by this experience."

Max released the older man's hand. "I appreciate your coming so quickly. Please call me Max."

"Roland." The middle-aged man pulled on protective gloves before handling the box. He examined each side as though checking for markings before looking at the contents. "What's the story here?"

Max drew a deep breath, further expanding his broad chest. "About six weeks ago, someone broke into my condo. The strange thing is, it's as though they had a key. The locks weren't damaged."

Roland's perpetual frown deepened. "Then how do you know it was a break-in?"

Max rubbed the back of his neck as he paced away from the glass doors. His footsteps were muffled as he crossed the warm-gold-and-burnt-umber area rug. "Because they tossed the place. They went through my stuff—the kitchen, the bathrooms, everywhere. They slept in my bed. And they took an old cell phone."

Roland jerked his square chin toward the inside of the box. "Is that the cell phone?"

"Yes." Max looked over his shoulder. "My deodorant went missing after the second break-in about a month ago."

"Were those the only items taken?" Roland looked around the room before crossing to the coffee table.

"Yes." Max watched Roland examine the paper in which the

stalker had wrapped the box. "The NYPD believe it may be an obsessed fan, but I don't know how they're getting through the building's security, much less into my home."

Alexis wrapped her arms around her waist. Her blood chilled at the thought of someone being so obsessed with the celebrity chef that they'd break into his home, sleep in his bed and steal his deodorant.

Creepy.

She glanced at Aaron beside her. His eyes were wide with disbelief as he listened to Max's recount.

Alexis stepped closer to him and lowered her voice. "Aaron, please remember not to discuss anything you hear about our guests with anyone. Not one single person. Everything that happens at the resort is confidential."

Aaron closed his gaping mouth and offered Alexis a weak smile. "I promise. I won't tell a soul. But this is just so...*cray*, right?"

Shrugging her eyebrows in silent agreement, Alexis returned her attention to Roland and Max. Mariposa's guests—actors, musicians, public servants, athletes—had had their share of wild encounters with fans, nonfans and the media. That was the number one reason so many of their guests checked into the resort. It wasn't just the exemplary menu from their Annabeth restaurant, the relaxation offered by the myriad spa services, the stunning views from their hiking trails or the pampering they received from their accommodations and the staff. It also was the ability to be anonymous at the resort. The respect for their privacy. The seclusion of the high-security, ultra-exclusive grounds.

But Aaron was right. Max's situation was super creepy.

Roland scanned the brief ominous note that had been included with the mailing. "Have you received any other strange messages or phone calls?"

Max shook his head. "No, this is the first time anyone has contacted me."

Alexis shivered again. She wished none of this had happened. That no one had broken into Max's home, that the package had never arrived, that the note had never been written.

Roland looked at him from over his shoulder. "Does the NYPD have any leads?"

Max dragged a hand over his close-cropped hair. "None."

Roland put the single sheet of plain white paper back into the box. "I'll look into this package with our mailroom and our post office contact. And I'll keep both of you apprised of what I learn." His look included Alexis. "Sorry, Aaron." The security director's stern look eased a little as he broke into one of his rare smiles.

Aaron waved both hands. "It's all good. I get it."

Roland's muscle memory returned his features to their usual serious setting. He pulled his wallet from the inside pocket of his uniform jacket. "In the meantime, I'd encourage you to update the NYPD on this development."

Max inclined his head. "I'll do that."

Roland handed Max his business card. "Here's my contact information, in case they have questions for me."

Max took the cream card and examined it. "I appreciate your help."

Roland turned to leave. "I'll brief my staff and let them know about the possible threat. We'll keep an eye on you—without being intrusive. And we'll keep you updated whether we discover anything or not."

"Thank you." Max sounded relieved and grateful.

Alexis approached him. "Max, if there's nothing else, we'll leave you to update the NYPD and settle in. If you do decide to get some rest before dinner, I recommend turning the Do Not Disturb switch on your phone."

Those dreamy milk chocolate eyes caught hers. "Thank you for everything, Alexis. You've helped to put my mind at ease."

The pulse at the base of her throat fluttered. "Of course." She swallowed. "We take our guests' safety very seriously."

Even those without dreamy eyes and New York accents. In addition to keeping Max safe, Alexis was keenly aware that a threat to one guest could affect the well-being of others at the resort—clients as well as staff.

* * *

"We're so glad you arrived safely." Max's mother, Erika Ross-Powell, spoke on a sigh of relief.

"We thought we'd hear from you hours ago." Maxwell Powell II spoke at the same time.

Max had called his mother after Alexis, Roland and Aaron had left late Friday afternoon. Erika had put him on speaker so his father could join the conversation. As usual, they talked over each other. Max mentally shrugged. It was a family trait. He and his sisters did the same thing.

Erika admonished her husband. "MJ, he's calling us now."

"MJ" was short for Maxwell Junior, which was his father's designation before Max's birth.

Max sat on the edge of the mattress and surveyed the bedroom as he spoke with his parents. Its decor was similar to the sitting area: bamboo flooring, ceiling and furniture. Instead of artwork, the north-facing wall had a large picture window that framed the mountain ridge. The scent of wildflowers came from the three vases placed around the room, one on the dressing table facing the bed and one on each nightstand.

"Sorry I didn't call sooner." He absently stared at the colorful area rug beneath his loafers. It was identical to the ones in the sitting area. "I met the resort's senior concierge. We discussed some of the tasks I'll need help with while I'm here."

And he'd had a suspicious package to deal with. He didn't want to get into that, at least not with his parents. Not now. He wasn't withholding information. He didn't have anything to share. In fact, he had more questions than answers. How had the stalker known where he would be or when he would arrive? Had the thief planned to return his stolen items all along? Most importantly, who was harassing him and what did they want? He'd keep the incident to himself for now. His parents would only worry, which would increase his stress.

"How beautiful is the resort?" Erika's question replaced his troubled thoughts.

Max imagined his mother holding the phone between herself and his father, her eyes wide with excitement. "It's very beautiful." He rose from the mattress and crossed to the window.

Once again, the view stole his breath. "Adam and his siblings have a lot to be proud of."

"Try to find time to relax and unwind." Erika was in full-on Mom Mode. "You've been under a lot of stress and working so hard for so long. You deserve to have at least a little fun."

"Your mother's right. You're there." MJ paused as though he was sipping a beverage. Was it coffee? His father was addicted to the stuff, but probably not. It was after seven over there. His mother cut off his supply after 4 p.m. "You might as well enjoy yourself."

"It was nice of Adam to invite you to the resort and give you a discounted rate, but you're still paying something." Erika's tone was gentle persuasion. "Make the most of it."

An image of Alexis appeared in Max's thoughts. "I promise to try."

Max wandered the room. He ran the tips of his fingers over the bamboo dressing table as he eyed the matching nightstand. The design was calming and intriguing.

"How are you feeling?" Erika asked.

Max could almost hear her concerned frown. He sensed her grip on the phone as though she was wrapping her arms around him.

"I'm fine." He hesitated. "A little tired." By not telling them about the mailing, he'd already lied by omission. He wouldn't add another sin to the list.

"Couldn't you sleep on the plane?" MJ sounded surprised. "I know it was a long flight."

"You know he's never been able to sleep on a plane." Erika laughed. "It used to drive me nuts. Miri and Melly would fall asleep as soon as the plane took off. But not Max. He'd stay awake the whole time, which meant one of *us* had to be alert the whole time."

Those family trips were great—once they got off the plane. Max still envied his sisters' ability to sleep during the flights.

"Have you heard anything more from the police about those break-ins at your condo?" MJ's abrupt change of subject caught Max off guard.

"No, they don't have any updates." Before calling his parents, Max had spoken with the officers assigned to his case about the package. They'd told him they didn't have any new information on the investigation. Somehow Max didn't think his outdated cell phone or used deodorant stick was a priority for them. "I've asked the building manager and a neighbor to keep an eye on my condo until I get home."

"The attractive young woman who lives across the hall?" Erika's sly tone hinted at the ulterior motive for her question.

His mother was anxious for all her offspring to give her grandchildren. His older sister, Miriam, was the only one married. She worked with their mother, who was a casting director. Miri and her husband, Odell, weren't in a hurry to have kids. Neither Max nor his younger sister, Melanie, were in a relationship. In addition to designing jewelry, Mel was an up-and-coming actress. Like Max, her focus was on building her career. Her dedication was paying off. She'd landed a supporting role as an FBI agent in a new crime drama. With the success of their first season, the show had been renewed for two more seasons. Max was as excited as if he were in the cast.

MJ had wanted Max to join his production company, but Max's first love had always been cooking. Owning a restaurant had been his dream. MJ had finally accepted that, giving him ideas and suggestions along the way. His father had been thrilled when a studio had offered Max his own cooking show. MJ had declared they were now a show-business family.

Max shook his head, more amused than exasperated. "That's right, Mom. My very attractive neighbor—who's happily engaged and planning her wedding to someone else—is keeping an eye on my condo."

"Son, I've been giving some thought to the second season of your show." MJ offered another drastic subject change. Max braced himself for his father's input. "You should tape the show in front of a live audience."

All at once, the fatigue of the travel, time zone change and weeks of restless nights crashed into him. Max's body was heavy with it. His eyes struggled to stay open. "Dad, I'm not really up to talking about plans for next season right now. I'm pretty—"

MJ's enthusiasm couldn't be stopped. "What do you think of the idea? It's a good one, right?"

Max rolled his shoulders to ease his tension. "Dad, you have years of experience in both television and film production. You know opening a show's production to a live audience would be expensive. We'd have to double our security, add bathrooms and offer audience members at least water if not snacks."

"You could recoup all those costs by charging for the tickets. People would pay good money to watch you cook in person."

Oh, boy.

"Why would anyone pay to watch me cook in person when they could attend tapings of late-night talk shows for free?" Max returned to sit on the edge of the bed. "And what if no one came?"

"It's worth the risk, son." MJ's tone brushed aside all Max's concerns. "Having a live studio audience would add energy to the show. Trust me. I know this. As you said, I have a lot more years of experience in the TV and film industries than you do."

Those words put Max's back up. "I know, Dad, and I respect your experience. But the show has been successful. Our viewing audience has consistently put us in the top ten ratings."

"Yes, and that's wonderful. But that was only the first season. Don't you want a long-running program?"

"Yes, of course, but—"

"*Non*-celebrity cooking shows are beating you in the ratings." MJ paused again as though taking another sip from a beverage. Maybe it was coffee. His father sounded overcaffeinated. "Historically, they do better anyway. You have to beat them at their own game. That's why you have to return your show to the people. Put them in the center of your program."

"You want me to change the format of the show?" The muscles at the back of his neck were knotting. Why didn't his father have more faith in his ideas? What was he doing wrong? What could he do better? What more could he possibly do to prove himself to his parent?

Erika intervened. "MJ, let Max get some sleep. First your own restaurants, then the cooking show and now a publishing contract. No wonder you're tired. We're so proud of you, hon."

"Of course we're proud of him." MJ sounded like he was only half listening. "But think about the idea, son. You're doing great! But you could do even better. There's room to grow."

Max had been hearing those words all his life. They were his motivation—and his burden. When would success be "good enough"?

"I don't think the show's producers would want to break the bank on adding a live audience, Dad. The show's not a comedy." At least it wasn't intended to be.

MJ tsked. "If they give you any pushback, just remind them they have to spend money to make money."

"Let him rest, MJ." Erika's tone was firmer this time. "Hon, we'll let your sisters know you landed safely. That way, they won't text you while you're trying to sleep."

"Thanks, Mom." He loved being part of a close-knit family. It was great knowing there were people who were always looking out for you—except when that concern prevented his sleep.

"Your mother's right. Get some rest, son. We'll talk more about the studio audience idea after you've had a chance to rest."

"All right, Dad." Max appreciated the warning.

"You've been scamming our guests." Alexis stared across the rectangular blond wood conference table at Mark Bower late Friday afternoon. The twenty-something-year-old was the newest addition to her concierge team.

Leticia Bailey sat between them at the head of the table. The tall, slender personnel director wore a striking mustard pantsuit with an ebony shell blouse. Long thin dark brown braids framed her diamond-shaped brown face.

Mark's round glass-green eyes flared wide with surprise. He obviously hadn't seen this coming. Alexis clenched her teeth. How long had he expected his clandestine operation to last? She relaxed her jaw and once again thanked the good fortune that had allowed her to uncover his dealings before they'd gone any further.

He shot a panicked look at Leticia before answering Alexis. "No, I haven't."

Alexis heard the fear in his words. Her muscles trembled with outrage. She wanted to shout at Mark that he was a liar. But he'd already damaged her professional reputation and caused her to question her own judgment. She wouldn't let him take her self-control, too.

She drew a long breath of the cool, citrus-scented air and tightened her grip on her temper. "I heard you speaking with the Elliots at the paddocks."

The horse paddocks were in the northern part of the resort. Earlier in the week, Alexis had taken one of her exploratory late-morning walks around Mariposa, checking on guests and waving at coworkers. That's when she'd overheard Mark speaking with the Elliot family. Mr. Elliot was a famous television star. He'd come to the resort with his wife and their four pre-teen children.

"You were spying on me?" Mark's shaggy sandy-blond hair swung forward as he leaned into the table. At least part of his anger seemed manufactured to put her on the defensive. He failed.

Alexis's voice was tight. "The Elliots sounded so happy that you were able to get their event tickets. It's such a nice feeling when guests appreciate our work. Then I heard you tell them that as usual, you'd added the cost of the tickets to their resort bill, but you were invoicing them separately for the service fee to reduce their tax burden. Imagine my surprise. As you know, we don't have a service fee."

Leticia tapped the manual on the table in front of her. Her chunky bronze earrings, a match to her necklace, swung as she turned her head toward Mark. "You signed a statement attesting to your having read the employee handbook. The handbook explicitly states staff are not permitted to accept any type of gratuity related to or in the course of employment."

The Coltons' legal counsel insisted on that specific language to ensure that clause encompassed bribes from the media and paparazzi.

Mark's prominent Adam's apple bobbed. "Well, yeah. I... I read it."

"And you went to all the new employee orientation seminars." Leticia flipped through several sheets of paper. "Your signature appears on each of these attendance certifications, confirming you attended and understood the policies, benefits and conditions of employment covered during the sessions. So you are aware soliciting and/or accepting gratuities in any form is cause for immediate dismissal."

"That policy exists for many reasons." Alexis clenched her hands together on the table, entwining her fingers. "First, this is an all-inclusive resort. Our guests have prepaid for every service, meal and activity available to them at the resort. Second, we don't want employees to be tempted to do anything inappropriate in exchange for a bribe. This is another way we protect our guests' privacy."

Mark spread his thin arms. "But I didn't do anything inappropriate." His voice rose several octaves.

Leticia didn't bat an eye. "You violated personnel policies. Policies you acknowledged receiving and understanding. Therefore, your actions were very inappropriate."

Inappropriate in every way. And Alexis had to admit to Laura Colton—her friend, direct supervisor and co-owner of Mariposa—the mistake she'd made in hiring Mark.

Alexis's skin burned at the unpleasant memory. "We also know this wasn't a one-time mistake or oversight. I spoke with several of the guests who'd been assigned to you." She pressed her palm on top of the documents that stood in a tidy stack in front of her. "They all signed these statements, attesting they'd paid you several so-called service fees for event tickets and restaurant reservations you'd made for them."

Mark interrupted. "They gave me those tips to thank me for my trouble. Some of those tickets and stuff weren't easy to get, you know."

Alexis's face burned with anger at his continued lies. "Every one of their statements makes it clear you told them they had to pay you a service fee."

"Alexis is right." Leticia gestured toward her. "But even if your clients had offered you a gratuity of their own will, you were required according to our employee handbook to decline the gift. Your response should have been some version of, 'Thank you, but the resort's policy prohibits me from accepting gifts.'"

Alexis was grateful for Leticia's support and her further clarification of Mariposa's policy, but she sensed Mark wasn't ready to admit his guilt.

He divided his scowl between her and Leticia. "But I'm still on probation."

"All the more reason to expect you to know and respect the rules." Leticia shifted on her chair to face Mark. "If you're willing to so blatantly disregard the rules at this stage of your employment, how much worse could your actions become?"

"That's not a chance I'm prepared to take." The possible answers to Leticia's rhetorical question could cause Alexis's head to explode. "Mark, your services are no longer needed. You can pack your belongings. Security will escort you out."

His jaw dropped. "You're firing me?"

Alexis's eyes never wavered. "That's right." Her words dropped into the thick silence.

Her sense of failure was complete. She'd hired someone who'd repeatedly flouted Mariposa's employee policies.

Alexis's eyes drifted toward the view outside the room's floor-to-ceiling tinted windows. The timing couldn't have been worse. The resort's event manager was getting ready to retire. Alexis had applied for the position. It would be a promotion, which she believed she was capable of and ready for. But after this experience, would Laura, Adam and Joshua agree? Would they ever trust her judgment again?

"It was one mistake." Mark's lips tightened.

Alexis returned her attention to him. "And you made it repeatedly."

Mark's wiry frame stiffened with outrage. "You've always resented me."

Alexis narrowed her eyes at his change in tactic. He'd gone from defense to attacking her directly. "What makes you say that?"

"You've felt threatened by me from the day I entered your department two months ago." He jabbed a finger toward her.

His eyes were hard with anger and resentment. "You knew I was a better concierge than you could ever be."

She would have laughed if she hadn't been so angry. "I hired you because I thought you would be a good addition to our team. I realize now I made a mistake."

"You're lying." His voice shook. Was it anger or anxiety? "You resent me. You treat me differently from other people in the department. I'm not the only person who's noticed it, either. Everyone else has, too."

Alexis's anger was giving way to disgust. "That's not true, Mark. You're making up these allegations to strike back at me, but it won't work."

"No, I'm not." He stabbed a finger toward her. "I want to file a complaint against my manager."

Leticia looked confused. "Mark, you no longer have a manager. You no longer work for the resort."

Shock wiped all expression from his thin, pale features. "What?"

Leticia stood and crossed the room. Opening the door, she invited the two young security guards who waited in the hall to join her before turning back to Mark. "Please remember you signed a nondisclosure agreement, stating you wouldn't share information about Mariposa's guests. That agreement is legally binding and enforceable even after your employment ends."

Mark stood. His eyes were dark with hatred as he stared down at Alexis. "You haven't won."

"You still don't understand." Alexis rose, straightening her shoulders. "This isn't about winning and losing. This is about right and wrong. What you did was wrong. The fact you have the nerve to lie about your actions proves you know that."

He glared at her for several moments more before turning to leave. His movements were stiff as he approached the door without looking back. Leticia and the two guards followed him out.

As they disappeared beyond the doorway, Alexis braced both hands on the smooth, cool table and shook her head. Laura may not fault her for hiring Mark, but Alexis blamed herself. How could she have missed the signs that Mark was a grifter?

"How are you feeling?" The question startled her.

She looked up to find Roland standing just inside the room. She found a smile for the older man. "What are you doing here?"

"Checking on you. I know how upset you are about this business with Bower."

Her smile faded. "Can you blame me?" She stopped beside the director of resort security. "Fortunately, the guests didn't seem upset or resentful. It probably helped that we reimbursed them for the fraud. But we can't be certain whether they've forgiven us unless they come back."

"Don't be so hard on yourself." Roland stood back so Alexis could precede him from the room. "He's only been here two months. You caught him and now he's gone."

"I hope he hasn't done lasting damage to Mariposa." Alexis looked up at her coworker. "How long will we have to deal with the fallout from this situation?"

Chapter Three

Max drifted out of a half-remembered dream. Far in the distance but lurching ever closer was an inescapable force that sounded like a ringing phone. Groaning, Max rolled toward the disturbance and lifted his eyelids just enough to locate the device.

With an effort, he stretched out his left arm to clutch the receiver. He croaked into the phone, "Hello?"

There was a brief pause almost like a gasp before a young woman spoke. "Mr. Powell, this is Clarissa at the front desk. I'm so sorry to disturb you."

Max cleared his throat. "It's all right, Clarissa. Alexis suggested I turn on my Do Not Disturb switch. I must've forgotten. What can I do for you?"

A relieved sigh proceeded Clarissa's next words. "You have a visitor, Sarah Harris."

Max was still groggy. Had he misunderstood? "Sarah? She's here?"

"Yes, sir. She's waiting for you at the front desk." Clarissa sounded determinedly upbeat.

Max rolled onto his back. Oh, for the love of everything holy. For a second, he considered asking Clarissa to tell Sarah he'd checked out of the resort and returned to New York. That way, he could go back to bed. But then his annoyance turned inward. Sarah was upset. Her marriage was ending. She was probably looking for someone other than family to whom she could just vent. He shouldn't be churlish. Surely, he could spare a few minutes—or even an hour—for a colleague in need.

He tossed off the bed's soft gold coverlet. "I'll be right there. Thank you, Clarissa."

"You're very welcome, Mr. Powell." Relief was evident in her young voice before she ended the call.

What time is it?

Max retrieved his watch from beside the resort's landline and blinked until the LED numbers came into focus. It was a few minutes after five o'clock Friday evening. He'd slept for less than an hour. Swinging his legs off the side of the bed, Max canceled the alarm he'd programmed on his phone. He'd set it for six o'clock, which would have given him enough time to get ready to meet Adam for dinner later this evening. He climbed out of bed and into black slacks, a white shirt and a slate gray jacket. That attire would be suitable for both his meeting with Sarah and dinner at the resort's fancy restaurant.

The golf cart was fun to operate and, as Alexis had promised, the directional signs leading him from his bungalow back to the L Building were frequent, well-lit in the waning daylight and easy to follow. Max was walking into the building within minutes of leaving his bungalow.

"Max!" Sarah ran forward, then launched herself at him.

He caught his breath and a lungful of her jasmine-and-lemon perfume. Max withdrew Sarah's arms from around his neck and stepped back, putting an arm's length of space between them. What had gotten into her? They had a professional relationship. Why had she leaped into his arms as though they shared something much more personal?

"Hello, Sarah." Max took another step back as he looked uneasily around the lobby. His eyes connected with Alexis's. *Perfect.*

She inclined her head with cool professionalism before returning her attention to the older woman standing beside her. The stranger looked like wealth and influence. There was something familiar about her. Max narrowed his eyes. She reminded him of Glenna Bennett Colton, Adam's stepmother. He'd seen photos of her.

Max pulled his eyes from Alexis and looked down at Sarah. She was frowning in Alexis's direction. "Sarah, what are you doing here?"

His administrative assistant turned her back to Alexis and beamed up at him. Her brown eyes glowed in her round porcelain face. "I'm here to collect on that drink you promised me, silly."

Max searched his memory. He was certain drinks had not been discussed in their earlier conversation.

He scanned their surroundings, careful to avoid attracting Alexis's attention. From what he'd seen so far, this main building was the largest on the property. Like his bungalow, this one-story structure had bamboo flooring and ceilings. Nature featured as its main decor. Vases of fresh flowers had been placed around the reception and lobby areas, and large square windows displayed mesmerizing views to the resort's east, west and south.

Max turned away from the bar on his right and gestured toward the open-air lobby opposite it. "Let's sit down."

Sarah raised her right arm as though preparing to point out the bar beside them. But something in Max's set features must have convinced her to join him in the lobby. She led him to a cozy bamboo love seat. Max swallowed a sigh. He would've preferred the individual armchairs but at least they weren't on the barstools.

His administrative assistant looked like a different person. She'd freed her shoulder-length red hair from the clips that usually kept it off her face. Tonight, her tresses were styled into a blowout. Heavy makeup emphasized her round brown eyes and turned her pink lips cherry red. Her crimson minidress looked more like a negligee. Had her divorce rattled her more than she was letting on?

Max angled himself to face her. His back was to Alexis. Was she still in the lobby? "Sarah, how did you know where I was staying?"

She shrugged her shoulders, which were bare except for thin

red spaghetti straps. "You said you were staying at a resort in Sedona. I took a chance that it was this one." She took his right hand from his knee and cupped it between hers. "Where else would someone with your celebrity status stay?"

He took his hand back. Max's eyes dropped to the sterling silver bead bracelet he'd given her—and the other women on his production team—for Christmas. It was an understated design.

Max ignored her reference to his celebrity. "Sarah, I'm sorry you and Steve are getting a divorce. Are you sure the two of you can't work things out? Do you want me to speak with him, let him know you and I aren't involved in any way outside of work?"

Irritation flickered briefly in her eyes before she masked her emotions. "I'm done with Steve. If he doesn't trust me, that's his problem." Sarah stood, offering him her hand. "Let's get a drink and toast my soon-to-be-single status."

"I don't think that would be a good idea." Max wondered if she'd already had a glass or two.

Sarah laughed, pointing toward the bar across the lobby in front of her. "What do you mean, silly? The bar's right there. You won't even have to drive home after."

"But you will." Max came slowly to his feet. Before he could continue, Alexis's voice came from behind him.

"Excuse me." Her soft, husky syllables commanded his attention and made his knees shake. "I'm sorry to interrupt—"

Sarah shoved her right hand onto her hip. "Then why are you?"

The aggression in her voice surprised and embarrassed Max. "Sarah—"

Unfazed, Alexis continued. "The resort's amenities are for guests only. I'm afraid people who aren't guests of the resort can't enter beyond the L Building's lobby. I'm sorry."

Sarah gave the resort's senior concierge a stony stare. "Why not?"

Max swallowed a sigh. "Sarah, the resort's rules—"

Alexis interrupted him. "It's all right, Mr. Powell. It's a fair question."

Max narrowed his eyes at Alexis. *Mr. Powell?* Earlier, they'd been Max and Alexis. What had changed?

She turned back to Sarah. "Ms. Harris, non-guests aren't permitted on resort grounds or to avail themselves of resort amenities, including our bar and restaurant, because they aren't clients. It wouldn't be fair to our registered guests to allow visitors to take advantage of services they're paying for. I hope you can appreciate that."

"No, I can't. Your rules are ridiculous." Sarah raised her voice. She flung a hand toward Max, barely missing striking him. "Do you even know who this is? This is *Maxwell Powell III* of the *New York* Powells."

If mortification was fatal, Max would be a corpse on the ground at Alexis's sexy nude pumps. "Sarah, you're making a scene."

"I don't care." Nevertheless, she lowered her voice. "They need to give you the deference you deserve. Is this a resort or some sort of cult camp?"

At Sarah's insult, fury flashed in Alexis's champagne-hued eyes. Max felt a stirring of anger as well. His friend put a lot of time, effort and talent into transforming the once-modest hotel into an exclusive getaway for the rich and famous. He was proud of Adam's accomplishments and didn't appreciate Sarah's denigrating comments.

He faced Alexis. "Thank you for making us aware of the resort's rules. Of course, we'll respect them." The temper in Alexis's eyes drained and was replaced by gratitude. He wanted to keep looking into them. But with an effort, he shifted his attention to Sarah. "I'll take you to your car."

Sarah's jaw dropped. "But—"

Max took her arm and walked with her to the entrance. He felt the eyes of other guests following them across the lobby. This was not how he'd wanted to start his working vacation. He'd come to the resort to relax. Instead, drama had followed him.

He pushed through the glass doors. "Are you all right to drive or should I call you a cab?"

"I'm not drunk, Max." Sarah's voice was tight. She looked

over her shoulder back toward the L Building. "You should file a complaint against that woman."

"She was doing her job. *We* were the ones in the wrong." A mild breeze snuck under Max's sports jacket. It would have been calming if it weren't for the waves of aggression rolling off Sarah and the responding irritation scratching under his skin. "I wish you'd told me you were coming, Sarah."

"I wanted to surprise you." She lowered her voice. "I wanted to see you."

"I'm sorry you're upset about your divorce, but I can't meet with you today." He retained his hold on her arm as she led them to her car. "I have another engagement."

Sarah scowled. "Well, I'm not sure how long I'll be in Arizona." She stopped beside an older-model white Toyota Corolla hatchback. "I mean, I have an open invitation from my relatives to stay as long as I'd like, but I've been thinking of taking a real vacation. Maybe to Hawaii."

Max released her arm. "I think that would be a good idea. Being away from familiar people and places might help you put things in perspective."

Sarah pouted. She put her hand on his chest and gazed up at him. "No, Max. What I need right now is a friend. That's what you've always been to me. A friend."

Something in her voice, in her touch, made him uncomfortable. No, they'd never been friends. She worked for him. He didn't want to blur those lines.

Max stepped back, breaking Sarah's connection. "Drive safely, Sarah." He turned to leave.

"Call me, Max." Her voice carried to him as he walked away.

Seriously, what had gotten into her?

Max walked back to the L Building Friday evening in a cloud of confusion. The only explanation for Sarah's uncharacteristic behavior was her divorce. Steve's accusations must have hurt her much more than she was letting on—maybe even more than she admitted to herself. For him to accuse her of cheating on him must have felt like the biggest betrayal. His lips tightened, thinking about the attack against *his* honor. He didn't appreciate it and he certainly didn't deserve it.

"Excuse me." A female voice scattered his thoughts.

He looked up to see Glenna Bennett Colton emerge from the main building. She gave him a tight smile as she walked past him toward the main parking lot.

"Pardon me." Their exchange pulled him out of his fog.

From the corner of his eye, Max caught a glimpse of a bronze skirt suit. Alexis was walking across the parking lot.

"Alexis." Max hurried to catch up with her.

She turned to him, a polite smile fixed in place. "Hello again, Mr. Powell. Is your bungalow comfortable?"

He stopped a little more than an arm's length from her, watching a cool breeze tease wayward strands of her raven hair forward. He curled his fingers into his palm to keep from brushing them back.

Max offered her a curious smile. "It's Max. Remember?"

Her bright eyes danced with mischief. "That's a relief. Max-well Powell III is a mouthful."

Max's cheeks warmed with embarrassment. Why had Sarah made such a public display of his identity as though anyone would—or should—care?

"Trust me. I know." He straightened his shoulders and held her eyes. "I apologize for Sarah's rudeness. She's been under a lot of stress but that doesn't excuse the way she acted toward you."

"I appreciate that." Alexis pulled her black purse farther onto her shoulder. "But you aren't responsible for her behavior."

"I feel responsible, though, since she works for me." Max gestured toward the lot. "May I escort you to your car?" It wasn't dark yet, but the sun was starting to set, and the shadows were growing longer.

"You may." Alexis turned.

"May I take your briefcase?" He offered her his hand.

Alexis blinked. She handed him the accessory. "Thank you."

Max glanced at Alexis from the corner of his eye as they walked across the asphalt parking area. He was thirteen again, experiencing the same anxious and excited feelings he'd had when he'd walked a girl he'd liked home from school.

Just breathe, Powell. "I had the impression you were aware of Sarah before you joined us. You addressed her by her last name without an introduction."

Alexis's lips twitched as though she struggled against a smile. "Clarissa, the front desk agent who processed your registration, called me. She was concerned Sarah might not appreciate all the resort's rules."

A weight pressed down on Max's shoulders. He didn't want to imagine what Sarah had done to raise Clarissa's concerns. "I'm sorry about that."

"Apologizing again?" The teasing glint in her eyes brushed the responsibility from his shoulders.

Max spread his arms. "I know I'm not responsible for Sarah, but everyone at the resort—you, Clarissa, Aaron, Roland—you've all been so welcoming. You don't deserve Sarah's rudeness."

"I'm glad we've made a good impression on you." Alexis stopped beside an older-model silver compact sedan. "In light of the suspicious package you received, we have to be even more aware of the resort's security rules and your safety. Frankly, we have to be extra careful about the welfare of everyone at Mariposa—our guests and our team. If someone has malicious intentions toward you, they could endanger everyone on the property."

"I hadn't considered the effect the threat would have on other people." Max stared across the lot, picturing a shadowy figure romping around his bungalow and stealing his stuff. He'd carry that burden for the rest of his life if anyone came to harm because of this stalker.

"Roland spoke with everyone who'd handled the package since it was delivered to our mailroom." Alexis extended her hand for her briefcase. Max reluctantly gave it to her. "There wasn't anything unusual about its arrival. Our postal carrier doesn't have any additional information on it."

Max didn't think they would. "I appreciate Roland's checking. He's very thorough." He tucked his hands into the front pockets of his black pants. "The NYPD's investigation is stalled. I appreciate your concern, and everything you and Roland are doing to solve this mystery."

This was much more than a mystery. He wasn't searching for misdirected mail or lost keys. It was a threat. Someone was following him. Who and why?

"Of course." Alexis again adjusted her purse strap on her shoulder. "The resort has exceptional security. We take our guests' safety very seriously. If you have any concerns or if there's anything you need, just let us know. Everyone here wants to make sure you enjoy your Mariposa experience."

Max heard the sincerity in her voice. "I appreciate that. And I'll make arrangements away from the resort to meet with Sarah. I'll abide by the resort's rules."

"Even though you're *the* Maxwell Powell III?"

"I'm just Max." He liked the way her eyes twinkled like stars when she teased him.

Alexis's chuckle strummed the muscles in his lower abdomen. She deactivated her car locks, then turned to set her briefcase and purse on the front passenger seat. Alexis closed the door before circling the car's hood as she moved to the driver's side. "I'll see you bright and early Monday, Max."

"I'm looking forward to it." Was his grin as goofy as it felt? "The project, I mean. I'm looking forward to getting started on the project."

Alexis waved before disappearing inside her vehicle. Max backed away from her sedan. He watched her pull out of her parking space and drive away.

Although he loved his career, this was the first time in a long time he was looking forward to a Monday.

Try having a vacation during your vacation.

Max received the text from his older sister, Miri, on his way to the resort's restaurant Friday evening. She'd copied their youngest sibling, Mel. Miri was the last person to get on his case about relaxing. Max paused to respond to her message.

When was the last time you & Odell took a break? Oh. Right. Your honeymoon 4 yrs ago. Farmers market tomorrow. Should be fun.

Miri responded with the eye-rolling emoji. Sounds like work.

Max chuckled, then put his cell on Mute before dropping it in his front pants pocket. He continued to the restaurant, Annabeth, where he was meeting Adam for dinner. Despite their demanding careers, they'd stayed close after graduation through calls, videoconferencing, emails, texts and occasional greeting cards. But it had been too many years since they'd seen each other in person.

He walked into the five-star restaurant and took a moment to enjoy the image of the vast, free-form pool with the stunning mountain ridge beyond. Every view of the mountains from the resort was gorgeous. He believed Alexis when she said the sights never got old.

The restaurant was quiet and classy with low lighting and white linens. As with the rest of the resort, the decor was tasteful and minimalistic with bamboo ceilings and flooring. The area was spacious but gave a sense of intimacy.

The kitchen was also in this building. Adam had told him it prepared the meals for the restaurant, pool service and any private meals guests might request be delivered to their bungalows, including the resort's signature champagne breakfast. Curiosity drove Max forward, eager to get a glimpse of the kitchen. A large hand caught his upper arm, stopping him in his tracks.

Adam's voice was thick with amusement. "I promise to give you a personal tour of the kitchen. But would you mind if we ate first? I'm really hungry."

"Adam, it's good to see you." Max returned his friend's embrace. "It's been too long."

"Yes, it has." Adam gave him a chiding look. "And I don't want to make it even longer by having to search for you in the kitchen."

"I don't know what you're talking about." Max stepped back to get a better look at his former college roommate. "The video chats aren't as good as speaking face-to-face. You're aging well."

In his tan business suit, Adam looked as fit as he'd been in college. A couple of inches shorter than Max, Adam was broad-shouldered but lanky. His deep blue eyes and tousled blond hair had attracted a lot of attention around NYU, but he'd only had eyes for his college sweetheart, Paige Barnes.

Adam briefly squeezed Max's shoulder. "You look *exactly* the same."

Max saw beyond the smile and worried about the fatigue and strain on Adam's tanned features. "You look stressed and hungry. Let's eat, then you can tell me what's on your mind."

Adam's broad brow creased. "I'm fine."

Max arched an eyebrow. "Try that on someone who hasn't known you for almost two decades. We roomed together for four of those years. I can read the signs."

Their host appeared. After greeting them, he led them to a window booth toward the center of the room. From that position, they could see the entire restaurant. Max wondered whether this was Adam's regular table.

After settling into his seat, Adam opened the menu but didn't look at it. "One of my concerns is the threatening message that came with the unmarked package that was waiting for you at the registration desk."

Max shouldn't have been surprised that Adam had been apprised of the situation. He looked up from his menu. "Roland told you?"

"He and Alexis." Adam's frown deepened. "You'd told me about the break-ins, but you didn't tell me the thief was stalking you. Should you hire security until this person's caught?"

"I live in a supposedly secure building." Max laid his menu down. "I was going to move before this trip, but my family thought I should take some time to relax first since moving is stressful."

"They're right." Adam hesitated. "I'll have one of our security guards accompany you when you're off-site."

Max started shaking his head before Adam finished speaking. "We don't have to go that far. This is a working vacation.

The only time I'll be off-site is when I go to the farmers market. The rest of the time, I plan to be in your resort's kitchen."

"Are you sure?" Adam didn't seem sold on the plan.

"Yes. But if I change my mind, I'll let you know."

Their server arrived to take their drink orders. They both asked for iced teas.

"Now tell me what else is on your mind." Max lowered his voice. "Is it your mother's remembrance?"

Annabeth Colton had died seventeen years ago this coming Sunday. Adam had been fourteen. Since he was the oldest, he had the clearest recollections of Annabeth and did his best to share them with his siblings to help keep her spirit alive.

Annabeth had been buried in a secluded section of Mariposa Resort & Spa. She'd loved the resort and had helped create wonderful memories here for her children. During the Colton siblings' remembrance ceremony, they went to her grave site together and placed bouquets of mariposas, their mother's favorite flower, on her grave.

Adam's shoulders rose and fell as he drew a deep breath. "This time of year is always difficult for Laura, Josh and me. And somehow my father always manages to find a way to make it even harder."

"What do you mean?" Max braced himself for the bad news.

Adam hesitated as though gathering his thoughts. "My father's lost all his money. He's trying to raise cash by taking the resort away from us."

Max's eyes widened with shock. He hadn't expected any of that. He reeled from the news that Clive Colton was broke. But the fact he would try to take away the legacy his children's mother had left for them made his skin burn with anger.

He struggled to clear his mind. "How could your father do that? I thought your mother specifically entrusted you, Laura and Joshua with the resort?"

"She did." Anger simmered in Adam's blue eyes. He masked it when their server arrived with their drinks and took their orders.

Max had been looking forward to the meal from this five-star restaurant but now he'd be satisfied with a sandwich—

made with fresh bread. He was much more interested in what Adam had to say and with what was going on with the resort, his friend's first love. Adam had started making plans for Mariposa's future while they were still in college. Maybe before that.

Shortly after they'd graduated, Adam had relocated to Sedona and taken legal control of the resort—at the cost of his personal life, including a future with Paige. He'd become general manager in addition to equal partner with Laura and Joshua. Laura was the resort's assistant manager and Joshua was the activities director.

Adam had dedicated his life to Mariposa. He'd put business before pleasure time and time again. His efforts and sacrifices had paid off spectacularly. Mariposa's unique location, stellar reputation and spectacular security allowed for a very private and highly sought-after experience for its wealthy clientele. And Clive wanted to take it away from him and his siblings.

Adam continued. "My father's the head of Colton Textiles."

"I remember. It's an elite importer."

Adam took a sip of his drink. "He's run his business into the ground. He can't pay the bills. He's laid off almost a third of his staff but even that hasn't helped his bottom line. The company's on the verge of bankruptcy. The only thing that might save Colton Textiles—or at least delay the inevitable—is a large influx of cash."

Max swallowed some of his iced tea, hoping to dislodge the knot of anger from his throat. "Is that where you, Laura and Joshua come in?"

"Yes." Adam ran the tips of his fingers over his glass. "My father came to me about a month ago to ask for a loan."

When Adam paused again, Max prompted, "But you knew if you gave him a *loan*, you'd never see that money again. And, even more importantly, he'd keep coming back for future *loans*."

Hence Adam's reference to Clive's cash influx only staving off the inevitable. Max had heard rumors in the business industry that Clive's father-in-law and his deceased wife had been the real geniuses behind the fabric import company.

Adam took a drink of his iced tea. "You're right. That's exactly what I'm afraid would happen. But when I refused to give him money—let's call it what it is—he showed me the land ownership papers for Mariposa. The land our resort is built on is held in trust by none other than Colton Textiles."

"Then whoever owns the company owns the land." Max watched Adam's nod of agreement. "How is that possible? Your mother wouldn't leave the property to your father, at least not without telling you."

Adam grunted. "I don't think she knew. My father admitted to sneaking the provision into paperwork my mother had signed while she was ill. Even then, seventeen years ago, he'd known he'd need money to help save his company."

"That was low." Max modified his language. His friend was already hurting. He didn't want to pile onto Adam's pain with the string of obscenities pounding against his skull.

"That's one way of describing it." Adam stared into his glass.

Max rubbed the tension from the frown between his eyebrows. "Can you buy him out?" He knew it was a futile question. If the Colton siblings were in a position to buy the land from their father, his friend would have led with that.

Adam shook his head, confirming Max's suspicions. "We can't afford the price he's named. It's a huge amount and he's not negotiating. Our only hope is to go into partnership with another business. Laura, Josh and I are looking for a company capable of purchasing half ownership of the resort. This will give us the cash we need to buy the property from my father. But we want a company that will still allow us to have control of the resort."

"A silent partner." Max shook his head, heartbroken for his friend. "I'm so sorry, Adam."

"So am I." Adam sighed. "The situation's not ideal. It's not what we want or what we ever imagined happening, but it's better than losing the resort, which is what would happen because Clive is definitely not playing fair."

An understatement. Max leaned into the table. "How can I help?"

Chapter Four

"Suz and I have been to Out with Friends during our trips to New York a few years ago." Alexis's mother's voice swung with enthusiasm. "We didn't see Max, though. Such a pity. We're planning another trip to New York in the fall. Maybe we'll see him then. What's he like?"

Alexis and her mother, Catherine Allen-Reed, were clearing the dishes after their regular Sunday dinner at her mother's home.

Catherine's question tugged Alexis from her thoughts. Today was March 16, the anniversary of Annabeth Colton's death. Laura had been twelve years old when her mother had died of pancreatic cancer seventeen years ago. Laura, Adam and Joshua would have held their annual private remembrance ceremony for their mother that morning. Today was the only day of the year the three siblings took off from work. How were they?

A ridiculous question. Alexis's father had died from cancer when she was seven. Her sister had been killed by a distracted driver a year after that. Their deaths were hurts that never went away. But loved ones made the pain a little easier to bear.

Alexis gave Catherine an indulgent smile. Her mother was a huge fan of the celebrity chef. "Mom, you know I can't talk about the resort's guests. In fact, I shouldn't have told you Max was staying at Mariposa."

Her mother looked much younger than her sixty years. A couple of times, they'd been mistaken for sisters. They were about the same height. Catherine managed to look both stylish and casual in a loose-fitting pale rose blouse and slim black jeans. Her mother's active lifestyle kept her fit and strong. Her still-dark raven hair was styled in a simple bob that framed her smooth, delicate golden-brown features.

"Don't worry. I haven't told anyone else, not even Suz." Catherine waved a slender dismissive hand. Her bright hazel eyes, which Alexis had inherited, sparkled. "But surely, you can tell me just a little bit. Is he nice? Polite? Does he have a good sense of humor?"

Suzanne Moore was her mother's best friend. They'd been close all Alexis's life. Suz had been a rock for her and her mother during her father's long illness and death. The two women had become inseparable after Alexis's older sister, Kaitlin, and Aunt Suz's husband had died. Suzanne's only child, Jacob, was one of Alexis's best friends.

"He's very nice." Alexis remembered his touch as he'd helped her out of the van. "And very polite. His parents raised him well."

She stiffened at the memory of the threatening note. She wouldn't tell her mother about that, though. It would be an invasion of Max's privacy, which was taboo at the resort. The Colton siblings as well as their employees signed nondisclosure agreements to secure their guests' confidentiality.

"Ah." Catherine started the dishwasher. "That's encouraging. He seems polite on his show but one never knows whether it's just an act. You know I've never missed an episode of *Cooking for Friends*."

Cooking for Friends was the only cooking show her mother watched and she was obsessed. Although she recorded each episode, she still arranged her schedule to avoid conflicts with the live viewing. On more than one occasion, she and Aunt Suz had hosted watch parties and invited their friends. Alexis couldn't think of a single program that inspired as much commitment from her parent.

"I know, Mom." Alexis dried the last pan and stored it in

the cabinet under the sink. "You talk about Max's show all the time. How could I *not* know? You're such a foodie. But why don't you ever try his recipes during our Sunday dinners?"

"Because sadly, they would be wasted on you." Catherine sniffed. "Your idea of fine dining is thin-crust pizza."

"I love the way you know me." Alexis wrapped her right arm around her mother's slim waist to give her a quick hug. "I much prefer your home cooking or a basket of burger and fries to a spoonful of tiny food I can't pronounce."

"Where did I go wrong?" Catherine led Alexis into her living room. They settled next to each other on the off-white, fluffy sofa. "Now you know why I save the fancy cooking for my dinner parties with Suz and the other ladies."

Once a month, her mother, Suz and four other women, all foodie friends from church, took turns hosting a dinner party. The ladies had been getting together for decades. The events gave these like-minded single mothers an opportunity to try elaborate recipes and share investment advice, career guidance, retirement strategies and parenting tips.

"You know, Suz and I will be eligible for early retirement in a couple of years." Catherine's cautious tone and change of subject put Alexis on alert. It was unusual for her blunt-speaking mother to weigh her words.

"That's exciting, Mom. I'm happy for both of you." She searched Catherine's expression for a hint of the direction this conversation would take. "You'll have a lot more time for your trips. Maybe you could travel abroad, too."

"That's true. You know how much I love to travel." There it was again, that hesitation in Catherine's voice. "And international trips would be exciting. We were also considering possibly relocating."

"Relocating?" Alexis blinked. "You and Aunt Suz are thinking of leaving Sedona? When? Why? Does Jake know?" If Jake knew and hadn't told her, the two of them would have to have words.

"It's just a possibility, Lexi. Nothing's definite." Catherine took Alexis's hands in her own. "Suz and I wanted both of you to have plenty of notice that this was something we're think-ing about doing."

She held her mother's hands a little tighter. "But why would you leave Sedona?"

Her family's roots grew deep in Sedona. Her parents had been born and raised here. They'd gotten married and started a family here. Alexis and her mother had buried her father and then her sister here. This was home.

Catherine gave her a gentle smile. The expression showed she understood how difficult change was for her daughter. "I agree Sedona is lovely. Suz and I have enjoyed raising our chil-dren here. But there are a lot of places that are just as lovely. A few are even lovelier and have more to offer. Some of them are close to the water. We want to allow ourselves the free-dom to at least consider moving to one of those other places."

Alexis released her mother's hands and leaned into her em-brace. "You're right, Mom. You and Aunt Suz deserve the freedom to pursue whatever makes you happy—as long as it's within the law."

Catherine chuckled, just as Alexis had intended.

She kissed her mother's cheek. "Thanks for giving me the heads-up."

Catherine gave Alexis a big hug before letting go. "Of course, dear."

Her mother's condo had an open floor plan with an abun-dance of natural light. As the sun set, Alexis rose to help her mother close the faux blond wood blinds around the living and dining rooms.

"You should experience Max's restaurant at least once." Catherine spoke over her shoulder as she closed the blinds behind the sofa. "He and his staff create dishes that bring food-ies from all over the world to his upscale restaurants in Man-hattan and Fort Lauderdale. And that was before he started his cooking show on that streaming channel."

Alexis closed the blinds near the fireplace. "It's probably even harder to get a table now."

"I'm sure it is." Catherine sounded as cheerful as though she benefited from Max's success. "His show has developed into almost a cult favorite. He has so much energy and enthusiasm."

"Really?" Alexis wondered whether she should start tuning in. She usually found cooking shows boring with a capital *B*. Maybe Max would change her mind. Or maybe she was making excuses to look at him without his being aware of it.

Did that sound creepy? Maybe a bit.

Her mother was still talking. "He's been getting a lot of traffic on the internet. And he's made appearances on talk shows and morning news programs. His cookbook's going to fly off the shelves. I can't wait to preorder it."

"How do you know about his internet traffic?" Was her mother tracking him, too?

Catherine either didn't hear Alexis's question or she chose to ignore it. "There's a lot of gossip about his personal life. Columnists and celebrity watchers are trying to start rumors about who he's dating but they haven't been able to connect him with anyone. There was a brief mention of perhaps something going on between him and his assistant, but I don't think those rumors lasted even a day."

A frown tightened Alexis's brow. She swallowed the denial in her throat. "There were rumors about a relationship between Max and Sarah Harris?"

Catherine's eyes widened with surprise. "How do you know Max's assistant?"

Alexis shook her head to clear her thoughts. "It's resort stuff, Mom. I can't talk about it."

"I understand, Lexi. The resort's guests pay a lot for their privacy. Although sometimes I wonder whether you work for some national spy agency." Catherine rolled her eyes as she returned to the sofa. "At the end of last year, an anonymous source had started a rumor that Max was involved in a *very personal* relationship with Sarah, who's a married woman, by the way. There wasn't anything to substantiate the gossip, no photos of the two of them together in public. There weren't any photos of the two of them working together, either. So as quickly as the rumors started, *poof*, they also died down." She snapped her fingers.

Alexis sat on the sofa, shifting to face her mother. "Perhaps someone from Max's organization tracked the source of the rumors and put an end to them."

She'd heard of the rich and famous having the resources to do that sort of thing. Thinking about Max's encounter with Sarah at the L, she was certain there wasn't anything romantic between them. Sarah had thrown herself—literally—into Max's arms when she'd seen him, but he'd quickly untangled himself from her embrace. According to Clarissa, he hadn't sounded pleased at Sarah's arrival, either. That was the reason the registration desk clerk had contacted Alexis about the situation. She'd wanted backup in case Sarah became disruptive, which she had. Kudos to Clarissa for planning ahead.

"It's possible Max had someone shut down the rumors." Catherine shrugged a negligent shoulder. "But I've read on the internet that Max's fame has brought *a lot* of gossip and fans who have very little respect for his personal boundaries."

Was Max's increasing celebrity the reason the stalker had latched onto him? It made sense. She and the rest of the resort staff would have to be aware of that possibility. They'd hosted high-profile guests before but, to her knowledge, they'd never had a stalker follow that guest or contact them at the resort. Fortunately, their security was tight. Although there weren't any security cameras on the grounds—again for the benefit of their guests' treasured privacy—Mariposa had guards on duty 24/7/365.

They'd have to remain vigilant for Max's sake—as well as the rest of their guests.

"Max? Max! I thought that was you."

The familiar female voice commanded Alexis's attention as she and Max crossed a four-lane street in downtown Sedona early Monday morning. She located Sarah Harris, waving at them from the curb they were approaching. Behind Sarah was the entrance to the Sedona Family and Community Farmers Market. Alexis's heart sank but her professionalism kept her shoulders squared and her brow smooth.

Today, Sarah's bright red hair fell in large, loopy curls to her chin. A slight breeze teased it. A knee-length old gold dress hugged her full figure. Max stepped up to the curb. Immediately, Sarah wrapped her arms around his neck.

Alexis's eyes widened in surprise. She stepped to the side to give them a semblance of privacy.

Max gently freed himself from her embrace. He circled Sarah and put an arm's length between them. He looked uncomfortable as he adjusted his dark sunglasses and black ball cap. "Sarah, hi. This is a surprise."

"I know, right?" Sarah stood with her back to the street. She held on to his hands. "Although I should've guessed you'd be here since you'd need to buy ingredients for your recipes."

Max tugged his hands free and gestured toward Alexis. "You remember Alexis Reed, the senior concierge with Mariposa."

Alexis could have done without Max drawing the other woman's attention to her.

Sarah's expression went from open and friendly to closed and hostile in a New York minute. "Of course."

Alexis inclined her head. "Good morning, Ms.—"

Sarah turned back to Max, effectively cutting Alexis off. Her pale, round face glowed with warmth and admiration. "Since we're both here together, I'll help you collect the ingredients you need. It'll be fun."

Alexis struggled not to let her temper at Sarah's dismissal show. It wasn't easy. If she strained a muscle during the effort, she'd file a worker's compensation claim.

"That's not necessary." Max inclined his head toward Alexis. His eyes were masked behind his shades' dark lenses. "Alexis is helping me."

Through her own sunglasses, Alexis watched a frown roll quickly across Sarah's face. It disappeared like a computer glitch. In contrast, it was hard to read Max's expression since his ball cap and shades obstructed his features. Did the celebrity chef realize Sarah had a crush on him?

"Nonsense." Sarah's laughter was forced. Alexis was sure of it. "*I'm* your assistant. Of course *I'll* assist you. It's *my* job."

Alexis expected Max to acquiesce to Sarah. She was preparing to be sent back to Mariposa. Disappointment tightened the muscles in her back and shoulders. Was it resentment at the thought of being set aside like damaged luggage after she'd gone to the trouble of adjusting her schedule to accommodate Max's needs? Or could it be envy at the thought of the other woman spending time with Max? She tried to deny it to herself, but the truth was part of her had spent the weekend looking forward to showing Max around the market this morning. She stepped toward the crosswalk, ready to make as gracious an exit as possible.

Max's words stopped her. "The show's on hiatus, Sarah. I've made other arrangements for my needs but thank you for your offer." He stepped closer to Alexis, lightly resting his hand on the small of her back. "Please excuse us."

Apparently, Sarah wasn't one to take no for an answer, at least not the first time. Instead, she moved to block them. She put her hand on Max's shoulder. "If you're working on recipes for the show, I'd like to be a part of that, Max. Please. Don't shut me out. Working with you while we're both here will be good for me. It will help keep my mind off the other issue I'm dealing with."

Her last statement caught Alexis's attention. Max had told her Sarah was going through a difficult time. Alexis should make a greater effort to be more patient and understanding toward the other woman.

Max stepped back, startling Alexis from her thoughts and breaking his connection with both her and Sarah. "Spend time with your family, Sarah. That's why you're here. At a time like this, you need their support."

Sarah rolled her eyes. Frustration poured off her. "My family's getting on my nerves. What I need is some time away from them." She fixed a pretty smile on her face. "You promised me a drink. When are we going to get together?"

Alexis's head was spinning from Sarah's rapid mood swings. She'd moved briskly through flirtatious, wheedling and frustration all while anger simmered right beneath the surface.

Max sighed. "I'll call you once I have a better idea of my schedule. In the meantime, get some rest, Sarah. You need to take care of yourself."

Sarah split a look between Alexis and Max. Her eyes were dark with resentment. After a brief pause, she nodded. "All right. I'll wait for your call, but don't make me wait too long." She gave him a tight smile before moving to the corner. Her gait was stiff.

Max's warm hand settled again on the small of Alexis's back. "I'm sorry to have taken up so much of your time with those negotiations. Sarah means well."

Alexis shook her head. "Please don't worry about it. It was nice of Sarah to offer to help you. Have the two of you worked together long?"

Max walked with her toward the collection of temporary booths, tables and tents that comprised the farmers market. "For a little more than two years. I hired her as my assistant for the show. She helped us get the project up and running."

"That's wonderful." From his tone, Alexis was certain he had no idea of his assistant's personal interest in him. It was so obvious, though. How could he miss it?

They entered the main market area. As always, Alexis was transported by the sights, sounds and smells of the vendors' products. It was crowded today, although not as packed as it had been yesterday when she and her mother had bought produce for the week.

At one of the vendor booths, Alexis lifted a packet of strawberries. She held it close to her face. The sweet, juicy fragrance filled her senses. She closed her eyes and allowed herself a moment to enjoy the experience.

She didn't have her mother's love of fussy little meals served on ridiculously large plates for exorbitant amounts of money, but she did share Catherine's love of fresh, organic fruits and vegetables. Alexis breathed the ripe clementines and grapefruits that surrounded her. Scallions, garlic, chili and cayenne woke her senses. The crisp, clean scents of broccoli and carrots made her mouth water.

"From your glowing expression and the bounce in your step, I have the feeling you've been here a time or two before." Max's gentle teasing was like a hug.

Alexis laughed to cover her discomfort. She hadn't meant to

let her professional mask slip so far. "My mother and I come here every week in season. We love it. What do you think of it?"

Max wore a plain black T-shirt and smoke-gray shorts. Alexis wondered if he thought those clothes, in addition to his sunglasses and ball cap, would allow him to blend into the crowd. If so, he was mistaken. The simple clothes drew attention to his tall, leanly muscled physique. Nearby shoppers were giving him second and even third looks. Max either hadn't noticed or he was pretending not to.

"I think produce that elicits a reaction like yours must be worth its weight in gold." He tossed her a smile and extended his hand. "May I get those strawberries for you?"

Alexis's fingertips itched to trace the deep dimple in his right cheek. His teeth were perfect. His deep voice wrapped itself around her, inviting her to... What had he asked her?

Alexis stepped back to clear her thoughts. Her laughter was even more nervous and embarrassed this time. "Thank you but I can handle the strawberries. I'm here to help with your cookbook recipes. Remember? What can I help you look for?"

Stop mooning over the man!

This wasn't a social outing. Mariposa's general manager himself had assigned her to help one of their many high-profile guests with a work project. Completing this task satisfactorily would provide another example of the exceptional service she offered the resort's guests and would be one more step toward proving herself deserving of a promotion to a management position, specifically the event manager's job.

Besides, Mariposa had hosted plenty of attractive celebrities: actors, models, singers, athletes. Alexis had never lost focus before. What made this guest different?

Her eyes moved from his clean, chiseled features to his long, lean physique.

Exactly.

Max shifted to face the produce. His stance brought him closer to her. Alexis recognized his fresh-mint scent above the smells of the fruits and vegetables. Was it his cologne, aftershave, deodorant, soap?

"This cookbook is the first in a series I've proposed, putting regional twists on fine-dining favorites, sort of like Manhattan clam chowder and New England clam chowder, or the one thousand and one ways to make mac 'n' cheese."

"That sounds interesting." Alexis approached the produce vendor and paid with cash for the strawberries.

"Thanks. I hope it will be." Max paused in front of a display of limes. He lifted one from the basket and gently squeezed it.

Alexis studied his sharp sienna features softened by full lips and wished she could draw.

Max turned and met her eyes. "Think fast."

Alexis gasped as a small lime cut through the short distance between them, flying toward her face. She caught it inches from her nose with both hands. Max burst into laughter.

She gaped at the celebrity chef. "Suppose I'd dropped it?" She sent the vendor an apologetic look. He forgave them with a wave.

"I'd have been embarrassed for you, but I would've paid for it." Still chuckling, he turned back to the produce. "Luckily, you have good reflexes." He selected more limes and added asparagus, a red onion and herbs. He handled the onion while giving her a considering look. "Think—"

"Don't." Alexis held up her left index finger.

Max shrugged, but his eyes twinkled with mischief. He paid for his items before leading her to another spice vendor. "And we're off."

Alexis's muscles remained on high alert. She hadn't expected this playful side to the soon-to-be published author. Was this his personality or were the scents of the farmers market making him giddy? She was beginning to suspect the sweet aromas of the fruit and the tangy scents of the vegetable were having an effect on her—although she never felt this way when she came to the market with her mother.

She watched Max touch and feel the coriander leaves. "What are you making?"

His lips curved into a smile. The teasing lilt in his voice invited her to join his game. "It's a secret."

That was disappointing. "Could I at least have a hint?"

He handed the herb vendor a credit card to pay for the cumin, mustard and coriander. "Nope."

She was more deflated than she'd thought she'd be. "All right, Chef. What about protein? Do we need the fish or meat market? Or both?"

Max took his purchases and his credit card receipt, then allowed Alexis to lead him from the table. "The Annabeth chef said she'd buy extra meats for me. I asked her to add whatever I use to my bill."

Alexis led Max out of the consumer pedestrian traffic before facing him. "Then I guess we're done."

Max patted her shoulder as he shook his head. "No, young padawan, we've only just begun."

Alexis arched an eyebrow. "Was that a *Star Wars* reference?"

He smiled with pleasure. "Yes, it was."

Shaking her head, Alexis walked past him and toward the crosswalk. With her back to Max, she freed the grin she'd been holding back since they'd started shopping. What a nerd. She could understand why Sarah had fallen for him.

Less than half an hour later, Alexis pulled into the parking lot in front of the L. Max wanted to get right to work on the recipe he was creating for his cookbook. Alexis felt the excitement shimmering around him as he sat on the passenger seat of her silver four-door sedan. He hadn't told her anything about the dish. Instead, they'd talked about Sedona and Mariposa. She'd described the advantages of the resort's proximity to Red Rock State Park, which was on the outskirts of the city. The park was close enough to allow Mariposa to benefit from its bird-watching and hiking trails. For those guests who occasionally wanted to venture off the property, Sedona was renowned for its New Age shops and its vibrant arts community, which supported a number of wonderful art galleries.

As Alexis pulled into a parking space near the front of the lot, she locked eyes with Mark Bower, the resort's recently fired concierge. He stood to the right of the L's entrance. Alexis suspected he was waiting to confront her. Her suspicion was confirmed when he straightened away from the building as she and Max emerged from her car.

Mark strode toward her. His steps were long and determined. The late Monday morning sun touched his sandy-blond hair. "Alexis, I want to talk to you."

Beside her, Max stiffened at Mark's aggressive tone. She turned to him. "I'm sorry, but may I ask you to wait for me in the lobby? I won't be long."

Max stared at Mark as though memorizing his description for a police report before facing Alexis. He'd taken off his shades. His beautiful brown eyes were dark with concern. "I can stay."

Mark frowned at Max's words. "This is a private conversation."

Ignoring Mark, Max repeated his offer. "Do you want me to stay?"

He was offering her a choice, which was empowering. She chose to let Mark know she didn't regret her actions. "No, but thank you. I won't be long."

Max took a moment, searching her expression. Alexis gave him a confident smile. She didn't have anything to worry about. She wouldn't speak for Mark.

Max finally nodded his acceptance of her decision. He gave Mark a deliberate look as he stepped past the other man. But instead of entering L, Max stationed himself three stingy strides from Mark. He was far enough to give them privacy but close enough to intervene, if necessary.

Alexis returned her attention to Mark. "Why are you here?"

Anger snapped in his green eyes. "Why do you think? I want my job back."

Mariposa paid generous salaries. It wasn't a surprise Mark wanted to return to his position with the resort. He'd realized he wouldn't be able to get another job in hospitality that paid nearly as well.

Alexis strained to keep her voice even. "You're no longer eligible to work at Mariposa. I removed you from your position on Friday for cause."

"You mean you fired me." A flush filled his thin, fair features. He flicked his right index finger straight up. "I made *one* mistake, and you fired me. Just *one*."

Alexis's mind still reeled when she considered what she'd found during her investigation into Mark's transgressions. Her body shook with something stronger than fury. "You made that *one* mistake over and over and over again. If I hadn't overheard you, you would have continued to make it."

It had been Alexis's responsibility to tell Laura that someone Alexis had hired had scammed their guests. Her skin burned with embarrassment. Laura had commended her on the way she'd handled the situation, but Alexis still felt guilty. There never should have been a situation to handle.

"I told you I wouldn't do it again." He stood several inches above her. "It's not as though anyone got hurt."

Alexis's eyes widened with disbelief. He still hadn't digested the magnitude of his betrayal even after she'd laid it out for him in painstaking detail during their meeting with the personnel director Friday afternoon.

She unclenched her teeth. "Mark, you violated the trust our guests put in us. You broke the trust the resort put in you. You've lost my trust completely."

"But—"

Alexis was too angry to listen. "Your job was to get tickets to events, concerts and shows for our guests. You were supposed to make reservations for them at restaurants and theaters. Simple. Straightforward." She fisted her hands to keep her body from shaking apart with anger. "You receive a salary way above the industry average to provide those simple and straightforward tasks for our guests. But you decided on your own to upcharge them directly for your services."

Mark's nostrils flared. "They didn't seem to mind."

Alexis saw red. "You took advantage of our guests. As Leticia and I reminded you Friday, during your orientation, you were told such actions were grounds for immediate termination. It's also in your employee handbook."

"I want my job back." Mark stepped forward, shouting at Alexis. "Now."

Alexis didn't back down. But before she could respond, Max's back appeared in front of her.

"Back. Off." The chef's impossibly broad shoulders blocked Mark from her view.

"You need to mind your business." Mark sounded less than certain.

"You need to mind your manners." Max's body radiated the heat from his temper.

Alexis stepped out from behind him. "Mark, I've made myself clear. The Coltons signed off on your dismissal. HR processed your termination. You're no longer employed by this resort. You're not welcome on this property. Leave. Now."

Mark looked from Max to Alexis. "We're not done."

"Yes." Alexis held his eyes. "We are." She took a breath to clear her head. "If you're seen on these grounds again, security will escort you off and I'll file the police report for trespassing myself."

She watched Mark turn and stomp his way across the parking lot to a cherry red pickup truck. It looked fully loaded. What were the payments on that thing? No wonder he was agitated about losing his job. Her muscles were still shaking with anger as she watched Mark climb into the truck's cab and drive off at a speed way above the limit.

"Are you all right?" Max's question refocused her attention.

She faced him. "I appreciate your concern, Max. But there was no need for you to intervene. I can take care of myself."

His frown eased. "I'm sure you can. That doesn't mean I'm going to stand by and do nothing when I see someone being attacked by a bully. What's his issue? He doesn't seem like an ex-boyfriend."

Alexis's eyes stretched wide with incredulity. "He's not. He's an ex-employee who wants his job back. You heard me. That's not going to happen."

Max nodded. "I see. What did he do?"

Alexis turned to lead him into the L. "It's a resort issue."

"I understand." He offered her a smile. "I admire your discretion. I'm sure all your guests do." Max sobered. "But,

Alexis, he's furious and he's threatened you. Promise me you'll be careful."

His concern touched her heart. Alexis nodded. "I promise."

Max shook his head as he matched his strides to hers. "First, I receive a threat and less than a week later, you receive one, too. What are the odds?"

Alexis shivered with foreboding. She would think those odds would be slim to none.

Chapter Five

"Lunch is served." Max's voice rang out from Alexis's office doorway early Monday afternoon.

She looked up from her paperwork. Max had covered his black T-shirt with a navy blue chef's smock. The color warmed the sienna tones of his skin. Her eyes dropped to the food trolley he'd wheeled across her threshold. It held two place settings.

"Wait. What's all this?" Alexis suspected she already knew the answer to that question. Beneath those silver domes were the meals Max had created using his new recipes.

"Your lunch." He removed the first cloche with a flourish. "Dry-rub chicken breast with grilled asparagus." Bright lights danced in his eyes.

Alexis pulled her attention from the chef and switched it to their lunch. A row of thinly sliced grilled chicken breasts were beautifully arranged in the center of the very large plain white porcelain plate. Asparagus spears, seasoned and grilled, lay across their width. The steam billowing up from the plate filled Alexis's office with the scents of chili, cilantro and mustard.

The meal smelled wonderful and looked tempting. It seemed moist, well-seasoned and hot. But Alexis's mind brought an image of her homemade Italian sub on whole grain bread served with a dill pickle spear and a bag of barbecue potato chips. She'd made the lunch with the fresh ingredients she'd bought from the farmers market yesterday. That had to count for something.

She stood from her desk. "Oh, wow. Thank you so much." She gestured toward the plate. "Your presentation is so beautiful. I'm really impressed."

"Thank you." Max grinned. "I hope you enjoy the meal." He gestured over his shoulder toward the small Plexiglas-and-sterling-silver conversation table behind him. "Do you mind if I set up over there?"

Alexis blinked. He was going to eat with her. Of course he was. There were two settings. *Duh.*

She placed her palms flat on her desktop to keep from wringing her hands. "I didn't realize you were cooking for me."

"Of course. We're in this together." Max transferred the place settings to her table without waiting for her reply. "I want your feedback on the recipes before I finalize them for the cookbook."

He what? Oh, my. Adam hadn't said anything about that.

Alexis hurried around her desk toward him. Her palm landed on the back of his hand as he reached for the second plate. The heat from his body rose up her arm and settled in her chest. Alexis couldn't move. She couldn't speak. Max stilled and lifted his eyes to hers. Seconds felt like minutes. She took an awkward step back, breaking their contact.

Her voice was husky to her ears. "The thing is, I'm not really into fancy foods. I'm more of a tacos-and-chips kind of person. Perhaps Laura would make a better taste tester for your recipes."

Max straightened, shaking his head. His eyes were full of questions she didn't want to read. "You've lived in this area all your life. I trust your feedback to help me with the regional flavors in my recipes."

Alexis couldn't think of an excuse that wouldn't make her seem churlish. Accepting defeat, she settled into the chair beside her. "All right. But I'll have you know, I eat meals that aren't specifically regional, too. In fact, I brought an Italian sub and barbecue chips for lunch."

"That's good to know. It shows you enjoy variety." Max spread the white linen napkin across his lap.

Alexis did the same, then sliced into the chicken breast. The knife slipped through the poultry as though it were cutting melted butter. It freed more spices: peppers, paprika and brown sugar. She took a bite. Cayenne, garlic and kosher salt teased her taste buds. The chicken melted in her mouth.

She closed her eyes in delight. "Mmm. Delicious."

"Really?" He sounded skeptical. He cut a slice of the chicken.

Alexis's eyes popped open. "Really." But she could tell he didn't believe her. "My mother's a big fan of your cooking. She's been to your restaurant in New York and has watched every episode of your show at least twice. She and her friends try your recipes during their monthly dinner parties."

"Alexis." He gently interrupted her nervous chatter. "What's wrong with the food? I can tell you're holding back. This cookbook is very important to me. I'd appreciate your honest reaction no matter how hard it might be to hear."

Alexis sighed and set down her silverware. "There isn't anything *wrong* with your food. It's just that, if you're going for a Southwestern style, you're not quite there. Yet."

"All right." Max leaned into the table. "How far off am I and what do I have to do to hit the target?"

Alexis selected an asparagus spear with her fork and held it up. "First, your choice of side. Asparagus doesn't really say 'Southwest.' It says 'California' or 'Washington.' Maybe 'New York.' In any case, it's more reminiscent of the coasts than the Southwest. You may be trying to add a twist to your recipe with the seasonings and the style of cooking, but when I see asparagus spears with a Southwestern meal, I think the chef hasn't made a connection with the region. It's like cosplay on a plate."

"That's a good point." Max inclined his head. "What else?"

Alexis saw the intensity in his gaze. Being the focus of his attention made her restless. "The seasonings. You're giving me a sample of the heat, but Southwestern cooking packs more of a punch. You need to really pour it on."

"This is great feedback. Exactly what I need to know. I'll go back to the drawing board and try again." Max picked up his knife and fork, and sliced more of the chicken breast.

"Please, not on my behalf." Alexis looked at him in dismay. "I'm not the audience you're cooking for."

"You're exactly the audience I want—people who love Southwestern cooking."

Alexis studied the entrée. It looked wonderful, smelled delicious and tasted great. She just wasn't into fancy meals and expensive restaurants. She preferred taco shacks and bar food, places where she didn't have to wonder which fork to use or wine to choose. Give her a highly caffeinated, carbonated beverage and she was good to go. She returned her attention to Max. She enjoyed visiting his world, but she preferred living in hers.

She lowered her silverware with a sigh. "Let's be honest, Max. With all due respect, I would probably never go to your restaurant."

Max cocked his head, giving her a curious half smile. "Why not?"

Alexis used her hands to illustrate her points. "In my experience, upscale restaurants serve you a little bit of food." She held her hands inches apart. "Then present you with a great big bill." She increased the distance between her palms. "If I'm going to spend that much money on a meal, I want to leave feeling full."

Max chuckled. "We'll have to agree to disagree."

"If we disagree, why do you want me to be your recipe tester?"

"Because you've presented me with a challenge, and I can never back down from one." The look in his dark eyes made her pulse skip.

Max was referring to his cooking, but Alexis was awakening to a challenge of her own. Her growing attraction to her client.

Max left his bungalow late Friday afternoon and went in search of Alexis. He'd seen her around the L during the week as he contrived to take breaks from his work that might coincide with her arrival to her office, her lunch breaks or her leaving work for the day. But he hadn't spoken with her since Tuesday afternoon when he'd served her his second attempt at a Southwest-inspired chicken dish. He'd incorporated her feedback, but he still hadn't won her over. Max hadn't worked this hard to impress someone with his cooking since he'd first started in his career. Alexis was shoving him out of his comfort zone. That realization brought him up short. Had he been taking the praise and rave reviews for granted? Had he lost his edge?

Arriving at her office, Max squared his shoulders, then knocked softly on her open door. Her eyes widened in surprise when she saw him. She seemed to relax when she realized he'd left the food trolley behind.

"Come in." Alexis gave him a welcoming smile. "How can I help you today?"

Max sat on the burnt-umber guest chair closest to the window in front of her white modular desk. "What are you doing tomorrow morning?"

She tilted her head. "Why?"

"I thought we could go hiking on the trails you'd told me about Monday." *I really want to spend time getting to know you.* "Consider it a thank-you for helping me with my work and giving me so much of your time."

Alexis grinned. Her full, bow-shaped lips parted over bright white teeth. "I thought the lunches you made for me Monday and Tuesday were your way of saying thank you."

Max leaned back against his seat, balancing his left ankle on his right knee. "I mean a non-work-related thank-you."

Alexis's brow furrowed but her bright eyes twinkled with amusement. "You want to thank me for giving you my time by taking up more of my time?"

This wasn't going the way he'd imagined. "Do you have other plans?"

"Actually, I do." Her bright eyes teased him as though saying, *Come strong or don't bother.*

Challenge accepted. "Let me rephrase that. Do you have other plans that can't be moved so you can go hiking with me tomorrow morning?"

"No, I don't."

"Then come hiking with me."

She still hesitated. "Max, Mariposa employees are not supposed to fraternize with our guests."

"We're not fraternizing. You're going above and beyond helping me with my work. I want to thank you. It's just a friendly hike out in the open. It'll be fun."

"All right, Max." Alexis's smile was uncertain. "A friendly hike on the open trail. I'll see you tomorrow morning."

"Great. I look forward to it." Max stood to leave before she could change her mind.

But not before he realized she'd added another challenge to his list. How was he going to get to know Alexis if spending time with her was against the rules?

"I don't know whether it's the hike or the scenery that's taking my breath away." *Or the woman I'm hiking with.*

Max stopped beside Alexis at an overlook just off the hiking path early Saturday morning. From their vantage point, he enjoyed the majesty of their surroundings. Rich red earth covered the hiking trails and the mountains circling them. Wisps of bright white clouds streaked the wide blue sky.

"It's the scenery." Alexis moved away from him and closer to the guardrail that bordered the edge of the overlook. She shoved her hands into the front pockets of her black hiking shorts, which hugged her slim hips and displayed her long dancer's legs. Her lemon yellow T-shirt highlighted her skin's warm gold undertones. "It always takes my breath away."

Max drew a deep breath, catching the woodsy, cedar scents of the nearby foliage, which Alexis had identified as manzanita and juniper trees. They were beautiful. "You were right. I could never get tired of this view."

Alexis beamed at him from over her shoulder. Her eyes sparkled like stars. Max could gaze into them all day. A cream tennis cap helped protect her skin from the sun's rays. She'd gathered her shoulder-length raven tresses in a ponytail that waved in the mild breeze. The style emphasized her classic features, which were free of makeup. This moment would make such a beautiful photo, especially with the mountains in the distance behind her. Max had a feeling Alexis would object to having her picture taken, though, and he didn't want to make her uncomfortable.

She turned back to the overlook. Pulling her right hand from her pocket, she pointed straight ahead. "Red Rock State Park. Oak Creek cuts through it. You should visit while you're here."

He exhaled, feeling more relaxed than he had in years. "This view is therapeutic. I can better appreciate why my family's always after me to take a vacation. They were happy last night after I texted them that I was going on this hike with you this morning."

Alexis turned toward him. "You've mentioned your family's concern about your not making time to relax before. When was the last time you went on vacation?"

"It's been a while." Max rubbed the back of his neck as he tried to calculate the passage of time. "A few years, perhaps. Between the restaurant and the show and now the book contract, I've been a little busy."

Alexis tilted her head with curiosity. "Why open restaurants and do the show? It seems like just one of those enterprises would be a lot of work. You're doing both. Why not focus on just one?"

Max let his right arm drop back to his side. "I think Jay-Z put it best. I'm not a businessman. I'm a business, man."

Alexis rolled her eyes. "Still, while you're here, you should at least take a few hours each day to enjoy the resort's amenities—the spa, pool, horseback riding. It would be a waste if you didn't."

"All right." Max raised his hands in surrender. "Which ones would you recommend?"

Feigning offense, Alexis gasped, pressing her right hand to her chest. "*All* of them. As the senior concierge, I've used all the amenities so I could personally recommend them to our guests."

Max grinned at her playacting. "How long have you worked at the resort?"

"Seven years." Alexis exhaled. "I love it here. I love what the Coltons have built and I'm proud of the role I've had in it."

His senses drank in her expression. It was more than contentment. It was happiness radiating from the inside out. "My mother always repeats the maxim, 'If you do what you love, you never work a day in your life.'"

"It's true." She held his eyes. "Do you love what you do, Max?"

He didn't have to think about it. "Yes, I do. I'm exactly where I want to be, doing exactly what I want to do."

"I feel the same. But whenever I feel stressed, all I have to do is look out a window." Alexis faced the overlook. "Who could be stressed with a view like this?" She set her forearms on the guardrail.

Then everything happened so fast. Max saw the guardrail collapse beneath Alexis's touch. He saw her throw up her arms as her body tipped forward.

He heard her scream.

Before he could think—before he could breathe—he leaped forward. Max caught Alexis's wrist as she fell over the edge. He tightened his grip as he landed on the ground, coughing as he inhaled the soil.

His heart was in his throat. He swallowed it down. "I've got you." His voice was breathless.

"Oh. Oh." She was panting. Max stretched forward to get a better view of her. Alexis tipped her head back. "Don't let go." Her voice was thin with fear.

"I won't." Max's mouth went dry. Beneath Alexis was a sheer drop of several feet onto a pile of large, sharp rocks. He extended his right arm. "Give me your hand. I'll pull you up."

Her eyes widened with fear. "I don't want to pull you over."

Max forced a confident smile. "My luggage weighs more than you do. Give me your other hand."

She offered her hand. He took her wrist. He felt the tremors of fear racing up her arms. Max closed his eyes and prayed for her safety and his strength. Alexis steadied herself with her feet on the side of the hill, using her legs to push herself up as Max pulled her.

Max rocked his hips to draw himself backward. "I've got you. You're doing great."

Undergrowth dug into his thighs and torso. Rocks cut into his flesh. His shoulder muscles burned. He gritted his teeth and carried on. Her breaths were amplified in his ears.

"Just a little farther. We're almost there." *God, please don't let anything happen to her.*

Suddenly her weight was lifted from his arms. Max looked up and saw Alexis crawling toward him. He released her wrists and rose onto his knees, drawing her to him. She was shaking so hard, he thought she'd fly apart. Or maybe they were both shaking. He tightened his arms around her. Now that they were on solid ground, Max could admit—to himself at least—that he'd never been more afraid in his life.

He squeezed his eyes shut. "You're going to be all right. I've got you. You're going to be all right." He crooned the words against her ears. He didn't want to let her go.

Alexis leaned back to look up at him. Her eyes were wide. Her pupils were dilated with fear. "You saved my life." She pressed her face against his chest and tightened her arms around him.

He kissed the top of her head and held her until they both stopped shaking. Max took a deep breath, filling his senses with the faint wildflower fragrance of her perfume. He exhaled as he helped her to stand with him. Max looked her over. There were several thin scratches on her right cheek. Deeper scrapes on her right thigh, both of her knees and shins were bleeding. He saw the bruises that were starting to form on her wrists and his heart clenched.

He brushed his left hand over the marks. They were roughly the size of his fingers. "I'm so sorry."

Alexis bent her head to catch Max's eyes. "You saved my life. I can't thank you enough." Her voice quavered. She looked down at his legs. "You're hurt, too."

Max looked down at his wounds. "It's nothing. Let's get you back to the resort." He offered his left arm to steady her. "I believe the brochure says there's a medical clinic on-site."

"You're right. It's in the L." Alexis took a step forward. With a sharp hiss, she tightened her hold on his bicep.

Max glanced down at her legs. "Is it your ankle?"

"I think I twisted it." She gingerly rotated her left foot. "Yes, it feels tender."

"I'll carry you back to the car." Max bent to lift her.

Alexis stopped him with a hand on his shoulder. "I can walk, if you let me lean on you a little."

"Of course." Max wrapped his left arm around her lithe waist. "We need to get you to urgent care."

Alexis reached up to put her arm on his shoulder. She nodded her agreement but didn't look happy about it. He couldn't blame her. This wasn't the way he'd seen their day together ending. This certainly wasn't the way he'd hoped to get her into his arms.

Moving slowly in deference to Alexis's injury, it felt like it took twice as long to get back to the L late Saturday morning as it had hiking the trail to the overlook. When Max finally pushed through the main building's entrance, near pandemonium broke out. Resort employees from the reservations desk, the concierge counter, the bar and other areas hurried toward Alexis. Their eyes were wide with shock. Their brows were creased with concern.

"Alexis, are you all right?"

"What happened?"

"Are you okay?"

Alexis stiffened against him. She drew her hand from his shoulder. Her smile seemed stiff. "I care about all of you and appreciate your concern but, please, let's not agitate our guests."

Clarissa rested her hand lightly on Alexis's left shoulder. "But what happened?"

Alexis glanced at Max before answering. "I fell during our hike."

Max felt the eyes of the guests in the lobby area on them. He sensed Alexis's rising tension and knew she didn't want to be the center of this distraction.

He shared a smile with the small group of caring coworkers around them. "Ladies and gentlemen, thank you for your concern. I'll help Alexis to the clinic now. We can talk later."

Alexis gave him a grateful look. He helped her past her colleagues, across the lobby and down the hall toward the clinic.

She braced her arm on his shoulder again. "I should've gone home and taken care of these scrapes and wrapped my ankle myself."

Max's arm reflexively tightened around her waist. "After a fall like that, it's better to have a professional examine you to make sure you're okay."

She gave him a side-eyed stare. "Then they should check you out, too."

Max frowned as they reached the blond wood door to the little clinic. "I suppose that's only fair."

The clinic was the last office in the administrative hall. The cozy space was cheerful and bright with homey touches. According to the resort's website, it had a small staff, which included physician's assistants, nurses and nurses' aides. They were available 24/7/365 to assist guests as well as employees in the event of a sudden illness or injury. Max admired the forethought Adam and his siblings had in offering these services on-site. He just hadn't imagined needing to use them.

A middle-aged woman at the front desk sprang from her seat as soon as Max assisted Alexis across the bamboo threshold. Her dark brown eyes widened. Her thin brown face cleared of all expression as she rushed toward them.

"Alexis, honey, what happened?" She was several inches shorter than Alexis. Her slight accent tagged her as a Southern transplant.

Alexis's smile seemed more natural this time. "Nurse Zoe Morgan, this is—"

"Chef Max Powell. I love your show." Zoe's eyes dropped to Max's legs. She hissed in empathy. "You're pretty banged up, too, Chef."

Max could imagine he and Alexis looked like they'd limped away from a terrible accident, which they had. "We fell during our hike."

Zoe motioned them to nearby visitors' chairs. "That must've been some fall." She waited for Max to assist Alexis onto one of the chairs before she knelt in front of them. With a gentle touch, she examined first Alexis's legs, then Max's. With a sympathetic wince and a sigh, Zoe pushed herself to her feet. "Since Alexis looks a little worse for wear, I'll bandage her up first, then I'll come back for you." She waved Max back to his seat when he started to rise. "I'll help our friend into the exam room. I'm stronger than I look."

Max watched Zoe assist Alexis across the reception area, ready to lend a hand, if they needed one. They didn't. As Zoe closed the door behind them, his cell phone rang. It was Adam. Strange. He'd been about to call his friend.

"Hey, I—"

Adam interrupted. His voice was tense. "Where are you?"

Max frowned. "I'm at your clinic. Why?"

"We're on our way."

Max's confusion doubled. "Who's we?" But Adam had hung up.

Minutes later Adam, Laura and Joshua arrived at the clinic. They wore almost identical expressions of concern and dismay. Max stood in time to catch Laura as she flung herself against him.

"Thank you for saving my friend." Her voice shook with emotion. She hugged him tightly before stepping back.

Adam's eyes were on Max's wounded legs. "For crying out loud, Max, you and Alexis could've been killed."

"How did you know about the accident? I was about to call you." Max shifted his attention from Adam to his siblings.

There was a strong family resemblance among the Coltons. Laura, the middle child, stood a step behind Adam. She was a tall, blue-eyed blonde. Her pale pink skirt suit emphasized her peaches-and-cream complexion. Beside her, Joshua, the youngest, was the same height as Adam but he wore his dark blond hair longer. He was the only sibling not wearing a business suit. His lanky form was clothed in khaki, knee-length shorts and a mud-brown polo shirt tagged with the Mariposa Resort & Spa logo.

Joshua tapped his cell phone screen before turning it toward Max. A video played with an off-screen voice narrating the events. The caption read, "Celebrity Chef's Heroic Rescue."

Max stiffened with surprise. "How could they have posted the footage so quickly? Is that from a drone?" He hadn't noticed one near them. But then, he hadn't been aware of anything but Alexis and their efforts to get her to safety.

His eyes stretched wide as one of the most frightening experiences he'd ever had replayed on some internet entertainment news site. Max's blood turned to ice as he watched himself leap across the screen like a professional football receiver going after an impossible pass. He saw himself securing his hold on Alexis and helping her to safety before they collapsed in each other's arms. Max locked his knees to keep from collapsing back onto the chair behind him. The video ended with Alexis and him limping back down the trail.

"I think so." Joshua glanced at his phone screen. "What happened to the guardrail?"

Max met the younger man's wide blue eyes. "It collapsed when Alexis leaned against it."

The blood drained under Joshua's healthy tan. "How's that possible? I checked it just last night. I checked all of them. They were solid."

"I believe you." Alexis's simple words came from across the room. Zoe had bandaged her deeper cuts and wrapped her ankle. Alexis held a cane in her right hand. Zoe stood beside her with a first aid kit.

Laura led the group to her. She rested her hands on Alexis's shoulder. "How are you?"

"I'm fine." Alexis managed a smile.

Zoe snorted. "She'll need to stay off her ankle for a day or two." She dragged a seat to Max and waved him toward the chair behind him. "Let's get you cleaned up now."

Max took the seat Zoe indicated, then rested his legs on the one she'd pulled over. Zoe sat beside him to tend his injuries. The iodine stung. Max gritted his teeth and tried not to flinch. He looked up and caught the empathy in Alexis's eyes. This must have been what she'd gone through.

Alexis nodded toward Joshua's cell. Her voice was stiff with dread. "Is there a video of the accident?"

Joshua returned his cell phone to the front right pocket of

his shorts. "I'm afraid so. We've been able to prevent drone operators from flying their machines directly over the resort. But this one looks like it was over Red Rock State Park, which is illegal. I'll file a report about it."

Alexis rubbed her eyes before looking back to Max. "I'm so sorry for this invasion of your privacy."

Max could feel her frustration and anger from across the room. "All that matters is that you're safe."

"I'm glad you're both going to be okay." Joshua took a step back, jerking a finger over his left shoulder. "I need to repair that guardrail and check the others before there are any more accidents."

Max watched the youngest Colton stride from the room. Joshua had said the guardrail had been secure when he'd checked it last night. Like Alexis, Max believed him. Then why had it broken free of its restraints and fallen down the hill so easily?

"You're good to go, Chef Max." Zoe's pronouncement broke his train of thought. She packed up her first aid kit.

"Thank you very much, Nurse Zoe." Max tossed her a smile before switching his attention to Alexis and her cane. "If you don't mind my driving your car, I'd be happy to take you home."

Alexis balanced her cane as she rotated her left ankle. "I'll be fine but thank you for offering. I should get going. I need to warn my mother about the video before she learns about it from someone else."

Laura stopped Alexis with a hand on her left forearm. She looked at Max. "I think you should let Max drive you home, Alexis. You're injured and you've had a horrible scare. I'd feel better if he was with you."

"So would I." Adam shoved his hands into the front pockets of his pale suit pants. "We want to make sure you get home safely."

Max looked between the two Colton siblings. He heard the sincerity in their voices. They were serious about their concern for Alexis's well-being. Then why did he also have the feeling they were trying to play matchmaker?

"Sorry, Alexis." Zoe crossed to the exam room doorway

where Alexis still stood. "It's four to one. And I'm sure it would be five to one if Joshua were still here."

Alexis shook her head with a smile. "All right. I surrender." She turned that powerful smile on Max. "I don't mind your driving my car, if your offer still stands. But you'd have to pick me up for work Monday morning."

Laura frowned. "But Zoe said you need to stay off your foot for a few days."

Alexis tilted her head. "And I'll be able to do that at work. I have a desk job, remember?"

Laura turned to the nurse. "Zoe, what do you think?"

Zoe snorted. "You know how stubborn Alexis can be. I think we should take the win with her agreeing to let Max drive her home." She pinned Alexis with a look. "As long as you promise that the only walking you'll do is to the bathroom and back to your desk."

Alexis's eyes widened in what Max could only describe as indecision. "I can only promise to try my very best."

Zoe sighed, shaking her head as she disappeared into the exam room.

Max stood. "I'll take you home."

Those words made him almost lightheaded with longing. He hoped it wouldn't make him unsafe to drive. He'd had more than enough excitement for the weekend.

Chapter Six

"Chef Max is driving me home." In his peripheral vision, Max saw Alexis hold the phone away from her ear as a scream emerged from the mic. "Yes, Mom. He's in my car with me now."

Max chuckled. He hadn't expected that information to prompt such an extreme reaction from Alexis's mother, or anyone's mother, for that matter.

"Mom, please don't call Aunt Suz." Alexis rubbed her eyes with the thumb and two fingers of her left hand. She listened in silence to the voice Max could just make out through her cell phone. "Because there's no reason to worry her. Just as there's no reason for you to worry. I only called because I didn't want you to be caught off guard if you saw the video before we had a chance to talk."

Alexis tapped Max's right arm, then signaled for him to get into the left-turn lane. He followed her instructions. She'd been using hand motions to direct him to her condo since she'd called her mother after they'd pulled out of the resort parking lot. Max didn't mean to eavesdrop on her call, but the one-sided exchange made him smile. It reminded him so much of his conversations with his family.

"No, Mom. I'm sorry. I didn't mean to imply you wouldn't have the right to freak out over the video. Of course you would."

More silence. The voice on the other end of the line came across as a high-pitched murmur. "Yes, please, let's have Sunday dinner at my house this weekend. I'd like that." While Alexis listened to her mother, she pulled an electronic door opener from her purse. "No, please don't call Aunt Suz. I mean it, Mom." A shorter pause. "Because Aunt Suz will want to call to check on me and I'd really like to get some rest."

Alexis tapped his arm again, then pointed to a condo on the right side of the street. She depressed the device to raise the garage door.

"Thank you, Mom. I really appreciate that. Okay. Bye. Yes, I'm home now. B—" Alexis paused again. "I will. Bye." She disconnected the call. "My mother thanks you for driving me home."

"Please tell your mother she's very welcome." Max parked Alexis's car in her attached garage.

As she depressed the button to lower the unit's automatic door, Max hustled to the passenger side to assist her from the seat. He feared she'd hurt herself trying to get out on her own. As he suspected, she was already trying to manage with the help of her cane. He'd only known her eight days, but he'd already picked up that she was determined not to lean on anyone, ever.

He offered her his right hand. "Let me help you."

"I'm usually a lot more graceful." Alexis lightly took his hand. She steadied her cane before pushing herself up and out of the seat.

Max searched her quietly determined expression. "You're doing fine. Better than fine."

"I also apologize for being on the phone with my mother during the entire drive over here. I feel so rude."

"You weren't rude. I understand. My parents are the same way."

With his hand on the small of her back, Max escorted her across the threshold of the garage entry door. It opened into her kitchen. One could tell a lot about a person from their kitchen. Alexis's was spotless. It had updated blond wood cabinetry and

flooring, granite kitchen countertops and stainless-steel appli-
ances. But the space was short and narrow.

Her refrigerator was dotted with magnets in the shapes of
colorful fruits, vegetables and wildflowers. Potted herbs sat on
the window ledge and measuring spoons stood in a container
near the stove. Max smiled to himself. He suspected Alexis
enjoyed cooking but didn't entertain a lot.

He followed her from the kitchen. Alexis moved cautiously,
perhaps because she was still getting used to the cane. He was
ready to catch her if she stumbled. They walked through the
dining area and into her family room. Max was struck by the
amount of natural light filling Alexis's townhome. The open
floor plan welcomed the early afternoon sunlight. Rays danced
against the blond wood flooring and spun back to the warm
cream walls and pale tan furnishings. Red, orange and grape
accents drew his eyes to the curtains, rugs and throw pillows
that beckoned him farther into the space.

"Your home is so welcoming." Max's eyes swept the photos
arranged on the mantel on the opposite wall. There were several
of her with a woman who looked a lot like her. Her mother?

"Thank you." Alexis's cheeks pinkened with pleasure. "The
few hours I do get to spend at home, I want to feel as relaxed
as possible."

"I can relate to what you're saying. You want your home to
be a sanctuary." That was one of the things that bothered him
the most about the break-ins. The thief had intruded on a space
he'd considered his retreat.

Max shoved his hands into the front pockets of his shorts.
His eyes dropped to the wounds on Alexis's legs. "Alexis, I'm
so sorry about the accident and your injuries, about the entire
experience. I feel responsible. Hiking had been my idea. If I
hadn't talked you into it, none of this would have happened."

Alexis held out her hand, palm out. "That's ridiculous. This
was an accident. Nothing more. None of this is your fault, and
I'd agreed to go hiking with you."

Max ran a shaking hand over his close-cropped hair. "I've
never been as scared as I felt when I saw you falling over the
edge of that cliff."

Alexis's knuckles turned white with her grip on her cane. She began to visibly shake. Max rushed forward to catch her as she started to crumble. He helped her to the tan cloth couch beside her.

"I'm sorry." She repeated the words in a voice as thin as a spider's web.

Drawing her into his embrace, Max pressed her head to his shoulder and stroked her right arm. "Don't. You have nothing to be sorry for. I'm the one who put you in danger. I should be apologizing to you."

Alexis pulled back to meet his eyes. "No, none of this is your fault. It's just... If one small thing had been different, I could've died today. If I'd been hiking alone. Or if you hadn't been able to catch me. Or if you hadn't been able to hold me." A violent tremor rolled through her.

Max held her more tightly. "But you weren't alone. And you were able to help pull yourself by climbing up the side of the hill. You were strong and calm the whole time. Your courage helped me keep it together."

Alexis took a shuddering breath. Her muscles were taut. "I may have seemed calm on the outside, but I was quietly having a meltdown on the inside." She held his eyes. "Thank you so very much for saving my life."

The look in her bright eyes was more than gratitude, more than caring. It was hypnotic. Max felt himself leaning closer. Alexis's eyes darkened. They dropped to his lips. Max's pulse leaped once. He pressed his lips to hers. They felt warm and soft. He stroked his tongue across her lips. Their taste was sweet, intoxicating. Alexis's body softened in his arms. She parted her lips to let him in. Max's body warmed in response. He swept his tongue inside her mouth. She caressed it with her own. The muscles in his lower abdomen quivered. Her arms wrapped around him. The scent of her perfume filled his head. He heard the pulse drumming in his ears.

Or was it a fist pounding on Alexis's door?

The doorbell chimed incessantly, accompanied by a demanding male voice. "Lex. Lex. Let me in."

Alexis started in his arms, then pulled back. Her eyes

seemed dazed as she looked at him. She licked her lips and his muscles ached. "Excuse me. I should get that."

He stood with her. He cupped her left elbow, providing some small support as he accompanied her to the front door. Whoever had come to see her wasn't letting up on the noise. The wannabe guest continued pressing the bell and calling her name.

Alexis's scowl grew ominous. She started speaking before she opened the door. "Jake, what is wrong with you—"

A tall, broad-shouldered man strode forward. He enveloped Alexis in a bear hug, rocking her from side to side. "Lex! Thank goodness you're safe."

Max's eyes widened. His jaw dropped. He let his arm fall to his side and stepped back.

Who was this?

The tall, good-looking man finally gave Alexis some breathing room, but Max noticed he kept an arm around her shoulders.

The new arrival was about Max's height, six foot two, lean, with fair skin and coal black eyes. His thick, tight, black curls were shaped into a trendy fade.

"Max, I'd like you to meet Dr. Jacob Moore. He's an accounting professor at Northern Arizona University in Flagstaff and a dear friend." The warm smile Alexis gave the other man filled Max with envy. "Jake, this is Maxwell Powell. He's a chef and host of *Cooking for Friends*. He's also a guest at Mariposa."

Jake's balanced features brightened with a huge grin. His perfect white teeth were gleaming testaments to the benefits of good oral hygiene. "You're the dude who saved my girl." He pulled Max into a bear hug. "Thank you so much, man. From the bottom of my heart."

My girl?

Max patted Jake's shoulders before stepping back. "Of course."

Disappointment drained the oxygen from the room. Why hadn't he considered that Alexis—beautiful, brilliant, charming and funny Alexis—would be in a relationship? Why hadn't that possibility occurred to him before he'd kissed her? But...

She'd kissed him back. He turned his attention to Alexis. She was still looking at Jake.

"Did my mother call you?" she asked.

Why was she acting like nothing had happened? She'd kissed him back, knowing she had a boyfriend. Apparently, that didn't matter to her. Had he misjudged her?

Jake locked her front door before maneuvering himself between Max and Alexis to help Alexis back to the sofa. "Your mother called my mother, who called me."

"I specifically asked Mom not to call your mother." Alexis looked to Max. "You heard me ask her not to call Aunt Suz, didn't you?"

"I did." What was happening right now?

Jake continued. "I promised Mom I'd check on you, but you know she's going to call you later." He propped the cane against the side of the sofa and positioned one of the pillows on the coffee table. Max gritted his teeth as he watched Jake lift both of Alexis's legs onto the pillow, then kneel beside her. He stared at her bandages. "Lex, your legs are a mess."

"Thanks." Her tone was dry.

Jake didn't seem to hear her. "I thought I was going to have a heart attack watching that video."

A part of Max wondered if he should excuse himself. A larger part wanted answers to a myriad of questions, starting with why had Alexis kissed him back?

Alexis sat up on the sofa. "You didn't send the video to my mother, did you?"

Jake gave her a sarcastic look. "Of course not. That video should come with an H rating for being hazardous to your health." He pushed himself to his feet. "Do you need anything before we leave?"

We? Max glanced at the other man. Who said *we* were leaving?

Alexis swung her legs off the pillows and reclaimed her cane. "No, I'll be fine." She pushed herself to her feet. "Max was going to use my car to get back to Mariposa, though."

That's right. Her car keys were still in his pocket. Max

started to assure her that he'd take good care of her vehicle, but Jake spoke first.

"I'll run you back to the resort." Jake jerked his thumb toward the front door.

Max stiffened. He didn't want to accept a ride from Alexis's boyfriend, especially not with Alexis's taste still on his lips. He turned to her, but her serene expression seemed to approve of Jake's plan.

He searched his mind for an excuse out of the situation. "I don't want to leave you stranded. How will you get to work Monday?"

Alexis waved a dismissive hand. "I'll be fine to drive myself by Monday."

Max frowned. Was she really that unbothered by the fact that they'd exchanged a passionate kiss while she was in a relationship with another man? What was he to think of this?

"Max has a good point." Jake tipped his head toward Max beside him. "I'll swing by and drive you to work Monday morning. We'll have to leave a little early, though, so I can get to my office on time."

Alexis rolled her eyes. "Fine. You both can stop playing nursemaid now."

Defeated, Max returned Alexis's car keys. "I hope you're feeling much better by Monday."

"Thank you." Alexis dropped her keys into her shorts pocket and glanced at his wounded calves. "I hope you are, too."

She smiled at him, but her eyes seemed wary with curiosity. It was as though she sensed something was bothering him but didn't know what it was. How could she miss it? The six-foot-two-inch source of his problems was literally standing between them.

Max followed Jake to the door. On impulse he turned back to Alexis before leaving. "If you need anything, please call me."

She smiled again. "I promise."

Max nodded, then turned away. But how could he trust someone who would kiss him the way Alexis had when she was already involved with someone else?

* * *

Max walked into his bungalow after bidding goodbye to Jake. Within five minutes of being in the car with the other man, he found it hard not to like him. He was good-natured, intelligent and interesting. He could understand why Alexis would be with him. Max bit off a curse. He threw his knapsack to the ground and marched across the great room to stare at the mountainscape through the sliding glass doors.

But why had she kissed him back? He wasn't mistaken about that. He could still feel her tongue on his. He couldn't be wrong about her. Alexis wasn't the type of person to make out with one person when she was dating another.

Why did this hurt so much? He'd only known her eight calendar days.

The knock on his door rescued him from his thoughts. Max checked the spyhole, recognizing Joshua on his doorstep. Another man was with him. The stranger was tall and muscular, and carried what looked like a black gym bag. His white face was covered by a full brown beard and moustache. Piercing green eyes locked onto the spyhole as though the stranger could see him. Who was he? Max opened the door to find out.

"Noah Steele. Max Powell." Joshua tossed him a poor imitation of the usual charming Colton smile as he crossed the threshold. "Do you have a minute?"

This was Laura's boyfriend, the homicide detective. He wore straight-legged black jeans and a loose black T-shirt. Adam had filled him in on the murder investigation in which his sister had been involved. He didn't think Adam had recovered from the scare, but he knew his friend had been impressed by the detective. He also was pleased his sister was happy and in love.

"Sure. Have a seat." Max locked up before joining the two men. They'd taken seats at the dining table just inside the bungalow. He sat beside Joshua. "What did you learn about the guardrail?"

Joshua sighed. His frown was still in place. "Tell us exactly what happened."

Max looked from Joshua to Noah and back. "You saw the video. Alexis turned toward the guardrail. She rested her forearms on it—barely—and it crumbled like pieces of a jigsaw puzzle." He briefly closed his eyes. "She started to go over the edge."

"And you caught her." Noah's voice was reassuring. "She'll be all right."

Max nodded. "Yes, she will. But what happened? What caused the railing to fall apart?"

Noah glanced at Joshua before responding. "Sometime between six o'clock yesterday evening when Joshua last checked the rails and nine this morning when you and Alexis went on your hike, someone shaved the rods. They shortened them just enough so that they weren't actually fitted together. They just looked like they were. They did the same thing to several other guardrails on that path."

Max's brow knitted with confusion. "Someone sabotaged the rails?"

Noah unzipped the gym bag he'd set beside his chair and pulled out a large evidence bag. Max glanced at the tattoos on his arms and the side of his neck before turning his attention to the bag. It contained one of the rails.

Noah pointed to it. "You can see where the rod was shaved. The edges are uneven."

Looking closely, Max could see what Noah described. He looked between the two men. "Were all the rails tampered with like this?"

"I'm afraid so." Joshua's voice was tight with anger.

"Who knew you were going hiking?" Noah asked.

Max gestured to Joshua beside him. "Joshua and Alexis. I mentioned it to my family but they're in New York." He shifted his attention back to Noah. "But anyone could have been on that trail. What makes you think whoever tampered with the rail was targeting Alexis and me?"

Joshua nodded toward the detective sitting across from them. "I gave Noah the suspicious package that was waiting for you when you arrived. Because of that note, we don't believe the guardrail was a coincidence."

Max had his doubts. "The person who sent the box is probably connected to the break-ins at my condo in New York. But no one has threatened me."

Noah held his eyes. "The threats could be escalating, meaning the break-ins could have been the start. I'm going to dust the package for prints and compare them against a national database."

Max went cold. "And Alexis could be hurt the same way she was today." He stood to pace the great room. His strides carried him toward the wall beside the sliding glass doors. "But how could the stalker have gotten into Mariposa? The property's secure."

Joshua sighed. "I haven't figured that out yet, but I'm on it. No one in our employ would provide access to people who don't work here or who aren't guests."

Max turned to pace back to the table. "If someone's targeting me, I need to leave the resort." He shoved his fists into the front pockets of his shorts. "I don't want to put Alexis—or anyone else—in danger."

Noah stood. "I understand your concern, Mr. Powell—"

Max shook his head. "Max, please."

Noah nodded. "Max. But I think you should stay at the resort. If someone is trying to harm you, we have a better chance of catching that person here."

Max continued pacing. "If this attack is connected to the break-ins, then the danger started in New York." He turned when he reached the front door.

"But it escalated here." Noah crossed his arms over his chest. "I can contact the detectives assigned to the case in New York and keep them apprised of our progress. They're welcome to come lend a hand, if they want to. But what happens in Sedona gets handled in Sedona."

"I agree with Noah." Joshua spread his hands. "Besides, where are you going to go? If you return to New York, you'll be putting your family in danger. If you go somewhere else, you won't have any backup."

Max rubbed the tense muscles in his neck. "You have a point. There aren't any good solutions."

Joshua stood from the table. "If someone's after you, Max,

leaving Mariposa will only prolong the situation. Noah's already opened a case. We can keep you safe here. And if Alexis is in danger, we'll bring her into the resort, too, until the case is solved."

Alexis's safety was all that mattered. If they could guarantee that, then he would stay. "All right."

"Why am I not surprised to find you here?" Laura's question preceded her as she walked into Alexis's office before 8:00 a.m. Monday. Her light blond bob swung just above her shoulders. Her azure coatdress made her eyes seem bluer.

"Maybe because you know I work here?" Alexis watched her friend and direct supervisor settle into one of the two visitors' chairs in front of her desk.

Laura coupled her sigh with a long-suffering look. "Do you want me to ask the nurse on duty to take a look at your ankle?"

"No, thank you." Alexis angled her head to check her injured joint. She'd propped it on a tall, empty box she'd found in the supply room. "It feels better. I'll go to the clinic if I have any pain." She wished Zoe was in today, but she was sure the nurse had left detailed notes in case someone needed to follow up while she was out of the office.

Laura pointed to her. "I'll hold you to that."

"I offered to arrange for another concierge to accompany Max to the farmers market this morning, but he said the chef was going to get his ingredients for him." Which meant she wouldn't be seeing Max today. She shouldn't feel so disappointed. It was inappropriate. Max was a guest at the resort and her client. They weren't friends—or anything more. Although after their kiss, the boundary lines had never seemed so blurry.

Alexis gave her friend a searching look. "So, I'm fine, but I can tell you're not. Something else is on your mind. I can hear it in your voice."

Laura sighed. "Noah believes the guardrail collapsing wasn't an accident. He's concerned the person who sent the package to the resort for Max tampered with the rail, intending for him to fall over the cliff."

Alexis's hand flew to her mouth as she gasped. "Oh, no.

That's horrible. Max didn't mention any of this to me when I spoke with him this morning. What are we going to do?"

"Max was thinking of returning to New York, but Noah convinced him to stay at Mariposa. We have twenty-four-hour security and Noah's already started investigating." Laura held Alexis's eyes. "We also prepared a bungalow for you. We're concerned whoever's targeting Max may also go after you since you've been spending time with him."

"I don't think I'm in danger." Alexis shook her head even as a chill seeped under her skin. "I didn't have any strange or threatening events this weekend. But I agree with Noah. Max will be safer here."

"Alexis, one weekend isn't a good test of your safety." Laura leaned forward in her seat as though trying to emphasize the urgency of the situation. "And why should we take the risk? Everyone agrees you should stay here for however long it takes to find Max's stalker. If it makes you feel better, think of it as saving time on your commute to work."

Everyone? How many people had the Coltons told about the incident? Although with the video circulating the news channels and the internet, they probably wouldn't have had to tell anyone. Alexis believed it was the video that had put her in the position of having to field questions from her neighbors, church congregation and everyone she'd walked past on her way to her office this morning.

"All right. I'll accept your offer of staying in the bungalow until the stalker's found. Thank you." Alexis tilted her head to the side, giving Laura a thoughtful look. "What else is on your mind?"

Laura stiffened as though in surprise. Then she relaxed back into her seat. "Your perception is one of the many reasons I love our friendship." She sighed. "My brothers and I just learned Clive owns the land Mariposa is on."

"What?" Alexis's lips parted in shock. "I thought your mother left the resort to the three of you. Why would she have left the land it sits on to your father?" It was disconcerting that Laura referred to her father by his first name, but considering she and her brothers didn't have much of a relationship with their sole surviving parent, it made sense.

Laura's peaches-and-cream features tightened with temper. "We think Clive tricked our mother into signing the land ownership papers to him while she was sick. Her chemo treatments really sapped her energy. She wouldn't have been able to read the documents clearly."

Alexis shook her head in disgust. "That's reprehensible."

"That's Clive." Laura's voice dripped with contempt. "He offered to sell the land to us, but he's asking for more than we could afford—and more than the land is worth. But if we don't give him the money, he's threatening to sell the land to someone else."

Alexis went cold as she realized what Laura wasn't saying. If Clive Colton sold the land on which Mariposa was built, the Colton siblings would become tenants of the new property owners. Such a drastic change for the business would inevitably change the resort's operating structure.

Her head was spinning. "Why is your father doing this?"

Laura drew a breath. "Clive is broke."

Another stunning revelation. Alexis winced, briefly closing her eyes. Clive owned half of Colton Textiles, a fine fabrics importer based in Los Angeles that he'd inherited from his father-in-law. The Colton siblings owned the other half.

Laura continued. "Colton Textiles is on the verge of bankruptcy. Clive's run the company into the ground. Now he needs a huge influx of cash just to keep it open. And he's decided that, if we don't give him money, he's going to take Mariposa from us."

The resort was named after Annabeth Colton's favorite flower, for crying out loud. The idea of Mariposa being stripped away from her children was obscene.

"Is there any way you could reason with him?" Alexis spread her arms to encompass the resort. "Mariposa was his deceased wife's dream. This is where they spent their honeymoon. It's where your mother has been laid to rest. Doesn't that mean anything to him?"

"Not at all." Laura shrugged. The jerky gesture was anything but casual. "None of that matters to Clive. All he cares about—all he's ever cared about—is money."

Alexis believed Laura. Still, she had trouble imagining a parent who would be so uncaring of their children's feelings and well-being. What kind of parent would deliberately destroy the legacy their children had inherited from their mother rather than support their offsprings' success? Apparently, the answer was a parent like Clive Colton.

"What are you and your brothers going to do?" Alexis's heart broke as she watched sorrow and distress settle like a mask over her friend's features.

Laura's eyes drifted away from Alexis. "We're thinking about going into partnership with another company."

The other woman made it sound like that plan would be their last option. Alexis could understand why. "You're considering giving another business part ownership of Mariposa?"

"We may not have a choice." Laura sighed. "If we sold a portion of Mariposa, we'd have the money to buy the land from Clive and we'd still be in a position to run the resort as we see fit."

Although not ideal, that strategy seemed to make the most sense. The bottom line was Laura, Adam and Joshua wanted to hold on to the legacy and the vision their mother had passed on to them. Laura had told her how much her late mother had loved the resort. She'd even shared some of the wonderful childhood memories she and her siblings had of the time they'd spent together on the property. The siblings had sacrificed everything, including personal lives, to build the resort into what it was today. They'd even built their homes on the property.

Together, Laura, Adam and Joshua had grown what was once a small hotel into an exclusive getaway for the wealthy and famous. The Coltons and their resort had built a stellar reputation, which they worked hard to preserve. Now their father had put them in an untenable situation that threatened everything—and everyone.

The Coltons treated their staff like an extended family, which had earned them loyalty and respect. If Clive sold the property, all their jobs would be on the line. Alexis didn't want to lose the resort.

She made Laura a promise. "I will do everything I can to help you and your brothers hold on to Mariposa."

To ensure the property was as appealing as possible to prospective partners, she'd have to help prevent any further scandals. The video of Max saving her from falling over the cliff came to mind. Well, no one said this would be easy.

Chapter Seven

"Lunch is served." Max's voice preceded him into Alexis's office early Monday afternoon. He wore his navy blue chef's smock with bronze pants.

Alexis looked up from her desk to find Max wheeling in a food trolley with two place settings, including large highball glasses of ice water. It was déjà vu all over again. "I didn't realize this was going to become a weekly appointment." She eyed the silver cloches covering the plates with a twinge of panic. What were they hiding today?

"People don't usually look so distressed when I cook for them." Max didn't sound offended. Thank goodness. Instead, he seemed amused. Alexis started to make an excuse. Max forestalled her by holding up a hand palm outward. "Honesty. Remember? My ego can take it."

Alexis gave him a crooked smile. "I'm sure it can."

"I need an ego if we're going to be friends." His brown eyes twinkled with disarming mischief.

Friends. Isn't that what she wanted them to be? But, oh, that kiss. Alexis kept her smile in place.

Max removed one of the cloches. "Portobello mushroom renello with black beans." He sounded so proud of himself.

A plume of steam wafted toward her. It carried the scents of cilantro, jalapeno peppers, onions, garlic and tomatoes. Delicious. The stuffed mushroom was topped with guacamole. It looked fresh and succulent. Max had garnished the plate with cilantro leaves and lime slices, which helped it look less empty.

Where was the rest of the food? "It looks wonderful."

Alexis pulled her purse from her desk's top left-hand drawer. She retrieved the greeting card in the hot pink envelope from the bag's center pouch, then stood to join Max at the conversation table. She moved with barely a limp.

"Thank you. I've passed the first test." Max watched her closely as he held the chair for her. "It was a good idea to wear sneakers today. How's your ankle?"

Alexis had felt awkward about wearing the black tennis shoes to work but they were much more comfortable than her pumps. And they almost disappeared beneath the hem of her black wide-legged pants.

"It's much stronger. Thank you." She settled into the seat closest to the door, then spread the napkin on her lap. "What about your injuries?"

"They look a lot worse than they feel." Max circled the table and took the seat opposite her.

"This is from my mother." Alexis offered him the card. "It's a thank-you-for-saving-my-daughter's-life card."

Max's eyebrows rose in surprise as he accepted the envelope. "That's so nice of her." As he read the message, his smile grew into a grin. "Your mother's very kind and very welcome." He set the card beside his plate.

"I'll let her know you appreciated it." She took a deep breath. The scent of the peppers, onions and cilantro made her stomach growl. She pressed a hand to her torso. "Excuse me."

"Bon appétit." Max waited for her to sample the meal.

Alexis's cheeks warmed under his scrutiny. She cut into the stuffed portobello mushroom and chewed. It was warm and spicy, but still not spicy enough. "You're getting there. It's delicious, but you have a little room to add more seasoning. And it needs cheese."

"It's still too bland?" Max looked and sounded disappointed.

"Food should be seasoned with abandon. And don't forget the cheese."

"Cheese. I'll make a note of that." The twinkle returned to Max's eyes. "Thank you for your candor, Alexis. You've been very helpful. Tell me, what's the most exotic meal you've ever had?"

Alexis eyed the black beans as she cut into the mushroom again. "Ever had or ever enjoyed?" His chuckle strummed the muscles in her lower abdomen. She caught her breath.

"All right. The most exotic meal you've ever enjoyed." He swallowed a forkful of the mushroom.

Alexis sipped her water as she considered his question. "That's easy—bacon and guac cheeseburger with seasoned fries."

Max watched her with a blank expression. "Are you kidding?"

"I'm totally serious." Alexis gestured toward her plate. "I mean, look at this plate. It looks like art, not food. You've got this ginormous plate and this itty-bitty food. Where's the rest of it?"

"That's called 'presentation.'" Max spread his hands. "Part of the enjoyment of dining is the way the food is arranged on your plate."

Alexis shrugged her eyebrows. "I understand that. But could you present across a larger part of the plate? If I have to work half a day or more to pay for one meal, I want to leave feeling full." She tried the black beans. They were delicious but could use a bit more salt.

"Point taken." Max inclined his head. "But remember, when you're dining out, you're not just paying for the food. You're paying for an entire experience—the quality of the service, the ambience of the establishment as well as the freshness of the ingredients and the chef's training."

Alexis fought back a smile. She was enjoying this banter with him, perhaps too much. "You sound like my mother. I'll tell you what I always say to her. If I want an experience, I'll grab a couple of friends and a burger to watch a movie on a streaming service."

Max laughed. "You're a hard woman to convince but as I've told you before, I can't resist a challenge."

Alexis swallowed another forkful of the beans. "Is that the reason you're involved in so many projects—your restaurants, show and now a book?"

Max drank his water before responding. "My fifteen minutes of fame is almost over. Unlike Julia Child and Wolfgang Puck, most chefs won't be household names forever. I understand that. At the end of the day, everything goes back to the restaurants. They're my first loves. While the spotlight's on me, I want to make sure I'm doing everything I can to ensure their success for the long term."

"That's a solid plan." Alexis bent her head, pretending to focus on her meal, but her lunch companion was a major distraction.

Kind, courageous, attractive and smart. How was a person supposed to resist the full package that was Maxwell Powell III?

Max's voice interrupted her thoughts. "Laura told me you'd agreed to move into one of the bungalows until the stalker is caught. I'm glad." He held her eyes. "I'm sorry you've been pulled into this, though."

Alexis lowered her knife and fork. "I'm sorry someone's trying to hurt you. Do you have any idea who could be behind these acts?"

"No, I don't, and I don't know what I could've done to make someone so angry." Temper hardened Max's eyes. "And to think they've involved you in this… Saying sorry doesn't seem like enough. Have you told Jake you're going to be staying at Mariposa for a while?"

Alexis sensed Max's tension and wondered at its source. "No, but I told my mother. She's relieved I've accepted Laura's offer. I'm sure she'll tell Jake and Aunt Suz."

Max took another drink of water. "Jake seems like a nice person." Was he deliberately avoiding her eyes?

"He is." Alexis didn't date much, but every man who'd been interested in her had also wondered about Jake. She'd never lied about their relationship, and she never would. "He's like a brother to me. Our mothers have been best friends for decades. We grew up together."

Max's tension drained away and Alexis returned to her lunch. Their comfortable silence was broken by the occasional questions about their plans for the rest of the day, amenities at Mariposa, and Laura and Adam.

Alexis set her silverware on her empty plate. "Max, there's something we should discuss." His sudden stillness made her even more uncomfortable, but she steeled herself to continue. With Mariposa's uncertain future, Alexis couldn't risk having a relationship with a guest. If the media found out, the resort would be in the center of even more salacious gossip. And it would be all her fault. "You're a guest at Mariposa. You're also one of my clients. As much as I enjoyed our kiss, a romantic relationship between us is against the rules. It also would be inappropriate."

Max gave her his crooked smile. "I'll admit to being disappointed. I enjoy your company, Alexis, and I want to get to know you better. But of course, I'll respect your decision. Besides, my home is in New York and you live here. I've heard long-distance relationships can be brutal."

The regret in his dark eyes reflected the pain in her heart. Alexis clenched her hands under the table. She desperately wanted to change her mind.

Just kidding! Forget everything I said! Backsies!

Alexis looked away and rose from the table. "I've heard the same thing about long-distance romances."

Max stood with her. "So we'll settle for friendship?"

Alexis swallowed the lump of regret in her throat. *No! I want more.* "I'd like that."

"Good." Max returned their place settings to the trolley. "I meant what I said about your feedback on the recipes. Your honesty is invaluable, and I'm enjoying the challenge of trying to impress you." He chuckled. "See you later, Alexis."

"Have a good day, Max." She watched him disappear beyond her doorway before returning to her desk.

Her office felt so empty without him. Alexis dropped onto her black wheeled desk chair. She'd have to fill the void with work as she always did. The problem was that plan wasn't as appealing as it had been before she met Max.

* * *

"I'm surprised you've come in today." The cool, indifferent notes of Glenna Bennett Colton's voice made the hair on the back of Alexis's neck vibrate like an early warning system. In the back of her mind, the scene music for the *Wizard of Oz*'s Wicked Witch of the West played.

Alexis gave Clarissa an apologetic smile before cutting their meeting update short Monday evening. The reservations desk clerk returned the smile with a sympathetic look.

Straightening her posture, Alexis faced Laura's stepmother. "Good afternoon, Ms. Bennett Colton. Why are you surprised to see me?"

Glenna was a few inches taller than Alexis. Her blood-red, straight-legged pantsuit made a statement—not a friendly one. She briefly dropped her cool green eyes to Alexis's feet. "You don't usually wear sneakers to the office. I heard about your *accident*."

"You have? From whom?" Alexis couldn't read Glenna's pale features. How did Clive Colton's second wife feel about his plans to take Mariposa away from Laura, Adam and Joshua? She imagined Glenna supported Clive's decision.

"I'm sure you know the video's all over the news." Glenna's narrow shoulders shrugged beneath her cap-sleeved jacket. She wore it with a cream V-neck shell blouse.

"Yes, I've seen it." The memory of the recording made her mouth dry. One of the most terrifying experiences of her life had been captured on video.

Alexis had the uncomfortable sensation Glenna was trying to get information from her. The Coltons' stepmother had been spending a lot of time at the resort. What was she after?

Glenna swept back an imaginary strand of her bone-straight, bleach-blond hair from her face. "You seem awfully calm. You're very lucky Maxwell Powell III was with you. The incident could have ended in tragedy. You could have been killed."

Alexis shivered despite the comfortable temperatures maintained in the L. "Luckily, I wasn't. That's not something I want to dwell on."

"I'm sure you don't. I'm sure Josh wants to put the *accident* behind him, too. It doesn't reflect well on the resort."

"What do you mean by that?" Something in Glenna's tone made Alexis's back and shoulders tighten.

She gave a short, scornful laugh. "What do you think I mean? Last month, there was a murder investigation. This month, there was a near-fatal accident caused by negligence. Do you think these events put Mariposa in a *good* light? If I were you, I would demand Josh be fired. I don't know why you aren't."

Alexis unclenched her teeth. "The accident was in no way Joshua's fault."

Glenna arched a skeptical eyebrow. "Then whose fault was it? *He's* the activities director. As such, he's responsible for the safe conditions of all the activities—pools, saunas, *trails*."

A deeper voice flavored with a New York accent joined their conversation. "Yes, he is. And he's excellent at his job."

Alexis turned to see Max come to a stop beside her. He was wearing the bronze pants from when he'd served her lunch. The sleeves of his wine-red polo shirt hugged his well-defined biceps jealously.

She gestured toward him, fighting back a smile. "Maxwell Powell III, this is Glenna Bennett Colton."

The twinkle in Max's eyes promised retribution.

Glenna offered him her right hand. "I know who you are, Mr. Powell. I've seen the video of your heroic rescue of Alexis several times. Before that, I've had the pleasure of dining at your restaurant in Fort Lauderdale a number of times. Each was a transformative experience."

"Thank you. I appreciate that." Max released her hand. "Just as I appreciate Joshua's conscientiousness toward the well-being of Mariposa's guests."

Glenna's lips curved into a thin, condescending smile. "With all due respect, Mr. Powell, how could you possibly know whether Josh is conscientious? Your misperception of his abilities allows him to escape responsibility."

The corners of Max's eyes crinkled with amusement. "I've been at the resort for well over a week. I've observed Joshua at work. I also know how dedicated Adam, Laura and Joshua are to their mother's legacy."

Glenna's smile stiffened at the reference to Annabeth. "I wasn't aware Josh had so many champions."

Alexis inclined her head. "He's earned it. Joshua isn't to blame for the accident. That's a fact."

Glenna's sigh signaled the other woman was nearing the end of her patience. "On what are you basing that?"

Alexis glanced at Max. "We're not at liberty to say. If you want additional information, you should speak with Joshua."

Glenna scoffed. "Of course he would come up with some story to cover his negligence."

Alexis clenched her hands. "We're serious, Ms. Bennett Colton. Speak with Joshua. Or you could ask Laura and Adam. But as I said, neither Max nor I are at liberty to say."

Max inclined his head. "Alexis is right. If you have questions about the accident, speak with Adam, Laura or Joshua. Otherwise, it isn't fair of you to spread false rumors about Joshua."

Glenna split a considering look between Alexis and Max. "I see. Josh and his siblings are very fortunate to have such loyal friends and employees."

Alexis didn't respond. Neither did Max. Without another word, Glenna pivoted on her four-inch stiletto heels and walked past them toward the administrative offices. Alexis hoped she was taking their advice about speaking with Laura, Adam or Joshua. Or all three of them.

She drew her attention from Glenna and turned to Max. "Thank you for everything you said about Joshua. You're right. He takes his responsibilities seriously. He's very dedicated to Mariposa and our guests. It made me angry to hear Glenna disparage him as though he were a recalcitrant child."

Max raised his eyebrows. "I could tell. I was afraid for Glenna." He glanced over his shoulder in the direction Glenna had disappeared. "Joshua's a good guy. He doesn't deserve to have Glenna smear him, especially since she has no idea what happened or of the other events that are going on."

Alexis frowned, tilting her head. "Doesn't she?"

Max's eyes flew back to hers. "What are you saying?" He

searched her features as though looking for the answer to his question.

Alexis regretted her words. "Nothing. Never mind." She lowered her voice. "It's just that Glenna was quick to say Joshua should be fired. She said if she were me, she'd demand it. That really made me angry."

Max frowned. "She has no right to say that. She doesn't have any authority over Mariposa."

Yet.

Alexis considered Max, standing beside her. Had Adam confided in him about Clive Colton's money problems and his intentions toward Mariposa the way Laura had confided in her? She wasn't going to bring it up, just in case.

She adjusted her purse strap on her shoulder and glanced toward the hallway again. "Glenna has her own agenda and I'm certain whatever that agenda is, it doesn't bode well for Mariposa."

"I agree."

Alexis faced him, arching an eyebrow. "Did you just happen to be walking by just now?"

"No, I was looking for you. I thought you might be leaving for the day." Max gestured toward her briefcase. "May I take that for you?"

"Yes, you may. Thank you." Alexis gave him her briefcase, then fell into step with him as he escorted her to her car.

Max tossed her a smile that revealed the deep dimple in his right cheek. "'Maxwell Powell III'? You had to use my full name for the introduction to Glenna?"

Alexis swallowed a chuckle. "No, I didn't have to, but I really enjoyed it."

Max held the door open for her and she led him outside the building. "Are you moving into your bungalow tonight?"

Alexis's amusement vanished. "Yes, I am. But it's not my bungalow. It's a temporary living arrangement."

Max stopped beside the building's entrance and turned to face her. "I'm glad you accepted the Coltons' offer and that you're moving into your temporary living arrangement tonight." He hesitated. "There's an unknown threat out there.

We don't know whether it's connected to my stalker or if it was an unfortunate coincidence. I feel much better knowing you're here with round-the-clock security at least until we can get those answers."

"So am I." It was unnerving hearing it in those terms. She forced her lips into a smile as she started walking again. "And so is my mother. But who could have sabotaged the guardrail?"

Max paced beside her. "It could be someone who wants to damage the resort's reputation. Or maybe someone who wants to hurt the Coltons personally."

An intonation in Max's voice made Alexis wonder whether he knew more than he was letting on. She was searching for a way to ask him when she caught a movement in her peripheral vision.

Mark Bower stepped out of his truck and into their path. "I see you brought your knight in shining armor." He turned to Max, gesturing back to Alexis. "I don't suppose it would do any good for me to ask you to let us talk privately."

Max gave the other man a stony stare. "No, it wouldn't."

"Why are you here, Mark?" Alexis was certain Max understood she didn't need a knight in shining armor. He knew she could take care of herself, but he was too much of a protector to step aside a second time.

Mark returned his attention to Alexis. "I want you to know I've hired a lawyer to get my job back."

She suspected her former staffer was bluffing. Although the resort paid very well, between legal and living expenses, it would undoubtedly cost Mark more to sue to get his job back than it would for him to find another suitable position. But since he'd turned this into a legal situation, she had to be careful how she responded.

Alexis adjusted her purse strap on her shoulder. "Thank you for letting me know. I'll brief Mariposa's legal counsel."

Mark's eyes shifted as though she'd given him a response he hadn't expected. "We can take care of this without our lawyers. I'd be willing to return to Mariposa on a probationary status. After a couple of months, you can reassess my performance."

Alexis had to bite her tongue to keep from saying anything

that could be used against the resort if Mark's suit made it to court. She decided to repeat herself. Her earlier response was innocuous enough. "Thank you for letting me know."

Mark's jaw flexed as though he was grinding his teeth. She sensed his tension and his anger. Alexis held his gaze without expression.

Finally, he nodded. "Good. You and your bosses can respond to my lawyer when you get her message." Mark turned and climbed back into his truck.

Max walked with Alexis past Mark's vehicle on their way to her car. "Do you think he's telling the truth about retaining a lawyer?"

Alexis was reluctant to discuss resort matters with a guest. But Max had been standing right there and he was Adam's best friend. She could trust him to be discreet with this matter. "I don't think so, but I could be wrong. I'll call Laura when I get home." She wanted to update her manager before she packed for her temporary relocation to the bungalow. "One thing I am certain of is that I can't trust him. Even if his performance is stellar during his probationary period, he violated our employee standards many times, and I couldn't be confident he wouldn't revert to that same behavior."

Max stopped beside her compact sedan. "Do you think Mark is upset enough over being fired that he'd try to take revenge against you or Mariposa?"

A chill raced through Alexis like a cold, foreboding wind. "Are you asking whether I think he could be capable of destroying the guardrail?"

Max flexed his shoulders. "He's a disgruntled ex-employee. I think it's worth discussing him with Noah."

"Yes, and Roland as well." She looked over her shoulder, catching sight of Mark's truck's taillights as he swung out of the parking lot. "But how would he have known you and I would be hiking Saturday?"

"Perhaps the guardrail wasn't tampered with as a way to

hurt one of us. If Mark were responsible, it might have been an attack aimed at the resort as revenge for his being fired."

It was a chilling thought, but a possibility they had to face. If Max's theory was correct, too many lives were at stake.

Chapter Eight

Laura entered Alexis's office early Tuesday morning, carrying two mugs of coffee. "Have you settled in okay at the bungalow?"

After placing one of the mugs on Alexis's desk, Laura took the visitor's chair closest to the office door. Her deep pink coatdress warmed her pale skin and highlighted her light blond bob.

Alexis hit a couple of keys on her laptop to save the document she'd been working on before spinning her black wheeled executive seat to face Laura.

Gesturing with the mug, Alexis smiled. "Thank you." She breathed in the dark roast coffee before taking a deep drink. The burnt-umber porcelain was warm against her palms. The caffeine gave her system a jolt. "And yes, the bungalow is very comfortable. Thank you. I can see why we have such a high percentage of repeat guests. And the work commute is a dream."

"Thank you for saying that about the bungalow. I'm glad you're enjoying it." Laura's blue eyes gleamed with pride over the rim of her mug. "How's your ankle healing?"

"I'm almost one hundred percent." Alexis was wearing her black tennis shoes again today. "Tomorrow will be the real test. I'm resuming my morning runs."

"Ooh. Ambitious." Laura gave her a narrow-eyed, skeptical look. "Try not to push yourself beyond what you're comfortable with."

"I promise, Dr. Colton." Alexis teased her as only old friends could. She lifted her mug, drawing Laura's attention to it. "For you to bring me a cup of joe means we have a lot to go over this morning. Where would you like to start?"

"We know each other too well." Laura settled back against her seat. "Thank you for calling me about Mark last night. I can't believe he's going to try to fight his dismissal. You have records of everything and so does HR. We have his signature on the orientation attendance sheets and the form asserting he'd read his employee handbook. We also have statements from several of the guests he up-charged for his services."

Alexis set her mug on her desk before clenching the arms of her chair. "As you know, I didn't want to fire him. But we can't have employees running cons on our guests." She was still outraged over Mark's behavior. His repeated demands to be rehired only made the situation worse.

"No, we can't." Angry color stained Laura's cheekbones. She lowered her mug. "Mariposa's brand is trust. Our guests trust us to ensure their privacy and security, to provide them with an all-inclusive vacation getaway and to not rip them off. Mark's scamming our customers betrayed that trust."

"Which is exactly what I told him." Alexis turned her attention to the window beside her conversation table. Red rock mountains circled the resort, but in her mind's eye, Alexis saw an image of Mark's expression when he'd told her he'd retained legal counsel. "I don't think he's hired a lawyer but it's better to be prepared in case he has."

Laura nodded her agreement. "I called Greg last night to brief him."

Alexis smiled with pleasure. "How is he?"

Greg Sumpter was the Colton family's private attorney. He also handled legal issues for the resort. Alexis always looked forward to his visits. He didn't in any way resemble her mental image of a high-powered lawyer. Unless high-powered lawyers wore cargo shorts and Hawaiian shirts. Really loud Hawaiian shirts.

"He's well." Laura gave her a conspiratorial grin. "He asked about Tallulah."

Rumor had it that Greg had a long-time crush on Tallulah Deschine, head of housekeeping for Mariposa.

Alexis's eyebrows stretched toward her hairline. "Of course he did." Her smile faded as she changed the subject. "Did you mention my concern about Mark to Noah? Actually, Max thought of it first. It was his idea." *Stop babbling*.

Laura's eyes twinkled briefly with amusement. Alexis could almost read her friend's mind. She was filing Alexis's awkward rambling for future reference.

"Yes, I did. He thought it was a good lead. He's going to question Mark and let us know what he learns." Laura shook her head. "Although I can't believe we have to worry about an angry ex-employee trying to damage the resort in addition to Clive's threats to take Mariposa from us."

Alexis's eyes dropped to Laura's hands wrapped around the mug. Her knuckles showed white. "It's a lot. I know. But our suspicion about Mark is just a theory. We could be wrong. Either way, I'm certain Noah will get to the bottom of this quickly."

Laura nodded. "You're right. Noah's very good at what he does."

"Yes, he is." Alexis knew Laura wasn't biased by the fact she and Noah were dating. Noah was a great detective. He was going to track down every viable lead.

"None of this has anything to do with the main reason I'm here, however." Laura crossed her right leg over her left and leaned forward on her chair. "I got a call from Valerie last night."

"Your phone got quite the workout yesterday between me, Greg, Noah and Valerie." Alexis pictured the redheaded, full-figured young woman who served as their daytime bartender.

"That's true. It was a long but very productive day." Laura sighed. "Valerie said she needed to take a few days off imme-diately—as in she's already gone. She has a family emergency."

"Oh, no." Startled and concerned, Alexis leaned forward into her desk. "I hope everyone's all right."

"So do I." Laura's thin, dark blond eyebrows knitted. "She didn't share any details, though, and I really didn't want to pry. I just wanted you to know she's taking time off."

Alexis sat back, searching her memory for her past conversations with Valerie. She didn't know much about the other woman.

"I understand." She waved a dismissive hand. "I wouldn't have pried, either. If she wants us to know what's going on, she'll tell us. I don't know anything about her family. Do you?"

Laura shook her head. "No, I don't know how many relatives she has or where they live. But I need to find a replacement for her yesterday." She gave a humorless laugh. "I wasn't going to deny her request for time off to help her family. I know how important families are."

"Of course." Alexis thought of her mother. She loved her Aunt Suz and Jake, but Catherine was her only living relative.

Laura continued. "Valerie didn't give me many details, like how long she'll be gone. She said she'd contact me when she has more information about her situation. In the meantime, we're short a bartender. I've found someone to cover her shift for a few days, but we need a backup in case she needs to be away longer."

Alexis realized this was another chance to prove she was ready for the promotion to event manager. She wanted to be promoted based on merit and not because Laura was her friend. This situation would give her the opportunity to demonstrate that she'd developed connections and had resources in the community. Those connections and resources would benefit the resort and support her in her role as event manager, if she was promoted.

She held Laura's eyes. "Let me take care of that. I have a couple of ideas."

Laura was shaking her head before Alexis finished speaking. "Alexis, I wasn't asking for your help. I can take care of it. You already have so much on your plate between working with Max and being short a concierge on your team. And you're injured."

"Really, Laura. I can handle this. It won't take long."

Laura spread her arms. "Alexis, I know you're interested in the event manager's position when Cheryl retires, but you don't have anything to prove."

Alexis sighed, trying to ease her impatience. "Laura, I'm serious. I can take care of this. I already have a lead."

Laura frowned. "You do? All right, if you're sure."

"I'm sure." A surge of excitement rushed through her. She was one step closer to her goal.

Max was torn. He stared at his ringing cell phone Tuesday afternoon. Should he answer Sarah's call? It was almost time for his daily accidentally on-purpose bumping into Alexis during her afternoon stroll through the L's lobby. He admired the efforts she made to stay connected with the resort's guests as well as her coworkers. It showed the pride she took in her work.

He picked up Sarah's call on the third ring. He'd keep their conversation short. "Sarah. How are you?"

"Max! It seems like you've been having a lot of fun at the resort." Her voice was sulky. "Have you forgotten about me?"

His brow creased in confusion. His eyes moved to the view of the mountain ridge framed by the French doors at the back of his bungalow. "How do you know what I've been doing?"

"Are you kidding?" Sarah sounded amused. "Ever since the video of you saving Alexis Reed's life, the paparazzi can't get enough of the two of you together at the resort."

Max's lips parted in shock. *Oh, no.*

Alexis was going to be irritated. Max clenched his left fist so tightly it hurt. Anything that threatened the safety and privacy of Mariposa's guests stirred her temper. He could imagine her reaction when she learned the media was recording drone footage of the two of them around the property. Would she insist they not spend any more time together in an effort to stop drawing attention to Mariposa?

Max rubbed his eyes with the fingers of his left hand. "Thank you for letting me know." How was he going to fix this?

"I'm surprised you haven't seen them." Beneath Sarah's voice, Max could hear traffic noise. Was she driving while using her phone again?

He turned away from the French doors and wandered the great room. The scents of the wildflowers were soothing. They reminded him of Alexis. He drew a deeper breath.

"You usually handle those types of things for me." Max knew the importance of using social media to build his brand and increase his audience, but he didn't enjoy coming up with content for those platforms. Sarah, on the other hand, was addicted to hashtags, views, likes and algorithms—whatever those things were. "Listen, Sarah, I'm sorry but I need to get back to work so—"

"When would you like to get together for that drink you promised me?"

Max briefly closed his eyes. He couldn't keep putting her off. "Why don't we meet for lunch Sunday?"

"That sounds great." There was a smile in her voice. "Where and when?"

Max glanced at his watch. "Where would you recommend?"

He needed to get moving if he were to have any chance of "bumping into" Alexis. He wanted to see her. Needed to see her. Even if it was a smile and wave from across the lobby, perhaps catch a trace of her perfume.

"Hmm." Sarah's hesitation spiked Max's impatience. "I'll ask my relatives for a recommendation."

"Great." He crossed to his front door. "Text me the time and place, and I'll meet you Sunday."

"I'll look forward to it." Her farewell sang in his ears as he ended the call.

Within minutes, Max was jumping out of his golf cart and hurrying into the L. To his relief, Alexis was speaking with Clarissa at the reception desk. He made his way to her.

She looked up as he approached and gave him the smile he'd been craving. Her black sneakers looked like they'd been made for her wide-legged slate gray pantsuit.

Alexis shifted to face him. "Hi, Max. How was your morning?"

Max greeted Clarissa before responding to Alexis. "Can I speak with you?"

Her smile dimmed. "Of course. Let's talk in my office."

Alexis said goodbye to Clarissa before leading him down the hallway. She lowered her voice. "Do you have more information on the accident or your stalker?"

Her limp was barely noticeable. His wounds were healing, too. He should be able to go back to wearing shorts in a day or two.

"No, but this is about something else." Max followed her into her office and closed the door. He waited for her to sit behind her desk, then took the visitor's seat near the door.

"This must be pretty serious." Alexis glanced toward the closed door. "What is it?"

Max braced himself. "There are videos of us together at the resort on the internet."

Her reaction wasn't what he'd expected. She sat back against her chair and frowned at him as though she didn't understand the words he was speaking. "Someone posted videos of the resort itself to the internet?"

Max nodded. "It's probably drone footage like the video of our accident."

"That's impossible." She straightened, spinning her chair toward her laptop. Rapid clicks sounded as her fingers flew across her keyboard. She shifted the monitor to face him. "My search brought back only the video of my fall and the ones from our own website. I've set up internet alerts to notify me when people post anything connected to Mariposa to the web. What made you think there were videos of us at the resort?"

Max stood, leaning over her desk to get a closer look at her monitor. "Sarah told me she'd seen them."

Had he misunderstood what his assistant had said? No, he was sure he hadn't. He felt like such a fool. Why hadn't he done a search for the videos himself? Because he'd been impatient to see Alexis, to be near her as he was now. He breathed in her soft wildflower scent.

Alexis waved a hand toward her laptop. "As I've said before, our guests' security and privacy are vitally important to us. How safe and secure would you feel if there were drones flying all over the property, recording your every move? Besides, drone recordings of private property violate the FAA's privacy guidelines. Our legal counsel would take care of that."

She looked up at him from over her shoulder. Her eyes hypnotized him. Her scent embraced him. Time slipped away. Her eyes dropped to his lips. Max stiffened. What would she do next?

Alexis looked away, breaking their connection. "Sarah was mistaken." She kept her eyes on her desk. "Other than the hiking footage, there aren't any unauthorized videos of the resort on the net."

Max felt empty as he returned to his seat. "Why are drones able to record footage from the hiking trail but not from any other part of the resort?"

"Legally, drone operators aren't allowed to operate on either property." She shrugged. "However, there are always people who are willing to take the risk, believing they won't get caught. Although our legal council eventually tracks them down, the violators just move their footage to another website."

Max set his right ankle on his left knee. "Maybe I misunderstood what Sarah said." Although he didn't think so. "I'll ask her about it when I see her Sunday."

Alexis gave him a quick glance, then tapped some computer keys. Her screen returned to her internet homepage. "You're meeting Sarah Sunday?"

"Yes, we're having lunch. Could you recommend a nearby restaurant?" He considered her delicate features. Was she avoiding his eyes? Why?

"It depends on what kind of ambience you want." She reached for some papers from a tidy stack on her desk. "If you're looking for something casual, I can recommend Tipsy Tacos. It's a Mexican cantina. A mariachi band plays there every Sunday evening."

Max watched Alexis rifle through the printouts on her desk. "That sounds appealing. We'd miss the band, though, since we're having lunch."

"There's also The Cloisters. It's a high-end restaurant and bar. I'm going there Thursday night."

Max stilled. "Alone?"

"Yes." Alexis stopped fidgeting and finally looked at him. "We need a bartender to fill in for one of our day shifts. I read about a talented, engaging bartender who works at The Cloisters. I'm going to check her out as a possible fill-in until our regular bartender returns."

Max heard the excitement in her voice. He scowled. "Do you think that's a good idea? Whoever's behind sabotaging the guardrail could still be after one or both of us. Under the circumstances, I don't think you should go off the resort alone."

Alexis's body seemed to relax. "There are always plenty of people at The Cloisters. I'll be fine."

Max spread his hands. "There may be a crowd at the bar, but what about when you're traveling to and from it? It's a bad idea for you to go alone. I'll go with you."

Alexis's eyes widened with surprise. For a second, Max thought she'd argue against his decision. Alexis Reed had a very strong, very stubborn independent streak.

But then she smiled. "All right. I don't think it's necessary, but you're welcome to join me. As a restaurateur, I'd appreciate having your opinion of the bartender."

"Great." Max rose to his feet. That hadn't been so hard. And he'd gotten a date out of it. Alexis may not call it that, but he would. "I'd be happy to give you my feedback. I should let you get back to work."

He sketched a goodbye wave as he turned to leave. His steps were much lighter now than when he'd first arrived. Thursday couldn't come fast enough.

Chapter Nine

"Between our losing Allison and your meeting Noah, I was half afraid our ladies' nights would come to an end." Alexis sipped her frozen margarita as she and Laura waited for their vegan tacos late Tuesday evening.

Laura drank her house margarita. "I'd never give up our ladies' nights. I don't think Allison would want us to, either."

Allison Brewer had been one of the yoga instructors at Mariposa. In the time she'd worked at the resort, Allison, Alexis and Laura had become very close friends. Her death earlier this year had left Alexis and Laura shattered and struggling to cope. Their grief had been magnified when they'd learned Allison had been murdered. Her body had been found in one of the empty pool cabanas as though the killer had just discarded her. Noah, who was Allison's foster brother, had gotten involved with the homicide investigation. Laura had helped him, which had scared Alexis almost out of her mind.

"You're right. Allison would've wanted us to continue this tradition. She looked forward to these evenings. So do I." Alexis raised her glass. "To Allison."

"To Allison." Laura touched her glass to Alexis's.

Alexis sipped her drink as she took in their surroundings. Taco Tuesday at the Tipsy Tacos. As usual the place was packed. Boisterous laughter and lively conversations covered the dining room. The rustic decor was fitting for a Mexican cantina. Wood carvings in vibrant colors decorated the stone walls. The floors and furnishings were built from aged brown wood. Sporting events, game shows and local news programs played on the televisions mounted around the restaurant.

The aromas of spicy salsas, melted cheeses and seasoned meats made Alexis's stomach growl. What would Max think of this place?

"I look forward to these dinners, too." Laura sighed. "For the longest time, our friendship was the only thing that kept me from being swallowed up by work." Her eyes flew up to meet Alexis's. "Don't get me wrong, the resort is very important to me. But now that Noah's in my life, I have more of a balance between my personal and professional lives. It's helped me with my work. Adam and Josh need to make that adjustment, too, especially Adam." A twinkle sparkled in her eyes. "So do you, maybe with Max?"

Alexis shook her head with a smile. "I knew you were up to something with your suggestion that I move into one of the bungalows."

"Oh, no." Laura held up her right hand, palm out. "I asked you to stay at the resort out of concern for your safety. Adam, Josh and Noah agreed with me. We don't know who destroyed the guardrail or why, or who the intended target was, you or Max or someone else at the resort."

Alexis inclined her head. "I appreciate your concern and I promise to be careful."

"Thank you." Laura's smile was soft with relief.

"In fact, Max is coming with me to The Cloisters Thursday night to observe the bartender I told you about. He didn't think I should go alone. He's also going to give me his opinion of her."

"Oh! I should have thought of that." Laura's hand flew to her mouth. Her eyes were wide with dismay. "I'm a horrible friend."

"You're one of my best friends."

"What was I thinking?" Her voice was muffled behind her palm. "Obviously, I wasn't thinking. I'm so sorry."

"Laura, stop." Alexis held up both of her hands. "I didn't

think about the stalker, either. This is a new experience for both of us. But luckily Max did remember and offered to be my wingman." She struggled not to squirm under the speculative look in Laura's eyes.

"Now, if your staying at the bungalow gives you more time with Max, that wouldn't be such a bad thing. Would it?"

Alexis remembered their kiss and the pulse at the base of her throat leaped. "Max is great. He's kind, intelligent, ambitious, funny." She cut the list of his attributes short before she started sounding like a besotted heroine in a rom-com.

Laura nodded. "And very attractive."

"Yes, he is." Understatement. "He also lives in New York, twenty-four hundred miles away. Approximately." She'd looked it up.

Their server arrived with their entrées, putting a pause on their conversation. Alexis thanked the young man before sampling one of the hot corn-shell tacos. They were filled with seasoned shredded chicken, tomatoes, lettuce, red onions, cheese, jalapeño peppers and black olives.

She searched her mind for a change of topic. Before she could think of one, Laura picked up their conversation where they'd left off.

"Fortunately, Max isn't in New York now. He's here." Laura had the air of a defense attorney, giving her closing argument.

Alexis had a few objections. "Exactly. Not only is he a guest, he's also my client. A relationship with him wouldn't be appropriate."

Laura giggled around another bite of her barbacoa taco. She swallowed before responding. "Alexis, you're people, not robots. We don't choose when, where or how we meet our soul mates." She hesitated. "I certainly didn't imagine myself finding Noah during the murder investigation of one of my best friends."

No one could have imagined that happening. "I don't know that Max is my soul mate." Her body warmed at the thought, though.

"How will you know if you don't give a relationship with

him a chance?" Laura arched an eyebrow as she sipped her drink. She obviously thought she was winning this debate.

Alexis wished it were that simple. "Max and I are from different worlds, Laura. He was born and raised in New York City. His father is a film producer, and his mother is a casting director. I was raised in Sedona by a single mother who works for the state of Arizona. He's a celebrated chef who owns two fine-dining restaurants. I'm a concierge who lives on burgers and fries."

"First, stop putting yourself down." Temper darkened Laura's sky-blue eyes. "It doesn't matter where you came from. What matters is where you're going. My father's proof of that. Everything he has was given to him and he's on the verge of losing it all. Second, Max isn't a snob. Adam wouldn't be friends with someone like that."

"Points taken." Alexis considered it a good sign that Max and Adam were such good friends.

Like Laura, Adam was a good boss. All the Coltons were. They never hesitated to roll up their sleeves and pitch in wherever and whenever help was needed. Their attitude helped inspire loyalty and commitment among Mariposa's staff.

Laura leaned into the table and lowered her voice. "What are you afraid of?"

Alexis stiffened. She placed her taco on her plate. "What makes you think I'm afraid?"

Laura cocked her head. "I know you. Come on. Spill."

Alexis's shoulders rose and fell with her sigh. "The men I've dated in the past haven't understood my career ambitions."

Another understatement. They'd resented the long hours she'd worked, and they'd tried to talk her out of going back to school for her MBA. Rather than giving up her goals, she'd ended those relationships.

"I remember." Laura nodded. "Their loss. But, Alexis, you don't know that Max will be like those other guys. He's ambitious, too."

"I know. That's not what I'm afraid of." She held Laura's eyes. "Suppose my feelings for Max make me give up my professional goals? If there comes a time when I have to choose between Max and my goals, which choice would I make and what would it say about me?"

"Seriously?" Laura smiled as though Alexis was teasing. She sobered when Alexis didn't smile back. "Alexis, you've never given up your dreams before. What makes you think you would this time?"

Alexis sat back with a sigh. "Because I've never felt this way before."

The Cloisters was crowded Thursday evening. Max wasn't surprised. The parking lot had been packed. Alexis had been lucky to find a spot toward the far end of the lot near some hedges under a lamp. He took a firm hold of her hand, drawing her close to his side to keep from losing her amid the masses. She looked up at him. Her bright eyes were wide with surprise and curiosity. Staring into them, Max could barely breathe.

She was so beautiful. Her wavy raven hair was thick and loose around her shoulders. His fingers itched with the urge to bury themselves into the heavy mass. Her little black dress skimmed her firm, toned figure. The scooped neckline gave only a hint of her cleavage. The long, wide sleeves billowed around her arms. The knee-length hem showed off her long, shapely calves. Her low-heeled pumps boosted her height to his chin.

Max gave her a reassuring smile, then set a course for the bar. As he cleared a path for them, he scanned the posh interior. They were surrounded by polished white oak wood, shiny bronze fixtures and soft black leather furnishings. The air was redolent with well-aged liquors, seasoned, high-quality hors d'oeuvres and money. The ambience telegraphed wealth and prestige. It was so different from Mariposa's warm, friendly environment. Could they find a bartender in this upmarket establishment who would fit into the resort's culture?

"Let's find seats at the bar." Alexis leaned against him to be heard above the instrumental music and murmurs of conversation.

Max felt her warmth against his back and a shiver went through him. Unable to form a response, he nodded. Was his palm sweating against hers? He found two seats together at the bar. Max could see his reflection in the gleaming, rectangular wood surface. Beneath the cylindrical bronze fittings, bottles of liquors and mixes arranged against the mirror on the back wall sparkled in the light. The action was happening at the center of the bar where a young woman moved briskly in the open space, taking requests and mixing drinks.

"Is that her?" Max held the back of Alexis's black leather barstool as she settled into the seat. She pushed her purse into the space on the seat beside her.

"Yes. That's Kelli Iona." Alexis watched her subject closely. "I recognize her from the photo in the magazine interview."

The young woman appeared to be in her mid-twenties. She was tall, perhaps five seven or five eight, and physically fit. She wore a double-breasted black vest over a crisp white oxford service shirt and what looked like black stretch service chinos. Her long, wavy brown hair was gathered into a ponytail holder that swung from shoulder to shoulder as she attended to her customers.

As though she had eyes in the back of her head, Kelli looked over her right shoulder toward Max and Alexis at the other end of the bar. "Welcome to The Cloisters! I'll be right with you. There are two customers ahead of you." Her smile was warm as though they were next-door neighbors, the good kind.

Max made himself comfortable on the barstool beside Alexis. "Take your time."

Maybe they could find a suitable bartender for Mariposa at this upscale bar after all. He should've known better than to have doubted Alexis.

"That was a good sign." Alexis folded her hands on the bar's smooth surface. "She acknowledged us as soon as we sat down."

"Yes, that's good customer service." And she'd greeted them with a smile. Max shifted to face Alexis. "How did you find her?"

Alexis glanced at him before returning her attention to Kelli. "She was profiled in an e-zine that covers local restaurants, bars and events. Her interview was very charming and personable. She started bartending after high school. She just recently moved to Sedona."

Max was impressed. "She must be good at her job, otherwise The Cloisters wouldn't have hired her."

He watched Kelli mix an order for one of the customers ahead of him. Her flair commanded her customers' attention. She selected a napkin from the top of a nearby pile, spun it in the air with a flick of her wrist, then tapped it onto the bar. Holding a bottle in each hand by their long necks, she free-poured the liquors into a silver mixer, then brought the bottles down and around to stop their flow. She added a few more ingredients, mixing them together with a quick stir. She transferred the contents into a highball glass and set the glass on the napkin.

"Very impressive. And quick." Alexis sounded like she was mentally applauding the bartender. "So far so good. She has one more customer before she gets to us. Do you have your drink order ready?" Alexis had asked him to request a complicated mixed drink to test Kelli's ability.

"Do you have one?" He lowered his voice and leaned closer. The pretense gave him an excuse to breathe in her perfume. He felt her warmth in the comfortably cool bar.

"Yes." She flashed a smile that dazzled him. "I had to look one up, though. I usually drink white wine. Or if I'm in an adventurous mood, a margarita."

"So you're experimenting tonight?" Max chuckled. "I may need to drive us home, then."

Alexis laughed. "Don't worry. I'll cut myself off if I start feeling tipsy."

Kelli appeared before them. Max sensed her energy. Her big brown eyes sparkled with excitement as though she was inviting them on an adventure. "Thank you both so much for your patience. What can I get for you?"

"You didn't keep us waiting long at all." Alexis returned the bartender's smile. "May I have an Aviation, please?"

Kelli raised her eyebrows. Her eyes glinted at the challenge. "A very good choice for the lady." She spun a napkin in front of Alexis, then turned to Max. "And what can I mix for the gentleman?"

"I'd like a Dark and Stormy, please."

Kelli's eyes widened with pleasure. She swung her right index finger between Alexis and Max. "I like these choices." She did her signature napkin spin for Max. "Ladies first."

Max watched Kelli collect the bottles of gin, maraschino liqueur, crème de violette and lemon juice. She free-poured the liquids into the silver mixer with a balance of deft precision and captivating flourish. She poured the mixture into a cordial glass, added fruit and floral garnish, then presented the glass to Alexis.

"Thank you." Alexis looked delighted.

"My pleasure." Kelli winked at her. She pointed at Max. "And now for your Dark and Stormy."

Max liked the drink but he'd only had it a few times. The last time had been years ago while training with a chef in the Caribbean. The drink only had two ingredients—dark rum and ginger beer—but finding the right balance of spicy and sweet was complicated. He watched her brisk, sharp movements as she made the beverage.

Kelli poured his drink into a cognac balloon glass and placed it in front of him. "What do you think?"

Max took a sip. His eyes widened in surprise. "Perfect."

"Yes." Kelli pumped her fist. "Thank you." She turned to Alexis. "How do you like your drink?"

Alexis nodded. "It's also perfect. Thank you."

Kelli's face glowed with pride and pleasure. "Thank you both."

Max slipped Kelli his credit card to pay for their drinks. The young bartender inclined her head before bouncing away. He watched as she stopped to check on another customer near the opposite end of the bar. An older gentleman sat back on his seat, revealing the guest Kelli was speaking with.

Max stiffened in surprise. "Isn't that Joshua?"

"Where?" Alexis followed his gaze. "You're right."

The youngest Colton was generous with his smiles as he chatted with the attractive bartender. She laughed at something he said before continuing to process Max's card and print his receipt.

Kelli returned to their side of the bar with Max's credit card and gave him his receipt. "I'll stop by to check on you, but if you need anything else before then, just give me a wave." With a wink and a smile, she turned away to check on her other guests. Max noticed she lingered a little longer with Joshua.

He took another sip of his drink. It was really good. "Does it look to you as though Kelli and Joshua have known each other for a while? It doesn't look as though they just met today. They're pretty comfortable with each other."

"You could be right." Alexis seemed to be nursing her drink, paying more attention to Kelli and her interactions with her customers. "She's very talented. This drink is delicious, and she has a great attitude. She seems to connect easily with her guests, and not just the male ones. I'm going to recommend Laura bring her in for an interview."

Alexis was right. More women than men sat around the bar and the women were just as comfortable with her. Kelli would be a wonderful addition for Mariposa, even for the temporary position. Max's only hesitation was Joshua.

He watched the younger man's interaction with Kelli. Other men tried to monopolize the bartender's time beyond ordering a drink. She put them off firmly but politely. However, she always had a few extra moments for Joshua. Did Joshua come to The Cloisters to see Kelli or was seeing the bartender an added bonus of the venue?

Max took another drink. "Joshua's attracted to her."

Alexis glanced down the bar. She must have seen what he saw. "It does appear that way."

"Doesn't he have a rule against dating employees?"

"That's what Laura told me." She returned her attention to Max. "You're not suggesting I tell Laura not to hire Kelli because her brother may have a crush on her, are you?"

Was he? "I think that's another consideration. Suppose there's something building between them. But because she comes to work at Mariposa, they have to pump the brakes on whatever that is. Is that something we're comfortable with?"

Alexis looked at him as though she questioned his sanity. "What I'm *not* comfortable with is not offering Kelli this chance just because of what may or may not be growing between her and Joshua. Kelli should decide whether she wants to accept this career opportunity."

Max raised his hands, palms out. He was embarrassed by how badly he'd misspoken. "You're right. It's her choice. But maybe you should tell Joshua you're recommending her for the fill-in position."

"I'll leave that to Laura. She's the assistant manager." Alexis still sounded more than a little perturbed by Max's suggestion. "I'll let her know we saw—"

"Max. Alexis. It's great to see you guys." Joshua's voice startled Max. Had the other man heard what he and Alexis were saying? Joshua's tone grew somber. "Have you both recovered from the accident?"

Alexis's eyes lit up. "Yes, thank you for asking. I've even started jogging again. My ankle's a little tender, but otherwise fine."

Joshua chuckled. "Of course you're running again. Nothing keeps you down, at least not for long." He glanced toward Kelli at the other end of the bar before addressing Max. "How're you, Max? I've heard Noah has a suspect who's not connected to that stuff in New York."

"I appreciate his looking into it." Max glanced toward Alexis. Her expression was tense. Was that because of Joshua's sudden appearance or their topic of discussion? "I know we're all looking forward to solving this mystery so we can put it behind us."

"Yes, we are." Joshua's eyes drifted back to Kelli as though he couldn't help himself. Max could empathize. He felt the same way when Alexis was nearby. "I hope you both have a good evening."

Max joined Alexis in wishing Joshua well before returning to their conversation. "Joshua couldn't keep his eyes off Kelli. But you're right. Kelli deserves the opportunity at Mariposa. She's an excellent bartender and the resort would be lucky to have her."

"I know." Alexis shook her head. "You're a hopeless romantic."

"I prefer to think of myself as a *hopeful* romantic." Max had more of his drink. It didn't pack as much of a punch as Alexis's laughter.

"Fortunately for Kelli, you're not the one making the referral. I am."

"Are you hopeless or hopeful?" Max held his breath.

Alexis took a moment to answer. "I prefer to think of myself as practical."

What does that mean? He exhaled. "Haven't you ever met someone who made you want to flush *practical* down the drain and follow your heart?"

Alexis shook her head. "Have you?"

I have now. "I haven't lost hope." Max cleared his throat. "Since we're here, would you like to get dinner?"

She smiled. "I'd love that."

And he'd love it if the night never ended. But for now, he'd hold on to *practical* with both hands and hope his heart could stand the wait.

The host led them to a table not far from the bar. With her decision about the fill-in bartender's position made, Alexis checked her evaluation of Kelli off her to-do list and focused on dinner with Max. That was definitely not a hardship.

The celebrity chef looked camera-ready in a casual brown suit. His black vintage shirt had a standing collar. He'd left the top button undone. The fabric stretched across his muscled chest. It featured a leaf embroidered pattern she'd dearly love to trace. Alexis curled her fingers under the table to resist the urge. His clean mint cologne was a distraction. So was his charm; the way he took her hand, held her chair, rested his palm on the small of her back. He made her feel like part of a couple. She hadn't realized how much she'd missed that. It was nice.

It also was scary. As she'd told Laura last evening, even if she decided to pursue a relationship with the charming chef, what would happen in three weeks when he returned to New York, leaving her behind? For tonight, she pushed the worry to the back of her mind.

They both chose the blackened salmon entrée. Descriptions of their days and their plans for the rest of the week carried them almost to the end of their meal.

"Where does love stand on your list of priorities?" Max's question caught her by surprise. Were they back to the hopeless romantic versus practical relationship debate?

A forkful of salmon found its way into Alexis's windpipe. She covered her mouth with her right hand and cleared it with a cough. That bought her a little time. "Excuse me?"

"Are you okay?" Max put his hand on hers where it rested on the table. His eyes were dark with concern.

"Yes, thank you." Alexis took a steadying breath. The scents of cayenne, thyme and oregano wafted up from her salmon. "Um, well, I've never really thought about where my love life was on my list of priorities." *Not until recently.*

His lips curved with amusement. "I think that answers the question of where it stands on your list. So, you and Jake have never dated?"

Alexis thought his tone was too casual. "No, we haven't."

"You've never been tempted?"

"I told you. Jake's like a brother to me and he thinks of me as his sister. Dating would be too weird. Although our mothers, who are both crazy impatient for grandchildren, have brought it up more than once."

Max smiled as he sipped his drink. "My mother wants grandkids, too. Mel and I have thrown Miri under the bus. She's the only one who's married."

Alexis's shoulders shook with amusement. "Oh, I'm sure she appreciated that. Well, Jake and I refuse to get married—especially to each other—just to satisfy our mothers' need to spoil our as-yet-unborn children."

Max lifted his glass in a mock toast. "Mel and I salute you."

Alexis arched an eyebrow. "So what about *your* love life? Where is it on your list of priorities?"

"The same." Max pierced his last piece of salmon. "I've been too busy building my restaurants to spend much time pursuing a relationship."

"I know what you mean." Alexis hesitated as she watched

Max put the forkful of salmon between his lips. The act seemed so intimate. She dropped her eyes and forced her thoughts into a semblance of order. "With all of your projects, I'm surprised you have time to sleep." She braced herself to meet his eyes again. "A relationship would probably put you over the edge."

His myriad business pursuits were additional reasons a relationship between them wouldn't work. She was building a career, but he was building an empire.

"My restaurants are my first love." Max nudged his nearly empty plate to the side. He folded his arms on the white cloth that covered their table. "I want people to think of Out with Friends as a place to go for a great meal and a good time."

"That's how my mother described it." Alexis admired people with a plan. She wiped the corners of her mouth with her linen napkin, then slid it and her plate to the side.

"My father had wanted me to join his production company, supporting documentaries and feature films that educated as well as entertained." Max stared at his glass of water, but Alexis suspected he saw a different image in his head. "I'm very proud of the company he built, but my first love has always been cooking. I hated disappointing him, but I didn't want to go into TV and film production."

"I seriously doubt your father's disappointed in you." Alexis paused as their server came to collect their plates and deliver their bill.

Max claimed the black leather check holder before Alexis could even move. He glanced at the receipt, then returned it to their server with his credit card.

He waited until the young man disappeared again before continuing. "My father's motto is, 'You can do better.' He's said that to me and my sisters all my life."

Alexis's eyes widened with surprise. "That's kind of harsh."

"Tell me about it." Max gave a humorless laugh. "My sisters and I think he's trying to encourage or maybe motivate us. I think he'd be surprised to know it's having the opposite effect." He sat back against his chair. "We've finally decided one of us should tell him. I think it should be my sister, Miri. She's the eldest."

"Or maybe the three of you should tell him together."

Max cocked his head. "Wouldn't that feel as though we're ganging up on him?"

"Not if you make it clear that your words are coming from a place of love."

"That's a good idea." Max's eyebrows knitted as he seemed to consider her advice. "I'll discuss it with them. Thank you."

"You're welcome." Alexis sipped her Aviator. She was alternating between it and ice water.

"What about you?" Max asked. "Where do you want your career to take you?"

"That's an interesting way to put it." She considered his questions. "Lately, I've started to feel as though I'm running in place."

"I can relate to that."

His understanding encouraged her to confide even more. "I've worked at Mariposa since I was in college. I started at the reception desk like Clarissa, then moved up to concierge. Now I'm the senior concierge. It's a supervisory position, but I'm ready to move into management."

Max's eyes gleamed with admiration. "Do you have a position in mind?"

Alexis nodded. "One of our event managers is retiring at the end of the month. I would love to be promoted into that position."

"Does Laura know you're interested in it?"

"We've discussed it." Alexis winced when she recalled the awkward conversation. "One of the drawbacks of having a best friend who's also your boss is the impression that perhaps my promotions were handed to me."

"What do you care what other people think?" Max shrugged his powerful shoulders.

"I know it shouldn't bother me, but I don't want other people's suspicions to undermine my position at the resort. I told Laura that, if I get the job, I don't want there to be any doubt that I earned it."

Max nodded his approval. "What do you need to do to earn it?"

"It's a matter of proving my project management and customer service skills." She gestured toward Max. "That's one of the reasons I was so happy when Adam trusted me to work with you on your recipes. It shows he believes I can provide you with satisfactory customer service."

"You've been better than satisfactory. Your feedback on the entrées has been critical to the success of my recipes."

Alexis shook her head. "You're being too kind."

"No, I'm not."

She ignored his interruption and continued. "I have to show I can coordinate with outside vendors." Alexis jerked her head toward the bar. "I'm hoping being able to refer Kelli Iona will score me some points with Laura."

"Your awareness of a talented bartender like Kelli has impressed me."

Alexis laughed. "You're good for my ego. I also have to bring my projects in at or under budget. To plan whole events at the resort or even *for* the resort would be so exciting. Weddings, anniversaries, family reunions." Her body vibrated with excitement. "I don't want to change the feel or flavor of the resort. But I would love for more people to experience it."

Max leaned into the table. His eyes darkened with an exciting emotion. He lowered his voice. "I love the sound of your voice when you're excited. The way your enthusiasm brings a sparkle to your eyes and a flush to your cheeks." He brushed the backs of his long, warm fingers across the side of her face.

Alexis felt a delicious shiver roll down her spine. "We agreed we should just be friends." Was that husky sound really her voice?

A ghost of a smile played with Max's full lips. He let his hand drop away from her face as he leaned against his chair. "We can still be friends."

Not if he kept looking at her like that. The heat in his eyes could make her forget her common sense.

Alexis cleared her throat and pushed away from the table. "We should get back to Mariposa."

Without another word, Max stood with her. He placed his hand lightly on the small of her back and escorted her to the parking lot. Alexis's steps were heavy with regret. The evening was coming to an end. It was better they said good-night sooner rather than later—before she did something she might regret.

Wasn't it?

Chapter Ten

Another beautiful night in Sedona. As Alexis walked beside Max, she filled her lungs with the cool night air. Beneath the scents of rich sauces, spicy poultries and fish, Alexis detected the fragrance of pines and juniper. In the clear, mid-March sky, the stars appeared like small diamonds scattered across blue velvet. A soft breeze threaded through her hair. The setting was too romantic.

Did Max feel it, too? Alexis slid him a look from the corner of her eye.

"Thank you again for coming with me." She stopped beside her car, which stood under a lamp in the back of the bar's rear parking lot. "You're great comp—" An object glinting in the bushes beneath the lamp distracted her.

Loud pops, two of them at first, rang out across the parking lot quickly followed by the screams and shouts of the people in the area behind them. Max grabbed her, using his body to shield her as he pushed her away from the car.

"Stay down." His words were curt and loud.

Alexis heard more popping. More and more. It seemed like the popping would never end.

They ran back to the bar, sticking close to the other parked cars. They stayed low, as low as possible. Their romantic surroundings had become a threat. The air smelled like gun smoke.

The stars were too bright. Alexis feared they'd give away their position. Each gentle breeze was the shooter's breath on the back of her neck. Alexis gritted her teeth. She prayed she and Max would make it back inside the bar without being shot. The establishment's entrance came into view. Max clasped her hand and sprinted beside her. She was torn between gratitude for his selfless protection and fear for the danger in which he was putting himself.

Behind The Cloisters' solid front doors, Alexis breathed again. But they still weren't out of danger. She pulled her cell phone from her purse and called for help.

"Nine-one-one. What is your emergency?" The dispatcher's voice was like air to a suffocating person.

Alexis gulped down her panic. "Someone's shooting at us."

"Noah." Alexis felt a rush of relief to see a familiar face in the midst of an unfamiliar and terrifying situation. The detective was walking across the lot toward her and Max. "I'm so glad to see you."

"So am I." Max's hand kept up a steady rhythm as he rubbed Alexis's upper arm. Was he aware he was doing that? Was he comforting her, himself or both of them?

"I heard the dispatch report over the radio that you'd called in a shooting." Noah came to a stop in front of them. He wore baggy blue jeans, a tight black T-shirt and a faded gray hooded jacket. "Laura would never have forgiven me if I didn't check it out. And she'll expect a full report when I see her."

He was probably right.

"I would be the same way." She was still shaking. Max tightened his arm around her waist, offering her comfort as well as support.

Alexis's eyes scanned the parking lot. She was struggling to make sense of all they'd been through. Uniformed officers were searching the immediate area. She'd overheard them discussing the fact that they'd found seventeen bullet casings. *Seventeen.* So many. And how had they not been hit by at least one?

While she'd called emergency services, Max had warned Kelli and the manager on duty about the shooting. They'd discreetly asked those guests who'd been preparing to leave to wait until after the police had secured their surroundings. Now dozens of their customers were cautiously stepping outside like penguins checking the water for sharks.

Alexis shifted her stance to take some of her weight off her left foot. Now that her adrenaline rush was over, she could feel her ankle throbbing. She'd run as fast as she could with Max back to the bar to escape the shooter. She hadn't given any thought to the injury she'd sustained during the previous attempt on her and Max's lives.

Noah shared a look between Alexis and Max. "Can you walk me through what happened?"

"Max and I got back to my car." She pointed toward her vehicle, which still stood under the lamp in the rear of the parking lot. "I noticed the light from the lamp glinting on something in the bushes. That's when I heard a popping sound."

Max picked up the recount. "Even as we ran back to the bar, I could still hear the gun firing."

Noah stepped back to get a better look at them. "Neither of you were hurt?"

Max squeezed Alexis's shoulders. "We're fine, fortunately."

"I'm fine, thanks to you again." Alexis's eyes lingered on Max.

Noah dragged his fingers through his thick brown hair. "It doesn't sound like an attempted mugging."

"It didn't feel like one, either." Max's voice was dry.

"Nothing was taken and your car's still there." The detective shook his head in amazement. "You're both lucky. Seventeen bullets. Someone emptied their gun at you. That's a lot of hostility."

"Hostility toward us?" Alexis took a steadying breath. "We can't be certain this was personal to Max and me. It could have been a mass shooter."

"I don't think that's what this was." Max's tone was pensive. "This was personal. The shooter was hiding in the bushes beside your car. They were aiming at us. At you. Then they left."

"I agree with Max. Although, since you two were together again, there's no way to tell which one of you the shooter was after. They could have been after both of you." Noah addressed Alexis. "What brought you to The Cloisters?"

Alexis glanced at the establishment over her shoulder. "We need someone to fill in at L bar temporarily for one of our regulars. I told Laura I'd check out one of the bartenders here to see if we should invite her for an interview."

Noah frowned. "Did you tell anyone besides Laura that you were coming here tonight?"

Alexis shook her head. "Just Max. There wasn't any reason to tell anyone else."

The detective addressed Max. "Did you mention it to anyone?"

Max also shook his head. "Only Adam and my family in New York."

Noah stared at the ground. Alexis could feel his thoughts churning. "Someone could have followed you from the resort. But they would've had to have been parked outside the grounds on the off chance that one or both of you would be going out."

Alexis heard the skepticism in the detective's voice. She wasn't buying that theory, either. "Have you spoken with Mark Bower?"

"Yeah." Noah shoved his hands into the back pockets of his jeans. "His alibi's weak. He claims the night the guardrails were tampered with, he was at the laundromat. There aren't any cameras at the one he used. He could've come and gone without anyone noticing. And we don't know what time the rails were cut."

"So he's still on the list." Alexis glanced up at Max. "I can't think of anyone else with a motive to do something like this. I don't want to think it could be Mark, either. I'm the one who recommended hiring him."

Noah turned to Max. "Have you thought any more about who your stalker could be?"

"I have no idea why someone would want to kill me." Max rubbed his jaw with his left hand. "And if that's their plan, why didn't they do it in New York? Why follow me to Sedona?"

"How are they tracking your movements?" Alexis spread her arms. "For that matter, how is Mark tracking my movements?"

"All right. I'll add this to our case file." Noah walked with them to Alexis's car. "In the meantime, I'll see how the search is progressing. Are you two okay to get back to the resort on your own?"

Max nodded. "We'll be fine. Thanks."

"Good." Noah's eyes scanned their surroundings again before he returned his attention to them. "Listen, I appreciate that you both have work to do but maybe think about staying on the resort until we find whoever's behind these attacks."

"That's good advice." Max lowered his eyes to meet Alexis's.

"I promise to be careful." She stopped beside her car and looked cautiously behind it. Max and Noah circled the vehicle. No one noticed anyone lurking in the bushes. She offered Noah a smile. "Thanks again. I'm glad you were here."

"I'm sorry this happened." Noah shook their hands. "It's a horrible experience. But please know I'm giving your case my full attention. Hopefully, nothing else will happen, but if it does, call me directly. And be careful driving home."

Alexis felt much better after his assurances. "Thank you for everything, Noah. Good night."

"Thank you." Max looked at Alexis. "Do you want me to drive?"

"No, thank you." Alexis engaged the keyless entry as she turned toward the driver's side door. "I can manage."

With a final wave goodbye to Noah, Alexis pulled out of the lot. She wasn't shaking any more, but her muscles were tight. Seventeen bullets had been shot in her direction. If Max hadn't pulled her away, would one of them have struck her?

Max broke the tense silence. "Noah's right. We shouldn't leave the safety of the resort anymore. At least not until this stalker is caught."

"I agree. When the guardrails were sabotaged, it was easier to think we weren't really the intended target. We were in the wrong place at the wrong time." Alexis released a shaky breath. "Having a loaded gun unloaded at me cleared up any confusion."

The rustling sound from the passenger seat indicated Max had shifted to face her. "I'm sorry you had this experience."

"I wasn't the only one running from bullets. I'm sorry this happened to you, too." She checked the traffic before merging into the left-turn lane. She stopped at the red light. "I wish we knew who's targeting us and what they want."

"So do I."

Alexis looked at the night sky and the mountains in the distance. The evening shouldn't have ended this way. She gripped the steering wheel and beat back the feelings of fear that were trying to take hold of her again. "Would you mind if we stopped by my condo so I could pack a few more things for my stay at the resort?"

"I don't mind at all."

"Thank you." When the traffic light turned green, Alexis pulled out of the turn lane and through the intersection.

Conversation was stiff and sporadic during the twenty-minute drive to her condo community. Alexis had the sense they were both still processing their terrifying experience. She pulled into her attached one-car garage and welcomed Max into her home again.

She was suddenly very tired. Was it the long day, the alcohol—or the shooting? "I could really use a cup of coffee. Would you like some?"

"Yes, please. If it's not too much trouble."

"It isn't." Alexis moved toward the coffee maker on the marble counter. "Why don't you have a seat. This shouldn't take long."

Behind her, Alexis heard Max cross to her dining table and pull out a chair. His steps seemed slow as though he was fatigued as well.

She was on autopilot as she moved around her kitchen, collecting the mugs from the cupboard and filling the carafe with water. Her fingers were clumsy as she tried to separate the coffee filters.

She laid her hands flat on the counter and stretched them before trying again. "Someone shot at us. I don't understand why." Her patience frayed, Alexis gave up and stuffed two or three of the thin white papers into the brew basket.

"I can't apologize enough." Max's words were heavy with regret. "It's my fault your life's in danger."

Alexis spun to face him. "No, it's not." That maneuver had taken its toll. Her knees were shaking again. She leaned heavily against the counter behind her. "The creep who's been following us around is entirely to blame. Besides, as Noah pointed out, we don't know whether that attack was directed at you, me or both of us."

"Do you really think Mark Bower would shoot you for firing him?" From his dubious tone, Alexis sensed Max didn't agree with that theory.

She found it hard to believe, too. Still… "I don't know."

Alexis fumbled for the tub of grounds she stored in the cupboard above the coffee maker. Her hand trembled as she measured the first teaspoon. She drew a breath to steady herself and caught the light, nutty aroma of the breakfast blend. The relaxation technique failed. The grounds were leaping from the teaspoon. Her breathing became more ragged. She needed to calm down.

Two large hands took hold of her shoulders. Alexis jumped and the coffee grounds scattered across her counter.

Max's voice came from behind her. "Lean on me. Just lean on me. I'm here for you."

She turned in his arms and stared up at him in amazement. "You aren't rattled?"

Max hesitated. "I'm a lot of things. Anxious, angry and chilled to the core." His eyes delved into hers. "Maybe I need to lean on you. Maybe I think we need to lean on each other."

"I was so scared." Alexis wrapped her arms around his shoulders and leaned into him. She tasted the tears she hadn't realized were falling.

"I know, sweetheart. I was scared, too." Max rubbed her back. His shirt was soft under her cheek. He'd hung his jacket on his chair. "I'm so sorry you went through that."

"I wasn't scared for myself. I was frightened out of my *mind* for you."

"For *me*? Why?"

Alexis leaned back in the circle of his arms. Swiping the

tears from her cheeks with the back of her right hand, Alexis glared up at his handsome, puzzled face. "Do you think you're bulletproof?" How could he be so brilliant, capable and creative about so many complicated things yet so silly about this? "You put your body between me and an active shooter." Her voice quavered. "If anything had happened to you, I would have lost my mind."

Max framed her face with his large palms. "If anything had happened to you, I would've lost mine."

He lowered his mouth to hers. Alexis's eyes drifted shut. She nibbled at his firm, full lips and shivered as those lips teased her own. Max stroked his tongue across the seam of her mouth. Alexis sighed as she sent her tongue to play with his.

From the moment she'd picked him up at the L Building and he'd strode toward her in his brown suit and black shirt, it had been hard for Alexis to remember the evening wasn't a date. They were friends and he'd offered to help her with a work project. Her mind was aware of those boundaries. But her body kept reacting to the sound of his voice, the dimple in his smile and the pull of his scent. Deep in her fantasies, she'd wanted the evening to end like this. Not with them racing away from gunshots.

Alexis parted her lips. Max deepened their kiss. He pressed her against him, molding her body to his. His tongue swept inside. Alexis shivered under the intimate caress. Her skin heated. Her pulse raced. Her body grew restless. She moaned deep in her throat. The pulse was loud in her head.

"I love the way you feel against me." Alexis spoke on a breath. She lifted on her toes to fit her body even closer to his. She opened her mouth wider and sucked his tongue inside her.

A ball of heat burst into flames inside Max. Pleasure, sweet and sharp, pierced him.

"And I love the way you feel in my arms." He slid his hands down Alexis's back, cupping her hips and lifting her from her feet.

"Wrap your legs around me, sweetheart." His words were

a whisper. Max pressed his lips against the curve of her neck. He breathed in her soft scent.

Without hesitation, Alexis wrapped her long, toned legs around him. She trailed kisses down his neck. Max shivered when she dragged her teeth lightly against his skin.

Four strides carried him into her dining area. Max lowered her onto the table. Her legs dropped away from him. Alexis pulled his shirt free of his pants and stroked her palms up and over his torso. Max's body burned. He drew a deep breath.

Reaching behind Alexis, Max released the zipper of her dress. He straightened and watched her bodice pool around her waist. The curves of her breasts rose above her demi-cup black lace bra. Max stopped breathing. He remembered the condom in his wallet and his palms dampened.

He also remembered Alexis racing away from gunshots, trembling in his arms, sobbing against his chest. She looked up at him. Her bright eyes were hot with need. Did she need *him*—or did she need to forget? The answer mattered. Very much. It would mean the difference between waking up to rejoice—or to regret. Max briefly closed his eyes. He gritted his teeth as he bit back a sigh.

Max wrapped his arms around her. He kissed her lips softly as he zipped her dress. It was one of the hardest things he'd had to do. His heart pounded against his chest as though in protest of his actions.

He spoke against her lips. "Why don't you pack your things, sweetheart? I'll make the coffee." He forced himself to let her go. Stepping back, he met her eyes. The heat in them was cooling. Confusion and disappointment took its place.

Alexis frowned. "I don't understand. What's wrong?" The uncertainty in her voice was like a gut punch.

He needed to have his head checked. Alexis wanted him. He was sure of that. And he wanted her so much more than he could express. Then why was he just standing there?

Max took a breath. "Alexis, someone tried to kill us tonight. It's unsettled us more than we probably realize. I don't think it would be a good idea for us to take such an important step in our relationship now, not after the shock we've had."

Alexis's lips parted in surprise. Max offered her his hand to help her off the table. She ignored him and stepped down on her own.

"Are you sure that's the only reason?" She adjusted her dress as she circled him.

"What do you mean?" Max turned to keep her in sight.

Alexis marched toward what he thought was her bedroom. Her movements were stiff and jerky. "I realize you're used to dating women in your same social circles. Is that the real reason you've decided not to get involved with me after all?"

Was she kidding? He wanted her so badly he could barely walk.

Max forced himself to follow her into the other room. That probably wasn't the best idea, but he wasn't going to let her accusation go unchallenged. "That's false and unfair. You're the one who wanted to just be friends."

"And you're the one who suddenly doesn't want anything to do with me." She pulled a large suitcase from the closet and started indiscriminately throwing clothes into it.

"Wrong again." He stood in the doorway, far from the bed. "But when we do make love, I don't want you to wake up with regrets."

Alexis stiffened at his words. She straightened from the suitcase and turned to him. "What makes you think I'd have regrets tonight?"

Max crossed his arms over his chest. "Like I said, too much has happened tonight. I don't want our first night together to be remembered as the night we had to run for our lives."

Her eyes moved over him as though she was imagining him naked. Max's groin stiffened even more. He bit back a groan.

Finally, she met his eyes. "You're right. Looking down the barrel of a gun affected me in ways I hadn't expected. I'm sorry I took my anger out on you and accused you of being a snob. I know you're not. I'm sorry."

Max didn't hesitate. "Apology accepted." He jerked a thumb over his shoulder. "While you pack, I'll make the coffee."

What he really needed was a cold shower. A long one.

Alexis hurried to the L lobby early Friday morning. Clarissa had called to tell her Jake was waiting at the registration desk. What was he doing here? He had class at the university on Fridays. Had something happened to her mother? To Aunt Suz?

She'd been stuck in auto-panic because of the shooting at The Cloisters last night. Alexis stumbled over nothing. Thank goodness she hadn't tripped last night. That could have made the difference between life and death. She had a flashback of gripping Max's hand as they'd raced across the parking lot. She'd run so fast, she'd felt like she was flying.

And now Jake was here unexpectedly. Alexis's palms were sweating. Her breath came in gasps. Her pulse was jackhammering at the base of her throat. She'd continue this way until he told her everyone was okay.

Jake stood beside the wall opposite the registration desk. His hands were in the front pockets of his gunmetal-gray slacks. In his navy sports jacket, gray tie and conservative cream shirt, he looked like a men's cologne model masquerading as a university professor.

As she reached him, Jake's tension slammed against her like an invisible truck. Her heart in her throat, Alexis stopped in her tracks an arm's length from him. The strain in his chiseled features eased as his coal black eyes examined her.

His voice was barely audible. "You look well—for someone who was shot at last night."

How did he know?

Alexis swallowed. First things first. "Are Mom and Aunt Suz all right?"

"For now." He took his hands from his pockets. "We need to talk."

Some of Alexis's anxiety eased. Their mothers were okay. Her pulse went back to normal, and she breathed again. It would take a minute for her palms to dry.

She led Jake to her office and closed the door. "How did you find out about the shooting?"

"Not from you." Jake stood behind the nearest visitor's chair. He'd shoved his hands into his pockets again. "A friend texted me this morning. He and his fiancée had had dinner at The Cloisters and were excited to have seen Chef Max there with an attractive woman. They'd enjoyed the evening—until the shooting in the parking lot. Seems that's not a regular occurrence at The Cloisters. Why didn't you tell us?"

Alexis's eyes widened with fear and dread. Us? "Did you tell our mothers?"

"Really?" Jake gave her a sarcastic look. "If I'd told our mothers, you would have heard from them by now. But stop changing the subject. How are you? What happened? And why didn't you tell us?"

"I'm fine," Alexis lied. She circled her desk to take her seat before her knees gave out. Seeming to take pity on her, Jake sat, too. "I was going to call Mom as soon as I figured out how to explain to her what happened. I'm still not sure how to approach it. Everything happened so fast. One second, I'm getting into my car. The next, there are these popping sounds and Max is pulling me to safety."

Jake closed his eyes and dropped his head. "Thank God." His voice carried a wealth of fear, relief and fear.

"We ran back to the bar and called the police. Noah Steele arrived with them."

"Noah? Laura's homicide detective?" His phrasing made Alexis smile. She really needed that levity, no matter how brief.

Alexis nodded. "He said they'd recovered about seventeen bullet casings beside my car."

"Seventeen?" The blood drained from Jake's face. He leaned forward in his chair. His voice was muffled behind his hands. "We could have lost you."

Alexis left her chair to kneel beside his. "But you didn't, thanks in large part to Max."

Jake straightened. His eyes were cloudy with fear. "I have to thank him. Although I would've preferred he'd talked you out of leaving the resort."

"He tried." Alexis returned to her seat. "The compromise was his coming with me."

Jake shook his head in exasperation, then straightened in his seat. "The shooter emptied their gun all in the same spot. Do the police think they were trying to kill you or scare you?"

"They don't know yet."

"Is this connected to the threats against Max?"

Alexis nervously patted the bun at the nape of her neck. "The threats aren't just against Max. I recently had to fire an employee. He threatened me."

"Alexis!" Jake sprang from his chair. "And you're only now telling me this? This drip, drip, drip of information is torture."

"I'm sorry."

"Does Aunt Cat know?"

"Not exactly." Alexis held up her hands in surrender. "But in fairness, we don't know who's behind these threats. It could be someone associated with Max. It could be someone connected to me. Or it could be someone who wants to damage Mariposa's reputation."

"By shooting at you? I don't know, Lex. That sounds a little personal to me." Jake served his sarcasm as he paced her office.

Alexis let his reaction slide. She understood where he was coming from. If their roles were reversed, she'd be freaking out, too. "The police are investigating. We know Noah's an excellent detective. And as I told you, I'm safe here at the resort. They have security checking the grounds 24/7/365."

Jake stopped and faced her. "You can hear how ironic you sound saying that after you were shot at with seventeen bullets last night, can't you?"

Alexis's face burned with embarrassment. She'd made a stupid mistake last night and had almost paid for it with Max's life. "I promise not to leave the resort grounds again until the shooter is caught."

Jake took his seat. "I agree the resort is a safe place for you to wait out this threat. I wouldn't want you to bring this danger to Aunt Cat, either."

"I wouldn't want to involve any of you in this." Alexis felt chilled. She pulled her scarlet blazer more tightly around her. "It would destroy me if something happened to you."

"And if anything happened to you, it would destroy *us*." Jake held her eyes, forcing her not to look away. "I understand you prefer to do things on your own. You're stubborn and hard-headed and—"

Ouch. "I prefer independent."

Jake continued as though he hadn't heard her. "—willful. But you've got to let Aunt Cat know what's going on and why. She deserves to know. How would you feel if she were keeping secrets like this from you?"

Alexis's heart stopped at the thought. "I wouldn't be happy about it. But, Jake, how do I tell my mother someone may be trying to kill me? My father died. My sister was killed. How much is too much?"

She dropped her eyes to her desk, but she didn't see the papers on its surface. Instead, she saw her father's and her sister's funerals. She remembered how frightened she'd been that her mother would be the next to leave her. So much fear.

"Your mother's a strong person." Jake's voice was gentle.

"Mom and I have spent so many years—decades—protecting each other. It's a hard habit to break."

"I know, but it's time." Jake shook his head. "Lex, of course Aunt Cat will be worried, but if you don't tell her—if she finds out after the fact or worse from someone else—she'll be worried, angry and hurt. Which would you rather deal with?"

"You're right. I'll call her before lunch." Dread, cold and heavy, was already building in her gut.

"Good." Jake pushed himself to his feet. "In that case, I'll leave so you can make that call."

Alexis stood. "That reminds me, I thought you taught a class on Fridays?"

"It's an afternoon class, which gave me plenty of time to come to your office and chew you out before making the hour drive to the university." Jake stepped aside so Alexis could open the door and lead him from her office.

"Lucky me." Alexis's voice was as dry as the desert dust.

"You're welcome."

Alexis smiled. "I'm grateful. I mean, I don't like having you call me out, but you're right. Mom and I have to stop keeping secrets under the guise of protecting each other."

Jake wrapped his arm around her shoulders. "You and Aunt Cat have a great relationship."

"I know." She patted Jake's back with her left hand. "So do you and Aunt Suz."

"I can appreciate this won't be an easy conversation to have but I think it will help make your relationship even stronger." Jake dropped his arm.

Alexis snorted. "We'll see about that. I just don't like disappointing her."

Jake stopped and turned to her. "None of this is your fault, Lex. How could you possibly disappoint her?"

Alexis squeezed Jake's right forearm. "You're right. Again. I'll just keep reminding myself I'm not to blame."

"Good. Make that your mantra." Jake started walking again.

As he passed the registration desk, he gave Clarissa a nod and a smile. The young woman blushed and lowered her eyes. Another admirer. Oh, brother. She joined Jake in the L's parking lot. His car was in the space closest to the main building's entrance.

"Drive safely." She gave him a hard hug. "And thank you again for coming to talk with me in person."

"What's family for?" He squeezed her back. "Call me if you need to talk."

"I will." She stepped back and watched Jake get into his car.

He waved before he reversed out of the parking space and drove off.

Alexis straightened her back and squared her shoulders. It was time to rip the bandage off and tell her mother someone wanted her dead.

Chapter Eleven

"How are you feeling?" Max stood on the threshold of Alexis's office late Friday morning. His knuckles still rested against the cool blond wood surface of her door.

Alexis looked up from her laptop. Her welcoming smile made her features glow and filled his body with warmth. It also eased his unrest, most of which had been stirred by the scene he'd witnessed between Alexis and Jake earlier in the parking lot. That had been quite the hug.

"Better." She spun her chair around and gestured for him to take the visitor's seat closest to her. "Please come in. And could you close the door? I don't want anyone to hear us talking about last night."

Her hair was pulled back into her customary bun, revealing her long, elegant neck, as well as her delicate sterling silver earrings and matching necklace. In his mind, he pictured the raven tresses as she'd worn them last night, loose and flowing around her shoulders. Over her ebony shell blouse, her scarlet blazer warmed her golden brown skin.

"Good point." Max shut the door, then settled into the chair.

"How are you?" Alexis asked.

Her office was pleasantly cool. The air smelled faintly of morning coffee, lemon cleaner and wildflowers.

"I feel better as well. Thank you." He rubbed his damp palms on the sides of his pant legs before gripping the chair's arms. "Although I'm sure it'll take a while for us to fully recover from being shot at. We're incredibly lucky."

Max looked into her eyes, searching for... He didn't know what. Some sign of lingering emotions from her meeting with Jake? Longing? Wistfulness? Love? Seeing Alexis in another man's arms had gutted him. Max knew Alexis thought of Jake as a brother. But how did Jake feel about Alexis?

"Yes, we were very fortunate." Alexis picked up a retractable black pen from her desk and rolled it between the palms of both hands. "I didn't thank you properly for once again putting yourself in danger to save my life. Thank you from the bottom of my heart." She smiled. "My mother and Jake thank you, too. Mom wants to send you something more than a card this time."

"Thanks aren't necessary." Max was uncomfortable with the admiration that warmed her hazel eyes to gold. "I did what anyone would have done."

Jake was grateful to him for helping to keep Alexis safe. That meant Alexis had told Jake they'd gone out together. How did the other man feel about that?

Alexis shook her head even as he spoke. "What you did took exceptional courage. Some people would have run—even out of instinct—and left me behind. Instead, you grabbed me and used your body to shield me. If anything had happened to you..." She dropped her eyes as her voice trailed off.

"I'm not a hero, Alexis." Max shifted in his chair. He wanted to put an end to this part of their conversation. "I can't speak to what other people may or may not have done under similar circumstances. All I know is that I wouldn't have been able to live with myself if I hadn't at least tried to help you. That's not the way I was raised."

Admiration softened to humor. "Then maybe my mother should send your parents that fruit basket."

Max widened his eyes, feigning surprise. "Well, if we're talking about fruit baskets, then she should definitely send it to me, especially if it's from the Sedona Family and Community Farmers Market."

Their shared laughter dispelled the rest of Max's unease.

He still had lingering doubts about Jake's role in Alexis's life, though. How could he approach his unanswered questions without sounding like a jealous jerk?

Was he being a jealous jerk? The uncertainty was brutal, but this was a new experience for him. He'd always had a hard rule against flirting with women who were already in relationships. If they were happy, he didn't want to sow doubt or undermine their commitment. Although he was still hesitant to be the reason a couple broke up, for Alexis, he'd throw reticence out the window. Max would fight for her love. He wanted to be with her—if that's what she wanted as well. Please let it be what she wanted.

Max sat back in his chair and rested his right ankle on his left knee. "How did your mother take the news about last night's incident?"

"Is *incident* really the right word?" Alexis shivered, putting the pen down. "I'm leaning toward near-death experience. I hated to burden her with it at work, but Jake convinced me I should talk with her before she found out from someone else. And he was right."

"Jake talked you into it? Was that the reason he was here this morning?"

Alexis hesitated, giving him a questioning look. "Did you see him? He didn't mention running into you."

Max fought a losing battle against the heat rising in his cheeks. "I saw the two of you as he was leaving. I didn't want to intrude."

"You wouldn't have been intruding." Alexis waved a dismissive hand. "I'm sure Jake would have liked to have seen you."

Would he, though? "I'm sorry. Perhaps next time. How did Jake find out about the shooting?"

"A friend texted him about it. In his text, he mentioned seeing you there." She gestured toward Max. "Jake put two and two together and was not happy that I hadn't told him about the attack myself."

"I haven't told my family, either." Guilt wrapped around Max like a wet jacket. "I don't know how."

"I understand." Alexis picked up the pen again. "Laura

called me last night. I had a feeling she would even though Noah said he'd fill her in on what happened. She wanted to speak with me anyway. She was very upset. I was exhausted after speaking with her, physically and emotionally. Perhaps her reaction is part of the reason I was reluctant to tell my mother."

"Adam called me last night." Max shook his head. "He was angry and shaken. After I calmed him down, I crawled into bed. I didn't want to think or talk about it anymore."

"Exactly." Alexis spread her arms. "It's not that we don't care about our families or that we aren't thinking of them. It's just, how do you tell the people who love you and worry about you all the time that someone's trying to kill you? Fortunately, the media reports didn't include our names. I admit if Jake's friend hadn't seen you, I still wouldn't have told him, my mother or my aunt Suz."

"You've already told your aunt, too?"

"No, but I'm certain my mother has by now. They work together at the same state agency. They're in different departments, though."

Max rubbed the back of his neck as he imagined filling in his family on the more distressing parts of his working vacation. "My family's in a different time zone. They're probably well into their day. But I doubt the shooting at The Cloisters would have made national news."

"Remember you're a national celebrity." Alexis shrugged. "Is your family on social media?"

"They all are." Max shook his head with a smile. "They compete with each other about followers, likes and reposts."

Alexis chuckled. "But not with you? Why not?"

Embarrassed, Max shrugged. "I'm an introvert in a family of extroverts. Sarah handles all the promotion for me, social media, the website, the fan e-newsletter."

Alexis's eyes dimmed. She dropped them to the pen quickly rotating between her fingers. "We already know one person recognized you at the bar. Suppose others did as well and some of them post about it on social media? Suppose in their posts, they include the fact they saw you at a location where there happened to be a shooting the same night? Your family might see it in their feed. Is that a risk you want to take?"

Max's muscles tensed at the image her words created. "Definitely not."

"Neither would I." Alexis's smile was soft with empathy. "I'll tell you what Jake told me. It's better for you to have that difficult conversation with your family rather than risk their hearing about the shooting from someone else. If that happens, not only will they be frightened for you, but they'll also be hurt and angry with you."

"I don't know how to tell them. Where would I even start?" Max had a fleeting image of his sisters and parents getting on the next flight from New York to Sedona. His family was that overprotective.

"How did you explain the unmarked package that arrived for you?"

Max sighed. He met Alexis's eyes with difficulty. "I didn't."

Alexis's eyes widened. "You didn't tell your family about the creepy box? Do they know about the break-ins?"

Max heard metal tapping nearby and realized he was drumming his fingertips against his chair's arms. He stopped. "They're worried enough about those. I had to talk my sister and her husband out of moving in with me until the thieves are caught."

Alexis's laughter startled him. "I like your family."

"You do? You can have them." Max squashed a smile. "I love them, and I like them, too, even when they're driving me insane. Because of the viral video, I had to tell them about our hiking accident. I didn't want them to stumble across the footage on their socials. As I expected, they freaked out and my busman's holiday almost turned into a family vacation."

Alexis gave him an encouraging smile. "Tell your family everything, Max. The sooner the better. It's not an easy conversation, but you'll feel better afterward."

He pushed himself to his feet, trying to burn the image of her smile on his mind. It would help him get through the upcoming call with his parents.

* * *

"Good heavens, Max. Are you all right?" His mother sounded out of breath.

It was late Friday afternoon in New York, which was two hours ahead of Sedona. He'd conference-called his parents after what would have been their lunch breaks. Like Alexis, he regretted burdening his parents with the news about The Cloisters shooting while they were still at work. But Alexis—and Jake before her, credit where credit was due—was right. He needed to tell his parents rather than risk their hearing about it from someone else.

Max stared at the French doors of his bungalow. Instead of seeing the soaring mountainscape in the distance, he visualized the frowns that were probably deepening the faint lines across his parents' brows. He clenched his right hand at his side, hoping to keep his anxiety from spreading throughout his body.

The conversation had gone pretty much as he'd anticipated. His parents had interrupted with frequent questions. He'd understood their impatience for information. He probably would have done the same thing, but it made his retelling even harder.

"Yes, Mom. I promise I'm fine." Max turned from the breathtaking view to pace the rest of the room.

"I need to sit down." Erika's voice echoed as though she'd put her phone on speaker. Max felt her anxiety through the satellite connection.

"Do the police have any leads?" His father's voice was both angry and impatient. Max imagined MJ was also pacing.

Max rotated his neck, trying to ease his tension. "They have a few theories, but not many solid leads."

"Do you want us with you?" Erika's voice was nearly normal again.

Max smiled. He'd anticipated that reaction as well. "No, thanks, Mom. As I said, the resort grounds are safe."

MJ expelled a breath. Max heard his father's fear and frustration in the sound. "And the Sedona detective—what's his name, Noah?—is keeping the NYPD informed?"

"Yes, Dad." Max stood to pace again. "But the NYPD's investigation has stalled."

"When you get back, you're staying with us until we can move you out of that condo and into somewhere safe." Beneath Erika's voice, Max heard the faint rumble of metal against plastic as though she'd rolled her chair across the plastic runner beneath her desk.

He imagined his tall, slender mother striding the confines of her executive suite, which was in an office building close to their family home in Queens and just a few blocks from his father's company. Max wanted to respond to her comment, but his father spoke first.

"He isn't coming home until this monster is caught." MJ's voice rose and fell in volume. That confirmed Max's suspicion that his father also was pacing while his cell phone was on speaker. A family trait.

Max started to agree with his father.

Erika interrupted. "How do we know this culprit is the same one who's been breaking into his condo?"

Max jumped into the conversation before his window of opportunity closed again. "If I'm the target of the threats here in Sedona, both Noah and the NYPD believe the break-ins are connected. However, there's a chance these threats aren't directed at me. The stalker might have a separate purpose."

Erika sighed again. "Well, whoever they are and whatever they want, let's hope they're caught soon. This has gone on long enough."

MJ grunted. "More than long enough."

Max cleared his throat. "I also wanted you to know my return to New York might be delayed even further."

Erika gasped. "Why? What's wrong now?"

That didn't come out the way he'd intended. Max rushed to reassure his parents. "Nothing's wrong. Well, nothing else is wrong. But the other producers and I are considering recording the second season of *Cooking for Friends* here."

"Why would you do that?" his father asked.

"Really?" Erika's response carried a wealth of speculation. "Would this change in venue have anything to do with your concierge, Alexis Reed?"

Max shook his head with a smile. "How did you guess, Mom?"

Erika's laughter was delighted and delightful. "It's your texts, silly. 'Alexis and I are going horseback riding. Alexis and I are going hiking.' And on and on. It takes a very special woman to convince my workaholic son to enjoy himself on his working vacation."

MJ chuckled. "Why didn't you tell me about your suspicions?"

"Why couldn't you figure it out?" Erika laughed harder. "Besides, I was waiting for Max to tell us himself. So, Max, tell us about her."

Where should he begin? "Alexis is smart, ambitious, caring. She isn't impressed by my so-called celebrity. In fact, she challenges me. She pushes me."

He loved that and he was starting to believe that wasn't the only thing he loved. His heart beat faster at the thought.

"She sounds remarkable." MJ's tone was warm with approval.

Erika sighed with content. "I'm looking forward to meeting her."

Max's eyebrows rose. "Slow down, Mom. Alexis and I are still getting to know each other. And I want more time with her."

MJ hummed. "And that's why you asked the other producers to consider taping the show there?"

Max wandered his bungalow's great room. "From a business perspective, I think it would be a good touch to locate the show here next season because our focus will be on Southwestern cuisine."

"Ah!" Erika exclaimed. "Because of your cookbook."

"Exactly." Max nodded. "But I won't deny that being with Alexis was the deciding factor."

"Well, between your cookbook's launch and meeting Alexis, I'm looking forward to your show's next season even more now." The smile in Erika's voice eased the weight from Max's shoulders.

"Using the entire season to promote your book is a solid business decision," MJ said. "It would be an even bigger boost to record each episode in front of a live audience."

"We can discuss that later, Dad." Not.

"When will the other producers make their decision?" Erika asked.

"Soon, I hope." Max sighed. "I mean, I know it sounds ridiculous. It feels ridiculous, too, to change my life for a woman I haven't even known for three weeks."

Erika tsked. "Three weeks. Three days. Three hours. Love's on its own schedule. It can take a while or it can be instantaneous, like it was for your father and me."

Max stilled. "It was love at first sight for you and Dad? Why didn't I know this?"

His parents had been happily married for more than thirty-six years. Max and his sisters had assumed his parents had been friends first and love had come later.

"We fell in love right away. When you know, you know." MJ took over the story. "But we waited until our careers were more stable to get married and start a family."

That made sense to Max. His parents were both very career-focused, and had met shortly after graduating from college. In contrast, he and Alexis were already building their careers. But he didn't want to get ahead of himself.

His mother's words claimed his attention again. "Don't worry about the quantity of time you and Alexis spend together. Focus more on the quality of time and on learning the most important things about each other."

Max frowned. "Like what?"

Erika lowered her voice. "What does she think about having children?"

Max closed his eyes and shook his head. "Mom, we're going to have to set some boundaries before you and Alexis meet."

Erika chuckled. "I'm looking forward to it."

That's what Max was afraid of.

"For the shooter to have fired seventeen bullets without any hitting you or Alexis makes me wonder whether the person was trying to kill you or scare you." Adam extended his hand, palm out. "Don't get me wrong. I'm glad neither of you were injured—or worse."

"Thanks for that." Max's voice was dry.

Adam ignored his interruption. "You have to admit it's strange. Either the shooter had never fired a gun before, or they deliberately missed seventeen times."

Max and Adam had finished dinner at Annabeth, the resort's five-star restaurant, Friday evening. The host had led them to Adam's regular table toward the center of the dining area, which had a view of the entire restaurant. They'd both ordered the herb-roasted chicken with asparagus spears, roasted potatoes, white wine and ice water. Max could still smell the cumin, olive oil, oregano and brown sugar.

Noah had been right about Laura demanding a full briefing on the shooting. Afterward, she'd texted the information to Adam and Joshua. Adam had called Max last night to ask three different ways whether Max was all right. He'd then made Max promise neither he nor Alexis would leave the resort grounds again until the stalker was caught and behind bars. Max had noticed there were more security officers patrolling the resort grounds today.

Max drank his ice water. "There's another possibility. The stalker didn't want to be seen. That's why they were in the bushes. They didn't expect Alexis to see their weapon glint under the lamp. Luckily, she did, and we were able to get away."

"That's a good point." Adam sounded pensive, as though he was mulling over Max's theory. "I still can't believe it happened."

"Neither can I." Max set aside his white linen napkin. "But I feel better knowing Noah is on the case. But let's talk about something else, please. Have you identified companies you might be able to go into partnership with?"

Adam sighed, allowing the change of subject. "There are a couple of companies on our list, but we haven't approached any of them yet. I guess a part of us hopes it doesn't come to that."

"I get it." Max inclined his head to indicate their surroundings. "This is your mother's legacy. She left it to you and your siblings. Of course, you wouldn't be in a rush to share it with anyone, much less strangers."

"Exactly. Thank you for understanding." Adam sipped his ice water. "In the meantime, we have another problem."

When it rains, it pours.

"What is it?" Max searched his mind, trying to anticipate what Adam was going to say.

Adam looked around the room. Was he checking on his customers' satisfaction or making sure no one was listening to their conversation? Or both? Adam lowered his voice. "I think we have a spy at the resort."

If he'd heard that declaration from anyone else, Max would've responded with skepticism. He'd need proof. But he'd known Adam Colton for more than a decade. His friend wasn't given to paranoid delusions. He was the opposite of that.

It angered him that someone Adam trusted would then betray him. "What's happened?"

A cloud swept across Adam's face. "Glenna and Clive have made comments about things they wouldn't have had any reason to be aware of unless someone at the resort had told them. It's suspicious."

Max brought to mind Mariposa employees he'd met during his stay, including Clarissa, Aaron, Roland, Zoe and, of course, Alexis. Could one of them be working against Adam and his siblings? It couldn't be Alexis. Not only was she Laura's friend, in the short time he'd known her, she'd proved her loyalty to the organization.

"But your employees sign nondisclosure agreements."

Adam had explained that, because of the high profile of most of the guests Mariposa attracted, he, Laura and Joshua thought it was important for everyone in the resort's employ to sign a nondisclosure agreement to protect their clients.

"It wouldn't be the first time an employee broke the rules." Adam folded his forearms on the table in front of him. "Alexis just fired someone for noncompliance with our employee rules."

Max clenched his fists as he recalled his encounters with Mark Bower. "And now that employee is suspected of trying to kill her. Could Mark be the spy?"

"I don't think so." The look in Adam's eyes was distant as though he was accessing a mental list of employees. "Glenna is referencing things that have happened since Mark was dismissed, like Alexis moving into one of the bungalows and Valerie suddenly taking time off. The leak would have to be someone in a position to overhear those conversations. It has to be someone who's here."

"That makes sense." Max continued to process this new, troubling situation. "What do you think Clive and Glenna are up to? Why would they want to have someone spying on the resort?"

Adam sat back against his chair, crossing his arms over his chest. Anger darkened his eyes and tightened his jaw. "They want information they could use against us personally. They also want to damage the resort's reputation."

That was what Max feared as well. "Which would make it harder for you to find a company to go into partnership with."

"Exactly. They're trying to sabotage us, putting us in a position where we'd have to give in to their demands. That's the bottom line."

Max considered his friend's situation in silence. "It's time to fight fire with fire. Since they have a spy, you need one, too."

Chapter Twelve

Max propped his hips against the half patio wall outside his bungalow, waiting for his video call to Sarah to connect early Sunday morning. His eyes took in the mountain ridge in the distance and desert plants around him. It had been a few days since someone had shot at him and Alexis outside The Cloisters. He'd tried to figure out a way to justify meeting Sarah for lunch when someone had made it clear they were determined to hurt him—or worse. Noah had promised to make this threat a priority. In return, Max and Alexis had promised him, Adam and Laura they wouldn't leave the resort again until the stalker was caught.

That meant he had to postpone lunch with Sarah indefinitely.

Sarah finally accepted the connection. Her face was flushed and her red hair tousled, as though she'd rushed to her phone. A cream patio door was framed behind her.

"Max! What a surprise." Sarah combed her fingers through her hair. "Hi. How are you?"

The memory of running from gunfire with Alexis rushed across his mind. Max shook his head to clear his thoughts. "Sarah, I'm afraid I have some bad news. I won't be able to meet you for lunch today."

"What?" Sarah's eyes stretched wide. Her jaw dropped. "Why not?"

"I'm afraid something's come up." He didn't want to discuss the dangers stalking him and Alexis. He'd told his family. He loved them and they had a right to know. Everyone else was on a need-to-know basis and Sarah wasn't on that list.

"*Something's* come up?" Her voice had risen several octaves. Her face was turning pink. "What is this *something*, Max? Does it have anything to do with Alexis Reed?"

Max's muscles stiffened. He didn't like his administrative assistant's tone. His eyes narrowed with a stirring of temper and a breath of outrage. "That's none of your business, Sarah."

"It is if you're breaking our date to spend time with her." Sarah bit the words. Her image shook as though her cell phone was trembling in her grip.

What had gotten into her? Could her family hear her? If so, they must believe, as Steve did, that he and Sarah had more than a professional relationship. For Pete's sake.

"Sarah, this wasn't a date. We don't have that kind of relationship. I was going to have lunch with you because I thought you needed an impartial person to talk with about your divorce. I was trying to be kind." Max heard her sharp intake of breath.

Sarah sniffed. "Well, thanks for that, Max. Thanks a lot. I'm sorry your *kindness* had to be canceled because of *something*."

"This isn't like you, Sarah." Max felt absolved from any feelings of guilt. Relief was the only emotion he had room for now. "I'm going to chalk your behavior up to your pending divorce. Have you heard from Steve? Is there any chance of a reconciliation?"

"For me and Steve?" She wrinkled her nose. "I'm not interested in Steve. Not anymore."

His eyes widened in surprise, then narrowed with confusion. That wasn't the reaction he'd expected from her. If she wasn't upset over her divorce, why did she need someone to talk to?

Max checked the time shown at the top of his cell phone screen. It was almost 9:30 a.m. "I'm sorry to hear you and Steve won't be able to work things out—"

"Are you really?" There was a suggestion in her voice.

"Of course I am." His eyebrows knitted. "I have a great deal of respect for the institution of marriage. My parents have been married for almost forty years. I want a marriage like theirs. I hate to see couples break up."

"That's sweet of you." A faint smile raised the corners of Sarah's thin lips. "But I realized that I'd made a mistake, marrying Steve. I couldn't stay with him anymore. Not when I'm in love with someone else."

He stiffened in surprise and a little disappointment. Perhaps his sisters were right. Perhaps he was a hopeless romantic. He refused to change. "I see. Well, I hope you'll be happy, Sarah. And again, I'm sorry about lunch, but I—"

She interrupted him. "Don't you want to know who I'm in love with?"

Max shook his head. "It's none of my—"

"It's you, Max." Sarah lowered her eyes as though she was suddenly uncertain. Her voice was soft. Her smile was shy. "I'm in love with you. I was going to tell you during our lunch date."

Max froze. He couldn't have heard her correctly. He shook his head in disbelief. "What did you say?"

Her smile grew. "I said I'm in love with you, Max. I've been in love with you since the first day we met. And I'll love you until the day I die."

Max's head was spinning. Phrases she'd said when she'd told him about her pending divorce came back to him. They were nearly muted beneath the cacophony of screaming voices in his head.

Steve's very jealous of you.

He's convinced we're having an affair.

He really *lost it when you bought me that bracelet.*

Max had one question: Had Steve become jealous of him before or after Sarah told her husband she was in love with Max?

He massaged the back of his neck, trying to ease the pressure building there. Max didn't feel equipped to navigate this emotional minefield. In fairness, he already had a lot on his plate with a stalker doing their very best to kill him and the woman he was falling in love with. He didn't want to hurt Sarah, but he wasn't willing to allow her delusions to continue beyond this phone call.

Max braced himself. He spoke with as much caring as he could muster. "Sarah, I'm sorry, but I don't share your feelings."

"Yes, you do, Max. I know you love me, too."

"No, I don't." Max clenched his left hand, trying to control the impatience that tore through him. "Sarah, I'm your boss. That's all I am. We work together."

"That's not true," she whispered. "You love me, Max. I know you do."

"No, Sarah, I don't."

"Could you...love me...in time?"

"I'm afraid not."

Sarah wiped tears from her eyes with her fingertips. Her nails looked freshly manicured. "We're good together, Max. I know you know that. Why are you denying it? You're always saying how much you rely on me and how much I help you."

"At work, Sarah." Max heard the bite of impatience in his voice. "We *work* well together. But I don't have those types of feelings for you. We need to keep things strictly professional between us for the good of the show."

"For the good of the show?" Temper hardened her voice. Outrage replaced her tears. "What about *my* well-being, Max?"

He took a mental step back. "I'm sorry if I did something to inadvertently mislead you about my feelings for you. That was never my intention."

Sarah stared at him through the video call screen. Anger built in her eyes. "Are you having a change of heart about me because of her? *Alexis Reed?*"

"Sarah—"

"Whatever you think you have with her now, that won't last." Her voice was almost a sneer. "Your life's in New York—your family, your show, your restaurants, your agent. That woman wouldn't last five minutes in the city."

It was getting harder to care about not hurting Sarah's feelings. "My personal relationships are not your business. If you're incapable of keeping things professional between us, then I'm sorry, Sarah, but I'll have to let you go."

"You're *firing* me?" Sarah's voice leaped up several painful octaves.

"We can't have a professional relationship if we can't keep personal feelings out of the office."

"You're actually firing me." She stared at him in disbelief.

"I regret things are ending this way, but I can't give you what you want."

Her scowl was vicious. "Yes, you can. But for some reason you're enthralled by that concierge. You're wasting your time with her."

Max had had enough. "I'll have my lawyer contact you about your separation agreement. He'll also arrange for you to clean out your office and he'll take your key."

"If that's the way you want it. Fine." She was visibly shaking. Her image on his phone's screen slid from side to side. "There's no reason for me to stay here any longer. I'll return to New York first thing in the morning. Your lawyer can contact me then." Sarah ended the video chat on her final word.

Max closed his eyes and expelled a weighty sigh. That could've gone better although he didn't know how. She'd blindsided him. He stood and walked back into his bungalow. He was confident he'd done the right thing. He and Sarah couldn't have continued to work together if she believed herself to be in love with him. His heart belonged to someone else.

The realization made his legs weak. Max dropped onto the nearest armchair. It was true. Alexis had laid claim to his mind, body and soul from the first time he'd looked into her big, bright eyes. It was irrational. They'd only known each other for three weeks, but he'd fallen completely—hopelessly—in love with her.

Now, what was he going to do about it? His home—his life—was in New York. Hers was here in Sedona almost twenty-four hundred miles away. How was he supposed to make that work?

Max was tempted to ignore the call when his father's number popped up on his cell phone screen late Monday morning. He'd been in such a good mood. He was in the Annabeth kitchen. The chef had brought back fresh produce from the farmers market. He'd checked and double-checked the recipe he was planning to make for his lunch with Alexis. It was more than her great feedback on his entrées. More than the way she challenged him to get out of his comfort zone. He enjoyed talking with her. He enjoyed being silent with her. He enjoyed *her*. It surprised him how much.

But the call was from his father and MJ wouldn't stop calling. The kitchen staff was preparing for lunch. Shouted commands, clanging pans and chopping knives would make it difficult for Max to hear MJ. Opening the rear exit door, he stepped into April's bright, warm late morning sunshine to take the call.

"Hi, Dad." Max heard soft music in the background on his father's end of the line. MJ had tuned his computer to his favorite jazz website.

"Max!" MJ's booming voice made it seem as though his father was standing beside him. "Have you thought any more about the ideas I gave you for your show? And feel free to take the credit when you present them to your producers."

He smothered a groan. Max had known his father would circle back to his ideas to revamp *Cooking for Friends*. He'd hoped MJ would wait until he'd returned to New York so they could discuss them in person.

"Actually, Dad, I've been focused on the cookbook recipes." He paced the length of the kitchen's exterior wall. It was several yards long, part shade and part sunlight. "I haven't made plans yet for the next season of the show. But I don't think it would be a good idea to make big changes after just one season."

MJ's sigh sounded like disappointment. "Max, you've got to keep all your projects moving. You can't ignore one in favor of another. I wouldn't have been able to build my production company by focusing on only one movie or TV show at a time."

Max felt nine years old again. "I have a different process. I like to focus on one thing at a time to make sure that thing is done well. Right now, I'm focusing on the cookbook."

And Alexis.

In the almost two weeks—eleven days to be exact—since the shooting at The Cloisters, they'd been spending time together every day. They'd taken the advice of their friends and the police and remained within the security of the resort. Last weekend, they'd gone horseback riding Saturday and hiking again Sunday. His stay was beginning to feel like a real vacation: fun, relaxing and exciting. Thanks to Alexis.

Fortunately, there hadn't been any other attacks or "accidents." Max was glad he and Alexis hadn't had to worry about their well-being. However, the reprieve prompted Alexis to start talking about returning to her condo. His growing feelings for Alexis weren't the reason Max didn't want her to go home. At least, they weren't the only reason. He didn't want Alexis to leave Mariposa because the stalker hadn't been caught yet.

"You sound like your mother." MJ's comment brought Max back to their conversation.

"Mom's a smart woman." Did he sound as defensive as he felt?

"Of course she is." MJ's voice was thick with humor. "She married me, didn't she?"

Max's tension eased. He laughed his appreciation of his father's response. He could imagine MJ behind his heavy oak desk, rocking back on his black faux leather wheeled executive chair and grinning at his own joke.

"Look, Dad, I've got to go. I've got to prepare another entrée. We'll talk about your ideas for the show when I get home, all right?"

MJ sighed. The squeak of his chair carried across the satellite towers. "All right. If you want to put off the show, we can do that."

Max closed his eyes and rubbed the back of his neck. His father had a way of expressing his disappointment without expressing it. "I'm not putting anything off. I'm scheduling myself. I have a lot to do and I'm trying to approach everything in a logical manner."

The silence on the other end of the line felt confused. MJ broke it. "I wasn't criticizing you, son. Your mother's always telling me I should choose my words more carefully."

Good advice. Thanks, Mom.

"I know what I'm doing, Dad."

"I know you do, son. Your mother and I are very proud of you."

Surprise widened Max's eyes and raised his voice a couple of octaves. "You are?"

More confused silence. "Of course I am. Why wouldn't I be? You're intelligent, hardworking, ambitious and the spitting image of me."

Max laughed. "You're proud of me even though I 'could always do better'?"

MJ snorted. "Everyone could always do better. *I* could do better every single day. That doesn't mean we haven't been doing great work."

Max exhaled. "I'm proud of you, too, Dad."

"I know."

Max rolled his eyes although his father couldn't see him. "Dad, I'm sure Miri and Mel would like to hear you're proud of them, too."

MJ's sigh was long and irritated. "What's wrong with you children? Of course I'm proud of you—all of you. If I weren't, I'd tell you."

Max's heart felt lighter now that his father was expressing his feelings in a way Max could understand. "We get a lot of criticisms from you, Dad. Once in a while, it would be nice to hear the positive reinforcement."

"Point taken. I'll make the effort."

Max grinned. "Thanks. Now I'd better get going. Give Mom my love."

"I will. Keep up the good work, son."

"You, too, Dad." Max disconnected the call.

He let his eyes sweep his surroundings and a smile settled on his lips. His father was proud of him. The day seemed a little brighter, a little more joyful. And the first person he wanted to share that joy with was Alexis.

"As your father said, what's not to be proud of?" Alexis beamed at Max as they sat in her office Monday afternoon. "I'm glad you cleared things up with him."

They'd finished lunch and had packed the dishes on the trolley. Max had made chipotle chicken with citrusy salsa. Alexis had been so enthusiastic about the meal—both the spice level and the side dish—that he'd considered taking a victory lap around her office. Not enough room, though. And she still complained about the presentation: *itty-bitty food on great big plates*. Next time, he'd use smaller dishes.

Max flashed a grin. "Now you're the one being too kind."

Alexis ignored him. "And thanks to you, I'm sure he'll have a similar conversation with your sisters."

"I hope so." Max settled back in his chair, placing his right ankle on his left knee. "It would mean a lot to them."

Alexis's smile faded. Max sensed the shift in her mood, and it worried him. What was on her mind?

She caught and held his eyes. "Noah called me this morning with an update about the case. I told him since I'd see you for lunch, I'd share his news with you."

Max frowned. "Judging by the look on your face, it's not good news."

"No, it's not." She squared her shoulders in her copper cotton long-sleeved blouse. The color made her eyes sparkle. "Noah said he's satisfied he's cleared Mark for the shooting Thursday night. Apparently, Mark has a strong alibi. He was barhopping with a group of friends. Noah checked with all four of them."

Max arched an eyebrow. "Barhopping on a Thursday night?"

Alexis shrugged. "Go figure."

"I sound old." Max sighed. He straightened in his seat and planted both feet on the bamboo flooring. "We can't connect him to the hiking accident, but he's cleared from suspicion for the shooting. So either there are two people out there who want us dead at the same time or someone other than Mark is responsible."

"We're back to square one. I was hoping to go home soon." Alexis crossed her right leg over her left. Tension radiated around her.

Max could feel it across the small conversation table. "I understand this is frustrating. I'm frustrated, too. But I'm glad you have a safe place to stay until the stalker's caught."

"Please don't get me wrong. I'm grateful to be staying at Mariposa." Alexis smoothed her hair, checking the bun at the nape of her neck. "I'm enjoying the bungalow. Who wouldn't like having someone come in and tidy up behind them every day? And you know I love the resort. The views are spectacular. The amenities are wonderful." She spread her arms to encompass their surroundings. "But none of this is home."

"I understand. There's a difference between being on vacation and being displaced because someone's trying to kill you."

"I miss my things. And I really miss my weekly dinners with my mother. Our videoconference dinners aren't the same." Alexis folded her arms beneath her chest. Her body language couldn't be any more closed off.

Max's concern increased. So did his guilt. "I'm sorry. I hate that you're caught up in this."

"Max, we've been through this." Frustration leaked into Alexis's voice. "This is *not* your fault. We don't know which one of us is the target. Maybe *I'm* the one who brought *you* into this. But either way, we're not at fault. The stalker is."

She was right. Max was glad she'd reminded him. "I wish I knew who that was."

"We all wish we knew." Alexis narrowed her eyes as she studied him in silence. "I can't stop thinking there's a connection between these attempts to harm us and whoever broke into your home. Why would they have sent you that package unless they wanted to get your attention?"

"But for what purpose?" Max stood to pace the confines of Alexis's office. "If they wanted to kill me, why didn't they do it in New York? They can't get to me at the resort."

"Maybe they didn't know that."

"I've always thought the thieves were random fans."

"Could random fans get into your secured building?"

"I wouldn't think so." Max spread his hands. "But the police questioned my neighbors and the guards." Alexis's silence seemed to speak volumes. "Just say it. I can tell something's on your mind."

Alexis hesitated. "Has Sarah ever been to your condo?"

Max pushed his hands into the front pockets of his black slacks. "A few times, either to drop something off or pick something up." He couldn't remember the number of times Sarah had come to his building.

"So your security guards are familiar with her." She paused again. "Did you know she's attracted to you?"

Max's muscles stiffened. "Do you think Sarah's the one who broke into my condo and sent the package to me?"

"Yes." She didn't look away.

Max's lips parted in surprise. He stared at Alexis, unable to gather his thoughts. "Sarah's married."

"You told me she's filed for divorce."

"I said I'm in love with you, Max. I've been in love with you since the first day we met. And I'll love you until the day I die."

Max wanted to run from those words. Instead, he paced Alexis's office. "You met Sarah less than three weeks ago. In that time, you recognized something I hadn't picked up on after working with her for more than two years."

"What are you saying?" There was dread in Alexis's words.

Max stood with his back to her. "It never crossed my mind that the obsessive fan who'd broken into my home twice could be Sarah. Nor did I think she could have mailed that box to Mariposa."

Alexis prompted him when he remained silent. "But now you do?"

He drew a sharp breath. The room smelled of cayenne peppers, citrus, tomatoes and wildflowers. "Yesterday, she told me she was in love with me."

"Oh, boy."

"How could she have known I'd be here?" Max turned to Alexis. "I never told her I was coming to Sedona."

"She's your assistant." Alexis's eyes searched his. "Did she have access to your emails or voice mail?"

Max dragged a hand over his hair. "No, I prefer to handle my communication myself. She didn't have any of my passwords. And nothing has ever been taken from my office."

"That's probably because there aren't that many people on your staff. If she took something from work, she'd be one of a handful of people you could accuse. But if something were missing from your home, there would be millions of suspects."

Alexis had a point. Now he felt worse. Max resumed his pacing.

Like her home, Alexis's office was clean and well organized. There were one or two invoices in her inbox. Several letters waited in her outbox, some in internal envelopes and others in Mariposa stationery.

Max's eyes swept her desk and the shelf above her computer, pausing briefly on framed photos he'd admired before. The pictures captured candid images of Alexis's family and friends through the years. She hadn't chosen to be in many of the pictures, which led Max to believe she'd been behind the camera for most of them.

He stopped to study the view from the floor-to-ceiling tinted window to the left of Alexis's desk. The sky was a clear, cerulean blue, dotted with thick white clouds and the peaks of majestic red rock mountains.

"There's no way Sarah could've known about our hike or that we were going to be at The Cloisters Thursday night." Max's thoughts were spinning.

In contrast, Alexis's voice was calm. "And yet somehow she knew we'd been spending time together at the resort."

"She said she'd seen a video of us."

"But there wasn't any such video."

"Why are you so determined to make Sarah a suspect?" He asked the question over his shoulder.

Alexis's sigh was soft and impatient. "It's too much of a coincidence that you're both in Sedona at the same time. Why are you so determined to ignore that?"

"Because I don't want to believe I hired someone who's trying to kill you." Battling frustration, Max scrubbed his palms over his face. "I don't have affairs with married women. Sarah and I have always had a strictly professional relationship. At least, I thought we had. But since we've been here, she's been acting differently toward me. I thought it was the stress of her marriage ending."

"But it wasn't." Alexis made it a statement, not a question. "Did the police question Sarah or anyone on your staff?"

"No, they didn't." That was still a source of frustration. Max understood the theft of an old cell phone and a deodorant stick wasn't a high priority, but someone had invaded his home.

"I think Noah should speak with her."

Max faced Alexis. "Did you tell him your suspicions about her?"

Alexis shook her head. "I wanted to speak with you first."

"Thank you for that." Some of his tension drained. "She may have returned to New York." Max crossed the office to resume his seat at the table. "When I told her I didn't love her, she became very angry. At that point, I realized we couldn't work together any longer. I told her my lawyer would be in touch with a separation agreement for her."

"You fired her?" Alexis's lips parted with surprise.

Agitated, Max spread his arms. "What was I supposed to do? She was bordering on unhinged. I've never seen her like that. She became a completely different person."

"I'm so sorry. Is that the reason you seemed distracted yesterday?"

"It was an uncomfortable situation." Max winced. "Nothing like that had ever happened to me before."

"I'm so sorry." Alexis's eyes were dark with concern. "Why didn't you talk with me about it? Talking often helps people to cope."

"I don't know." Max shrugged restlessly. On second thought, yes, he did. "I was embarrassed. I didn't want to hear you say I handled it badly."

"I understand, but I'm sure you handled it as well as anyone could. It was a difficult situation. I still think Noah should speak with her." Alexis stood, stretching to reach the writing tablet beside her desk phone. It had the Mariposa logo on it. She offered the tablet to Max. "Could you give him Sarah's cell phone number?"

Max took the writing tablet and retrieved his cell from his right front pocket. He wrote Sarah's contact information. "Of course. At least that way, we could put these questions to rest."

He searched for Noah's number in his cell phone. He was sure the detective would clear Sarah's name. Max couldn't believe there was any way he would have hired a killer.

Would he?

Chapter Thirteen

"We can't locate Sarah Harris." Noah looked at the group gathered in the L's small conference room Thursday morning. The detective was wearing a plain gray T-shirt and black straight-legged jeans. "Nor can we find any information that confirms she has relatives in the Sedona area."

Seated beside Max on the right side of the table, Alexis sensed his tension like a wall pushing against her. She wanted to reach out and squeeze his left forearm beneath his pale tan short-sleeved shirt as it lay between them on the rectangular blond wood table. But such a gesture between them wouldn't be appropriate right now.

Noah had asked to meet with Roland, Max, Alexis, Laura, Adam and Joshua to update them on the investigation into the threats against Max and Alexis. It had been three days since Max and Alexis had called Noah to give him Sarah's cell phone number and the highlights—or lowlights—of their last, contentious conversation. Max also had provided nonsensitive information to help the detective find her, including her description, her soon-to-be ex-husband's name and contact numbers, and Sarah's maiden name, Brockman, to help the police department identify her relatives.

"You think she lied about visiting family here?" Alexis studied Noah seated directly across from her. His tanned features looked strained. His green eyes were hard and focused.

He sighed. "We spoke with Steve Harris Monday. He was positive Sarah didn't have relatives in Sedona."

Max gestured toward Noah seated diagonally across the table. "They've been together since high school. He would know."

Noah continued. "We still spent the past two days calling every Brockman listed in the Sedona area. No one knew a Sarah Harris who grew up in New Jersey and now lives in New York."

Max sat back in his chair, crossing his arms over his chest. "She said she was returning to New York Monday. Maybe she did."

Noah didn't look convinced. "She lied about staying with relatives. I'm not sold on her keeping her word about leaving Sedona. But I'll ask the NYPD to check."

Laura was seated between Adam at the head of the table and Noah on her left. Her violet blouse deepened her blue eyes. "And she hasn't returned any of your calls?"

Noah's expression softened when he met her eyes. "No, she hasn't. We've called early in the morning, late at night and several times throughout the day. We weren't going straight to voice mail, which means she was letting the phone ring. Each time, we left messages. Now her mailbox is full."

Roland was on Alexis's right in his security director's uniform. "She's either ditched her phone or she wants you to think she has. Can you track it?"

Noah gave the security director an appreciative look. "We've requested a warrant for that. Hopefully, the court will approve it."

"We can't forget that Mark Bower's still on the suspect list, too." Max looked from Noah to Alexis. "Sarah didn't have access to the trail, but Mark would have."

"Speaking of tracking cell phones, there's something I've been wondering about." Alexis caught Max's eyes before returning her attention to Noah. "We can't explain how the stalker knew where Max and I would be and when—the hiking trail, The Cloisters."

Max swept his right hand around the table. "The only people we've shared our plans with other than our families have been Adam, Laura and Joshua. Since we'd texted our families, is it possible someone's hacked our phones?"

Noah frowned. He shared a look between Alexis and Max. "I suppose it's possible. Do you both have iPhones?" He waited for their nods of confirmation before leaning into the table. "Find your International Mobile Equipment Identity number under General Settings. Now dial hashtag zero six hashtag into your phone. Does the number that came up match your IMEI?"

"Yes." Alexis nodded. She felt a wave of relief. "Thank you."

"Mine doesn't." Max looked at Noah. "Does that mean someone cloned my phone?"

Noah frowned. "I'm afraid so. Someone's been monitoring every text and call you send and receive."

Seated on Noah's left, Joshua gestured toward Max's phone. "It must have been Sarah. She could've been keeping tabs on you for months. Did you have any idea she'd been spying on you?"

"None." Max looked at Alexis. "I can't wrap my mind around this. How could I have been so blind?"

"You've always been trusting." Adam's voice was low. "But that's not a bad thing."

"It was this time." Max rubbed the back of his neck. "I'm so sorry, Alexis, for putting you in danger."

She couldn't hold back any longer. She leaned forward and squeezed his bicep. "This isn't your fault. You don't have anything to apologize for. This is all Sarah. I'm confident Noah will find her soon and we can start putting this behind us."

His eyes smiled at her before he addressed Noah. "What do we do now?"

Noah nodded toward Max's cell. "First, we break the connection between your phone and whoever's cloned it, presumably Sarah. You'll need to contact the manufacturer's support team."

"I'll do that right away." Max turned off his phone, then slipped it into his front shorts pocket.

A little more of Alexis's tension drained. She glanced around the table at Laura, Adam, Roland, Max and Joshua before meeting Noah's eyes. "Since it sounds like we have a strong suspect for these attacks, could I move back to my home?"

Beside her, Max stiffened. Across the table, Laura frowned. Alexis hoped their reactions wouldn't influence Noah's opinion.

The detective shook his head. "I'm sorry, Alexis. I understand you're getting restless. I would be, too. But it would be best for you to stay at the resort. Neither you nor Max will be safe until we have the stalker in custody." He looked at Joshua to his left, Laura on his right and Adam at the head of the table. "If you don't have any objections."

"None at all." Laura's voice rose above her siblings' responses.

Adam turned to her. "Alexis, Noah's right. Stay here for as long as you need to."

Joshua sat back in his chair. "I agree."

"All right." Alexis struggled to mask her disappointment. At least Laura and Max were happy. "Could I at least resume my Sunday dinners with my mother? Having dinner via videoconference isn't the same."

Noah's eyebrows knitted. "I suppose that would be all right. As long as you don't have the dinners at your home. I doubt the stalker knows where your mother lives."

"I'll call Mom to let her know." Alexis beamed at Max. He didn't seem to share her enthusiasm. Her smile faded.

Noah rose to his feet. "If you don't have any other questions, I'd better get back to work. Thanks for your time."

Roland led the group from the conference room. Laura joined Noah. The Colton brothers followed them.

Max touched Alexis's arm to detain her. "Could we talk in your office?"

"Of course." Alexis noted the somber look in his eyes. This didn't bode well.

Max followed Alexis back to her office late Thursday morning. He breathed her scent as he reached forward to open the door for her. With her permission, he closed it again behind them. His eyes swept her slim, toned figure in her black pantsuit as she walked to her chair. She was beautiful, but he couldn't let his attraction to her distract him.

He clenched and unclenched his hands. The conversation they were about to have wouldn't be pleasant. His muscles pushed him to pace her office. But he chose to sit in her visitor's chair instead.

Alexis pulled her executive seat farther under her desk. "What's wrong?"

"I'm concerned about your leaving the resort Sunday evening." Max forced himself to speak calmly even as his pulse galloped with panic at the thought of Alexis being in danger. Again. "We have ideas about who's responsible for the threats, but no one's in custody yet. Suppose the stalker's watching your mother's house?"

"They don't know where she lives." Alexis picked up the pencil on her desk and rolled it between her fingers. "I haven't been to her house since before my accident. The weekend I was injured, my mother and I had dinner at my house."

"I understand you miss your weekly dinners with your mother but the stalker's still running around out there." Max jerked his chin toward the window.

"*Do* you understand?" Alexis's eyes darkened with disappointment. She stared at the pencil as though it could show her the future. "Your stay at the resort was planned. You packed everything you needed for your six-week stay. You know when you're going home, and your family knows when they'll see you again. As much as I love Mariposa, I'm not comfortable living my life day to day. It's been almost three weeks."

Max felt a stab of guilt. He lowered his eyes and stared at the bamboo flooring. "I'm sorry about everything. I'm sorry you're in danger and that your life has been turned upside down." He raised his eyes to hers again. "I know you don't blame me, but I still feel responsible."

"You've really got to get over that." Alexis shook the pen at him. "By assuming responsibility that's not yours, you're absolving the actual guilty party. That's not right."

Max considered her words. "Good point. Thank you."

Alexis searched his features. He didn't know what she was looking for. "I know I pushed you to have Noah add Sarah to the list of people to investigate for these threats. But I hope she's innocent. I don't want her to have lied to you or sabotaged the guardrail or shot at us or cloned your phone. That kind of betrayal would really hurt."

Max was a little overwhelmed hearing the list of grievances he and Alexis had against the stalker. It was long. "I appreciate that but she's already lied to me. I had no idea she had romantic feelings for me."

"You mean a crush on you." Alexis leaned against her chair, still playing with her pencil. "I could tell the first time I met her."

"You could?" Max's eyebrows knitted. "I wish you'd told me."

"I didn't think it was my business." Alexis spread her arms. "But if I had, would you have believed me?"

Max thought about it for a while. "Honestly, no. I don't believe Sarah tampered with the guardrail or shot at us, either. Seriously, we've worked together for more than two years. She's never shown any signs of violence."

Alexis tilted her head. "You don't think she could be the stalker?"

"No, I don't."

"She kept her feelings for you a secret for more than two years." Alexis laid the pencil on her desk. "Don't you think it's possible she kept other things a secret from you, too?"

Max arched an eyebrow. "Like her hobby as a metalsmith or her aspirations to be a sharpshooter?"

"I don't know about the sharpshooter." Alexis's tone was wry. "If that had been her, she fired seventeen bullets without hitting us. Thank God."

He massaged the back of his neck. "I'm sorry. I didn't mean to be short with you."

She gave him a dismissive wave. "I understand. This is a sensitive subject. Someone you know and trust—or trusted— is suspected of trying to kill you."

"And you."

"Do you now think she could be the one who broke into your condo?"

"I don't know. It's possible." Max rubbed his eyes. "I remember her humming songs that were also on my playlist. I thought it was a coincidence." He sprang from his seat, trying to escape his mistakes. He paced Alexis's office. "Adam's right. I'm too trusting. If I'd put all this together before, none of this would have happened."

"Let's not go there." Alexis looked up at him as he paused beside her. "And although I really appreciate your concern, I'm having dinner with my mother—in person—on Sunday."

Gritting his teeth, Max returned to his seat. "Alexis, I—care about you very much. I would never forgive myself if anything happened to you."

Alexis's eyes widened. Was it surprise or pleasure? "I care about you, too, Max. I promise I'll be careful. If you'd like, I'll call you at your bungalow to let you know when I arrive and when I get back." She smiled at him as though she'd offered him the perfect solution.

Not even close. "If you're determined to go off the resort property Sunday, then you leave me no choice."

"What does that mean?" Alexis's tone warned him to proceed with caution.

Max drew a breath. The air was scented with strong coffee and soft wildflowers. "I'm inviting myself to your mother's home for Sunday dinner."

Alexis blinked. "You want to have dinner with Mom and me?"

"That's right. I'd feel better if I were there to watch your back." He hesitated. "If you don't mind."

"Are you kidding?" Alexis clapped her hands together and laughed. "My mother would love that. She's such a big fan. I can't wait to tell her."

Max smiled, but reluctantly. Alexis's enthusiasm was flattering. And her words were very kind. But they couldn't lose sight of the still-looming threat.

"Slow down, Allyson Felix." Max referenced the track-and-field Olympian. "I'm looking forward to meeting your mother and enjoying her cooking. But we need to be careful. I'll arrange a car service to pick us up from the resort and bring us back after dinner. Sarah—or Mark—may be familiar with your car. In case they're watching the resort, I don't want them to see your car leaving and follow us."

"That's a good idea. Thank you." Alexis reached for the phone on her desk. "I'll call Mom to let her know you're coming."

Max saw the excitement in her eyes. If he'd known how happy his visit would make her, he would have invited himself to their dinner weeks ago.

He stood to leave. "Please let her know I appreciate her hospitality and that I'm looking forward to meeting her."

"Of course." Alexis was waiting for her call to connect.

Max was more agitated as he left Alexis's office than he'd been when he'd arrived. He was going to meet Alexis's mother. Alexis loved her mother. What would he do if her mother didn't like him?

The atmosphere in the conference room Friday morning was electric with curiosity. The table was bathed in the sunlight that slid in through the room's floor-to-ceiling window. Alexis felt as though they were meeting on a stage under a spotlight.

The invitees hadn't been given much information about the purpose of the meeting. The group email had only asked that they join Laura, Adam and Joshua in the conference room at 9:00 a.m. Alexis considered the other Mariposa team members seated around the table. Their positions gave her a hint of the meeting's agenda. She wasn't sure why she'd been asked to attend, but she wanted to help Mariposa in any way she could.

Laura sat at the foot of the table. She wore an A-line soft pink dress and nursed a cup of coffee. Roland was on Laura's left in another crisp security director suit. His right hand was wrapped around a bottle of carbonated soda as though he feared someone would take it from him. Beside Roland, Leticia gave the security director's soda bottle a dubious frown. The personnel director wore a white, red and green floral coatdress. Adam sat at the head of the table in a smoke gray pin-striped suit. Like Laura and Joshua, the eldest Colton sibling had brought a mug of coffee to the meeting. Greg Sumpter, the resort's legal counsel, was on Adam's left. His loud Hawaiian shirt challenged Leticia's attention-grabbing dress. Joshua sat beside Alexis. His tan polo shirt was embroidered with the Mariposa logo.

Adam started the meeting. "We appreciate your dropping everything to join us. This is a very sensitive issue. As such, please do not discuss it with anyone outside of this group or where you could be overheard."

"That sounds serious." Greg was tall and fit with brown hair and green eyes. Alexis couldn't remember ever seeing him in a suit.

"*Very* serious." Joshua glanced at Greg's clothing. "Do you own any quiet shirts?"

The other man crossed his arms over his chest. "Jealous?"

Adam's blue eyes, so like Laura's, moved over them, one person at a time. "Laura, Josh and I suspect an employee is discussing events that occur at the resort."

Alexis heard the anger and disappointment in his voice.

Leticia straightened on her black-and-sterling-silver chair. Her eyes were wide with shock as they moved from Adam to Joshua and Laura. Her accent exposed her North Carolina roots. "But everyone who works for Mariposa has signed a nondisclosure agreement, including you three."

Greg grunted. "If this is true, it wouldn't be the first time someone violated a nondisclosure agreement. They're legally binding documents but they don't have superpowers."

Roland stroked his goatee. "What kind of 'events'?"

Laura wrapped her palms around her coffee mug as though she was trying to warm herself. "The kind that could damage Mariposa's reputation and make our guests uncomfortable. Details about the investigation into Allyson's murder." She nodded toward Alexis. "The sabotaged guardrail and Max's mysterious box."

Leticia waved her hands. Her long nails were polished red and green. "Okay. But why do you think someone's discussing things that happen *on* the resort with people *outside* of the resort?"

Joshua's tone was dry. "Because Clive and Glenna have made comments and asked things about the resort and those events in particular that tipped us off that they know more than they should."

Adam continued. "But they're coy about where they're getting their information."

Joshua expelled a breath as he leaned against his chair. "We need to get to the bottom of this. We've built this resort on a reputation for security and privacy. This leak is undermining our brand."

Laura looked to Alexis before turning her attention to the rest of the group. "We've been able to keep these events out of the media so far, but we're running out of time."

Alexis stared into her coffee mug, searching for ideas on how to expose the leaker. She was coming up empty.

Greg's question broke her concentration. "Why don't you plant a false rumor with people who could be the leaker and see which one gets back to Glenna and Clive?"

Alexis looked up from her mug. "I don't know if that would be a good idea." She shared her attention with Laura, Joshua and Adam. "If the media's already giving us extra scrutiny, it wouldn't be a good idea to *add* rumors. We should concentrate on shutting down the leak. Perhaps we find out which employees Clive and Glenna spend the most time with."

"I like that plan." Adam nodded his approval.

"So do I," Joshua agreed.

Laura touched her shoulder. "This is one of the reasons we especially wanted you to join us, Alexis. You have a good rapport with everyone. Could you subtly ask around to see if Glenna or Clive have been spending more time with a particular employee?"

"Of course." She would start with the concierges. For her own peace of mind, she needed to clear her staff as soon as possible.

"Great." Adam shifted his attention to Leticia. "Could you review the personnel files to see if anything jumps out at you?"

Leticia arched a dark eyebrow. "You mean in case someone would be susceptible to Clive and Glenna bribing them? I'll take a look, but I'm not sure I'll find anything."

Adam's shoulders moved in a restless shrug. "I know it's a long shot, but I appreciate your checking." He moved on to Roland. "We'll keep you apprised of the situation in case we need your help with an internal investigation or if the situation becomes volatile."

Roland inclined his head. "I'd appreciate that."

Adam's eyes dropped to Greg's shirt. His lips twitched as he resisted a smile. "We'll keep you in the loop as well in case we need you to intervene with the media or if we need your legal expertise to remove the employee once they're identified."

"Sounds good." Greg tapped the table.

Adam stood. "That's it, everyone. Again, thank you for your time."

Alexis started to rise. Laura's hand on her shoulder stopped her. "Could you give me a few more minutes, please, Alexis?"

"Sure." She settled back on her chair and watched as Roland, Leticia and Greg filed out of the room.

Adam paused beside her and gave her a warm smile. "Thanks for all you do, Alexis."

Her face heated. "You're very welcome, Adam. If there's anything else you need, please let me know."

"I will." He smiled at Laura before leaving.

Alexis looked up as someone patted her shoulder.

Joshua winked at her. "Great work as usual."

Her face was still warm. "Thank you, Joshua. I appreciate that." After he left, closing the door behind him, she turned to Laura. "What did you want to talk with me about?"

Laura gave her a somber look. "It's official. Cheryl has submitted her paperwork for her retirement."

"That's wonderful. I'm so happy for her." Alexis felt a rush of joy. Cheryl had been with Mariposa almost from its opening day. She was a resort treasure. Then almost immediately, panic set in. She was out of time to prove herself capable and ready to fill the other woman's shoes.

Laura smiled. "So are Adam, Josh and I. Adam's going to

send a companywide email Monday, announcing Cheryl's last day, which is April thirtieth. We want to keep the focus on her until then. After she leaves, we're going to announce her replacement."

"You've already made a decision?" Alexis could barely breathe.

"We have." She paused. "Adam, Joshua and I are offering the job to you. We think you would make an excellent event manager. You're thorough, customer-focused and imaginative, and you inspire loyalty in your staff. You'd be perfect for the position."

"What?" Alexis's jaw dropped. Was she floating? "This is wonderful. Laura, thank you so much for this opportunity. I'm thrilled to accept your offer. Thank you."

Laura stood with Alexis and embraced her. "Alexis, I'm so happy for you but I'm even happier for the resort. You're the perfect person to replace Cheryl."

"Thank you so much. This is amazing." Alexis stepped back.

"Remember, please don't tell anyone yet. Cheryl knows we're offering you the position but we're keeping the focus on her for now. We'll announce your promotion May first. Until then, you can tell your mother so you can celebrate." Laura gave her a sly look. "And, if you want, you can celebrate with Max, too."

Alexis smiled. "As it so happens, Max and I are having dinner with my mom Sunday."

Laura gaped at her. "What?" She tugged Alexis back to her seat. "Spill."

Chapter Fourteen

"You didn't have to go to all this trouble for me—the roses, the dinner, the dessert." Alexis sighed as she stood beside Max on his patio late Friday evening. The sound pooled in Max's lower abdomen.

Alexis was wearing her little black dress that skimmed her lithe figure and showed off her shapely calves again. Max had another flashback to her demi-cup black lace bra. He gave himself a mental shake and sharp scolding.

"You keep saying that. It wasn't any trouble. I love to cook. And Annabeth's kitchen had all the ingredients I needed, even for the dessert. And I found itty-bitty plates for the entrée."

Alexis's laughter was soft and low. Max swallowed to ease his dry throat.

The trolley with their meal had been magically cleared away. Only the scents of the garlic and rosemary Cornish game hen, roasted asparagus spears and oyster stuffing remained. He'd made the arrangements for the celebratory meal after Alexis had called to tell him she'd gotten the promotion she'd been working toward. He'd been so happy, he'd been unable to concentrate. All he could think about was doing something to make the day even more special for her.

"Thank you so much for everything." She turned to him.

"The meal was delicious. The roses are beautiful, and the company's even better."

The evening's lengthening shadows highlighted her delicate features. Max wanted to caress her cheek, run his fingers through her hair as it flowed in waves to her shoulders. He stuck his hands in the front pockets of his steel gray slacks.

"You're welcome. I know you said we could celebrate your promotion during dinner with your mother on Sunday, but I couldn't wait. I wanted to do something now. And since you're not comfortable dining with me in Annabeth—"

"I've explained employees and guests aren't supposed to fraternize—"

"I know." Max held up his left hand. "The alternative was to have dinner in my bungalow."

"This was so thoughtful of you." Alexis wrapped her arms around herself.

"You're cold. We should go inside." Max placed his hand on the small of her back.

"Not yet." Alexis turned back toward the view. Beyond the red rock mountain ridge, the sun was setting in a wash of indigo, orange and gold. "Let's watch the sunset first."

Max hesitated. He felt her muscles shiver against his palm. "All right." He put his right arm around her shoulders and drew her near to share his body heat.

His temperature rose when she cuddled closer and put her left arm around his waist. Happiness wrapped around him like a soft blanket. He enjoyed the silence as they watched the sun slip behind the mountains.

"What drives you, Alexis?" His voice was low.

She stirred against him. "What do you mean?"

"This promotion was so important to you. You said you don't want to stand still when it comes to your career. You want to keep moving, keep advancing. I admire that about you. I was wondering why. What drives you?"

She was silent for several beats. Was she going to ignore his question?

"An inferiority complex." Her words were so stark and unexpected, Max thought he'd misheard her.

He shook his head in confusion. "Why would you feel inferior to anyone?"

Alexis let her arm drop away from his waist. A cool breeze came between them. "My mother and I didn't have a lot of money. I couldn't afford to go to fancy schools. I went to community college. My wardrobe wasn't full of designer labels. Most of it came from secondhand shops. So I felt I had to prove myself." She shrugged her right shoulder. "I still feel that way. I had to be the valedictorian of my high school class. I had to make the dean's list every semester in college."

"Valedictorian? Dean's list? I feel intimidated." Max was only half joking.

"Oh, please." Alexis gave him the side-eye. "I've read your bio. You've been graduating the top of your class since elementary school."

"Day care, but I don't want to brag."

She laughed as he'd hoped she would. "I've never shared that with anyone before, not even my mother. She's worked so hard and sacrificed so much for me. I didn't want to risk making her feel bad."

"Thank you for sharing your feelings with me. I won't betray your trust." Max's heart was full. He was both proud and humbled by her confidence in him. "May I ask about your father, or is that too personal?"

She arched an eyebrow at him. "You've seen me in my underwear. I think you can ask me about my dad." But she took a deep breath before answering. "He died from cancer when I was seven. My older sister was killed in a hit-and-run by a distracted driver when I was eight."

Max's heart clenched with pain at her loss. "I'm so very sorry, Alexis."

"Thank you." Her voice was husky.

Max felt her struggling with her grief as though she was trying to put it back into a box. He studied her profile, wishing he could say something more meaningful and helpful than "sorry." He reached out to touch her hand. She wrapped her fingers around his and held on.

After another moment of silence, she faced him. "So I

told you about my inferiority complex. What's your deep, dark secret?"

Still holding her hand, Max escorted her back into his bungalow. "This is going to sound really stupid." He stepped aside so she could enter first.

She looked at him over her shoulder. "And mine didn't?"

He took a moment to secure the French doors before turning to face her. "I have stage fright."

Alexis stared at him. "You're a celebrity chef. How could you have stage fright?"

He spread his arms. "I told you it was stupid."

"That's not what I meant at all."

Max looked at Alexis, trying to really see her for the first time. The confident woman she projected and the insecurities she tried to hide. "I think, in a way, we're more alike than we may think. You feel like you have to prove yourself. Sometimes I feel like I'm a fraud."

Her eyes stretched wide. "Why would you think that?"

"Sometimes I don't know who I really am." Max moved his shoulders restlessly. "When people meet me, they see The Celebrity Chef. But I'm just Max. I think that's what's causing my anxiety. Am I giving people what they want? If I am, then am I losing Max?"

Her eyes darkened with pain. For him? "How do you film a weekly TV show with stage fright?"

"It's not easy." His voice was dry. "My mother suggested I pretend I'm in the kitchen of my condo, talking with friends as I get ready for a dinner party. That helps. And the editor does a great job putting the show together in post."

Alexis's smile was tender. "Well, if what we're seeing on TV is you, pretending to be in your kitchen, then what you're giving us is Max, who happens to be a very successful celebrity chef."

Her words made him feel like he could breathe again. "Thank you. I'd never thought of it that way."

"You're amazing. Do you know that? You've managed to create a hit show despite your anxiety."

Max gave her a wry smile. "My father thought the ratings

would be even better if I taped the second season in front of a live audience."

Alexis gasped. "Oh, no. He doesn't know about your stage fright?"

Max's smile disappeared. "Absolutely not. I asked my mother never to tell him, either in this life or the next."

Alexis's laughter filled his bungalow and his heart. "I admire you even more now."

He closed the distance between them and took her hand again. "Because I have a successful show?"

She dipped her chin and gave him a chiding look. "Because when you want something, you make it happen even if that means overcoming significant challenges. Not only did you survive but you thrived. You're very impressive."

He stepped even closer, until he felt the warmth of her body, and looked into her eyes. "I feel the same way about you, Alexis Reed. When *you* want something, you make it happen, like your promotions. You've impressed me." His voice was low and deep. He didn't recognize it.

"Is that all I've done?" Her words were barely audible.

"No, it's not." He caressed the side of her face with the backs of his fingers. Her skin was so soft, so smooth, so warm. "You've challenged me. Distracted me. Invaded my thoughts and my dreams." He took the hand he still held and raised it to his shoulder. "And you've made me yearn for you."

Max pressed his mouth to hers. His body tightened at the feel of her soft moist lips against his. He wrapped his arms around her and held her closer. He never wanted to let her go. He wanted to go to sleep with her in his arms and wake up the same way. Max ran his palm down her back and cupped her hips. Alexis moaned deep in her throat. His body burned. She rose up on her toes to fit herself against him. His heart skipped a beat. She opened her mouth to welcome him in. Max swept his tongue past her lips to explore her touch, her taste, her moisture.

Alexis slid her palms up and over his chest to twine around his shoulders. Max shivered under her caress and deepened their kiss. Alexis chased his tongue with her own, taunting and teasing him. She moved against him restlessly. Each wiggle and roll made his pulse pound louder in his head. Alexis raised her left knee along the side of his leg. Max thought his body would spontaneously combust. He cupped the back of her thigh. The feel of her stocking against his palm sketched heated images in his mind. His hand followed the garment under the hem of her dress. His finger traced its edge between the nylon and her skin. Alexis shivered in his arms like a leaf tossed on a breeze.

She pulled away. "Max." She breathed his name, then stopped.

"Alexis." He forced himself to give her space, but he couldn't let her go. "What is it? You can tell me."

She took another breath and lifted her eyes to his. "You're going back to New York soon. You're going home and my home is here. I'm sorry, but I don't think we should start something we both know can't go anywhere."

He dropped his arms from her waist and took several steps back. His movements were robotic. Max turned to pace away from her. He needed to clear his head.

With his back to her, he nodded. "All right. I respect your feelings." He took a breath, straightened his shoulders and managed to smile. "Let me take you back to your bungalow."

Alexis's smile looked stiffer than his felt. "No, that's all right. It's not far and security is everywhere." She crossed to his side table and collected her purse.

Max followed her. "I'll take you back, Alexis. If I stayed home while you drove a golf cart to your bungalow alone at night, I'd disown myself."

And the cool night air would do him some good.

"Restaurants, cooking show or cookbook." Catherine sat beside Alexis on her tan sofa late Sunday evening. She leaned forward toward Max seated on the love seat beside her. "Which do you prefer?"

The evening had started on an awkward note. Seated beside Alexis on the back seat of the car service he'd arranged for them, Max had felt Alexis's tension like a third passenger in the sedan. After their heated kiss Friday evening, Max thought they'd needed to spend Saturday apart. Apparently, so had Alexis. Neither had called, texted or tried to see the other.

In other words, Saturday had been horrible. At least from Max's perspective.

Max had missed Alexis more than he could describe. He'd missed hearing her voice, looking into her eyes, seeing her smile, being in her company. Sunday couldn't come fast enough.

But when he saw her again, he'd followed her lead as to how to approach their relationship. Her greeting had been perfunctory. Her smile had been polite but distant. She hadn't touched him. He hadn't touched her either, not even accidentally on purpose. The next move would need to be hers. Or at least that's the mantra he repeated to himself during her mother's fabulous six-course meal.

Catherine had served the sixth course, her homemade pecan pie, with coffee in her spacious living room. She must have worked all weekend, planning and preparing the celebratory dinner for her daughter.

He considered Catherine's question. "The restaurants, show or book? I enjoy them all equally. With the restaurants, I get to cook for people. Through the show, I teach people how to cook for themselves. And I'm having a great time with the cookbook because..." His voice trailed off as his eyes met Alexis's. "Because I enjoy experimenting with new recipes."

Catherine beamed at him. Her smile was as transformative as Alexis's. Max was fascinated, watching mother and daughter next to each other. They looked so much alike: the same lithe, dancer's build, golden brown skin and long-lidded, hazel eyes. They were similarly dressed in dark wide-legged pants and pastel blouses. They even had similar mannerisms. But Catherine's raven hair was a bob that framed her delicate face. Tonight, Alexis wore her hair in loose waves that tumbled to her slender shoulders.

Catherine stood to put her cup and saucer on the blond wood coffee table in front of her. "My friends and I were so excited to learn that your cooking show was extended to a second season. We enjoy trying your recipes during our monthly dinner parties." She returned to the sofa and crossed her left leg over her right. "When are you going to open a restaurant in Sedona?"

"Mom!" Alexis gasped. She sent an apologetic look at Max before addressing her mother. "You just got through the long list of projects Max is juggling. Why are you adding more responsibilities to his list?"

Catherine scowled. "Because it's very expensive to fly to New York every time I want his food."

Max laughed. "Actually, my lawyer and I have been discussing opening a third restaurant. But it's only an idea at this point. I'm using the show and cookbook to help increase demand for the two that I have now. Once the demand has grown, we'll identify a third location."

Catherine raised her hand like a good student asking for the teacher to call on her. "I'm putting in a push for Sedona now."

"I promise to keep it in mind." Max inclined his head. He was at ease in Catherine's company. She was warm and charming. Alexis, on the other hand, was a challenge. In her company, Max was forced to keep his wits about him.

Alexis pinned him with her eyes. "I've read several interviews with you but none of them explain how you got started in your career. They describe how you started your restaurants or your show, but not where you got your love of cooking."

Max cocked his head. "It's interesting that you worded your question that way, my 'love' of cooking. For me, cooking is an expression of love. My family's kitchen was the warmest room in the house. I don't mean the temperature. I mean it's where we spent most of our family time. We started the day together with breakfast. We ended the day together with dinner, and then my parents would go back to work. We celebrated birthdays, holidays, graduations, my parents' anniversary in that kitchen. That's where I found my love of cooking, from my family's kitchen."

"Those sound like wonderful memories." The coolness in Alexis's eyes began to warm. "I agree that cooking is an expression of love."

"Really?" Catherine looked at her daughter as though she

didn't know her. "Then why are you always eating burgers and fries?"

Alexis shrugged. "Because I love them."

Catherine put a hand over her face. "I don't know where I went wrong."

Max laughed. "There's nothing wrong with having burgers and fries once in a while. They could be cooked with love, too."

"Ha!" Alexis pumped her fist triumphantly. "And that was from the great Chef Max."

"Fine." Catherine threw up her hands. "I will bow to his greater culinary wisdom. But mark my words. When you love someone, you cook for them. You don't pull up to a fast-food window and place two orders for burgers and fries."

Alexis pulled her attention from Max. Her voice and expression seemed subdued. "I promise, Mom." She stood, gathering the tray that held the remains of their dessert course. "It's getting late. We should be going, but first I'll load the dishwasher."

Max rose, too. "I'll help."

"Oh, no." Catherine and Alexis spoke at once.

Catherine continued. "You're our guest. Please make yourself comfortable. It won't take us long to clean up."

Alexis nodded. "In the meantime, you can request a car service to pick us up. That way, we won't have to wait long for it to arrive."

"A car service?" Catherine waved a dismissive hand at Alexis. "Take my car instead."

Alexis hesitated. Max could sense that she wanted to say yes. "How would you get to work tomorrow?"

"Suz could take me to work in the morning." Catherine spoke over her shoulder as she went to the coat closet near the front door. She pulled her purse down from the top shelf and fished out her car keys. She returned to the living room to give the keys to Alexis. "And she could drive me to the resort to collect my car at the end of the day. It's not a problem. I'd do the same for her."

"If you're sure it's not too much trouble, I'd really appreciate it." Alexis looked at Max. "I'd like to stop by my place to get a couple of things on the way back."

"Of course." Max turned to her mother. "Thank you, Catherine." She'd insisted he call her that. "But you realize now there's nothing to keep me from helping you clean up."

He led the way to her kitchen, trying not to think about what happened the last time he'd stopped by Alexis's condo.

Alexis lived close to her mother. Max could probably jog the distance in little more than an hour. It took minutes for Alexis to drive it. Using the electronic device from her purse, she opened her attached garage. She pulled her mother's sedan through, then welcomed Max into her condo.

"Can I get you anything?" Alexis asked over her shoulder.

"No, thank you." Max looked at the soothing tones of her decor. "I don't want to dilute the memory of your mother's six-course meal. Thank you again for letting me invite myself to your Sunday dinner. I had a great time."

"I'm glad." Her face glowed with joy. "I think meeting you was the highlight of my mother's year. Thank you for answering all her questions so graciously."

Let her set the tone.

"I had fun." The room seemed to have gotten warmer. Max put his hands in the front pockets of his dark brown pants. "Your mother asks good questions."

"Yes, she does." Alexis led him into the dining area. "She also has good insights. It must be a maternal superpower."

Max kept his gaze averted from the dining table and the memories it held. He frowned, sensing Alexis's discomfort. "What do you mean?"

She clasped her hands together, then let them drop to her sides. "She said when someone cooks for you that means they love you. My mother and I usually cook our Sunday dinners together. We plan our meals, then we buy our ingredients at the farmers market. We usually go back to her house to cook because she has the bigger kitchen."

"I'm so sorry." Max rubbed his neck, pacing away from her. "This stalking situation has disrupted your life even more than I realized."

"That's not what I'm getting at." Alexis swept her arms

before her like a conductor bringing a song to an end. "My mother and I cook for each other every Sunday because we love each other." She took a step toward him. "Friday, you cooked for me."

Max's mind went blank. "Alexis—"

She held up her hand and took another step closer. "We haven't known each other long, less than a month. But I realized yesterday when I had time to think that, even if what we have can't go anywhere, for the rest of my life, I would regret never having been with you."

Max took the final step, removing the distance between them. "So would I." He cupped her cheek with his right hand. "So would I, sweetheart."

He touched his lips to hers. There would be time later to tell Alexis he was falling in love with her. For now, he would show her.

Alexis rose up on her toes and fitted her body to his. She sighed against his lips. Max opened his mouth and let her in. Her exploration was slow and gentle, soft and sweet. Max drew her tighter against him and lost himself in the feel of her. The scent of her.

Her tongue stroked against the roof of his mouth, then withdrew. Needing more, Max followed, sucking it back. Alexis pressed against him, moaning her pleasure. Max captured her tongue again, wanting to hear that sound once more.

Her fingernails pierced his cotton shirt and dug into his shoulders. Max's muscles shivered at the touch. He freed his mouth from hers and buried his face in the thick dark mass of her hair. He breathed deeply, drinking in her scent, soaking up her warmth. He tried to calm his racing pulse. He didn't want to lose control. He wanted this night with her to last.

Alexis's teeth grazed his earlobe. Her voice whispered in his ear. "Take me to bed."

Was he dreaming? Max squeezed his eyes shut as desire tightened his muscles. Those words from her lips were the sweetest sounds he'd ever heard.

"Like music to my ears." He swept Alexis into his arms and carried her through the door he remembered led to her bedroom.

With her hand cupping the back of his neck, she pulled his head down for another mind-blowing kiss. Her taste was intoxicating. It cleared his mind of everything but the two of them. The way they fit together. The way they felt together. The way they tasted together. Nothing had ever been better. Nothing ever would. In her arms, he knew exactly who he was and who he wanted to be: hers.

Max stopped at the foot of her bed and gently released her. Alexis's thigh stroked his hips as her legs lowered to the ground. Max's muscles shook. His blood heated even more.

Breaking their kiss, Alexis leaned back to search his eyes. Her cheeks were flushed like a pink rose. Her eyes shone like stars. Her lips were swollen with passion. "Do you have protection?"

"I do." Thank goodness.

She gave him a smile that made his desire throb. Holding his eyes, Alexis pulled his cream polo shirt from the waistband of his dark brown pants. He felt her palms stroke up and over his torso as she removed it, letting it drop to the floor. Max's stomach muscles trembled. He locked his knees to keep his legs steady.

He removed her mint green blouse. His breath caught when he revealed her demi-cup black lace bra.

Max raised his eyes to hers. "Did you plan this?" His voice was a curious whisper.

She gave him a seductive smile. "It may have been in the back of my mind."

Max swallowed. Hard. He was glad he hadn't known what she was wearing when they'd met at the L. They may never have made it to Sunday dinner. His fingers shook slightly when he reached behind her to unclasp the bra and free her breasts. They were firm, full and round. *Perfection.*

He drew her into his arms, lowering his head for another taste of her lips. The feel of her soft, warm skin rubbing against his bare torso made his body burn and his pulse race. He pressed her closer to him. Alexis raised her arms and wrapped them around his shoulders.

"Alexis." He whispered her name against her lips, still unsure of whether he was in a dream.

Alexis drank her name from his tongue. The feel of Max's hardening erection against her stomach made her thighs quiver. She reveled in the feel of his hard, hair-roughened chest pressing against her soft breasts. She felt his nimble fingers at the waistband of her pants, unfastening them and tugging them down. Breaking off their kiss, she quickly helped him. She stripped off her underpants, socks and shoes as well. Then she watched as he removed the rest of his clothing.

His body was art. Alexis's eyes moved over his proud shoulders, sculpted pecs, flat stomach, narrow hips and long, powerful legs.

Dropping to her knees in front of him, Alexis stroked Max's thighs. His muscles were hard and tense beneath her palms. His skin was warm. She reached up and caressed his thickening erection. He was hot, smooth and heavy moving against her palm. Her body moistened. His moan echoed in her ear, emboldening her. Alexis braced both of her hands on Max's thighs, then leaned forward to take him deep into her mouth. The muscles in his legs shook beneath her touch. His harsh breaths urged her on. Alexis drew him in, stroking him with her tongue.

"Stop." Max sounded breathless. Stepping back, he grasped her arms with unsteady hands and helped her to her feet. "You are so beautiful."

Alexis saw her beauty in his eyes.

Max urged her onto the mattress then drew her to the edge of the bed. He knelt in front of her and moved in. Excitement made Alexis's body pulse. She pressed her knees against his sides. Max reached out and cupped his large palms over her sensitive breasts. Her back arched, pressing her against his magical touch. His rough hand smoothed down her torso. Alexis felt her heart beat against it. Her breath came in gasps. Her stomach muscles quivered at his touch. Moisture pooled inside her as desire built.

Max lowered his head to place kisses just beneath her navel.

Her legs went lax. His hand cupped the juncture between her thighs. His fingers played tauntingly in her nest of curls. Alexis moved restlessly against the mattress.

"Max. Touch me."

"Where?" His breath blew against her navel.

Alexis whimpered. "There." She lifted her hips, trying to get closer to him. She ground her teeth when he remained out of reach.

"I will, sweetheart."

"Now, Max. I need you now." Her body was moving of its own volition. Her hips pumped. Her back arched. Her body strained.

"Like this?" Max slipped two fingers inside her, stretching her.

Alexis gasped and closed her eyes, pressing her head back into the mattress. Her muscles clenched around him. Max continued to slide his fingers in and out of her. Her nipples tightened, responding to his rhythmic touches. Her legs parted, urging him to join her.

Max's voice coaxed her. "Look at me, sweetheart."

She opened her eyes and looked at him. The heat in his dark gaze singed her. She'd never felt this rush of heat and need before. The connection was more than physical. It was beyond intense. It was all-consuming.

"Come inside me, Max. I want to feel you in me."

The heat in his eyes blazed brighter. He reached behind him, drawing his wallet from his pants pocket to find his condom. Alexis helped him roll it onto his erection, eager to make this final connection with him. It was the closeness she'd fantasized about. Here, she felt equal. Not less than. Not lacking. Never inferior. In Max's arms, she found a place where she could belong.

He rolled with her onto the bed. Pulling her into his arms, he held her close. Max pressed his lips to hers and entered her with one long, deep thrust.

It was too much.

Alexis's lips parted on a silent gasp. Her body shook and tossed as waves of pleasure rocked her. Max stilled. He tightened his arms around her, caressing her, soothing her until she stopped shaking and could breathe again.

And then he moved once more.

With her. Against her. Deeper and deeper. Max's eyes locked on hers. He slipped his right hand between them and touched her. Alexis moaned as he teased her, stoking the embers that still burned inside. She could feel the moisture flowing from her.

Alexis wrapped her arms and legs around him, holding him even closer. With each of his thrusts, her breasts trembled, rubbing her sensitive nipples against his chest. Alexis arched her back, bringing her breasts closer to Max's lips. He bent his head to suckle first one, then the other. Her nipples pebbled, pleading for more. He kissed them. Alexis twisted and writhed beneath him. Her muscles clenched around his erection, pulling him deeper, holding him tight.

Her pleasure was building to a crescendo. Her hips pumped, greedy for more. Max kissed her again, sliding his tongue into her mouth the way he worked his body into hers. He pressed into her, caressed her. Her muscles tightened and strained, twisting her higher and higher until her restraints broke. His body stiffened. Her muscles tensed. He buried his face in the curve of her neck. She pressed her face against his shoulder and held on tight as they exploded together.

Chapter Fifteen

"There's a video of us at The Cloisters." Alexis handed Max her cell phone Monday morning.

They were standing in the dining area of his bungalow. Alexis was too agitated to sit. She watched him press Play on her cell phone to activate the file. It was a short video. Her body was shaking with outrage. She turned to pace the great room. There was no need for her to watch the clip again. She knew what he would see.

It was a poor-quality video, which was surprising considering even cell phones produced high-quality recordings these days. It started with the interior of The Cloisters. The camera framed a wide shot of the bar. Then it zoomed in on Alexis and Max. Their seats were close. There was an air of intimacy as they talked and laughed together. From the camera angle, it looked as though they were in each other's lap. Several times, the camera closed in on their drinks and the modest neckline of Alexis's dress. The message was a clear condemnation of their behavior and a sly inference on their relationship.

The camera followed them across the bar as they were seated for dinner. The video made an abrupt cut, then ended with Max embracing Alexis in the parking lot. The video title read, "Companionship among the Amenities Offered at Mariposa."

The day had started so well. She and Max had showered together. She'd made him breakfast. Then they'd driven to Mariposa. When they'd arrived at the resort, they'd parted at the parking lot, careful to avoid public displays of affection.

And now this.

Trying to temper her emotions, Alexis drew a deep, steadying breath. Beneath the scent of the fresh-cut flowers in the vases around Max's bungalow, she detected his clean, minty scent. It soothed her, at least for a little while.

Max watched the video in stunned silence. When it ended, anger simmered in his eyes. "This was posted today?" He returned her cell phone.

Alexis pocketed the device. "Yes, I got the alert a few minutes ago."

Max rubbed the back of his neck. He wore a brick red short-sleeved shirt with gray cargo shorts. "How did they know I was a guest at Mariposa?"

Alexis flung her arm in the general direction of the nature trails. "From the hiking accident video. *Celebrity Chef's Heroic Rescue* must have a million views by now." She stopped pacing and covered her face with her left hand. "I can't believe this." She dropped her hand and faced Max. "Did you see anyone at the bar pointing a cell phone at us or any kind of camera at us?"

"No, but that doesn't mean there wasn't one or a dozen nearby." Max continued pacing. "The paparazzi are ubiquitous."

Alexis sighed. "So I've heard. But I can't see them going into the bar to record a video of you, then posting it. The Cloisters is private property. They could be sued."

"You're right." Max paused beside one of the bamboo armchairs, propping his hip against it. "Whoever shot that video wouldn't want to be seen. But why would they wait so long to post it? It's been almost three weeks since we went to The Cloisters."

"Really?" She turned to him in disbelief. "Is that what you got out of this? Why did they wait so long to post such an inflammatory video?"

Max raised his hands in surrender. "Hear me out. If you

went to all the trouble to make a secret video designed to show people in a bad light, would you wait three weeks to post it?" He had a point.

"No, I wouldn't."

"Then why would they?" Max gestured toward her front right pocket where she'd stored her cell phone.

"Because the timing is significant." The pieces were coming into place in Alexis's mind. Now if she just knew what the picture was supposed to be. What were they after?

"What's significant about it?" Max straightened from the side of the chair. "Could there be a connection to your promotion?" A flash of worry flew across his dark eyes.

"It could be. But the only person who'd want to hurt me professionally is Mark Bower. At least that I know of."

"And he has an alibi for that Thursday night."

"Besides, the only people who know about my promotion are the Coltons, Cheryl, you, my mother and me. How would the person behind this video have found out?"

The memory of her Friday meeting with the Coltons, Roland, Leticia and Greg wormed its way into her mind. Was it possible that Clive and Glenna's spy was somehow involved in this video post? Was this an attempt by the couple to destroy Mariposa?

Alexis wasn't free to discuss the resort's suspicion that there was a spy in their midst, not even with Adam's best friend. But if Adam wanted to share the information with Max, then that decision was between the two of them.

Max's voice distracted her from her thoughts. "I don't think there's anything that would connect this timing with my projects."

Alexis nodded distractedly. She took a few more paces around the room, conscious of Max's eyes on her. This wasn't the way she'd planned their "morning after." It had started with plenty of promise for romance. Then it had taken a steep nosedive.

She turned to him and stilled. It would be foolish not to bring up the one person who'd been top of mind in the other threats. "Is there anyway Sarah could be involved?"

He stared at the bamboo flooring as he considered her question. Several seconds, perhaps half a minute, ticked by. "If she was the shooter, I don't think she would've had time to record video from inside the bar, then get in position to try to shoot us."

"I disagree." Alexis shook her head. "She would've had plenty of time while we were eating dinner."

"What about the image of us embracing at the end of the video? How did she get that recording?"

Alexis shrugged. "She could've been hiding somewhere across the street when she took that photo. The police were looking for a shooter, not a celebrity chef fan recording an unauthorized video."

"All good points, but I don't believe Sarah's involved." Max crossed his arms over his chest. "She's returned to New York, remember?"

"Until the NYPD confirms that, I'd rather err on the side of caution." She took a shaky breath. "And if we're right that the motive of their timing was to hurt my promotion, then it looks like they've succeeded."

Max frowned. "What do you mean?"

Alexis let her head drop back as she expelled a frustrated breath. She didn't want to have to deal with this. Not now, not ever.

"I'm going to have to show this video to Laura at least, if not all the Coltons." Alexis strained to keep the panic from her voice. "This video puts Mariposa in a very negative light and it uses me to do that. The inference is that I'm a prostitute. The defamation is intended to hurt me and it's succeeded."

Max joined her, taking both of her hands in his. "I'm so very sorry, sweetheart. When we find the person responsible for this, I promise you, we'll make them pay. I promise."

"How? By suing them and exposing that video to even more people?" Alexis snorted. "Let me sleep on that." She gently drew her hands from Max. "I'd better talk with Laura now. The sooner I get this over with, the better."

"Do you want me to come with you?" His dark eyes searched hers.

Alexis would remember the care and concern in his eyes for the rest of her life. "No, thank you. I'd rather handle this quietly."

He escorted her to the door. "Let me know how it goes and whether you need to talk. Okay?"

"Thanks. I will."

Alexis got back into the golf cart she'd borrowed and returned to the L. She had a pretty good idea of how the fallout from that vile video would affect her professionally. It wasn't going to be good. What she didn't know was how it would affect her and Max personally.

Once again, the video loaded onto Alexis's cell phone. She sat quietly on one of the burnt-umber guest chairs on the other side of Laura's white modular desk Monday morning. Her friend's office was comfortably cool, but Alexis's palms were sweating. She was so tense, if a breeze blew through the room, she'd shatter into dust. Alexis stared blindly out the window beside Laura's desk, mentally working on a way to explain this media fiasco.

The video started and Laura gasped. "What the—" She cut herself off as the video continued. Had she been reacting to the title screen?

Alexis's stomach muscles were tied in knots. She retreated to her thoughts while she waited for the video to end. It shouldn't be much longer now.

Laura's eyes were wide as she looked from Alexis's phone to Alexis. She'd pressed her hand to her chest over her pale silver blouse. "This is reprehensible."

Her friend's reaction was worse than she'd expected. Alexis wished the floor would open up and consume her. She briefly closed her eyes, swallowing in an effort to ease her suddenly dry throat. "Laura, I'm very sorry. The video's—"

"*You're* sorry?" Laura gasped again. "What do you have to be sorry about?" She returned the phone to Alexis. "You should sue."

The conversation had taken an unexpected turn. Alexis was having trouble keeping up. "You said I should sue?"

"Absolutely." Laura waved a hand toward Alexis's phone. "That's libel. In fact, they've defamed Mariposa, too. I'm going to discuss this with Adam and Josh. I think we should sue."

Alexis held up her hand. "I'm not sure I want to draw additional attention to that video. It's highly insulting."

Laura's voice softened. "I understand, Alexis. But they could be counting on your being too uncomfortable to speak out. You wouldn't be speaking out alone. And they shouldn't be allowed to get away with this."

Alexis's eyes were drawn back to the scene outside the window. The red dirt trails, desert foliage landscaping and the ever-present mountains. "Max thinks I should sue, too."

"He's right." Laura still sounded upset. "I'm going to discuss this with Adam and Josh. Unless they have valid concerns against suing, I'm going to ask Greg to look into this. I won't allow you or Mariposa to be bullied."

Squaring her shoulders, Alexis met Laura's eyes. "I'm sorry my actions have put Mariposa in this position."

Laura frowned and shook her head. "You didn't do anything wrong. I remember the plans we made for you to go to The Cloisters to check out their bartender Kelli Iona. You were doing me a favor and I'm grateful to you. That ridiculous video is deliberately and maliciously misrepresenting the purpose for your visit."

Alexis felt weak with relief. "Thank you for understanding and believing in me."

"Do you think I don't know you?" Laura giggled. "You don't have anything to worry about."

Or at least, there wasn't anything *more* for her to worry about. "I appreciate that."

Laura sobered. "Do you have any idea who could be behind the video post?"

Alexis crossed her right leg over her left and leaned forward. "I met with Max right before I came here. We discussed Mark Bower and Sarah Harris. It could also be Clive and Glenna. Max thinks it could be the paparazzi."

"You don't sound like you agree with that last one." Laura

stretched forward and pulled a pencil from her holder. She wrote down their brief list of names.

Alexis spread her hands. "I think it's a long shot."

Laura nodded. "But this is a good start. I'll share these names with Noah. He'll probably want to speak with both of you."

"I'm happy to speak with Noah, if he thinks it will help." Alexis shrugged. "But I don't know what else we could add. I feel helpless. Someone's trying to harm me, but I don't know who or why. You'd think if someone hated you enough to want to harm you, you'd have some idea of who that person was."

"This situation is very scary. We have to do everything we can to keep you and Max safe."

"Thank you." Alexis exhaled a frustrated sigh. "I want this to be over so we can go back to normal."

Laura leaned into her desk, folding her arms on its surface. "We all do. We're worried about you and Max."

"That makes me feel worse, knowing I'm the cause of other people's anxiety. Getting the promotion was a bright spot in all of this. I would've been devastated if I'd lost that opportunity, especially over that defamatory video."

Laura looked shocked. "Even if your visit to The Cloisters wasn't work-related, I'm not going to hold you accountable for what you do in your private life—unless it's illegal. And falling in love isn't illegal."

Alexis gaped. "Well, I don't know if you could say—"

"Don't try to deny it." Laura held out a hand, stopping her. "I've seen the way the two of you are together and the looks between you. I'm very happy for you."

Alexis sighed, dropping her eyes to the bamboo flooring. "I don't know if there's anything to be happy about. He's going back to New York in two weeks."

"Alexis, you're the most determined person I've ever met. We've had clients who've asked for the impossible and you've never blinked. You find a way to make it happen. I know you." Laura pointed at her. "If you want something, you'll make it happen. If you want this relationship to work, you'll make it work."

Her friend made it sound so easy. Alexis wanted to believe it could be—but suppose it wasn't. "A relationship involves two people. Suppose *I* want it to work, but it's not as important to him."

"Then that would make him a fool."

Alexis gave the other woman a chiding look. "Laura—"

Laura sat straighter on her chair. "I'm serious, Alexis. You're intelligent, kind, hardworking, ambitious and loyal."

"You make me sound like a Saint Bernard."

Laura ignored her. "If he doesn't see that in you and do everything he can to build a life with you, then he's a fool who doesn't deserve you."

Alexis smiled as she stood to leave. "I appreciate the pep talk."

Hopefully, she won't need it again in two weeks.

"Someone took video of you and Alexis at The Cloisters, then posted it online?" Adam stood still beside Max. His eyes were wide with disbelief and outrage. "That's a massive invasion of privacy. You should sue."

"That's what I think, but Alexis is embarrassed by the video." Max started walking again. Adam kept pace with him.

They were strolling the resort grounds Monday morning. Mariposa was picturesque. A mixture of delicate vistas and bold terrain. This morning, a subtle, warm breeze pushed webs of cirrus clouds across the bright blue sky. Max thought being outdoors would help clear his mind. It might also help Adam. Since he arrived at the resort, Max had sensed something had been weighing on his friend's mind beyond the threats from his father. Adam had dodged every attempt he'd made to get him to open up, though.

"I'll talk with Laura and Josh about it." Adam sounded annoyed and determined. "Unless they have a substantial objection, I'll speak with Greg about filing a suit. You think Mark or Sarah might be involved?"

"It also might have been a member of the paparazzi." Activity near the outdoor pool drew Max's attention. Private cabanas and deck chairs surrounded the large outdoor pool. A stunning view of the surrounding rock formations stood in the background.

"It could also be an attempt by Clive and Glenna to undermine Mariposa's reputation." Adam's statement drew Max's attention back to their conversation. "Have you given this information to Noah?"

Max was irritated that he hadn't thought of that himself. "No, I've been so concerned about Alexis's reaction to that video. I didn't think about updating Noah. I'll do that as soon as I get back to my bungalow."

Adam glanced at him. "Do you want me on the call with you? You seem a little distracted."

Max rubbed the back of his neck. The restless feeling was building again. "I'm supposed to leave in two weeks. Suppose the case isn't solved by then? I can't stay here indefinitely, but I can't leave while Alexis is still in danger."

"You're my best friend, Max." Adam stopped again, turning to face him. "Your safety is very important to me. Stay here as long as you need to."

"I appreciate that, Adam." Max started moving again. He couldn't control the frustration in his tone. "But the sooner this case is solved, the sooner everyone will be safe."

"By 'everyone' you mean Alexis."

"If Sarah's the stalker as we suspect, then Alexis is in danger because of me." The thought filled him with anger and shame.

"You're wrong." Adam's voice was firm. "If Sarah's behind these attacks, then Alexis is in danger because of *Sarah*."

"I'm not completely blameless. If I hadn't been so blind, I'd have realized Sarah had issues." Max surveyed the pathways, buildings and bungalows in the immediate area.

Was it his imagination or were there more security guards on the grounds lately? Was it all because of the threats or was something more going on?

Adam's assessment of their surroundings seemed more critical than admiring. Was he checking to see whether repairs or improvements were needed? Max thought everything looked perfect.

Adam addressed Max. "I hope the case is solved before you

leave. I hope it's solved today. But what then? Will you and Alexis keep seeing each other?"

Max blew a breath. "I want that very much, but my life is in New York, and she seems rooted in Sedona."

Adam chuckled. "You wouldn't be the only couple in history who'd need to manage a long-distance relationship. It's not ideal, but other people have made it work. If she's important to you, you can make it work, too."

"Distance isn't the only problem." Max glanced toward the hiking trails far in the background. Even though he and Alexis had gone hiking after the accident, he didn't think he could look at a trail without remembering her fall. "I'm growing the restaurants, starting a second season of the show and I have my first-ever publishing contract. I don't know if this is the best time for me to start a relationship, especially a long-distance one on different time zones."

He and Adam walked together in silence for several strides, each caught up in their own thoughts. Usually, physical activity helped him think. It put things in perspective and made him feel better. That wasn't happening today. He still felt overwhelmed, agitated and lost.

Adam finally broke the companionable silence. "Max, I'm going to give you some advice—don't make the same mistake I did."

"Which one are you talking about?"

Adam gave him a sour look before facing forward again. "I've seen you and Alexis together. There's a strong connection between the two of you. Laura and I were right. You make a great couple."

Max stopped in his tracks. "You set us up?"

"Of course we did." Adam waved his hand. "Keep up. We all think Alexis is a wonderful person. If you agree, you need to find a way to make a relationship with her work. There's more to life than your career. Success doesn't mean anything if you don't have someone you love—and who loves you back—to share it with."

"You're thinking about Paige, aren't you?"

Adam sighed. "I have a lot of regrets in my life. I think not pursuing a relationship with her is the biggest one."

Max silently agreed with his friend. "What happened between you?"

Adam's shrug was more of a restless movement than a gesture of confusion. "I thought my family needed me and I didn't want to hold Paige back. You and Alexis are in a different place in your lives and careers than Paige and I were. Still, don't make the same mistake I made. Don't turn your back on happiness."

Max knew that was the most he'd get out of his friend on the topic of Paige Barnes, at least for today.

But his friend was right. Alexis was special. She was worth whatever effort was necessary to make a relationship with her work. She was the kind of woman he'd change his life for.

He needed to tell her that.

Chapter Sixteen

Why was her condo's management office calling her at work in the middle of the morning?

Alexis accepted the call on her work cell phone late Monday morning. "This is Alexis Reed. How can I help you?"

"Ms. Reed, this is Orlie. I'm new with the Red Dust Realty Property Management Group Office. I'm afraid I have some bad news for you, ma'am. Your condo was broken into this morning."

"Oh, no." It doesn't rain, but it pours. Alexis stood, preparing to leave her office. "How much damage did they do?" She tapped some keys to lock her computer.

"I'm afraid quite a bit, ma'am." Orlie's tone was full of regret. "The police are here with me in the management office. I know we're interrupting you at work right now, ma'am, and I apologize for—"

"No, I appreciate your call, Orlie." Alexis grabbed her bag from her top desk drawer.

Was it possible the break-in had something to do with the stalker? Alexis didn't believe in coincidences.

"It's no problem, ma'am. But do you think you might be able to get away for a short bit? The police would like to get a report from you about what the thieves might have taken."

"I'm on my way, Orlie. I should be there in about twenty minutes."

Orlie breathed a sigh of relief. "Oh, that's wonderful, ma'am. I appreciate your time."

"And I appreciate your assistance. Thank you, Orlie. I'll see you soon."

Alexis hurried out of her office. She sent a text to Laura as she strode down the hall. Her boss needed to know she was leaving the office to deal with a home emergency. Under the circumstances, Alexis was sure Laura would understand.

She paused briefly to leave a message with one of the clerks on duty at the registration desk. "Hey, Clarissa. My condo manager just called. Someone broke into my unit."

Clarissa's naturally sunny disposition clouded over at the news. "Gosh, I'm sorry, Alexis."

"Thank you. I sent Laura a text about it and I'm on my way to check it out."

"Okay. Be careful." Clarissa waved. "Drive safely."

Aware that Sarah, Mark or some yet-unknown stalker suspect could be watching the resort, Alexis drove her mother's car. She should be back in plenty of time to return the vehicle to Catherine. All the way to her condo, Alexis chided herself for the break-in. Although she didn't know what more she could've done. She'd put a hold on her mail, left the exterior lights on, left a couple of interior lights on and asked her mother to drive by at least once a day.

She wished she'd called Max before she'd left, but she'd been in a hurry to deal with her condo situation. She'd call him after she spoke with Orlie and the police.

Alexis arrived at her condo in less than the twenty minutes she'd promised Orlie. She slowed as she approached the driveway to her garage. That was strange. When she'd asked how much damage had been done, Orlie had replied, "Quite a bit." Leaning forward in the driver's seat, Alexis scrutinized her condo. It didn't look damaged at all. The garage door and all the windows were intact. Her front door...was it ajar?

What was that about? Were the police holding a sale with the remainder of her belongings?

Alexis parked her mother's compact sedan in her driveway instead of opening the garage. She was anxious to lock her condo. She jogged up the four steps to the front door. It was open perhaps three inches. Alexis cautiously pushed it open all the way. She waited to see whether an intruder would welcome her into her own home. Nothing.

She stepped over the threshold. Still nothing. No police officer. No property manager. Alexis started to feel uneasy. She wasn't convinced her muscles would listen to her if she urged them to move one more time. But they did.

Another, longer step placed her in the entryway. The door slammed behind her. Alexis jumped a foot off the floor and spun toward the sound. Sarah Harris stood in front of the now-closed door. The tall, full-figured woman wore black biking shorts that ended at her knees and a midriff-baring blue cap-sleeved cropped shirt. In her right hand, she held what appeared to be the largest knife from Alexis's butcher's block. Her pale round face was a mask of jealousy and anger.

Alexis's shaking started slowly but was building. She exhorted herself to remain calm and confident. "Good morning, Sarah. So you do know where I live. I'd wondered."

Without a word or a sound, Sarah charged at Alexis, knife raised. Shock gripped her. She quickly shrugged it off. Fight or flight? She'd choose fight every time. She had no doubt if she tried to run from Sarah, the other woman would stab her in the back. That's not the way she imagined herself dying.

Alexis grabbed Sarah's knife arm with both of her hands. "Drop the knife, Sarah! What good is killing me going to do?"

No response. Instead, Sarah grunted, growled and panted like a person possessed.

Alexis had never been so afraid in her life. Not even when she'd fallen off the side of the cliff or when she was being shot at. Was that because in both cases, she hadn't been alone? Max had been with her.

Alexis battled fear and Sarah. The other woman was as strong as she looked. Maybe stronger. Alexis could barely move her. She gripped the other woman's arm as hard as she could with both of her hands. Sarah would not let go. She squeezed and squeezed and squeezed. She tried to hurt Sarah to force her to drop the knife. It wasn't working.

"You pretended to be Orlie to lure me here?" Between terror and exertion, she barely had breath to speak.

Sarah replied with more grunts, growls and pants. She brought her other arm into the struggle. She seemed to want to drive the knife into Alexis's chest. Alexis saw the blood-thirst in Sarah's eyes. They were wide and filled with hate. The pupils were dilated. Alexis was losing ground. The knife was coming closer and closer to her skin. In desperation, she kicked out. Sarah lost her balance, knocking over a chair. Falling to the floor, she finally released the knife.

Alexis kicked it away. She dropped to the floor, straddling Sarah's hips and pinning her arms down. "What is wrong with you? What do you want?"

"To kill you." Sarah spoke in a growl.

Alexis had deduced that much. "Why?"

"You stole my man and my job. I. Am. Going. To. Kill. You."

Sarah surged up, dislodging Alexis. Alexis's flailing arms knocked over another chair. Was Sarah's delusion giving her strength? Sarah reached for the knife. Knowing if Sarah reclaimed the weapon, she was going to die, Alexis struggled to drag the taller, stronger woman back. She grabbed Sarah's arm and caught her bracelet. The jewelry broke in her hand.

Sarah's scream of rage came from deep inside her. The sound was like that of a mortally wounded wild beast. Alexis's blood ran cold. Sarah pushed her backward. She saw the other woman's fist coming toward her. She tried to block it, but Sarah was too fast. Alexis's head snapped back. Everything went dark.

Chapter Seventeen

Max knocked briefly on Laura's office door. "Good morning, Laura. I'm sorry to interrupt you, but have you seen Alexis? She isn't in her office or her bungalow."

Laura's concerned expression made Max worry more. "She sent me a text. Someone broke into her condo. She's meeting with the police at the condo manager's office."

A break-in. Guilt weighed even more heavily on him. He crossed the threshold into Laura's office. "How long ago did she send the text?"

Laura checked her cell phone. "About thirty minutes ago. She should've reached her condo by now. I can text her for an update."

"No, that's okay." He stepped back, preparing to leave. *A break-in? When a stalker was after her?* "I'll call her. I had my service provider help me reset my cell phone."

Laura gave him a knowing smile. "Would you rather go to her?"

"Yes, I would." Max shrugged. He was restless. Something didn't feel right. He felt an urgent need to see Alexis. Now. "Between that video and this break-in, she's had a tough morning. I'd like to be with her. Unfortunately, that's not possible because I don't have a car."

"That's sweet." Laura's smile widened. "And I would love

it if my friend had someone with her to help her deal with the fallout from this break-in. Why don't you borrow a Mariposa jeep? It's a twenty-minute drive. I'll call the grounds service and ask them to lend you one."

Max's body eased with relief. "Thanks, Laura. I appreciate that."

He drove his golf cart to the grounds department. The young woman who set him up with one of their jeeps looked like a college student. Max was fairly certain he could find Alexis's condo, but he didn't have time to waste. He used an app on his phone to direct him.

He arrived in a little more than twenty minutes. What he found made his blood run cold. No one was around; not the police, condo management or Alexis. Her garage and front doors were wide open. There wasn't a car in the driveway, garage or parked on the street.

What was going on? Where was Alexis's car?

Max jogged up the front steps. He raised his hand to knock on the door—and froze. Several chairs had fallen over. Or had they been thrown over?

"Alexis?" He entered the condo, careful not to touch anything. "Alexis?"

Panic was trying to grab him. He beat it back. Max searched her bedroom, the bathrooms, the dining area and the kitchen. Nothing. He checked the area near the fallen chairs. On the floor, half-hidden by one of the chairs, was one of the bracelets he'd given to the women on his show's production crew.

Sarah.

It was getting harder to stave off the panic.

Max used one of Alexis's paper towels to handle the broken bracelet, then went in search of the condo office. It was dark, dusty, stifling and stank of cigars. He tapped the service bell twice for assistance.

An older woman walked up to the scarred and dusty desk. Her nametag read Orlie. "I heard you the first time. Whaddya need?"

He took a breath and forced himself to speak patiently. "One of your tenants said you'd contacted her at work earlier this morning to report she'd had a break-in."

Orlie was shaking her head before Max had finished speaking. "Not me."

Ice collected in his veins. "Are you sure? The tenant is Alexis Reed."

Orlie frowned at him. "Well, I don't know who'd have told you all that bunk, but *I'm* telling you, we haven't had any break-ins since I've worked here. Someone's got their wires crossed. Anythin' else?"

Max's heart was pounding. Thoughts were screaming across his mind. "No, nothing else. Thank you."

He pushed his way out of the management office and got Laura on the phone.

"Hi, how is she?"

Max's voice was grim. "She's missing."

"What?"

"The condo manager said she never called Alexis. There haven't been any break-ins at the condos."

Laura gasped. "Do you think the stalker has her?"

Max thought of the broken bracelet in his shorts pocket. "I know she does. I need to find her."

"Wait." Laura's voice was breathless. "We gave each other permission to use the locator app to find our phones."

"Thank goodness." Max climbed back into the jeep.

"Come on. Come on." Laura spoke under her breath. "Got it! I'll text her coordinates to you and Noah. Max, please find her."

"I will." His words were an oath and a prayer.

Chapter Eighteen

"*Sarah!* What are you doing?" Max raced through the trees into the clearing.

The scene unfolding in front of his eyes had been pulled from his worst nightmare. Alexis knelt at the end of a cliff. Max knew a rock-filled river lay at its base. She'd been gagged. Duct tape bound her arms behind her back. Sarah stood over her. She held a gun against the back of Alexis's head.

Max had never known he could be terrified and enraged at the same time. He drew a deep breath to settle his nerves. The solid scents of desert foliage and red dirt steadied him. What was he supposed to do? Culinary school didn't offer classes on de-escalating hostage situations. Frantic, he searched his mind for a plan. Two things were helping him keep it together. The first was his love for Alexis. He needed this woman in his life. The second was the knowledge that Noah was on his way. If he could keep Sarah talking until the cavalry arrived, Alexis would get out of this alive

"*Sarah!*" He called to her again as he ran toward her and Alexis. "What are you doing?"

"Max?" Sarah jerked Alexis to her feet. "Why are you here, Max?"

Alexis struggled to get her feet under her. Max gritted his teeth at Sara's continued mistreatment of her. Her gold pantsuit was torn and covered in dust as though she'd fallen several times during the hike to this area. Her arms and cheeks were scratched. One of her shoes was missing.

"You know why I'm here." Max walked closer. Only thirty yards separated them now. But it was still too far. He had to get a better look at Alexis. Was that a bruise on her jaw?

Sarah's smile was bitter. "Oh, I get it. You're here for *me*. Right? Because you care so much about *me*. Because *I'm* the one you really love. And I was wrong to think you were in love with Alexis." Her words taunted him. "Were you going to use that script, Max?"

"No, Sarah." Max clenched his fists at his sides. "I'm here for Alexis. Let her go!"

"No!" Sarah growled the word in a voice Max didn't recognize. "Why should I let her go? Why do you care about *her* and not *me*?"

"For one thing, she wouldn't try to kill the woman I love." Max paced forward. In his peripheral vision, he saw Alexis look at him as though surprised, but he couldn't think about that now.

Sarah held the gun in the air and pulled the trigger. "Don't come any closer or the next one won't be a warning shot."

Max's temper spiked in equal measure to his fear. "What do you want, Sarah? Why are you doing this?"

I can't keep her talking for much longer. Where is Noah?

"Why am *I* doing this?" Sarah screeched. "This isn't *my* fault. This is *your* fault. I did everything for you! Everything! I kept your schedule. I brought your supplies. I made your appointments. You said I was indispensable."

Max frowned. "That was your job, Sarah. You got paid to do those things."

She ignored him. "I even ended my marriage for you. And for what? So you could spend time with some cheap woman you got from that resort?" Sarah waved the gun toward Alexis.

Max's heart nearly stopped. His eyes flew to Alexis. She was glaring at Sarah. She must have realized as Max had that Sarah was indeed the person behind the defamatory video.

They could deal with that later. For now, Max needed to

know that she was all right. "Put the gun down, Sarah. *Now.* And let Alexis go." He was so angry. And so afraid. He wasn't doing this right.

Dear God, please don't let me get Alexis killed.

"I will not." Her voice was thick with hatred. "You betrayed me."

"If you think I betrayed you, then deal with me and let Alexis go. Take me!" Max saw Alexis's eyes widen. He heard her voice in his head, *Are you crazy?*

"Maybe I should kill both of you." Sarah's smile was mean.

Max was winging this. "That would be in keeping with your deceit."

"What?" Sarah lowered the gun. "How have I deceived you?"

Max walked forward. "You claim to love me, but you don't. You love The Celebrity Chef. You love the fame and fortune. The perks that come with the persona. But you don't know anything about Max."

"That's not true." She waved the gun at him. "I've read every interview about you. I know everything there is to know about you." Sarah pointed the gun at the sky and fired another bullet. "Stop! Moving!"

Max stopped. "You know everything about me? Then tell me, why did I become a chef?"

Sarah frowned. "You already know why you became a chef."

Max spread his arms. "I want to hear it from you." *Please, God, let this work.*

Sarah looked at Alexis, then back to Max. "You became a chef because you wanted to open a restaurant."

"That's not true." Max shook his head. "So you see? You don't love me. You only think you do. Let Alexis go."

"I do love you!" Sarah screamed. "Why won't you believe me?"

"Police! Freeze!" Noah's voice carried from the tree line behind Max. It was loud and firm.

Max heard the detective's footsteps as he ran forward to join him. Relief lifted the weight from Max's back. He started to turn toward Noah, but Sarah's scream distracted him.

"Why won't you believe me?" She pointed her gun at him.

Before Max or Noah could react, Alexis launched herself at Sarah, knocking her to the ground as the gun went off.

The sound of that discharge would feature in Max's night terrors for years.

"Alexis!" Max charged toward her. Her body was so still as she lay on top of Sarah.

Max dropped to his knees beside her as Noah reached Sarah. The detective pulled Sarah out from under Alexis and took her into custody.

"Alexis. Sweetheart, are you all right?" Max searched her for injuries. He found scratches and bruises, but no bullet wounds. Thank God.

Alexis was trying to talk through the duct tape Sarah had used to gag her.

"Sweetheart, this is going to hurt." Max took a corner of the tape with his still-shaking fingers and pulled as fast as he could.

"Ow." Alexis gasped. Her hands flew to her face to rub her cheeks. She scowled at Max. "I said, please take me home."

Noah returned, hunkering down beside them. He held up a retracting knife. "What say we cut you loose first."

Max turned to him. "Thank you, Noah. For everything."

Noah smiled at him as he cut Alexis free. "I think Alexis is the one you should thank. She saved your life." He straightened and disappeared.

Max helped Alexis to stand. "Alexis." He had no other words.

She cupped the side of his face. "You came for me. Thank you."

Wrapping his arms around her, he lifted her to his lips and kissed her until their fears drained away.

Chapter Nineteen

"When I heard your voice shouting at Sarah, I wanted to cry with relief." Alexis shivered at the memory. Max tightened his arms around her. "But at the same time, I wanted to scream at you to run away. I didn't want you putting yourself in danger. Again."

"There was no way I was leaving without you." Max could no longer even imagine a life without her. They sat wrapped in each other's arms on Alexis's love seat Monday evening.

He gently took Alexis's small, pointed chin, turning her face into the light so he could better see the bruise on her jawline.

"Sarah was freakishly strong." Alexis sounded tired. "And she'd become unhinged. I wonder what led to that."

"I don't know if we'll ever learn the answer." Max felt a wave of sadness. Had she always been troubled? If so, why hadn't he noticed it during the two years they'd worked together.

Alexis's condo was eerily quiet in the aftermath of the parade of family and friends who'd come to check on her once they'd heard about her kidnapping. The well-wishers included her mother and her aunt Suz, Jake, Laura, Adam, Joshua, Roland, Clarissa and a number of other Mariposa colleagues. Some had brought flowers, cards or candies. A couple of people had shown up with burgers and fries.

Max put his arms around Alexis again, careful not to hurt her. Her body was soft and warm against his, reassuring him she was real, and she was here. "I've never been so afraid in my life as I was when I saw Sarah holding that gun on you and realized she planned to throw you over the cliff."

Alexis shivered again in his embrace. "And I've never been so afraid as I was when I heard you offer to take my place." She tilted her head up to hold his eyes. "Please don't ever do that again."

"Hopefully, I'll never have another opportunity." Max kissed the top of her head. He kept touching and kissing her. Was he comforting her or himself?

"I'd hoped once the case was solved, everything would return to normal." Alexis drew a shaky breath. "But I have a feeling I won't feel normal for a while."

"Neither will I. But we'll get through this together." Max caught his breath at the hope in Alexis's eyes.

She raised her arm and stroked a finger down the right side of his mouth. "I hope it won't be too long before I see that dimple again." Her words made him smile. "Ah. There it is."

He kissed her forehead. "Your wish is my command."

Silence lingered over them for moments. It felt comfortable to lean on each other as they sank into their own thoughts.

Alexis sighed. "Max?"

"Hmm?"

"When Sarah asked why you loved me and not her, you said because I wouldn't try to kill the woman you love."

Max's muscles tensed in preparation for her obvious question. He prompted her when she remained silent. "That's right."

Alexis cleared her throat. "Did you say that because you were trying to save my life, or did you say that because you're in love with me?"

Max shifted to face her. His arms were cold without her in them, so he took her hands. "Alexis Reed, I fell in love with you the first moment I met you. Like a fool, I didn't want it to be true. I should have been smart enough to realize it without your being in a life-or-death situation." He paused to help Alexis wipe the tears from her cheeks. Were those tears of joy or regret? He grasped his courage in both hands and continued. "You once said the two of us want different things. I don't think that's true. I think we want the same thing—to be together. And we're the kind of people when we want something, we make it happen. Alexis, I've never wanted anything more than to have you in my life."

Alexis gave a watery laugh. "I confess, I don't think I fell in love with you in the *first* moment we met, but I fell pretty quickly."

Max kissed the back of her right hand. "I know how much you love Sedona."

"And I know your family, home and work are all in New York." She sounded disappointed.

Max smiled. "My family could come to visit. In fact, my mother's excited to spend time at Mariposa. And although my work is primarily in New York, that doesn't mean it can't be moved, at least temporarily."

Alexis gave him a curious smile. "What are you saying?"

"The producers have agreed to film the second season of *Cooking for Friends* here in Sedona."

Alexis's eyes widened. "They did?"

Max nodded. "I floated the idea to them a couple of days after the shooting, when I realized I'd fallen in love with you."

Alexis gasped with pleasure. She launched herself into his arms and covered his face with kisses in between exclamations of joy. "This is so wonderful. My mother will be thrilled. I can't believe you'd do something like this. Did you do this just for me?"

Max smiled into her eyes. "I did this for us." He grew serious. "You're my heart. You're my world. You're the one I want standing beside me in good times and in bad. I would change my life to be with you, Alexis."

Alexis wiped the tears from her eyes. "Maxwell Powell III." She paused when he chuckled. "You're everything to me. And

I would willingly change my life to be with you, including eating itty-bitty Veronica Forand food on great big plates."

"Now, that's love." Max pressed his lips to hers and tasted their forever.

* * * * *

Don't miss the stories in this mini series!

THE COLTONS OF ARIZONA

Colton's Deadly Trap
PATRICIA SARGEANT
January 2025

Colton At Risk
KACY CROSS
February 2025

Colton's Reel Danger
KIMBERLY VAN METER
March 2025

MILLS & BOON

The Twin's Bodyguard
Veronica Forand

MILLS & BOON

Veronica Forand is the award-winning author of romantic thrillers, winning both the Booksellers' Best and the Golden Pen Award for the novels in her True Lies series.

When she's not writing, she's a search and rescue canine handler with her dog, Max.

A lover of education but a hater of tests, she attended Smith College and Boston College Law School. She studied in Paris and Geneva, worked in London and spent several glorious months in Ripon, England.

She currently divides her time living between Philadelphia, Vermont and Cape Cod.

Books by Veronica Forand

Harlequin Romantic Suspense

Fresh Pond Security

Protector in Disguise
The Twin's Bodyguard

Visit the Author Profile page
at millsandboon.com.au for more titles.

Dear Reader,

Siblings are both amazing and frustrating. My brother is one of my best friends and also the person who can antagonize me more than anyone else. His antics occasionally make me wish for a sister, a wish that inspired the creation of twin sisters Allison and Zoe Goodwyn. Allison is focused on getting ahead in her job as an investigative reporter, while Zoe, an elementary school teacher, drops everything to help out both her sister and their father. In *The Twin's Bodyguard*, Zoe takes on Allison's identity in order to save her sister's life.

She transitions out of her role as a teacher into the world of television news. She not only takes over her sister's wardrobe but picks up a sexy bodyguard, Noah, along the way. While Noah's protecting Zoe, his belief in her shifts her self-image and allows her to step out from her sister's shadow.

This is book two of the Fresh Pond Security series, which can be read as a stand-alone. However, this book does expand on some plotlines introduced in book one, *Protector in Disguise*, Fiona and Jason's story.

I love hearing from my readers, so feel free to visit me at www.veronicaforand.com and leave me a message.

Enjoy the thrill!

Veronica

For Steve

When they handed out older brothers,
I hit the jackpot.

Thanks for the laughter, the scotch
and always having my back.

Chapter One

For as long as Zoe Goodwyn could remember, she'd put the needs of her twin sister, Allison, first, even if it meant sacrificing her own needs. She'd given up career opportunities and even let go of a boyfriend or two to remain in their hometown to care for their father. Her latest sacrifice seemed mild by comparison—abandoning plans with friends to catch the ferry from Nantucket and watch her sister's dog.

Stepping off the bus into the heart of Boston, Zoe shielded herself from the city's loud energy, a sharp contrast to the meditative qualities of waves breaking on a sandy beach and the call of seagulls darting across the sky. The salt air in Boston felt invigorating, but the bags of trash waiting for pickup added a somewhat sour city smell that wrinkled her nose. Although Zoe enjoyed visits to Boston, she preferred when Allison traveled to Nantucket so Zoe could remain in her zen place. Not that she entirely disliked the city. Just city people. People acted differently in large groups. They had more of a survival of the fittest mentality. She preferred any groups around her to be under the age of ten. In fact, her third-grade students were her favorite people. Everyone else brought too much with them. Too much noise, conflict, gossip, expectations, and superiority. She slipped away from the crush at the bus station while texting her dad that she'd made it into the city.

Zoe relaxed as she reached her sister's neighborhood. Few cars ventured down the one-way cobblestone road to the three-story brownstone. Pausing in front of a florist, she bought a bundle of white and pink peonies before traveling the final block to her destination. Flowers always made everything a touch brighter and more fragrant.

A woman, dressed in a pale blue shirtdress and walking a large white dog, waved from across the street. "Allison, I loved your report on stolen pets. Keep up the good work." As a young and energetic investigative reporter for a local news channel, Allison had minor celebrity status in the city. She thrived among people and could persuade anyone to hand over their most personal stories. She also loved getting in the middle of complicated issues.

Normally, Zoe would ignore people confusing her for her sister, but she couldn't make her sister appear unfriendly. Trying to explain that she was not, in fact, Allison, was always too much of a chore. Not many people knew about Allison's sister, and Zoe liked it that way. Her baseball cap, ponytail and sunglasses should have kept her identity hidden. This was her sister's neighborhood, however, so perhaps, people could see through a disguise here. She waved and mouthed thanks to the woman, who smiled and continued down the street with her dog.

Once inside the building, Zoe heard howling. Marlowe. Mrs. Peterson, an older woman with a tousled, pewter bob and a charming disposition, never disciplined Marlowe when she watched him. She preferred the bribery method in restraining him. Zoe entered the apartment and was greeted by one very excited beagle. As soon as the door closed behind her, she let go of her suitcase, kicked off her red Mary Janes, never allowed on the perfectly waxed floor, and headed to the kitchen to put the flowers in a vase. Marlowe's intensity didn't slow. His tail wasn't wagging. Instead, he appeared distressed. He was always happy to see her, so his behavior caused her to pause and crouch down to his level.

"What's the matter, little man?" Zoe asked the shaking beagle. Normally, he'd greet her between blistering romps around the foyer, into the kitchen, over the living room furniture and right back to her side. Now he didn't leave her side.

She dropped the flowers on the counter and scanned the room. The kitchen and living room seemed as sterile and minimalist as always, but quiet, except for Marlowe.

"Mrs. Peterson?" she called out, as Marlowe continued his barking. He nearly tripped her as she tried to walk into the room. "Go to bed." She pointed to Marlowe's bed and looked around for Mrs. Peterson. She paused and stared him down. He popped into a down position on his bed, but as soon as she walked further into the apartment, he bounded to her side.

Turning away from him, she took a deep breath.

The energy inside the apartment felt unfamiliar. Something was off. Whatever created the tension in the room lifted the hair on her arms and made her almost turn around and run back out the door. But Mrs. Peterson had to be here because Zoe could smell hints of the jasmine perfume she always wore.

Marlowe rushed ahead, barking and winding up again. Zoe stalled at the door to Allison's study. Papers and drawers and files had been tossed all over the floor. Marlowe skittered back into the hall away from Mrs. Peterson, who was face down on the floor.

Zoe rushed over to her. It appeared as though she'd fallen or maybe collapsed. A good-sized gash was on the back of her head, matting her hair with blood.

"Mrs. Peterson, are you okay?" she asked, knowing she wasn't. Marlowe rushed toward her, barking louder. Zoe wanted to comfort him but had to focus on the unconscious woman in front of her.

"You're here?" A gruff voice came from behind her.

Before she could turn, the stranger's hand reached around and covered her mouth with a cloth. She tried to push him away, but his grip was strong and her ability to fight was fading. Her eyes closed, the barking grew faint, and everything went black.

Chapter Two

Noah Montgomery sat inside his car, listening to Vivaldi and snacking on M&M's, almonds, and raisins for hours. He'd already placed two discreet cameras at the back entrances to the apartment complex he'd been assigned and had parked near the front entrance to watch for anyone coming and going.

Allison, the woman whose apartment he'd been tasked to watch, had already walked by his car, carrying flowers and a duffel bag with her brown hair up in a ponytail covered with a baseball hat and wearing sunglasses. Even with the attempted disguise, he'd recognize her from the news. She'd strolled along as though she had no worries in the world, but according to their client, she had a target on her back. Allegedly, she'd uncovered a bribe in the local government. Although the source of the bribe was unknown, there were rumblings in underground channels placing Allison at risk. Not that she'd appeared anxious or even more cautious than the average person. Perhaps she was unaware of the risk or welcomed dangerous assignments.

When he called Jason, the operational leader, to tell him that she was back, Jason seemed incredulous.

"She is? Meaghan last tracked her to Rhode Island," Jason said.

Rhode Island was only an hour from Boston, so she could have easily driven back from wherever she'd gone.

"I don't know where she was, but she's here now."

"Fine, keep an eye on the door. I'll send Meaghan to stay on her," Jason said.

Noah had spent years at a desk as an analyst for the NSA—he wanted fieldwork, not more sitting. "I can enter an apartment just as well as Meaghan can."

"You're on the building, she's assigned to the person. If Allison leaves again, I still need someone watching all the exits. Keep an eye on the outside for anything unusual."

Noah's gaze had remained on the front entry and on the camera feeds of the back of the building. "Understood," he said, through clenched teeth. This was supposed to be the year he took on more adventurous assignments. As soon as Jason approved his request.

Having been stuck at a desk for the past few months after a gunshot wound, he'd been happy to get out of the office to handle surveillance work. Granted, he'd prefer interacting with people in more direct fieldwork, but at least he was no longer in his office twelve hours a day. Having arrived at 1:00 p.m., he couldn't be certain who had come and gone in the morning, but Jason had made it clear that he remain outside the building in the background.

This was Noah's first assignment with their client EON, the Eclipse Operations Network, a shadow agency that stepped in when a case needed specialized teams outside of regular law enforcement channels. When Fiona, a former member of EON, joined Fresh Pond Security, EON saw an opportunity to use the team as an alternative arm of their group. It paid much better than security guard and protection work, but the assignments often had vague instructions and unclear goals.

The team had been hired on this case to investigate bribes running between City Hall and some sort of criminal enterprise. EON wanted the name of the entity making the bribe. After years of monitoring these types of organizations when Noah was an analyst at the NSA, he understood how difficult it would be to find enough evidence for charges to stick, but he'd do his part sitting inside his car, watching the comings and goings of Allison Goodwyn, the investigative reporter who had broken open the case.

But ten minutes later, everything changed. A food delivery guy carrying two bags entered the building when a woman and a young kid exited. He was dressed in jeans, a gray T-shirt, and heavy leather work boots that nobody in their right mind would wear for Uber Eats deliveries. The muddy boots seemed more appropriate for a construction site. His suspicions raised, Noah contacted Jason again and explained the situation. Although he didn't have the actual field experience of his colleagues, the majority former law enforcement or military types, he could analyze a situation better than most. And his instincts screamed to follow that guy.

"I can wait for Meaghan or go inside and get a closer look," he said, trying not to overstep his position, but knowing damn well that something was off. "All of the cameras are recording and Calvin has the feedback at the office, so we shouldn't miss anything on the outside."

There was a pause and then Jason replied, "Meaghan's delayed. Go ahead and check on Allison's well-being."

Noah didn't have time to feel relieved. He left his car, only to be stopped by the locked front door. "Damn it," he cursed under his breath.

As he stood and waited for someone to let him inside, he tried to listen through the door for anything that sounded off. The only sound coming from the building was a barking dog. After what felt like forever, he lucked out when some business suit of a guy exited the building more focused on his phone than on whom he was letting inside the building. Noah bolted past him. Too much time had lapsed for a simple food delivery. He dashed upstairs and could hear the muffled sounds of a struggle in the location of the barking dog.

He tried the apartment door. After rattling it enough to know it was locked, he backed up a few steps and then used his stronger leg to kick in the door. His hip throbbed with a sharp pain that shot through him as every muscle propelled him forward, but the door burst open. As the door slammed into the wall, he paused at the scene inside the apartment. The fake delivery man, a huge guy with a scowl on his face, stood with an accomplice, another burly guy in jeans and a T-shirt, who must have entered the apartment before Noah had been sent to monitor the place. Allison was unconscious and being dragged across the rug toward the front door. A beagle ran around the men, barking and growling.

Noah pulled out his weapon. "Stay where you are." He pointed his gun but didn't have a good enough shot to guarantee he wouldn't hit Allison. Although he seemed the same height as the men, he had more lean muscle than pumped-up gym muscle. But he'd handled burly guys in hand-to-hand combat in training, outwitting them in tactical situations when his strength wouldn't match his opponents.

Instead of rushing them, he grabbed a large blue vase from a side table with his free hand and tossed it at the man closer to him.

The guy deflected it toward the wall where it smashed into an explosion of glass fragments. To avoid the glass, the men dropped Allison. The beagle bit into the pant leg of one of them, who kicked back and forth trying to get free. His partner pointed a weapon at the dog, which sent Noah rushing forward to the asshole. With his focus on rescuing Allison and saving the dog, one of the men came from behind and clocked him in the head with a very large fist. He fell, curling under his shoulder to limit the impact of the fall. By the time he righted himself, the men had rushed out the door. Allison, her hat knocked off and part of her shirt ripped, remained out of it in the middle of the floor on top of bits of glass.

He knelt by her and checked her pulse. She was alive. Phew. That would take a whole lot of explaining if he'd failed her, although he had an even bigger question. Where the heck was Meaghan? She was supposed to be trailing and guarding her all day. Meaghan had fantastic instincts when it came to the protection of her subjects. Yet, in this instance, she wasn't in sight. Instead, Allison had been left alone to be attacked and almost kidnapped.

The beagle's incessant barking started to push Noah's last limits. Exasperated, he shouted, "Quiet!" To his surprise, the dog obeyed. "Good dog," he whispered, his heart still pounding from the rush of adrenaline.

He called Jason and updated him on everything that happened. "Have you heard from Meaghan?"

"She's been caught up in something going on in Rhode Island." Jason provided no more insight into Meaghan's failure to be there, so Noah didn't question him further. He had enough going on.

"Do you want me to call an ambulance or take Allison to a hospital?" Noticing a rag next to her, Noah lifted it. Soaked. He could smell the sweet smell of chloroform and pulled it away from his nose quickly. "I think she was drugged. Chloroform is my best guess."

"They wanted her alive. Otherwise, they would have shot her and been done with it. They'll be back. We need to increase security on her. Bring her in. I'll have our medical team look at her. We can't trust anyone," he responded.

The beagle circled Allison, his body shaking. From the glass on the floor to the risk someone would return to shoot the little guy, Noah made a decision.

"I need to bring in Allison's dog too," he told Jason. The dog had also been sort of a hero, slowing the attackers down, and he was currently licking Allison's face. They probably needed each other.

"A dog?"

"Protecting the person includes protecting everyone they love."

Jason exhaled loud enough to send Noah's stomach to the floor. "Fine."

After he hung up, Noah searched around for the dog's leash. Instead of a leash, he found the body of an older woman. He braced himself for the fallout and then called Jason back.

Because they were being paid by someone deep in the government to look into corruption, the team had to handle this fiasco with finesse. Two team members arrived to help transport an unconscious Allison to their medical center so her name would not be listed on a hackable hospital databank. The dog accompanied Noah to headquarters. He preferred to ride on Noah's lap, which was not going to happen, so he created an area in the back seat where he could fasten the harness. As Noah drove, the dog got into his M&M's. He called his sister, a longtime dog owner, to confirm that the dog would not, in fact, die after ingesting three candies and then he met with Jason.

The minute he saw Jason's expression, he knew he was in trouble. The beagle did not pick up on the same cues and rushed over to the man who could make or break Noah's career, tail wagging and whining in an excited manner. Jason rubbed his head, but then stood up out of the dog's reach and focused on Noah.

Before Jason had a chance to criticize him, Noah said, "We would have been better off if I'd followed Allison into her apartment immediately."

"Except we were hired to watch over things, and now we've taken custody of the person we were supposed to be watching, never mind having to place an untraceable call to 9-1-1 to get local law enforcement to investigate a scream from Goodwyn's apartment so they can locate the body." He shook his head.

"Is she okay? Not the neighbor, but Allison."

"Dr. Morgan thinks she'll be fine after she sleeps off the chloroform. Good job figuring out what drugged her. It saved Allison a whole battery of blood tests."

"Do you want me back at the apartment?"

"Not right now. The place is crawling with a whole department of forensics ready to get out of the office for the day. Just stay here and help Calvin do some analysis. Maybe talk to Allison when she wakes. You have the friendliest face of all of us, including Meaghan. She's beautiful, but damn she could stare a person into an early grave. I'll have her step in to watch over her when she gets back."

Noah frowned. He'd just fought off two armed men and stopped a kidnapping and was still deemed a second stringer.

Chapter Three

Zoe woke with a bear of a headache. Used to living in a resort town where drunk tourists caused most of the problems, she hadn't expected to find both an unconscious woman and a burglar in her sister's apartment. But she did. The sensation of large hands wrapped around her neck crept over her sanity and made her stomach twist. She blinked her eyes open and looked around the unfamiliar room. Marlowe slept at the foot of her bed curled up tight like a doughnut. He was the only thing that looked familiar. The beige-painted room seemed sterile, hospital like, but not exactly. Maybe more of a hotel room with a small sitting area and a table, but there were no windows. *No windows?* That one fact unnerved her. The only things in the room that could be considered comforting were three paintings of a rocky coastline with pathways bordered by rosebushes. While they provided some color and interest, they couldn't transform the blandness of the room into an inviting space.

The door swung open and a woman dressed in a pink designer pantsuit and crisp white blouse entered. She was stalled by a visit from Marlowe, who had jumped off the bed to sniff the woman's legs. She greeted him with a rub under his chin, then turned her attention back to Zoe. "You're awake. Good. I'm Dr. Morgan." More fashionable than anyone Zoe knew in the medical field, the woman, no older than forty, wore her hair up in a messy bun and tortoiseshell glasses perched on her head. "How are you feeling?"

"Like I'm hungover." Her body had few actual aches and pains. Instead, she felt off internally, both physically and psychologically. Her attacker haunted her waking thoughts. Just the idea of a stranger putting his hands on her sent shivers down her spine.

The doctor nodded. "That's expected with chloroform."

The memory of a cloth covering her mouth before she passed out added to her queasiness. "Chloroform? How? Why?"

"Lots of questions that need answers. It seems you were drugged, but I did an exam and from what I saw, you're otherwise in good shape. Do you have any pain anywhere?"

"A smashing headache."

"Also expected. Drinking water will help."

Zoe stared at the person who called herself a doctor and paused. At present, Zoe didn't know whether she was a captive or in the basement room of a hospital, although not many hospitals allowed pets. "Where am I and when can I leave?" she asked.

The alleged doctor's lips pressed into a thin line. "Let me tell Jason you're finally conscious. He'll be able to explain more to you." With that, she moved toward the door.

Zoe needed answers. Who did this to her? What happened to Allison? Where was she? Then another question came to mind. "Wait. What about Mrs. Peterson? Is she okay?"

Dr. Morgan's dramatic pause said too much. "I'll let Jason talk to you about that too."

Zoe leaned back into the bed. So much had happened. She wanted to call her father. A retired chief of police, he'd be able to give her that calm reassuring voice that had been her backbone whenever life had become too much, but her phone wasn't anywhere near her. Several possible scenarios filled her mind. Was this a random act of violence? Had someone targeted Allison? If the man had been after Allison, was she still in danger? Where the heck was Allison? Where the heck had Zoe ended up? It felt like living through a true crime story, except this time, she was at the heart of the drama, without the protective screen of a television. Unlike Allison, who loved adventure and challenges, Zoe preferred tranquility and comfort. This was all way too much for her.

Adding to her confusion, a man with beachy brown hair casually tousled like a swimwear model entered her room, leaving the door open. His sun-kissed skin and relaxed demeanor suggested he spent plenty of time by the sea.

"Jason?" she asked, her voice tinged with hope and confusion.

He shook his head, his frown steady, or perhaps it was concern. Dressed in an untucked blue button-down and khakis, he looked more like one of the guys who weekended on Nantucket during the summer crush than someone who could assist with her current predicament. The fabric of his shirt hinted at a lean, athletic build.

He pulled up a chair beside her bed and sat down, his whole aura more compassionate than critical. "I'm Noah. Noah Montgomery."

She stared at him, trying to place his face. Her silence must have prodded him to explain himself.

"We met at your apartment. I guess *met* isn't the right word. I found you unconscious and being dragged out by two men. I made enough of a fuss to scare them off. Luckily, they left you behind." He shrugged modestly. "I wish I'd been able to stop them. It would make figuring out who they are easier. Unless you have any idea who targeted you. From the circumstances, they wanted you alive." He spoke as though her everyday life came out of a thriller novel, no shock or drama, just facts.

Marlowe jumped onto her visitor's lap, his tail wagging forcefully. Noah rubbed behind his ears and gave him a partial smile to calm him down. Marlowe settled.

Zoe felt comfortable in Noah Montgomery's presence as well, despite her unanswered questions. Yet something he said stuck out to her. She had assumed only one man had attacked her.

"They? I only remember one person in the apartment," she said, trying to make sense of it all. The memory of the man who had grabbed her from behind and tried to suffocate her sent a shiver through her again. She could feel him against her back and the large palm of his hand over her mouth. She couldn't remember anything after that. The knowledge she'd been violated washed over her, lifting her heart rate and shaking her well-being. Her current location, stuck in this cell of a room, offered no relief.

"I encountered two men when I arrived. They were carrying you toward the front door. I stopped them from taking you, but couldn't prevent them from escaping." He sounded annoyed with himself. Perhaps he was Allison's current boyfriend. She changed her partners the way most people changed their sheets. Monthly. And he was the right age. On second thought, this guy wasn't Allison's type. She preferred muscular guys forced to order bespoke suits because of their shoulder widths. This guy seemed more like a tennis pro. Athletic, but not in a hang-out-in-the-weight-room kind of way. He also didn't seem as condescending as Allison's typical man candy. Most of her exes looked down their noses at Zoe as though she were the sale rack version of her identical twin.

"Why were you in her apartment?"

He continued rubbing behind Marlowe's ears. "I'm with Fresh Pond Security. You have a target on your back, and we've been charged with keeping you safe. It's best if you remain out of sight for the next few days, at least until the threat can be minimized."

"Threat?" She tried to process everything, but her brain wasn't functioning at 100 percent with the drug clouding her thoughts.

"I interrupted whoever was in the apartment, but they're still out there. Do you have any place you can go until this dies down? If not, we have a secluded cabin in Maine," he said. His demeanor stayed relaxed, but those dark eyes held a seriousness that sent chills through Zoe.

Her heartbeat sped up as she processed his words. This guy with his wind-tousled hair thought she was Allison, and Allison was in trouble. Big trouble. And Allison needed protection to keep from getting attacked or worse. She'd always pushed for more and more dangerous assignments. While still in college, she'd found proof of sexual misconduct by the dean at her university. Protests erupted on campus on both sides, and the dean, his back against the wall, threatened to shut the whole paper down. His threats didn't intimidate Allison. She fought him until the day she graduated. Her story brought him down. Reporting the truth was her calling. If her current assignment had even higher stakes, Zoe was terrified for her.

"You're not law enforcement?" she asked the stranger, unease growing in her voice.

"No, but we work closely with law enforcement," he responded.

"So I can call the police to verify all of this." She glanced around for her phone again, not finding it anywhere.

"I'd prefer you didn't. If your whereabouts get to the wrong people, protecting you will become nearly impossible."

Panic set in. For some reason, she'd thought she was being held at a police station, sort of, but not entirely. Instead, she was trapped in this protection agency's office? She sat up. She needed to contact Allison.

"I can't protect you if you run," he stated, his tone firm yet devoid of aggression. "There's a whole team working to protect you. We can decide on the next course of action when we all get together. There's been a lot of rumblings about what you've uncovered. People will go to great lengths to keep that information hidden."

The words seemed benign enough, but something dangerous threaded through every word he said. Someone was after Allison and currently, this man thought she was Allison. Whether he could help her or not, she couldn't risk lingering a moment longer.

On the other hand, if he'd wanted to hurt her, he would have. They were alone, minus a dog who seemed to prefer his company to hers. If Allison was out there somewhere, these people would turn their attention to finding her and letting Zoe go. But Zoe couldn't unleash the hounds after her only sibling. Perhaps if they thought they had Allison, Allison would be safe.

Chapter Four

Noah had put hours and hours into his job, assuring he earned every dollar of his generous salary and proving himself an asset to the team. Lately, however, after the gunshot wound, he felt an even stronger need to demonstrate his worth. His last field assignment had been protecting Jason's son, Matt. That had been the day Matt was kidnapped and Noah was shot in the hip. Despite the team getting Matt back to safety, Noah couldn't forgive himself. This new assignment was a chance to start over. How hard could it be to protect a woman who regularly took on criminal enterprises and challenged the status quo?

Taking a deep breath to ground himself in his current assignment, he observed the woman in front of him. She wasn't at all what he'd expected after watching her on the news over the past few years. On-screen, Allison was poised and confident, her hair and makeup perfectly done, drawing viewers in with her calm assuredness as she reported stories. But here, as she moaned and stretched, waking her muscles from a drug-induced slumber, she looked soft and sweet. Without makeup, her natural beauty exuded a girl next door quality, so different from her on-screen persona. He'd expected confident, loud, and demanding. Instead, she seemed more reserved, although that could also be the chloroform wearing off.

Taking him by surprise, she stood, causing her dog to hop off his lap and stand at her feet.

"What are you doing?" he asked, prepared to catch her if her body hadn't regained its strength.

She grabbed a Black Dog sweatshirt from the end of the bed and pulled it over her head. "I need to get going. Thanks for everything."

She'd never get out of the locked facility, and trying would only cause her more distress than necessary, so he stood back and tried to act nonconfrontational. He wasn't her enemy and didn't want to act like one. She needed to trust him and the whole team.

"You aren't ready to get up and around. Why don't you wait for the doctor?" he suggested, hoping it might persuade her to stay.

"The doctor said all I needed was water. I think that means I can go as long as I hydrate when I get home." She sat on the edge of the bed and pulled on her shoes.

Noah couldn't allow her to leave, so he called Jason. "Our guest would like to leave. I was hoping you'd have the opportunity to meet her first. Can I escort her into the conference room?"

"Anything wrong?" Jason asked clearly sensing trouble.

"It would be easier to explain in person." Noah's eyes stayed on Allison, who had stood again and seemed ready to bolt.

"Sure. I'm in conference room three."

Despite being knocked out for almost an hour, their guest appeared stable enough. Until she wasn't. Her body swayed too far to the left and he dived several feet in order to stop her from crashing onto the floor.

Wrapping his arms around her, he curved into her fall and cushioned her impact with the floor. They landed together with a thud. Marlowe raced to them, barking. Allison didn't move. Her body pressed against his, her elbow digging into his side. Noah gently slid her arm from his rib cage and let out a deep breath. The pain from the hard impact made any potential meet-cute feel more like corporal punishment.

As the pain subsided, they both stayed still for a moment.

Their faces inches apart, Noah became acutely aware of every detail—the softness of her lips, the amber flecks in her eyes, the way her hair framed her face. Then Marlowe pushed his way in and licked her cheek.

"Um…thanks," she whispered, maybe to him or maybe to Marlowe. "I should probably stay seated for a while longer. You don't mind waiting here for a few minutes, do you?"

He couldn't suppress the smile. "I have nothing else to do but be your personal cushion."

The floral scent of her hair was intoxicating, her proximity overwhelming, and the feel of her in his arms relaxing and painfully heavy.

"Can I help you up?" he asked.

"Probably not, since I'm sitting on you," she said, her tone light.

"Perhaps I should rephrase. You're killing me. Can you get up?" he quipped, trying to keep their connection lighthearted.

She laughed and nodded, carefully shifting her weight. "I think I can manage that." With a bit of effort, she moved off him and sat down on the side of the bed.

Noah sat up, rubbing his side. "I think staying seated is a good idea. I don't know if I have it in me to catch you again."

"I don't have it in me to fall again," she said, her eyes meeting his with a grateful smile. "Thanks for catching me."

"Anytime," he replied. His heart raced at the memory of her in his arms.

They sat for a few moments in silence until the quiet became the largest presence in the room. Before he could break the awkwardness, she was back on her feet, but not steady at all.

"What are you doing?"

"I really need to leave," she insisted. "No offense, but this place feels more like a jail cell than a safe house. I'm highly claustrophobic and need windows. If you can offer me an arm, I'm sure I can walk out of here fine."

Against his better judgment, since she needed rest, not a stroll down the hall, he wrapped an arm around her and helped her balance as they strode the forty yards to the conference room. It was better than explaining to Jason why the person they were supposed to look after was struggling to escape. Marlowe, his leash dragging behind him, trotted next to them.

The hallway to the conference room was quiet, save for the soft hum of the air-conditioning. When they arrived, Jason looked up from a map on the table. With his black hair pulled back in a ponytail, Jason seemed more like a motorcycle gang leader than a former military officer and business owner. Despite the ribbing he caught from the rest of the team, he insisted his wife, Fiona, preferred it that way.

Dr. Morgan came from behind them and rushed to Allison's side. "You look dizzy." She glared at Noah as though he'd dragged her out of bed.

"I'm a bit shaky on my feet, but I insisted on moving around." She surveyed the room, her eyes scanning every door, every screen, every person in the area.

"Understood, but let's not overdo it." Dr. Morgan pulled out a chair. "Take a seat. Noah, why would you let her walk around?"

"It was not my choice."

The doctor shook her head, then turned to Allison. "If you need anything, have someone call me. I'll be down the hall."

After she left, Noah and Jason's attention turned toward their guest. Despite her lack of makeup or camera-perfect hair, Allison's appearance commanded attention, altering the room's dynamics.

"Are you Jason?" she asked.

"I am. You must be Allison," he said as he bent down to pet Marlowe. "I've already met this furry fellow. Not the best trained dog in the world, but his friendliness makes up for it."

She nodded. "He's only trained to live in an apartment and curl up on the bed at night."

"I'm sure he does a great job at that." Jason's phone rang. He acknowledged the room and then stepped out to answer it. When he returned only minutes later, his demeanor had changed. "That was Meaghan. She's held up for a bit."

He walked around to Allison and sized her up, as though she were now a criminal defendant. "Do you feel okay, Ms. Goodwyn?"

"Yes, but I'm ready to go home."

"I'm sure you are. Before you go, I'd love it if you could answer a few questions."

"Um. I'll try."

"Good. Have you spoken to Brendan Quinn about what you're accusing him of?"

She stared back at Jason frozen in silence as though she had no idea what he was speaking about. But she'd been the person who had stirred up this controversy after chasing down a tip from one of the clerks at City Hall.

"Yes or no?" Jason demanded.

She looked at Noah, but he had no idea if she'd seen the city council member. Part of him wanted to step in and comfort her, but Jason was never mean to anyone he was protecting. Something was wrong.

After an uncomfortably long time, she shook her head. "No."

"That's interesting. We received information that you cornered him in City Hall Plaza in front of a crowd of tourists, made wild accusations with no evidence, and left. That doesn't sound like a sound investigative technique. Do you have any idea how fast evidence can be buried?"

"I...um...no."

"No, you didn't confront him or you didn't know how fast evidence could be buried?"

"Both." She took a few deep breaths and stayed silent.

Jason leaned in, his gaze as dangerous as a crowbar. "People want you dead. Do you know that?"

She swallowed hard, then nodded.

"And you're prepared for attempts on your own life?"

"Absolutely." Her voice grew more confident.

Jason's expression remained intense. "What about someone in your family's life?"

The question hit her like a physical blow. She recoiled, as though struck squarely by that imaginary crowbar.

Chapter Five

Zoe had never been so scared in her life. This gangster of a man seemed to want her head on a platter. Not hers, but her sister's.

Noah, the one person who seemed trustworthy, stepped forward. "What are you doing? She's not the enemy. She was almost killed."

His boss completely ignored him and stared Zoe down. "Do you think they'll leave your family alone? They'll hunt down everyone you love and destroy them."

"I'll do whatever it takes to protect them." She meant every word, although she wasn't entirely sure what that would entail.

"I believe you, but I won't protect a liar. Until you come clean, you're on your own and so is your family." He crossed his arms over his chest and glared at her.

Zoe could feel the weight of Jason's stare boring into her. Noah stood beside him, his expression confused. He had no idea that she wasn't Allison, but Jason certainly did. She should never have lied. Lies were always discovered, as she said to her third graders all the time. She couldn't argue with Jason, because he had the truth on his side, so she chose to defuse the bomb in the only way she knew how, with the truth.

Defeat weighed her down as she sank back into her chair. "I'm not Allison. I'm Zoe, her twin sister," she confessed in barely a whisper.

"Right." Noah's expression turned skeptical.

She had hoped for understanding from him, maybe even some empathy. Instead, she received suspicion and doubt. He'd believed she was Allison and she'd lied to him. For some reason, losing the trust of this stranger bothered her as much as all the events of the past few hours…this was all too much. A tear fell down her cheek. She dropped her head to hide the mountain of emotions threatening to erupt.

"I like my privacy, and she likes her fame," she said.

Noah's brows lifted. "That's convenient. A sister who just happened to be in her apartment?"

"Yes. She asked me to watch Marlowe." Her shame turned to annoyance.

"And why should we believe you?"

"I have nothing to lie about. Someone attacked me in her apartment, and I thought Allison would be safer if I took on her identity." She always took care of Allison. She turned to Jason. "I'm telling you, I'm not Allison. I'm her sister, Zoe."

Noah maintained his stance. "We can't just take your word for it. For all we know, you want to play the hero and dig up more dirt, but that's only angering your enemies and people will die because of it. If they don't silence you, they'll end up silencing everyone involved in the scheme and that's a lot of deaths in Boston we intend to prevent."

"Check my driver's license. It'll prove my identity." Zoe spun around, forgetting she didn't have her phone or the attached wallet.

Jason, however, took a phone off the table—her phone—and handed it to her. He seemed to be the control center of the entire place. Her wallet was still attached to the back. She gave it to Noah, who took out her license. He examined it closely, comparing the photo and details with the person standing before him.

In the photo, she was smiling. A huge smile that generally wasn't allowed in government identifications, but the photographer had been a friend from high school and was making faces at her.

"Look at the name, the birth date. It's all there. I'm Zoe, not Allison," she said.

"It seems legitimate," he conceded, handing the wallet to Jason, who was calmly scratching Marlowe behind his ears. Marlowe's tail thumped in pleasure.

Noah studied the wallpaper on the phone. Zoe caught a glimpse of it and held her breath. The picture was of two high school– or college-aged women, unmistakably identical in their shared laughter. Both in graduation gowns and both seeming so young.

Grief flooded her eyes. "My mother took this photo. It was the last photo she ever took of us. She died a few weeks later."

"I'm sorry."

She shrugged. "It feels like a lifetime ago. My father and I live with her memory every day in the house she'd put her heart into."

He put the license back into its compartment and handed the phone to Jason.

"Incredible," Jason murmured, the word hanging in the air. "You look just like your twin. Identical?"

She nodded.

"You knew?" Noah asked Jason.

"Meaghan's with Allison right now." Jason handed the wallet back to her.

"Is she okay?" Zoe asked.

His interrogator demeanor had disappeared and his expression softened. "Meaghan found her in a small hospital ER in Rhode Island. She was hit by a car. Nothing life ending, but I think she'll be holed up in the hospital for a week or two."

Zoe nearly fell from her seat, but Noah shot out toward her and wrapped an arm around her to keep her steady. Jason looked as though he'd run in to help too if needed.

"Did someone target her?" Zoe asked, her expression falling.

"We don't know," Jason said. "Probably. A group of high schoolers who arrived to party in the parking lot for the last day of school must have scared away the car that hit her. It allowed her time to drag herself away from the area, which saved her life. Our team is already at the hospital. They blocked her name from reaching the computer so she is hidden for now. I'll have Calvin Ross, our chief of technology, scrub the medical records and Meaghan will remain with her."

"What about me?" Noah asked.

"Carry on watching over Zoe. With her looks, she could be easily misidentified as her sister. Since they'd targeted Allison in Rhode Island, the people in Allison's apartment wouldn't have been after her, so they must have been there looking for something. Maybe her evidence that linked Brendan Quinn to the person bribing him? Your appearance must have confused them. Even so, it's best you remained here."

Remain? Zoe recoiled from Noah as she realized that they intended to keep her in this basement. "I'm not staying here. I have to see Allison."

"Too risky," Jason replied. "I don't want anyone seeing you around there or you'll tip them off to your sister's location."

Zoe wasn't having it. "I have to be with her. She needs me. You can't keep me here. That's kidnapping."

Noah nodded. "Fine, I'll drive you."

A very chic woman, about five feet nothing, her blond hair in a ponytail, entered the room and pointed at Zoe as though she had heard the whole conversation. "We can hide her appearance. I think it's a good idea for her to see Allison. For both of them. Her presence will keep also Allison from bolting." She turned to Zoe and put out her hand. "I'm Fiona. I hope everyone is treating you well."

The more Zoe stared at the woman, the more familiar she seemed. Fiona? "Fiona Stirling, the author?"

"I try to keep my work with Fresh Pond Security quiet."

Noah stepped in. "She's more of a ghost employee."

"You're a security guard too?" Zoe couldn't believe such a successful author had to have a part-time gig to make ends meet.

Fiona laughed. "I like to think of myself as a consultant."

"You're one of my favorite writers," Zoe gushed. Fiona wrote amazing romantic thrillers that took place all over the world. Her presence increased her trust in Fresh Pond Security, despite having no other knowledge of her.

"Thank you. It's nice meeting you."

As people stood to leave, Zoe called out to stop everyone. "Wait. What about Mrs. Peterson? Is she here?"

Jason shook his head. "She's in the morgue."

The whole room stopped, all sight and sound frozen on those words. Her face fell and words failed her as she realized she too could have ended up in the morgue.

Chapter Six

Zoe remained silent as Noah drove to a small hospital in the southernmost part of Rhode Island. So many things had happened to her in the past twelve hours—almost kidnapped, assaulted, drugged. The frightening blur of chloroform and the terror of finding Mrs. Peterson's lifeless body haunted her. She stared out at the highway, trying to avoid the image of Mrs. Peterson's bloodstained hair. She was not cut out for all of this. She needed Allison.

"How long until we get there?" she asked, observing traffic crawling along the highway.

Noah continued watching the road. "Ten minutes."

Zoe couldn't wait. They'd been driving almost two hours. She tapped her fingers together until Noah turned and looked at her.

"It's rush hour. I can only go so fast without getting us killed."

"I know. It's just with everything going on, I want to see her with my own eyes to know she's safe."

He nodded. "We've got her under a false name, tucked away in a secluded room. We need to keep a low profile when we go in."

Touching the blond wig on her head, she mumbled, "I've never looked good as a blonde."

"It's not a beauty contest. You need to be unrecognizable, forgettable." He glanced over at her and nodded as though she'd achieved their goal.

"I'm perfect then." Dressed in a baggy URI sweatshirt, ill-fitting jeans, and oversize sneakers, she felt far from herself—let alone beautiful like Allison.

When they arrived, they slipped through the hospital's back service entrance and down sterile corridors to a small room where Allison lay.

The sight of her sister knocked her back. Allison looked like hell. Her face appeared pale and sickly with dark circles under her eyes. Her legs were immobilized, one in a full cast, and a bandage encircled her ribs. IVs and tubing appeared to anchor her to the bed. Zoe swallowed back the horror of seeing her sister so broken and banged up. Her fingers trembled as she took Allison's hand.

"How are you feeling, Ally?" Zoe's voice faltered as she took her sister's hand.

"Like I've been hit by a truck." Her usual flair for the dramatic was now a grim and sober reality.

"I was so worried about you." Zoe squeezed her hand. "I don't know whether to be thankful for you being alive or breaking down because of your injuries."

Allison closed her eyes for a moment. "Let's be thankful I'm not dead, although before they gave me the pain meds, I might not have minded."

"Don't say that." Zoe held back the tears forming in her eyes, as a lump formed in her throat. The idea of losing her sister left a huge hole inside her.

Noah introduced Meaghan, the person in charge of protecting Allison, to Zoe. She stood off to the side, a gorgeous tall sentinel in black cargo pants and a gray T-shirt. Although she seemed very beautiful, her demeanor remained calm, yet alert, seemingly ready to battle at a moment's notice. Her and Noah's presence made the room feel safer, protected.

As Zoe sat with Allison, she caught some of Meaghan and Noah's conversation.

"Nice seeing you back in action," Meaghan said, punching Noah on the arm.

"I'm just watching over Zoe for now." He sounded resigned in his role as chauffeur and guardian to Allison's sister. Not that Zoe blamed him. She wasn't in danger like Allison, and that's where all the resources should be placed.

"That's a step up."

"It is. Keeps me off of surveillance and more in the field. I honestly thought she was Allison when I met her."

Meaghan looked toward both sisters. "She does look similar, but you should be able to notice the difference. There are markers in each person and even twins carry themselves in different ways. Understanding people is a skill set you need to develop."

"I have years of analysis at my fingertips."

"Logic is only one tool in your belt, instinct is arguably the more powerful weapon." Meaghan spoke with a self-confidence that appeared earned through experience.

Noah frowned at her comment, then took a step back toward the wall and blended into the room, looking more like a boyfriend than a bodyguard. Bodyguards in Zoe's mind wore suits and earpieces, and never smiled, although she might be confusing them with Secret Service agents.

Zoe wondered about Meaghan's comments. Was she so dissimilar from Allison that their differences were visible? Probably. Allison stood taller, carried herself with more confidence, and could walk in high heels.

She stared at her sister's broken leg. She couldn't fathom the amount of pain Allison had been in. Their differences didn't matter when one of them was hurting. "Who would do such a thing to you?"

Allison shook her head, her expression falling further. "I have no idea," she whispered, pain evident in her voice. "I was meeting a source at the Enchanted Forest—an abandoned amusement park. I was supposed to meet someone with information on the bribes. Then everything went wrong."

Meaghan interrupted them. "I sent your statement to my boss, but he had some follow-up questions. Do you mind another round of questions?"

"Go ahead." Allison tried to sit up, but after wincing and letting out a moan that broke Zoe's heart, she remained in her current position.

"What we know so far is that you were found unconscious on the road about ten miles from here by a woman in an SUV. She called the police and they transported you here. No identification, no phone." Meaghan spoke methodically, like a police officer questioning a victim at a crime scene.

Allison tried to sit up again, the effort leaving her breathless. "I should never have gone alone."

"Why would the news station send you alone?" Noah asked.

"I'm pretty gutsy, but even I wouldn't subject myself to the ghosts of evil clowns without backup," Meaghan added.

"I've looked into stories alone before. Not in such isolated locations, but Glenn, my producer, sent me, insisting I go without the cameraman so I don't scare them off. I've always trusted him," Allison murmured, a hint of betrayal in her tone. "Now? I don't know."

"Do you know who you were supposed to meet?" Noah asked without the directness of Meaghan, less interrogation and more a conversation with a friend.

"I was supposed to meet someone who had information for me, but I received no name or description of the person. There was a source inside City Hall, a staffer who had sent invoices and a few other strange zoning requests. The papers are in my office. From what Glenn had said, I'd assumed the person I was meeting was a new source. But I should never have gone alone. I get that now." Her voice was filled with regret, something Zoe had never seen in her sister.

While Zoe sat beside her, the gravity of the situation sank in. Allison, the fearless journalist, seemed so vulnerable.

"I'm here for you," Zoe said. She squeezed her sister's hand and received a squeeze back.

"I know you are. Where's Marlowe? He needs to eat every four hours or he's a grouch." Allison looked around the room now completely consumed by the whereabouts of her dog.

"He stayed back with the team at headquarters. Just tell me what he eats and I'll have someone get it for him. He seems to have adopted Calvin, our chief of technology. He'll be spoiled," Noah replied.

"Thank you. He has raw hamburger mixed with peas for breakfast and a cup of his salmon kibble for dinner." Allison's demands probably came off as spoiled to Meaghan and Noah, but that was how Allison did everything—perfection or not at all.

Zoe never had the money to spoil her cat Dory the way Allison spoiled Marlowe. "I'm sure he'll be okay with some regular kibble tonight."

Allison, hating to compromise on anything, conceded with a sigh. "I suppose so. Do you know when I can go home?"

Zoe looked at Meaghan, who stared at Allison with a frown. And at that moment, Zoe realized Allison had no idea what had happened at the apartment. And Zoe wasn't going to tell her. Not right now.

"The doctor thinks you need to stay on bed rest for at least two weeks," Meaghan said.

"Two weeks? How can I continue my investigation?" She'd never been able to relax when there was work to be done. Zoe doubted Allison would be able to stay locked away without someone tying her to the bed.

"Is it that important? You were almost killed." Zoe had almost been killed as well, and Mrs. Peterson, well, Zoe didn't want to think about that memory at the moment.

"Yes. It makes a difference. If a bunch of thugs can run the city and bribe the government, then the city I love is going to spiral into someplace I don't want to live. I'm willing to risk my life for it."

Chapter Seven

With both side by side, Noah now saw the unmistakable resemblance of Allison and Zoe, despite the blond wig and baggy clothes Zoe sported. They shared the same long brown hair, same tawny eyes, same high cheekbones, and perfect lips. Not that he was focused on Zoe's lips, but they seemed as though someone had drawn them a perfect Cupid's bow. He shook his head to refocus. There were also significant differences between them that Meaghan had already hinted at. Meaghan, with her years on a police force, read people with decent accuracy. Allison spoke in a crisp, confident manner, while Zoe had a softer tone. Allison demanded. Zoe preferred to ask, even if she'd already made up her mind. Overall, however, they could switch places and be damn convincing.

Their resemblance meant Zoe was in as much danger as Allison if she walked out of here without protection. Whatever story Allison had found, it had tentacles. An internal investigation arm of the government wanted to have the whole story before people or evidence disappeared. They, whoever they were, had paid Fresh Pond Security to handle the investigation. After years of uncovering money laundering crimes by criminal organizations, Noah could sense the depth of the corruption. In addition to whatever was going on at City Hall, the atmosphere at Allison's newsroom reeked of a cover-up.

No responsible producer would send a young reporter on their own to an abandoned place unless they had ill intent or were an idiot. Which meant her producer had just become a person of interest, and maybe more people in the newsroom were associated with this. Payoffs for ignoring or shifting stories were not so unusual in parts of the news media.

Noah finally spoke his thoughts aloud, breaking the silence in the room. "How much do you trust your producer?"

"Glenn? He hired me years ago for my first job. I owe my whole career to him," Allison replied.

"Then why would he send you alone to such a vulnerable spot?"

"He told me something was brewing, and I wanted to break the story. I volunteered myself for the assignment."

Noah swallowed a curt reply to her obvious death wish. He didn't need to voice his annoyance that she disregarded all the warnings that had to have been going off in her head, because Zoe did.

"You volunteered to meet people in a secluded location? What were you thinking? I know your career is important to you, but you're important to me. You could have been killed." Zoe stared at her twin with her mouth open.

Allison, despite her injuries, seemed defiant. "I wasn't though."

"No, but Mrs. Peterson was," Zoe blurted out. "Someone has rummaged through all your papers at your apartment, and Mrs. Pederson was an innocent victim. And I almost was too. Don't you care about the bigger implications of this?"

Damn it. Zoe should have kept her mouth shut. Allison did not need to know about the murder of her neighbor. Not at this instant. But it was too late.

Allison flinched as though someone had struck her. "What? When? Why? Oh my God. I had no idea."

The alarms on one of her monitors screeched out what had to be her internal distress, and a nurse rushed in. "What's going on?"

Allison, now in tears, started choking.

"You'll all have to leave. She needs rest." The nurse did not seem at all impressed by her visitors' collective ability to rile her patient.

Zoe, now in tears as well, held on to her hand. "I'll be back as soon as things calm down. I promise." She reached over and hugged her, but was dragged away by the nurse.

"You too," the nurse said to Meaghan.

"I'm staying put." Meaghan remained leaning against the wall in the precise spot she was at when they entered the room. She was blessed with the ability to remain on her feet all day and show zero signs of wear.

The nurse scowled. Meaghan scowled back, but didn't move a fraction of an inch. Noah waited for a standoff, but the nurse must have known from the look on Meaghan's face, she wasn't leaving Allison's side.

Noah and Zoe walked past an abandoned nursing desk and a few medical staff pushing mobile workstations, allowing for staff to work more with less backup. A boom for the bottom line, but not for employee morale. Noah thought of his sister Elise slaving away in a hospital near San Francisco. A NICU nurse, she cared for the most fragile of newborns. She didn't make nearly enough to compensate her for her work ethic. Noah's salary was almost four times hers. Granted, he had bullets to avoid, but she fought infections and birth defects and cardiac issues. And her success rate was much higher than his.

Perhaps it was thoughts of his sister, but an emptiness followed him into the cafeteria. There were too many days when he had no idea how he could give any more of himself to this career. The men and women around him had far more experience than him, so he made up for it by working more hours. Yet, until he could be assigned to something that involved more people interaction, he wasn't going to get better. So far, his two big chances at showing his skills involved failing to protect Jason's son when he was kidnapped and foiling two kidnappers going after Zoe, but failing to stop the men from escaping.

He followed Zoe, looking down halls, listening for anything unusual, and making sure she was protected at all times. He dreaded the thought of letting someone else down. The cafeteria had a few medical staff lingering around, but not many other people. They both grabbed some coffee, he opted for a blueberry muffin, and she chose a cup of strawberry yogurt, courtesy of Fresh Pond Security.

He pointed Zoe to a table in the quiet corner away from the windows. She sat in a rigid plastic chair, her eyes red rimmed, her hands clasped tight around her coffee cup. He sat in a way that blocked her from prying eyes. Even with her disguise, she was at risk being out in the open. She had the kind of demeanor that caused people to take notice. Or maybe it was just him noticing her, feeling bad that she'd been dragged into such a mess because of the dangerous decisions of her sister.

Breaking the silence, Noah leaned forward and offered Zoe a piece of his muffin. "It's not great, but it's warm." His voice came through as a low rumble in the sterile coldness of the hospital.

Zoe managed a faint, grateful smile as she accepted the piece, the warmth from her coffee cup jumping from her fingers to his.

"Thank you," she murmured, her gaze meeting his long enough that he noticed the deep brown of her eyes, like polished wood, rich and inviting. Eyes a man could easily get lost in.

He nodded, his fingers lingering on hers for a moment longer than necessary. He felt gratitude from the slight smile she gifted him and the way she sighed as she swallowed the muffin as if thanking him for being there while her world crumbled around her. At least that was his interpretation. She could just be tired and her defenses had long since collapsed.

Leaning back in her chair, she closed her eyes and took a slow, deliberate sip of the coffee. He was staring. Uncomfortably. When her eyes opened, he looked down at his own cup while battling with the conflicting sides of his professional duty and the personal sentiments that had unexpectedly taken root over the last few hours.

Zoe shivered in the cold air-conditioned room, and he reacted without thought. He removed his jacket and gently draped it over her shoulders. As the fabric settled around her, some of the tension melted from her neck and jaw. She glanced up at him, and for a moment, the hustle of the hospital faded away.

They stared at each other, not a word said between them, but a thousand emotions, an acknowledgment of the danger, a concern for Allison, and something more that he refused to define because it would break protocol. Her appreciation for his gesture did nothing to send him back to a more neutral professional attitude toward her.

Zoe fiddled with the lid to her coffee cup, her mind probably down the hall where Allison lay recuperating. She'd seen a dead body, been attacked and drugged, effectively kidnapped by Fresh Pond Security, and seen her sister, not only injured, but in traction. Yet, Zoe wasn't crying in a ball on the floor or begging to be hidden away. She had guts.

Based on everything he'd gathered so far, this involved people willing to do whatever it took to stop the story and silence anyone who had information about the bribes. Allison had identified a key player: City Councillor Brendan Quinn. Noah's mind raced through a labyrinth of possibilities and scenarios. If only they could sneak into the news studio and uncover why the producer had sent Allison out alone. He could simply be a moron or be tied to something more sinister.

A plan formed in Noah's head. It seemed like a desperate shot in the dark at first, but the more he thought about it, the more the pieces fit together. Zoe, with her resemblance to Allison, could keep the investigation alive. Though dangerous, learning the bigger players now was better than hiding Zoe and Allison away indefinitely.

The clatter of trays handled by the kitchen staff and the distant call of a code from another part of the hospital created a disjointed soundtrack to his internal deliberations. It was risky, but so was allowing Allison's investigation to remain in limbo while she healed from her injuries.

"Did you ever switch places with your sister when growing up?" he asked, trying to sound conversational.

"Once when we were about five. Our mother knew instantly, so we never tried again. Allison walks and talks in a different way from me. Our looks are about the only thing we have in common." She shrugged, and Noah saw a woman who had lost out on a lot of fun. If he were a twin, he'd be in his brother's shoes all the time. How could she not take advantage of such a cool ability? It was a superpower.

"You don't think you could walk into that news station dressed as Allison and fool everyone?"

She clasped her coffee cup with her hands, considering the idea. "Not in a million years. I don't have a clue what she does at work. I teach elementary school, for Pete's sake, and I'm very camera shy. I've met her coworkers maybe twice at the most, and certainly not everyone at the station. I can't just step into her world. Those are big stilettos to fill, and I'm more of a Converse kind of girl." She paused as she realized the full extent of what he was asking. "No. I am not going to trade places with my sister."

"I get it," he said. "It was just an interesting thought, a way to find the people who want to hurt your sister. But you're right. It's a lot to ask. You don't even have the training for such an assignment." As he pondered it further, he knew she would have no idea what to do undercover. Too bad he couldn't transfer her looks to Meaghan, who would be more than competent in a den of wolves.

Zoe's gaze dropped to the cup she was holding. "I want her to be okay," she whispered. "But I'm not the hero of this or any story, Noah. That's always been Allison."

Guilt tightened Noah's chest as he nodded and squeezed her hand in understanding. "We'll find another way to help Allison, a way that doesn't ask you to be anyone but yourself." He helped her up and they walked slowly down the hall.

"No matter what happens, I want you to know that I'm here for you," he said gently as they paused outside Allison's room. "Not just as an assignment, but as a friend. We'll get through this together in whatever way works best for you."

"I'm an assignment, I get it. You don't have to placate me," she replied, but also offered him a weary but genuine smile. "But I appreciate it just the same."

A few hours ago, he'd have agreed that he was placating the woman who had been assigned to him, but now his feelings had changed. He genuinely wanted her to get through this in the safest manner possible. Not out of some duty, but because he had come to care for her. His feelings were not only ill-advised and impractical, but could be downright dangerous.

As they entered Allison's room, he cast a final glance down the hallway, sensing an impending threat. The distant rumbling of staff and various others approached. "Get inside. I'll wait here until the coast is clear."

She nodded and slipped inside, sitting next to her sister. The commotion grew louder, and Noah held his breath, braced for a fight.

Chapter Eight

Zoe sat with Allison in the now quiet hospital room. The rhythmic beeping of the heart monitor played a soft, persistent backdrop compared to the alarms going off only an hour before. Her sister seemed so vulnerable on the hospital bed with a tangle of IV lines and hospital sheets as pale as Allison's current complexion. Her lack of vigor, beaten out of her by a black sedan, made Zoe ignore everything Noah had said in the cafeteria. Instead of pushing Allison to continue her investigation, Zoe tried to convince her sister to hide out in Nantucket while she healed.

"Come on, Ally. It's not giving up, it's just…regrouping," Zoe implored, her voice a blend of concern and reason. "Nantucket would be perfect for you to recover, away from all this chaos. You could take a moment, breathe in some sea air, and—"

Allison cut her off with a resolute shake of her head. "I can't do that. This story is bigger than us. The moment I'm able to stand on my own, I'm finding out who bribed Brendan Quinn. No detours."

Zoe sighed. Allison's tenacity, her relentless pursuit of truth, made her an exceptional journalist, but it also painted a perpetual target on her back. "Please consider it. I'm worried about you." Zoe knew even as she spoke that Allison's mind was made up.

Her sister's expression softened momentarily. "We can plan a vacation just as soon as I finish this assignment." She was lying. She hadn't had a vacation for three years. There was always one more story to chase, one more opportunity she couldn't miss. But then she showed her true colors…"If you're going back to my apartment at any point, could you grab my laptop? It's in my office. I need to check a few things and send out some emails."

Before Zoe could respond, Meaghan interjected from her post standing by the wall. "That's not a good idea. You're off-grid right now, and that's the safest place for you. Any digital footprint, any hint of activity, and whoever's behind this will trace your location to this room number."

Allison's jaw set stubbornly, a look that didn't bode well for Meaghan. "I appreciate the concern, but I can't just lie here and watch TV. Someone tried to kill me. That's one hell of a story."

Meaghan crossed the room in a few decisive strides, her height impressive, her intimidation factor for someone so beautiful even more so. "I get it, I do. But your safety's my priority. My job. My paycheck. I have to insist you keep it low-tech for now. Notebooks, the back of napkins, anything that doesn't leave a trace. I won't have you adding risk to the hospital staff because you have a death wish."

"And if I fire you?" Diva Allison reared her ugly head.

Meaghan literally smiled at her. Not one of those mocking smiles that contained a threat. Nope. Meaghan wore a soft, pretty smile way more nerve-racking than one that challenged. "You're not my boss, so that would be difficult."

Allison wouldn't back down. "Who hired you?"

"A government agency that is looking for the same information you are. They tend to prefer other people do their dirty work, so they wanted you to finish the investigation, but obviously that won't happen. Instead, I'm here to protect you from whoever is trying to bury the story."

"And I can't investigate the story without my computer, so

you'll never catch who made the bribe," Allison said as though she'd won the argument.

Zoe looked between the two women, and chose sides. Meaghan. While Allison was an unstoppable force at work, Meaghan made more sense. A computer would be a homing beacon to the bad guys.

"Meaghan's right." Zoe's voice was soft but firm, as though trying to convince a child that he did have to share the new markers in the classroom. "I can help you do some groundwork off-grid. I have nothing else to do for a few weeks before I start at the summer camp."

"Not a chance. I won't have you running amok and scaring away all of my potential sources."

"I don't run amok with anything." She reached for Allison's hand, holding it gently. She didn't want anything to do with this investigation, but she had no choice if she wanted to protect her sister.

A huge commotion came from outside the door. Meaghan reached for a gun, which made this whole ordeal feel much more dangerous. The door swung open and Marlowe rushed inside with Jason trying to control his leash. Noah stood beside him and quickly shut the door after they entered. Marlowe jumped on top of the bed.

"Marlowe!" Allison's face lit up. The dog landed far more gently than expected. He remained by her side and sniffed around her casts before settling down at the foot of her bed as though he had one job to do and he accomplished said job.

Meaghan broke out into laughter.

"Why is the dog in the hospital?" Noah asked Jason.

"If I did that, you'd place me on probation," Meaghan said with a grin.

"Good thing I'm me then," Jason replied with more confidence than the whole room combined. "I thought Allison could use the company, and honestly, Marlowe was driving Calvin and everyone else crazy." Jason's brows furrowed. His tense expression seemed to make Meaghan laugh louder.

"I never would have believed you'd be taken down by a beagle." She walked over to Marlowe and patted his back.

"Marlowe's too smart to be an apartment dweller. He needs a job or time with his owner." He looked between Zoe and Allison and paused. "You two couldn't avoid being recognized as sisters, even with your disguise and Allison's black eyes."

The mention of a flaw in Allison's appearance had her grasping for the mirror on her table tray.

"But we have bigger issues to worry about. I noticed two thugs circling the hospital on my way inside. Calvin's running the plates, but in the meantime, we all have to leave."

"Leave?" Meaghan said, glancing down at Allison's casts.

"Yes. Before they can confirm Allison's location. I estimate that we have less than four minutes. Wait here." Jason turned and walked out of the room.

Zoe stared at the back of the man who had just told them they were all in danger before casually strolling away. From the look on Meaghan's and Noah's faces, their focus had sharpened, yet they remained calm and stayed in the room.

Just over a minute later, Jason returned. He tossed a pair of scrubs at Zoe. "Put these on," he instructed before leaving again. Moments later, he returned with what looked like a large gurney with walls, resembling a mobile casket... Zoe stared at the contraption, realizing with a chill that they would be placing Allison in it.

"No. I will not be carried in that dead body box," Allison protested, a squeamish look overtaking her features.

"You're not in a position to negotiate," Meaghan replied firmly. "You can be treated like a corpse, or you can become one for real. Since I'm not in the mood to fight our way out of here, I've decided for you." Meaghan positioned everyone around Allison to help lift.

Jason ceded authority seamlessly, allowing Meaghan to take charge. Zoe watched as they transitioned from a group of individuals to a cohesive team. Seeing them work together with such confidence reassured her that they had some control of the situation, which made her feel a bit less nervous.

The four of them pulled Allison's sheet tight and shifted her, sheet and all, onto the gurney. When Allison found some semblance of comfort, Meaghan lifted the walls and covered her. Allison was completely hidden, leg cast and all.

Jason assured Allison he'd get the dog to her when she'd settled in to her new location. Then he glanced down the hall. "It's clear," he whispered. "Good luck." With a casual stride, he departed down the hall with Marlowe walking at his side and disappeared.

"Are you ready?" Noah asked Zoe. He seemed concerned, but he stayed back, holding Meaghan's hand as though they were a couple. She was a bit tall for him, although that was probably the three-inch boots she wore. Something bordering on jealousy went through Zoe. She wasn't sure if it was the hand-holding or the fact that they were able to remain dressed in the same clothes.

The danger, however, propelled her forward. She nodded to her sister's bodyguards and maneuvered the gurney with surprising agility. As she began to turn to the right, Meaghan coughed from behind her. "Left." Zoe turned left.

A nurse walked down the hall past them, her face pressed into a phone with only the slightest glance in Zoe's direction. People don't tend to notice average, and Zoe felt about as average as one could get.

As they went through the Emergency Room exit, cool fresh air greeted them. She wasn't sure where to go until she saw the sleek gray hearse parked inconspicuously by the curb.

"Hearse?" she said as though to herself.

"Yep," came a voice from behind her.

Zoe pushed her sister up to the back of the vehicle and swung open the rear door. It held the lingering smell of lilies, probably the scent of a thousand flowers that journeyed with prior occupants to their graves. Zoe wouldn't mention that to Allison. This was already far too morbid.

She slid her sister and the gurney mattress into the back. And then heard alarms going off in the hospital. Her instinct was to run. Before she could react, Noah was at her side, helping her move her sister inside and closing the door.

"Where's Meaghan?" she asked.

"Driving." He stepped back and pulled Zoe with him as the hearse drove away.

A few seconds later, two men ran out the Emergency Room exit. They were definitely looking for someone. Zoe had no idea what to do, but Noah's proximity gave her an idea. She wrapped her arms around his neck, pressed him against the wall, and kissed him. It wasn't anything epic, mostly because her body was shaking from the fear of being caught, but there was comfort in holding a man who didn't seem nearly as scared as she was. He held her tight and absorbed her fears and worries until the footsteps faded toward the side parking lot. Even then, she remained with her lips on his, drawing support from his physical and mental strength.

"How are we getting out of here?" she asked, lips still touching, and body warmly wrapped within his arms.

"My car. We'll wait another few minutes and then stroll at a casual pace to the car, not a care in the world. Can you do that?" His arm held her so tight, she could probably lift her feet off the ground and he'd hold her up.

"Yes. Just tell me when to stop." And she kissed him again.

Chapter Nine

As Noah drove away from the hospital, he replayed kissing Zoe over in his mind. Actually, she'd kissed him and he'd enjoyed the hell out of it, even while trying to focus on her safety. Although he'd never forget how good her lips felt on his, his thoughts kept traveling back to the two guys who had been searching for Allison. He wanted to know who they were and how the team could protect Allison and Zoe while learning enough to shut down whatever criminal organization was involved.

"Are you okay?" he asked Zoe.

She nodded. Her face seemed flushed and her eyes betrayed her fear, no doubt from being chased down like prey. He didn't push a conversation because he had no idea what to say to her. So many thoughts twisted through him. So many emotions that he didn't want to be feeling—protectiveness, frustration, and an undeniable attraction to the woman he'd been assigned to protect.

Once in the underground garage at headquarters, Zoe lingered in the car, removing her wig wearily. Noah remained by her side as she strode with heavy steps toward the entrance. Her face was a blank page, drained of expression, as though she didn't have the energy to display any emotion.

When Zoe retreated to her room, Jason summoned Noah

to the conference room. The problems compounding in this assignment followed close behind Noah, taunting him and reminding him that his last case had been a disaster. He measured himself against the top performers of the team, all with years more experience than he had. He was not yet in their caliber.

"You look exhausted," Jason said.

"I'm good," Noah lied. He wanted a nap and a shower, but he couldn't show weakness. Not to Jason, a person who rarely skipped a day of work and always seemed ready for anything.

"How was Zoe while escaping the hospital?"

"She blended in as hospital staff and handled moving her sister into the hearse without a problem." Noah would not mention the kiss between them.

"Perfect." He gestured for Noah to take the seat across from him. "I need you to stay with Zoe for the next few days. Keep an eye on her until we can make sure whoever is behind this won't go after Allison's family"

No more surveillance. This assignment would set him up for something bigger. Maybe international travel. The only problem involved his attraction to Zoe. No matter what happened, he had to make his decisions based on what was best for the team. Not that he'd ever do something that would harm someone innocent in all of this. In fact, he could handle his assignment, care for Zoe, and maintain a wall of professional detachment. The stakes were too high, and Jason's trust too valuable to lose. "I can handle it."

"You don't need to be glued to her side 24/7. We'll rotate you out for rest, although right now we're limited in field crew, but Fiona and I are available to assist you if you need it." Which meant this was their biggest case if both Jason and Fiona, Jason's wife, were working on it. That made it even more important for Noah to handle it like the best of the best.

The door opened and Zoe entered, dressed in sweatpants and a T-shirt, her hair wet from a shower, her energy revived, and her appearance a most beautiful distraction.

"Can I come in?" she asked.

Jason nodded and pointed to the chair next to Noah. "I'm

sorry you had to be placed in such a tricky situation, but Noah told me you handled it well."

She stared at Noah for an uncomfortable minute, probably wondering what Noah had told Jason.

"You have the making of a spy. You moved your sister through the hospital with a calm that was impressive. And then we drove back here without incident. That's as good as it gets in terms of success." Noah didn't mention the kiss to assure her that he had skipped that aspect of their flight from the hospital.

"Thanks." She visibly relaxed. "I hope I never go through anything quite so crazy again. I could barely breathe by the time we got into his car. I just want to make sure Allison is okay."

"I have Meaghan online now. She and Allison are safe and Allison is set up comfortably." Jason turned an iPad toward them. The video call showed Meaghan in a nice-looking bedroom that seemed far better than the hospital where Allison had been staying.

"We're all settled. I'll keep you updated. Dr. M is here too, and can check in on her every few hours." Meaghan turned the video toward a queen-size bed with Allison resting on one side of it. She appeared comfortable and fast asleep. Marlowe, as asleep as his master, stretched out, his head resting against Allison's arm. Dr. Morgan, wearing her pink pants and a soft cream-colored sweater, stood next to her with a stethoscope draped around her neck.

"Where are you?" Zoe asked.

"I can't tell you. Her location is unknown to everyone but me and the good doctor. No one can leak information they don't have," Meaghan answered.

The stillness of the new room with Allison's soft breathing and the occasional beep of a monitor should give Zoe confidence that Fresh Pond Security was taking good care of her sister. However, from what Noah knew about Allison, she wouldn't take her forced time off easily. Once awake, she'd return to being the intrepid reporter who had uncovered the bribe at City Hall, even though her life had been nearly cut short at far too young an age. The threats would persist as long as Allison continued to pursue the source of the bribe, placing her sister at risk as well.

On this side of the monitor, Zoe stared at the screen, her brown hair up in a loose ponytail. Without the wig, their resemblance was even more striking. Noah's plan for Zoe to impersonate Allison to retrieve the notes and evidence in her office seemed like their best option for handling the case. It was a risk, but so was keeping the women in protective custody for an indeterminate time.

Now was the best time to get this plan in motion. Before Allison's absence brought her too much scrutiny. If Jason disagreed, they'd need a different means of finding the source of the bribe.

Breaking the silence, Noah leaned forward in his chair. "We need to obtain the information Allison left in her office. Calvin and his team as well as all of us could find out information that would lead to an understanding of whoever is behind the bribes and the attacks. We could break in, but I think there's a less risky plan. Zoe, dressed as Allison, walking in and out in under an hour." He turned to Zoe. "I know this is a lot to ask, but stepping into Allison's shoes might be our only chance to expose the corruption she uncovered."

Zoe's frown deepened, her annoyance at him bringing the idea up again visible. She responded before he could say anything else. Her frown making him almost regret his suggestion...almost. "What you're suggesting is insane. I'm a teacher, not an undercover agent. You can't seriously expect me to fool anyone into believing I'm Allison."

Jason nodded in agreement, his words a blow to Noah's confidence. "Zoe has a point. This plan is too high-risk. If there is a leak in the company, she would be at risk and so would our investigation. Without proper training, innocent people could get killed, and we could spook the very people we need to observe."

Noah felt Jason's words like a sucker punch. The complete rejection of his idea didn't bode well for his career goals. To be fair, Jason had watched Noah's failed attempt at saving Matt, Jason's son, from kidnappers.

Meaghan nodded in agreement with their boss. Her loyalty would always be with Jason, as he'd rescued her from a very bad situation at the police station where she'd worked, giving her more money and security than she'd ever received on the police force. "She's not trained for this kind of operation. This whole plan would be too much to ask of her."

"I'm not spy material," Zoe agreed. "I have a job and a life I love. Risking my life this afternoon was more than enough adventure for me for a whole lifetime."

Allison stirred and everyone fell into a charged silence. Even in her sleep, Allison commanded the room. Her bruised face wore a confident countenance and had the bone structure of a queen. Zoe did too, but she seemed afraid to step into her own power. She preferred a life on the sidelines, and he wasn't going to convince her otherwise.

She exchanged glances with Jason. "I'm sorry but I'm far more of a risk than I am a help."

Allison's wakening voice cut through the conversation. "Are you all out of your minds? Zoe, pretending to be me? She can barely stand in high heels, never mind speak in front of a camera."

Zoe's response came fast, as though a sibling rivalry reared its head in the middle of their debate. "Allison, I..."

"She could never be confused for me. Ever." Allison made a face that was as much an insult to Zoe as the words she spoke. "Zoe is... Zoe. She's not me. She's kind, gentle, not cut out for anything that involves bravery. No offense, Zoe. You see the best in people, believe in the goodness of the world. How can you possibly navigate the backstabbing world I walk through every day?"

She had a point. And part of Noah couldn't help but feel drawn to Zoe's inherent goodness, a quality too rare in his line of work. Yet, she'd also demonstrated nerves of steel when thrust into the middle of a crime drama. If she was falling apart, she did a great job hiding it.

"As much as I hate to say it, the more I think about it, the more I like the plan." Jason's deep voice rumbled across the room, taking back control of the situation. "As Noah mentioned, Zoe, you're rarely in Boston, and very few people know Allison has a twin. If we proceed, we need to meticulously plan every detail. The more I think about it, the more I agree with Noah. In and out quick and no one will be the wiser." He turned to Allison. "We know it's a risk. But Zoe's unique position could give us the leverage we need. And with more information, we can help break your story, handing you all the credit if you need credit. This isn't about throwing Zoe into the fire, it's about using the element of surprise to our advantage."

Zoe's eyes met Noah's. A storm of uncertainty clouded them. "But I'm not an investigator. I don't have Allison's instincts, her experience. How can I convincingly step into her life, her investigation?" She said it not so much as a rejection of the plan, but as an honest interest in the logistics of the assignment.

Noah paused and made sure to frame his next statement as perfectly as possible in order to keep her confidence up and not scare her away. "You're more than capable of handling an hour or so in a newsroom. I'm sure you paste on a happy face every day when you meet up with your students."

"I love teaching."

"Every day?"

She looked down. "Well, no, but..."

"Exactly. You have to pretend sometimes and the kids are none the wiser. You swallow down your emotions to provide for a solid classroom experience. And you do that for what, seven or eight hours at a time? That's not easy. You have an innate understanding of people and you have major problem-solving skills. What teacher doesn't? Trying to line up twenty kids when one goes rogue. How often have you handled something like that?"

He could see her mind racing. She knew how talented she was but in a different context. It wouldn't be hard to transfer those skills for a small portion of one day. Especially since she was pretending to be the person she was closest to in the world. "These aren't qualities you can teach or fake," he continued. "They're uniquely yours, and in this situation, they'll be a huge asset."

Allison tried to sit up, but was hindered by the weight of her leg cast. "That's a pretty picture you're painting. But be realistic. Zoe teaching third graders is not the same in any way as working at a cutthroat newsroom. She's not only never left her hometown, she never left the home where we were born."

"I stayed on the island, Allison, because someone had to remain with Dad after Mom died. You chose to leave and that left me with no choice at all. But I'm not complaining. I love my life and wouldn't trade it for all the fancy shoes in your enormous closet. That doesn't mean I'm some country bumpkin, and you're this international jet-setter. I'll have you know that school board meetings are vicious. Our new principal is set on dumbing down the curriculum in order to boost his class promotion rates and obliterate the budget, a plan I have been fighting every chance I get. I battle a whole lot of assholes every single day. A newsroom just might be a picnic for me." Zoe's voice carried a newfound edge of defiance. Allison's words must have stirred up a whole lot of resentment that had remained unsaid over the years.

The room stilled, the weight of her words hanging in the air. Noah's respect for Zoe lifted to new levels. She wasn't some pushover. She had more of a backbone than anyone had given her credit for, which made Noah's plan all the more plausible now. "Zoe, listen to yourself. This passion you have, it's exactly what we need. You're more like Allison than you realize."

Zoe hesitated, her retort wavering as she processed his words. She'd probably been told Allison was the golden child her whole life and moving out of that role into her own sunshine was a huge step.

"I have to admit, she's got spirit. Perhaps we were too quick to judge her capabilities earlier." Jason spoke with a hint of newfound respect for Zoe. He'd recently stopped judging people by their appearances after he learned that his very short, very curvy wife, Fiona, had been an operative for the government without Jason or anyone outside the smallest of circles knowing. She had been perfect for her job because many people looked her over with her Marilyn Monroe demeanor and assumed she had no idea what was going on around her. That allowed her to go places and do things without having any suspicion landing on her. A whole team from Fresh Pond Security had seen her in action and all agreed to never let their guard down around her.

"It's not just about her resemblance to you, Allison," Meaghan said. "It's about having the courage to stand up when it counts. And Zoe is showing a lot of grit right now."

Meaghan also told Noah she did not like working for divas. They thought they deserved to call all the shots and could place everyone around them at risk. Her annoyance with Allison didn't bode well for their time together in the near future.

Zoe, on the other hand, seemed to have everyone's well-being at heart in her actions. Noah would have mentioned the kiss at the hospital, where she shielded herself from view by two men and whatever weapons they carried, but he didn't want to embarrass her. Not that what she'd done should cause embarrassment, instead it proved that she had great instincts, but she seemed the type to ignore her success.

As the debate continued, with the whole Fresh Pond team defending Zoe, Noah observed a transformation in her. Her eyes lit up with a fire that had, until then, been mostly hidden, except for when she pretended to be Allison back at headquarters. Her performance proved she was more than capable of acting as her sister with the right motivation. She'd have gotten away with it if Meaghan hadn't checked in with Jason about her and Allison's location.

He watched as Zoe handled their compliments and observations. He could be a real bastard and push her decision from a solid "no" to a half-hearted "yes," but he hesitated, remembering Jason's son feeling safe under his protection before being kidnapped by a drug cartel. While he cared about breaking cases that could make the world safer for everyone, he needed to minimize the risks toward innocent people caught up in the chaos of the criminal world. If Zoe got hurt, he might never forgive himself. And the thought of any harm coming to her made him fearful of how he'd be able to handle the inevitable danger around them without compromising the case.

"I'm not going to let anyone take my place. That's illegal, impersonating a reporter," Allison said, her anger focused on Zoe more than any of the other people in both spaces.

Although she had a point, this was sanctioned by some high-level law enforcement agencies. Fresh Pond Security had a certain amount of protection offered to them as part of their arrangement. No one in the conference room would be indicted in their attempt to capture the person who bribed City Hall.

"You'd really have me prosecuted? When I'd do it to keep you safe?" Zoe asked, her brows lifted.

Allison clenched her hand into a fist. "I don't need your protection."

"No. You're doing a bang-up job of keeping yourself safe. You went to an isolated area where someone could have just as easily shot you in the head and left your dead body to rot." Zoe shook her head as though clearing the picture out of her mind.

Interesting, Noah thought. She actually made a statement in favor of stepping into the ruse.

Noah didn't shine any light on her sudden burst of courage. Instead, he spoke to Meaghan and Jason. "She'd be far more protected than Allison was at the Enchanted Forest. It's not like we'd leave her alone. She'd have someone accompany her at all times for safety."

Meaghan stepped forward before Noah could volunteer. "If Noah can stay with Allison, I can go with Zoe." Meaghan never begged off a current assignment, but in this case, being locked away with a demanding, drama magnet, Noah understood.

Jason, however, disagreed. "You're assigned to Allison. I like the idea of Noah posing as Allison's new boyfriend and accompanying Zoe to the studio." He looked over at Noah. "Act curious about all the inner workings of the studio. I want you inside that producer's office to see if we can dig up something that would explain why he'd risk Allison for a story. Allison can create a map and help you and Zoe familiarize yourselves with the office layout, names, and positions of people to avoid arousing suspicion."

Meaghan nodded in agreement. "Of course. Are you okay with this plan, Zoe?" she asked, ignoring Allison's huff from the bed.

Zoe ignored her sister as well, focusing on Jason. "No, not entirely, but maybe…" And at that second, Noah knew they had her.

His gaze lingered on her, relieved he wasn't going to be sent over to babysit Allison. He didn't want to leave Zoe's side partly because the thought of Meaghan spending more time with her annoyed him. He also wanted to keep an eye on her while she was in a vulnerable position. And now he had his chance.

"Good," Jason declared. "It's settled. We're going to call you Allison from the moment we leave the hospital. You have to hear that name and react as though it's yours. It might take twenty-four to forty-eight hours to get you to a place where you'll feel more confident."

"More confident in Allison's really high shoes?" Zoe asked.

"More confident interacting with anyone who might know Allison. Noah and our team will handle the logistics. Just stay by Noah's side. Then when you're done, we'll relocate you for a week or so until we see what comes of this."

"What am I supposed to do?" Allison said, her annoyance growing.

"Help your sister get the information she needs and rest. No phone, no emails, unless we're in the room monitoring what you say. For the time Zoe's in the newsroom, we'll transfer your cell number to a temporary phone that can't be traced. Your phone is going to be shut down with the card removed until everything is ready to return to normal."

"You can't take my phone. I have rights."

Meaghan stood at the foot of her bed, her brows furrowed. "You would place your career and your own happiness over your sister's safety?"

"That's not fair."

"That's the reality. I'll be here with you," Meaghan said with a placating smile. "We can have lots of fun together. Do you play cribbage?"

Allison shook her head, completely shut down.

"Great." Meaghan clapped her hands together. "I'll teach you. It's a life skill worth having. Like golf, but for rainy nights with wine."

Jason interrupted Meaghan's pep rally. "Before you pull out your cribbage board and a deck of cards, Allison needs to call her producer and tell her she's still gathering information and will be back in the office soon," Jason said. "You need to make this call right now from Meaghan's burner phone. You've already been out of contact for far too long. It's vital to keep them thinking you're still investigating."

"And lie to my producer? No. What if he's innocent and I lose my job?" Allison said, as though her actions had no impact on anyone else in the room.

Jason's expression was unyielding, which meant he was one hundred percent on board with the plan. Allison's reluctance was understandable, yet the urgency of their situation left little room for debate. "It's the only way to buy us some time. To keep them off Zoe's back and give her a fighting chance to dig deeper. Make it happen, Meaghan."

Meaghan nodded, her personality hardened into someone who didn't play games. "She'll make the call."

With a shaky hand, Allison took the phone, her voice barely a whisper as she dialed the number. "Fine, but if this blows up, it's on all of you." A hint of her usual fiery spirit burned the air even in her weakened state.

The room fell silent when she spoke to whomever was on the other line. "Glenn? Hi, yes. I'm okay. It was crazy. The person showed up, but drove off in a huff as though they chickened out... No we never had contact and I didn't get the license plate, but I was looking over my notes and I have a few more leads. I've been following up on each one. I should be back in the office in a day or two... No, I don't want to come in before I'm ready. I promise to keep in contact... No, I can't say more right now. Just know that I'm on it." Despite her condition, Allison played her part convincingly, setting up a situation where Zoe would be able to walk into the newsroom without too much interest pointed at her. Unless the coroner leaked Mrs. Peterson's death. That would create a whole bigger issue. One that Noah couldn't worry about at the moment.

Once the call was over, Allison's hand dropped to her side, the annoyance remaining in her expression.

Jason and Noah exchanged a glance, an unspoken acknowledgment that they'd willingly placed themselves one step too close to the cliff's edge.

"Okay. Go get some rest and I'll meet you in a few hours in Conference Room two." Jason waved Noah and Zoe from the room. "I have a few questions for Allison."

Noah turned to Zoe, who had been a silent observer during this exchange. "Are you ready? We've got a lot of ground to cover and not much time."

She nodded and glanced back at the screen. "Take care of yourself, Ally."

"I don't have much of a choice, do I?"

Zoe took a deep breath. "Okay, let's do this."

With that, Noah and Zoe stepped toward the door.

"Wait," Allison called out to them.

Zoe and Noah turned around.

"Be careful," she called out.

Zoe nodded and something just short of a smile appeared on her face. "I'll do my best."

Chapter Ten

Zoe stepped into the hallway with Noah, the tension from the discussions with Jason and Allison ringing in her ears. Despite the refreshing shower she'd taken earlier, her whole body felt like a plant that lacked water. Stepping into her sister's shoes presented an almost impossible task. Allison was right. Zoe had never mastered her sister's style and confidence. There was too much on the line for her to believe she could just wing it.

A short fashionable blonde wandered down the hallway. Jason's wife, Fiona. Dressed in jeans and a loose black blouse, she stood in heels without the slightest sign of distress. Fiona's self-assuredness unnerved Zoe.

"I heard about your harrowing day," Fiona said while holding Zoe's hands. "Jason asked me to stop by to see if you need anything."

Her voice faltered as she admitted, "I think I've made a huge mistake. I don't think I'm as capable as you all think I am."

"Nonsense. You'll be fine. Everyone starts somewhere, but let's not worry about that until tomorrow." Fiona handed her a business card. "You need a decent amount of sleep and a few moments to process everything. If you wake in the middle of the night and need to talk, don't hesitate to contact me. I like to be disturbed."

"Thank you."

"No worries. There's wine in the kitchen and herbal tea too if that will help you sleep. I'll see you first thing in the morning."

Zoe's nerves frayed. "You're leaving?"

"I need to get home to my son. You're safe here. There's not a safer place in the city, and Noah will be asleep in the next room. He's harmless toward people he likes."

Fiona didn't have to say anything for Zoe to trust Noah. She already did. He'd protected her, but he'd also volunteered her for the most dangerous job she'd ever held. "I don't know how I'll learn everything I need to know in a few days."

"Time is an advantage. We can make you into a replica of Allison with a month, but we need the information now," Fiona responded, her voice low and measured. "I agree with Noah about you giving us a tactical advantage. You know your sister, her mannerisms, her life. That's invaluable. But—" she paused, weighing her next words "—turning you into someone who can convincingly infiltrate a news station in a week will be a challenge."

Zoe's heart sank. The reality of Fiona's words hit hard. She was a third-grade teacher, not a spy. Her expertise lay in lesson plans, not espionage.

"I know. That's why I said I didn't want to do it," she murmured, glaring at Noah as her certainty faded. "I don't know why I agreed."

"You agreed, because it's the best way to keep you and your sister safe in the future. As long as these guys want Allison silenced, they will keep going after her, and you too," Noah said.

Zoe studied him a moment, then bit her lip. "I'll just be getting you inside the news station, right?"

"More or less," Fiona replied. "Once Noah is on the inside, it's up to you to keep a level head. Even if someone accuses you of being a fake, you need to hold to your part. While the physical danger is there, it's the psychological game that you need to handle."

Noah nodded. "I'll have your back and we'll have a backup team behind us as well. Success is getting the information we're looking for and leaving before anyone notices anything out of the ordinary."

"But that's the problem. I have no idea what is ordinary in Allison's job."

"We'll figure it out together." He smiled, but his words weren't reassuring.

Fiona looked between them. "On second thought, it could only benefit us to give you some extra training. Tactical and physical defense is important, but more important is the ability to think under stressful circumstances. And thinking out of the box. Zoe, you can leverage your unique insights into your sister's life. You need to think like her, anticipate how she would react. That's your real advantage here. Noah, you need to convince yourself that even without the on-the-ground experience the others have, that you are just as able to handle whatever is thrown your way."

Noah frowned. "I believe in my abilities. It's Jason who doesn't."

"You are so wrong. He would never let you do anything he thought you couldn't handle." She put two closed fists in front of them. "Before I let you go to your rooms, here's your first challenge as a team. Which hand has a quarter in it?"

"Seriously?" Noah asked.

"Seriously. You can work it out together, but one answer."

It was as though Zoe had been sent into another dimension. One where she had to solve puzzles as the clock closed in on midnight. She could not believe life had brought her here.

Noah seemed to be rolling his eyes but Fiona stood with conviction, her hands offering no clues. Zoe shook her head, trying to wake up her brain after an impossibly long day. Fiona definitely did not have the look of a woman kidding, so Zoe stared at her hands. She hadn't noticed Fiona holding a coin or anything else for that matter, although maybe she should have. If Fiona pulled it from somewhere, there weren't a lot of options. She was wearing a long-sleeve shirt and jeans, but she'd never placed her hands in her pocket.

Zoe shrugged. "There isn't a quarter."

Fiona smiled. "You need to make that decision with Noah."

"This is ridiculous. She's exhausted," Noah said, but continued staring at Fiona's hands.

"So make a decision."

Something about Fiona's self-assurance woke Zoe up from her fatigue. She looked over at Noah, her former protector and new partner. "Well?" she asked him.

"Fiona is known to carry a pocketbook that doubles as Noah's Ark. It has everything in it. I've never known her to carry anything in her pockets, although I have seen her pull a knife out of a boot before."

Fiona laughed in that way a goddess laughed at the silly things mere mortals said. "A quarter. You don't have to analyze anything else I may have on my person."

Zoe didn't know whether she should laugh, because, although Fiona didn't look like the type who would harm anyone with a knife, the glint in her eyes said that she most certainly would. Noah wasn't laughing and that said a lot too.

"Can you turn your hands over?" Noah asked.

Fiona complied. They both looked identical.

This was such a silly test. She either had a quarter or didn't and it was in her left hand or her right hand. Two things to guess.

"Where did you come from?" Noah asked.

"Picking Matt up from the library and dropping him off at home."

"Where is the library?"

"Concord."

"And you can pay for parking with quarters there still, which you would, because you hate leaving any technological footprint." Noah grinned, as though he'd solved the whole problem. It would make sense she'd have a quarter if she planned on parking there.

"True, but there are cameras set up that can pick someone up on Main Street."

Zoe wasn't sure whether Fiona was incredibly paranoid or she truly had that level of awareness about everything around her. "How much is parking?" she asked.

"One dollar for on street parking."

"Did you pay to park?"

"Matt, in his infinite wisdom, chose to wait at the curb."

Noah went into his own pocket, pulled out his car keys, and without the slightest preamble, threw the keys at Fiona as hard as he could. Zoe's mouth dropped open at her inability to even warn Fiona. Without the slightest shift in her stance, Fiona caught the keys with her right hand.

"One quarter, the left hand," Noah said as though he'd tossed her the keys gently.

Fiona opened her left hand and there was the quarter. She turned toward Zoe as though she was the bellman of a swanky hotel. "Let me walk you to your room."

Zoe couldn't respond. As a teacher, that would never be the way to solve a situation. Yet, it got the job done. She had to really rethink so much about how she got through life.

"Zoe," Fiona said as she walked down the hall, her expression softening, "this isn't about turning you into a soldier. It's about expanding the skills you already have. You're not going into the studio alone. You'll have us backing you every step of the way."

Noah followed them and Zoe glanced back at him. He seemed to have his own shadows following him. Did he think he lacked the skills for this job? Because he sure as heck saved her life.

Zoe's resolve wavered under the weight. "I'm not sure I can…"

Fiona interrupted. "Noah thinks you can give us an edge. And Jason trusts his instincts. I do too. We'll give you some basic training—enough to keep you safe and make you useful."

"But in a few days?"

"It's not ideal," Noah answered. "But Fiona is no mere instructor. She'll give you a crash course in tactical thinking, observation, and evasion."

"Flattering, but you'll be just as involved. You both have to trust each other." She gave them a wave. "I'm off. Make sure you get at least a few hours of sleep."

Noah escorted Zoe the rest of the way. Her room now had a bottle of water and a glass on the bedside table as well as fresh flowers in a vase. Peonies.

"My favorites," she said, stepping to them and lightly brushing a finger over one of the petals.

"You had some on the kitchen island at Allison's," Noah said. "I thought they'd cheer up your space. It can get a bit sterile in here."

"They're perfect." Zoe relaxed further when she saw two pairs of sweats, some T-shirts, and a duffel bag where she hoped she would find some toiletries. She turned to him. He leaned against the doorframe, not stepping inside the room, a very respectful thing to do. "I hope I don't let you down. You seem to have far more faith in my ability than I do."

"That will change over the next few days. In the morning, we'll assess your skills, see where you stand. Then, we can tailor your training to maximize your strengths and mitigate your weaknesses. You probably have a lot more skills than you know."

Their eyes met, and Zoe stepped closer to him, mesmerized by everything about him. She didn't care that the door was open, nor did she care about whatever she was being asked to do. She only thought about how beautiful his eyes were. He took a stride forward, the heat of his body radiating toward her. His hand reached up, almost instinctively, to brush a strand of hair from her face. Her breath hitched, her heart pounded in her chest. But then Noah hesitated, his hand lingering near her cheek. He searched her eyes, as if seeking permission, and Zoe leaned in, drawn by a need for something solid to hold as her world swirled around in chaos. She closed her eyes and waited, but when she opened them, he'd pulled back from her.

"Good night, Zoe," he whispered, his voice husky and low.

"Good night," she choked out.

After a lingering glance, he walked away, leaving Zoe standing alone at the door with a racing heart and a hunger for a not-so-chaste good night kiss. As she got ready for bed, her thoughts stayed on Noah and what his lips would be like on hers. If he'd wanted to release the stress she'd been under, he achieved his goal. She was still nervous about tomorrow, but now all she could think about was what would have been an amazing good night kiss.

Chapter Eleven

Noah had come so close to crossing the line with Zoe. She had somehow claimed his heart. And he'd been only one inch from claiming her mouth, but self-preservation kicked in before Jason could turn the corner and see him kissing the person he was supposed to be protecting. In another world, where he wasn't assigned to protect her, he'd have taken her in his arms and held her all night. But he couldn't. Not to mention that she was the type of woman who probably wanted a husband and kids. His current job required him to travel and be away for weeks and months at a time. Even if he wanted to be with his family, the logistics of his schedule would make it difficult. In other words, they'd be better off not going there.

Now that the case was back on with Zoe playing a significant role, he had to make sure the plan went off without any problems. His mind kept drifting back to her smile, the way her eyes lit up when she talked about her students. He went into his office and shut the door. He regretted involving her in this. She'd stepped into the crosshairs of some very dangerous people and should have been sent away to a safe place until the risk dissipated. Tomorrow, Zoe, a third-grade teacher, would begin a two-day training exercise that would never prepare her for the risk she'd accepted. In fact, she was more likely to get overwhelmed by too much information and forget what they taught her. As much as he wanted to figure out who was behind the bribe and the murder of Allison's neighbor, he didn't want Zoe hurt in any way.

A text message pinged on his phone from Finn. Finn Maguire had been Noah's closest friend since he'd moved to Boston and joined Fresh Pond Security, but Finn quit after Jason admitted he'd lied to the team about his identity, pretending to be dead so a drug cartel would leave his family alone. He wouldn't stay where he didn't trust the leadership, because he'd already been stabbed in the back when Finn's superior officer lied about Finn's involvement in something he had nothing to do with. The betrayal resulted in Finn's dishonorable discharge. Noah missed working with him.

The text message had a picture of a nice black Ferrari.

Noah: New wheels?

Finn: Just arrived on the lot for someone with two hundred thousand to spare.

Noah: I doubt I'll ever have that much in spare change. And worse, my assignment is hammering me. Do you ever miss it?

The phone rang.

"I miss it all the time. I'm not a born salesman but will manage until the next job comes along. What's wrong?" Finn asked.

Noah explained the situation without giving away the specifics. "Is it wrong to have someone so unprepared go into a deadly situation?"

"Does she want to do it?"

"She said she did, but it was after some arm-twisting." Even as Noah said the words, he could feel the hypocrisy. He'd pushed her into it, and her sister had helped provide the final jab. Zoe was the type of person who would sacrifice herself for everyone around her's benefit. Even if she was ultimately not acting in her own best interests.

"So you like her?"

"Wh-what?" Noah stammered. Finn's words lodged straight under his skin.

"I've always known you to place the good of an assignment over everything else. Not that you would go out of your way to hurt anyone, but the woman agreed to assist. Why the guilt?"

"I pushed her into it."

"Does it make sense for the assignment?"

"Yes, but…"

"And will you be with her to keep her safe?"

"Yes, but…"

"Seems to me that it's a no-brainer. And from what I know of Jason, despite the fact that he lied to us, he is a hard-core professional. He wouldn't send anyone into a dangerous situation without adequate backup."

"That's true."

"So put your energy into helping her get through the next few days, instead of stressing over what can't be undone. You're on this. I would trust you by my side any day." His words meant everything. Finn was the best of the best when it came to security and protection.

"Thanks. Any chance I can persuade you into coming back and standing by my side for a change?"

The pause was uncomfortable. Their friendship had meant everything and Noah could already anticipate his reply.

"Not this week. Catch you later, brother."

And then he was gone and Noah felt a bit more alone.

The next morning after little sleep, Noah ran into Zoe, dressed in jeans and a cable-knit sweater, in the kitchen. Her eyes sparkled with vitality, and her face glowed with a well-rested charm that accentuated her natural beauty. He felt over-tired and grungy. He didn't have a bedroom at headquarters, so he slept uncomfortably on the couch. Not that he minded much. He was working in the field again. And he would prove that he could handle bigger and bigger assignments. He didn't need rest. If Jason asked him to fly over a small building, he'd figure out a way to do just that.

Zoe held a coffee mug between her hands as though it were

a religious artifact. Noah's eyes lingered on her, drawn to the way her lips curved into a gentle smile.

"How are you feeling?" he asked, his voice softer than usual, betraying a hint of concern he couldn't fully mask.

Her eyes met his with a hint of a memory of the night before and what could have been if he'd moved one inch closer. "I just woke up, but I'm ready for a nap."

"Not until after the sparring," Fiona replied, walking in the door.

"Sparring? What happened to going in and out of the building?"

"You need some self-defense moves. Nothing dramatic, but I wouldn't feel right about sending you in there with no skills. I think you have some appropriate outfits in the closet in your room. There's a gym down the hall. See you in ten." Fiona grabbed an apple from a bowl of fruit and strolled out again.

Zoe refilled her mug and disappeared. When Noah saw her again, she was wearing a gray UMass T-shirt and black leggings.

"Are you ready?" Noah met her at her door after changing into a Salt Life T-shirt and board shorts. It wasn't the most appropriate gear for sparring, but he wanted her to feel comfortable with him.

"You look prepared to hit some waves," she said.

"I wish. I haven't had time in years to do anything other than a few miles of running."

"Where did you surf?"

"Long Beach. I grew up there." California was a totally different vibe from New England. Not better, not worse, just different.

"Why did you move to Massachusetts?"

"Jason offered me a job that I'd always wanted. So I picked up and moved." It was a chance to live outside the office. He only regretted it after being shot and sent to desk duty while healing.

"Do you miss the sun?"

"I miss my sister, otherwise, I'm happy here." He pointed down the hall, trying to get her to hurry—they were three minutes late. "Come on. Fiona, although new to the group, has the ability to make our lives miserable. We all fear her in a way."

"You fear Fiona? She's so tiny and doesn't appear the least bit athletic." Zoe, a woman who didn't seem that judgmental, was certainly judging.

"Underestimate her at your own risk."

Two hours later, Zoe would never underestimate Fiona again. She was on her back on the mat in the middle of the floor, panting as though she'd run a marathon while Fiona stood over her looking as though she'd just walked in from a hair appointment.

"Again," Fiona said to her.

"It's no use. I won't gain muscle memory in two days."

"Mind over matter. Besides, without any training, you'll be in a worse position."

Zoe stayed on the mat and shook her head.

"Let's see how you handle someone Noah's size." Fiona stepped back after throwing Zoe on the ground a hundred times, strangling her, and punching at her face and stopping millimeters short of breaking her nose.

Previously, Noah had been the attacker toward Fiona to show Zoe how to do the moves. Now he was stepping toward an exhausted and frustrated woman who had no energy to even feign a defense. He hesitated, not wanting to hurt her, but knowing she needed to be prepared. This was not the way to build trust with her, but Fiona told Zoe to get on her feet and for Noah to step behind her. He grabbed her ponytail, and instead of pulling away as she had on most of the previous attempts by Fiona, Zoe turned into him and slammed her fist right into his groin, then slammed her other arm into his back forcing him to the ground. The pain took Noah's breath away. Although he caught himself before he hit the floor, he released his grip on her hair. Noah stepped back, his eyes tearing and his vision off.

"That was perfect," Fiona said to Zoe, with no thought to Noah's pain.

Zoe rushed over to him and placed her hand on his shoulder. "Are you okay?"

He nodded and forced a lame smile. "That's exactly how you need to protect yourself."

He glared at Fiona, but she merely shook her head. "If you wore the correct gear, you wouldn't be bowled over. I think we're done for the day."

"That's it?" Zoe replied, her hand still resting on Noah's shoulder. "How is this going to help me act like Allison in the newsroom?"

"Take a shower and come back after lunch. We're done with self-defense, but you have a lot to learn before you go to sleep."

Zoe turned one more time to Noah. "I'm sorry."

"Don't be. You did everything right." He meant it. If something happened, she'd have to know how to defend herself. And Fiona was right, he hadn't anticipated Zoe's strength when arriving in the gym, but she had to fight like she meant it. And she did.

The first part of the afternoon was spent on beauty treatments with Zoe getting a manicure and pedicure as well as her hair trimmed and colored to add the subtle highlights of her sister. Noah worked with Calvin during that time getting more of the security logistics of the assignment.

When he returned to see Zoe in action, he stalled at the door. The chill Zoe who wore sweatshirts and baggy jeans was now dressed in a tight black pencil skirt and pale green silk blouse with black high heels. Allison's twin in almost every way, until she took a few steps in her shoes. He leaned against the wall of the conference room, arms folded, trying not to look discouraging. Or to laugh. The main problem was that Zoe looked like her sister, but her mannerisms were low-key elementary school teacher, not überconfident television personality. The mission hinged on how convincingly she could impersonate Allison, an idea that seemed more far-fetched with each passing moment. Her facial expression beamed self-doubt. How could identical twins have such opposite personalities? He'd always had a great head for problem-solving but here he missed the mark.

At least Fiona had accepted the position of taskmaster. Her easygoing manner never once showed the frustration that even the stylist Eleni exhibited when Zoe almost toppled into a chair when trying on a pair of her sister's heels. Clothes, shoes, and makeup boxes were strewn about the floor and table, a chaotic attempt to transform Zoe from a third-grade teacher into a savvy and sophisticated news reporter.

Fiona held up a tablet, playing clips of Allison on air. Zoe copied whatever Allison said and tried to gesture with her hands and assume her stance in a similar manner. Whatever she was doing seemed awkward and out of place compared to her sister. Which was strange, because the day before, as she handled all sorts of big issues, she'd acted far stronger and more competent.

Fiona had brought in a full-length mirror so Zoe could mimic her sister's facial expressions. She was trying too hard. Draped in a sleek blazer right out of Allison's closet, she faced her reflection with pinched lips and furrowed brows.

"You look like you hate everyone in the world. Can you lift your chin and smile? See how she commands attention? It's all in the posture, the eye contact," Fiona directed, tapping the screen for emphasis.

"I see it, but…" Zoe's voice trailed off as she tried to mimic the stance.

Eleni pushed forward and adjusted Zoe's posture. "Darling, it's like you're apologizing for existing. Shoulders back, chin up. You're a lioness, not a mouse. Show us fierce."

Zoe, still staring at herself, lifted her brows, shifted her posture, but made such a forced expression, she almost looked like a caricature of herself. "This isn't working." She attempted to stride toward Noah in her new high heels, wobbling slightly. "I feel more like a circus performer," she joked, trying to lighten the mood, until she tripped and fell into Noah's arms.

He held her a moment, before feeling the heat of Fiona's stare and the wilting of Zoe's confidence. Lifting her back to a standing position, he thought about the circus performers he'd seen in his life. They walked on high wires with more ease than she walked on the floor.

"I want you to stay in heels until you go to bed tonight." Fiona pointed at Zoe's feet.

"All day? Then I really will be like Allison because I'll end up in the hospital with a broken leg just like her."

"Doubtful. After a few hours, you'll get your balance. It's

like riding a bike. Once your body knows how to shift the weight to keep your balance, it will become one hundred times easier." Fiona turned to Eleni. "Thank you for your help. We could use your services tomorrow and the next day, before she goes into the newsroom."

"I thought Allison said her makeup gets done on the set."

"It does, but she always wears a base before heading into the newsroom. You have a simpler makeup style and you also need your hair blown out before you go." Fiona didn't seem to notice Zoe rolling her eyes. She'd endured an hour getting her hair styled. And tomorrow she'd do it again?

The long wavy hair that just yesterday had been pulled tight in a ponytail under a baseball hat looked good on her, but the maintenance wasn't worth it for most people. Noah was thankful for his shorter, low-maintenance style. A little gel, a quick minute under the hair dryer, and a swish of hair wax to keep his cowlick from running amok.

After Eleni left, their attention shifted to a mock newsroom setup. Each role and function appeared on a SMART Board with the current employees in each role at the studio. A Face Time video of Allison appeared to the right of the diagram, sitting at a table with a large window behind her. The background to the video seemed familiar. The cabin where Fresh Pond Security sent people who had to be removed from view for a while. Their other safe house, a very high-tech facility that seemed more like a dilapidated colonial farmhouse from the outside had been blown up at the time Jason and Fiona's son, Matt, was kidnapped. Allison, dressed in a sweatshirt with her hair put up in a ponytail seemed more like Zoe. It was as though they'd shifted bodies.

"I'm glad you could be here with us," Fiona said to the screen.

"It's no problem. I'm bored out of my mind." She turned her face toward Zoe. "You don't look anything like me," she said, causing Zoe's confidence to falter.

Noah wanted to strangle Allison. After spending all day trying to build her up, one comment from her sister could send her tumbling.

"Yes, you do look like Allison. Exactly like her," Meaghan said, appearing behind Allison. "Nice job. Love the highlights."

Zoe's expression brightened.

"I've been teaching your sister cribbage," Meaghan continued, deftly changing the subject. "She'll make a formidable opponent when she decides to focus." Marlowe barked in the background and she shook her head toward him. "I'll be back after I take this little monster outside." As Meaghan walked off-screen, everyone could hear her calling out to him, "Are you the bestest boy? Let's go outside for a minute and then we have to get back."

"How are you doing?" Zoe yelled toward the screen at Allison.

Her sister lifted her hands to cover her ears. "My ears work fine. My legs not so much. Let's get through this as I'm a bit dizzy from sitting up for so long."

Zoe nodded, but her energy seemed to have waned after Allison's attacks.

"The man with the dark brown comb-over is my producer, Glenn. He oversees the show, hands out assignments, and is generally my biggest advocate."

"But not your biggest protector," Noah added.

"That's not fair. He saw that I could get a big break from the meeting and I was more than willing to take that risk." Her defensiveness punched right back at Noah, not that her reaction changed how he felt about the guy. No reporter should go to such high-risk areas without a backup, especially a fairly young reporter whose biggest stories so far came from her university days.

Fiona gave him an icy glare, so he remained silent for the next few minutes as Allison went through the major players in the newsroom.

"Is Gretchen as off-putting as she seems or is that just her television persona?" Zoe asked about the morning anchor.

"At fifty-eight, she feels the daggers in her back. Her coanchor, Marty, is sixty-three, but he has no such pressure, despite both of them pulling in the same ratings. I'd put her name on a list of allies."

Zoe soaked up the information, her interest in the workings of the newsroom a thousand times higher than her interest in which color blue to wear with a black pencil skirt. Although her knowledge of the people was essential, she'd never get a chance to interact with anyone if she didn't succeed in mimicking her sister's mannerisms.

"And the camera and sound crew?" she asked.

"You should be familiar enough with each of them to be able to joke and smile. They're the unsung heroes of the place." Allison listed four camera operators and two sound techs who were particularly friendly with her.

Noah wrote down every person mentioned in a notebook. He'd memorize the details Allison listed about each part of the newsroom and the overall layout of the studios and then leave the notebook back at headquarters in order to have nothing on him that would implicate him.

They broke for dinner after Allison insisted she needed a nap.

"How are your feet?" Noah asked Zoe as she toddled to the kitchen. He wanted to keep their conversation on the trivial following the hours spent absorbing a mountain of data for this task.

"You put them on for even an hour and tell me how your feet feel." Her voice carried amusement laced with annoyance.

"I'm quite satisfied with my loafers." He strolled alongside her as she limped down the hall, now carrying her shoes.

"I bet."

They each grabbed some coffee and a sandwich from a tray someone had ordered for them. It was appreciated, as this assignment would take all of her concentration.

"Are you a fan of GDK news?" he asked about Allison's station.

"Not sure I'd say I'm a fan, but I find the station brings me the local news without a whole bunch of cooking segments and interviews with actors or writers. That's a huge time-saver," She shrugged. "So are you a fan of Allison and her station?"

"She's good at her job and the station is effective in their delivery," he conceded.

She smiled at that. "She *is* good at her job. I've always admired how natural she is in front of a camera."

From the sound of it, Zoe cared about Allison, but they didn't seem to share a bond. "How close are you?" he asked in search of a better understanding of their relationship.

"We're siblings. We're going to have good moments and bad ones. We share much more of a past than we do a present. Perhaps that's the way it goes for all siblings. Once work obligations, families, and babies take over, there's little room for connection." She bit into her sandwich, a bit of mustard touched her chin, but Noah held back taking it off with his finger. Instead, he handed her a napkin and pointed to it. "What about you? Do you get along with your siblings?"

"I only have Elise, my sister." More than a sister, a confidante and a best friend. "And we get along great. It might help that we live by different oceans."

"I'm not sure. I think the distance between Boston and Nantucket might make us even more estranged. Perhaps being twins makes it different for Allison and I. The expectations to be married to twin brothers and each have two point five kids and puppies from the same litter came at us hard."

"Is that what you wanted?"

She paused. Her mind filing through a thousand memories. "I never wanted to be her next-door neighbor, but I wanted more contact than she was willing to give. The only times she calls me is when she needs something, like yesterday when she asked me to watch Marlowe. I grab at those chances, because I'm terrified that she'll let me go if I'm not useful to her in some way, and here I am again, being useful." Her eyes showed a whole mountain of hurt.

He couldn't imagine straining to hold on to his relationship with Elise. He always knew she'd have his back and he'd have hers. There was no secret tally keeping score of favors done or contact made.

"I'm sorry. I sound like a jealous child, but I'm not jealous. Not of her money and lifestyle. I am jealous that her work gets the best of her and I end up with only the scraps." She put the half-eaten sandwich on her plate and took a sip of coffee.

After lunch, Allison never came back on-screen. Instead, Fiona quizzed Zoe one hundred different ways about the people in the newsroom.

"Who loved the Red Sox more than the Patriots?" Fiona asked.

"Marty," Zoe answered after a moment of recalling all the information that had been thrown at her that morning. "Once Spring training began, he knew all the baseball scores and almost ignored football."

"Perfect."

As the day progressed, Zoe's transformation became more pronounced. She channeled some of Allison's confidence, her walk in high heels though not natural yet was definitely more assured, her questions were sharp and insightful, and her Allison expressions seemed more natural.

Despite his initial reservations, Noah found himself impressed by Zoe's progress. Leaning against the wall in the conference room, he analyzed each step she took and each word she spoke. Better. Much better. The physical transformation was striking, but it was the subtle changes in her behavior that truly surprised him.

"You're getting there," he said as they wrapped up for the day.

Zoe flashed a tired but grateful smile. "Thanks. While I feel better than this morning, I couldn't walk into the studio in the morning and be anything near like Allison."

Noah pushed off from the wall, his skepticism waning. "I disagree. I have to admit, you're doing better than I expected. But remember, mimicking Allison is about more than looks and mannerisms. It's about mindset."

Zoe met his gaze. "If I could get into Allison's mind, I would be as successful as she is."

"Is that what you think? That she's more successful than you are? Tell that to the classroom full of children who were crying on the last day of school because you wouldn't be their teacher anymore."

"Only a handful of kids were upset. The rest raced off into the summer."

"You matter. Would you give up your life to have Allison's? Answer truthfully."

She tapped her fingers on the table and frowned. "I suppose not. I'd miss the stars at night and the sound of the ocean outside my window...and the children. So how does that help me turn into Allison?"

"You don't have to transform into Allison completely. Be as confident in your decisions as she is in hers. Be proud of who you are and what you've accomplished. Then take your own personal reservoir of confidence and act like Allison for one, maybe two days," Noah said, his doubts giving way to cautious optimism.

Chapter Twelve

Zoe fell asleep thinking about what Noah had said to her. She'd spent so long being jealous of her sister that she never thought of the wonderful life she'd made for herself on Nantucket. Instead of dreaming about being Allison, she dreamed of a simple coffee date with Noah, ending with a breathless kiss and a yearning for the one hole in her life to be filled.

At breakfast the next morning, she had a pop quiz on every part of the studio and the people there, including the security guards at the door to the building. Noah, seated across from her, his eyes occasionally meeting hers with a warmth that made her heart skip a beat, recited answers off the top of his head with an ease that only deepened her admiration of him. Although he would have to act ignorant of the workings of the newsroom as her boyfriend, he understood the place and the people more than she did.

When she went to the training room again, Fiona pushed Zoe further. She threw her down three times and lifted Zoe off the ground, making her kick like a toddler getting moved around by her mother. The problem was that Fiona was shorter than Zoe. Much shorter.

When Noah came at her, Zoe hesitated. She felt bad about the day before, until he pulled back her ponytail and wrapped his other arm around and covered her mouth with his free hand.

The action flooded back the fear and agony of having someone grab her from behind and drugging her in her sister's apartment. She stopped thinking and started thrashing her arms and legs, pulling away from Noah with every bit of strength she had. Her hair pulled even tighter until he let go.

Her breath came in short, ragged gasps, each one mirroring the frustration and doubt swirling inside her. The training room, with its huge blue mats and an entire weight area, felt like a prison. Fiona's instructions on self-defense were forgotten the second Zoe tried to put them into practice. Each attempt to replicate Fiona's and Noah's moves ended in bruises, falls, and a deeper sense of inadequacy.

"Focus. It's about anticipating your opponent's next move," Fiona reminded her, resetting her stance for what felt like the hundredth time.

"I'm trying, but my body and my brain aren't speaking the same language," Zoe confessed, her arms and legs aching.

"You did it perfectly yesterday," Noah said.

"But yesterday you didn't cover my mouth with chloroform."

He winced. The concern in his eyes tugged at her heart. Before he could say anything, the door to the training room opened, and Jason stepped in. He winked at Fiona, which might have been adorable had Fiona not spent so much time beating up Zoe prior to his arrival. His presence added to the pressure overwhelming her.

"How is our trainee?" he asked Fiona.

"I'm failing in every way." If she'd had even a speck of assurance in herself when she agreed to this, it was all lost with her poor defense skills and her inability to walk five feet in stilettos. "I don't think Noah and I can pull this off." She didn't want to throw him under the bus, but it had been his idea and it was a bad one.

"Would you feel more comfortable if I went inside with Zoe instead of Noah?" Fiona asked. "No offense, Noah."

Noah definitely took offense from the way his expression fell.

"That won't be necessary," Jason responded. "Noah will

handle this fine and draw a lot less attention than you will."
He strolled over to Noah's side. "Have you sparred with her?"

"A few times."

"Let me see how she's doing?" Jason pointed in Zoe's direction.

She almost fled the room. The thought of sparring with Noah again made her stomach twist, not wanting to hurt him, but needing to master everything she learned. Lose-Lose. She'd had a hard enough time with Fiona, knowing Fiona would throw her to the mat without any hesitation.

Noah approached her from the front, his face unreadable. Then he pulled a knife on her. An actual knife. What the heck? She stepped back, but he moved closer. Panic wrapped over her. Her foot slipped as she tried to execute a simple defensive move Fiona had made her practice twenty times, sending her crashing to the mat. The thud of her body hitting the floor echoed across the room. Noah, after putting the knife away, knelt down and put out a hand to help her up. "Are you okay?"

His touch, gentle and caring, sent a shiver down her spine. His pity, however, hit as hard as her fall onto the mat. She scrambled to her feet, her frustration burning her face. She turned to flee the room, but was blocked by Jason.

"You're not done. Show me what you've got," Jason said, more of a challenge rather than encouragement.

Fiona stood to the side, her perfectly curvy body and blond ponytail mocking her.

Zoe, wiping sweat from her brow, squared her shoulders, more to keep from crying than to build her own confidence. Jason approached her, no weapons, but his size alone intimidated her. Black hair pulled back in a ponytail, black T-shirt and jeans, he would be cast as a bad guy in any TV show or movie. As he stepped in to grab her shoulders, she went through her defensive motions again, every movement slow, predictable, and ineffective. Jason's expression remained impassive, but his disappointment was as palpable as the tension in the room.

Noah's eyes met hers. The flicker of concern he wore almost broke her resolve completely, yet something in his gaze, a silent encouragement made her ache with a myriad of unspoken emotions.

"I thought you said she was making progress," Jason remarked dryly, turning to Fiona.

Fiona defended her. "She is. These things take—"

"Time?" Jason finished for her, his skepticism clear. "We don't have the luxury of time. Brendan Quinn's chief of staff was murdered last night. It seems that whoever paid the bribe is sending a warning to Quinn to keep his mouth shut, no matter what. Quinn's family might be next. We need to cut the head off the beast or the morgue is going to end up with a waiting list."

Fiona shot him a look, as though he'd said too much, but Zoe caught the exchange. People were dying. And she was walking into the middle of this mess. Feeling the walls closing in, she excused herself, muttering something about needing a moment. She retreated to her room, her heart racing, her mind picturing a hundred ways to die by interfering with a criminal organization.

Alone, she sank onto her bed, head in her hands. The doubts that had been whispering at her now roared. Her life was literally on the line, including whoever came near her. This wasn't going to work. Even if she could figure out how to act like Allison, she was a liability.

She called her father. When she left to watch Marlowe, he'd told her to have fun. She'd since texted him a few times saying how great things were, at Jason's insistence. No need to force her father into the middle of everything, but she missed having his thoughts on her current situation. A former police chief in Nantucket, he was her biggest ally. Perhaps everyone else, including Allison, had been wrong about keeping him out of it. She didn't bother leaving a message when the call went to voicemail.

With a shaky breath, she dialed Allison next, but received her voicemail too. She left a message. "Hey there. They have me trying to act like you, but you are a one of a kind twin. And I doubt I'll ever be able to fill your shoes."

Hanging up, she sat in silence, the sense of isolation wrapping around her like an icy embrace.

Someone knocked on her door.

"Come in," she called out, because whoever it was, they'd barge in whether she wanted them to or not.

It was Noah. The sight of him freshly showered and dressed in navy khakis and a white button-down shirt, ignited something in her. He looked more put together, more striking than anyone else at Fresh Pond Security, besides Fiona, who dressed with a flair that outshone Allison.

"Are you okay?"

"No. I'm not prepared. And honestly, I'm not ready to die, and I'm not ready for my sister to die either."

Noah stared at her with an intensity she hadn't seen in him before. It spoke of pain, suffering, and a fortitude that seemed more like a brick wall than a ramming machine. And she knew he'd protect her to his last breath, whether she asked or not. "You're not going to die. And Meaghan is the best of the best. Your sister is safe." The silent promise in his eyes, a vow to protect her at all costs, suddenly had her fearing for his life. She didn't have him in any way but she didn't want to lose him either.

She stretched her arms overhead and winced. Even if she could remember the moves they'd drilled into her, she wouldn't be able to lift her arms to actually do the moves.

"You're using muscles you haven't used in a while, if ever. A hot bath tonight should ease the pain. You'll be fine tomorrow" He waved her to the door. "Ready for more training? I promise it won't involve being thrown to a mat."

"I don't think I'll ever be ready. I could get us both killed tomorrow." She needed to speak with Jason and convince him that she wasn't prepared. "Where's Jason?"

"He left for a meeting."

"Can you tell him I need him? Or even Fiona. I'm not ready to die."

"I'm not going to let that happen." Despite his appearance, all chill and casual, he did have an edge to him. And that should have made her feel more secure, but the only person in the newsroom she would be able to protect was her, and she didn't have an edge. She didn't even have a backbone, especially when murderers were involved.

"So many things could go wrong," she said on a sigh.

He stepped to her side. "Or we could pull it off beautifully and no one will be the wiser."

"That's a long shot."

His mouth lifted into a teasing smile. "I like betting on long shots."

By the end of the second day, Zoe was stronger and more of a mess. Jason's insistence on telling her about the murder at Boston City Hall destroyed her growing confidence. It didn't help that Allison had been on a phone call with her, whining about how Zoe had better not ruin her career while fishing for information that could help save Allison's life. Whenever Allison seemed bored, she entertained herself with bitter criticism of Zoe. According to her, Zoe had no ambition, no courage to go after her goals, no fashion sense, and an inability to attract the right kind of man, although Allison had yet to describe the type of man she should be attracting. To be fair, Zoe had committed herself to the wrong man back in college, someone smothering, who, in the course of three years of dating, had managed to strip Zoe of most of her self-esteem, but she'd found it again, most of it anyway. Besides, Allison had not been super successful with her string of boyfriends either. Once the men found themselves second to Allison's career, they tended to replace her with someone dedicated to inflating their egos.

Adding to Zoe's stress, she'd texted and called her father multiple times, but hadn't received a reply from him. Each unanswered call amplified her distress. When she called their neighbor to check on him, he didn't reply either. Noah found her sitting in the kitchen with Calvin, phone to her ear, a portrait of barely contained panic.

"I can't get through to him. What if something's happened? I need to go home." Her voice didn't waver on those last words. She'd decided on her next course of action and had fully committed to it.

Calvin shook his head. "The mission begins in the morn-

ing. We don't have time. I know Jason won't approve it. Can
someone you know go over to the house? We need to be practical," insisted the most practical person at Fresh Pond Security.

Noah stepped closer to her, his eyes never leaving her. "Calvin's right. We can't afford to lose you now. But," he added,
his voice softening, "we'll find a way to check on your father.
Trust me." He reached out, gently squeezing her shoulder, the
warmth of his touch a silent promise.

His touch provided enough reassurance to steady her beating heart. She nodded. "Okay," she replied. "I trust you."

As Noah turned to leave, his hand lingered on her shoulder. His hand on her at all wasn't necessary, but felt amazingly
right. The overwhelming sense of dread steadied, still there,
but grounded by a hero's touch. She wasn't in this alone, and
that made all the difference.

Chapter Thirteen

Noah, leaning against the doorway, crossed his arms. Zoe must be exhausted after all the training and the mental strain of the dangerous situation. The genuine concern etched on her face provided him a mountain of guilt, but this wasn't about making everything easy for Zoe. They had to get inside the news station soon. She wasn't as prepared as she could be, but prepared enough for the task at hand. "Calvin's right. We have a timeline. You know this isn't simply pretending to be your sister for a day. Every moment counts to find something that can help us."

Zoe spun to face him. "I'm not going anywhere until I hear my father's voice, or see his face. If I'm your only shot—which isn't true because you could break in, at some risk, but you could—then you need to go on my schedule. I'm not as ready as I want to be, and I'll be thinking of my father the entire time if I don't reach him soon. 'Trust me,' you said. Show me that I can trust you. If anything were to happen to him because I wasn't there—"

Her words gave Noah pause. He did want what was best for her well-being, and he'd told Jason about the situation with her father. They were already looking for him. If she didn't believe in herself, she'd never convince anyone else that she could handle this. Watching her struggle, Noah felt a twinge of empathy. He'd been in her shoes once, torn between his job and family. His mother had been in a car accident. He should have dropped everything and rushed to her side. Instead, he believed he could wait until the weekend to travel to see her. When he finally flew back to California, he'd been too late to say goodbye to his mother. She'd died from a head injury the moment he stepped on the plane. The memory still wrecked him, because at the time, he'd still been an analyst. He had no reason to stay at his desk and give more hours to his job. It wasn't as if anyone cared if he stepped away for a few days. There had been sufficient backups for him. He could have left. Zoe had even more reason to want to check on her father. If whoever had attacked Zoe at the apartment learned about the rest of Allison's family, they might harm them to stop her investigation. Besides, this wasn't Zoe's job—she'd volunteered to help. If she decided not to go through with it, there would be nothing they could do to keep her.

"I have been working on it, but let me get an update," he said and then stepped into the hall to call Jason.

"Is she ready?" Jason asked as soon as he answered the phone.

"Not really."

The silence on the other end of the line lasted decades. "What's her hang-up?" Jason finally asked.

"She wants to be sure her father is okay."

Jason was silent for a few seconds, then said, "Although I was hoping to keep her focus on the newsroom, no one on the team would be able to focus if they felt their family member was in harm's way. Go ahead and take the jet but be back in time for her to get some rest. There's a lot happening on that island and she should see it personally."

Noah couldn't believe his ears. They'd just acquired the Gulfstream after signing several more than lucrative government contracts. It made flying in and out of areas quicker and easier. Taking it for a quick flight to Nantucket seemed frivolous, but he accepted the offer anyway.

"Is there something I need to be prepared for over there?" he asked.

"You should be prepared for anything at all times."

"Not an answer." He'd worked with Jason enough to know that his boss held his cards tight as he manipulated everyone around him.

"Just keep her focused on the greater good. I'd prefer you to go in unaware. It will keep you honest with her." The big honesty line was a bit hypocritical, since Jason had hid his staged death from everyone around him for years. Noah had given him the benefit of the doubt and had chosen to stay with the team, while his best friend, Finn, had decided to leave because he'd lost faith in his boss. Although Noah had good relationships with Sam, Meaghan, Calvin, and the other members of the team, he missed Finn. They shared a comradery and friendship that was difficult to build in their field.

Noah returned to Zoe and Calvin. They were facing each other as though captains of rival debate teams. Calvin's fists were clenched together, while the color in Zoe's face was an alarming shade of red.

Calvin shook his head and stepped back as Noah arrived. "I can't believe you'd just quit after all you've already done. We don't have time for a Plan B. This could make Boston safer and keep your sister safe as well."

Zoe crossed her arms across her chest. "I said I would try. I never said for sure that I would do it. I can't believe you're bullying me. I'm not getting paid enough to have to deal with you. Oh, that's right. I'm not getting paid at all."

She did have a point, but Noah had high hopes that she'd help them anyway. Perhaps a quick trip to see her father would ease her fears.

Calvin appeared ready to challenge her again, but Noah stepped between them and cut him off. "Listen," he began, "what if I could get you to Nantucket and back quickly? We have a private plane. We fly out, check on your dad, and return right after. Would that put your mind at ease?"

Zoe blinked, the offer clearly catching her off guard. "You'd do that?"

Noah sighed, a decision made. "Ensuring your head is in the game by knowing your family is safe is just as important as a good night's sleep." Although they would hopefully be back in time for her to get some sleep too.

"Thank you, Noah. I... I appreciate this more than you know." There was relief in her words, and less strain than the one directed at Calvin, which had bordered on panic.

"No problem. Let's get you to your father, and then you can make your decision with a clearer understanding of everything going on around us." He turned to Calvin. "Can you contact Hanscom Field and make flight preparations?"

"For when?"

"Right now, and have them on standby on the island. This is a quick round trip. Jason's orders."

That last part took the thorns out of his request. It was Jason and Steve Wilson's company. What they said went, no arguments. Calvin nodded and turned toward his computer screen.

An hour later, Zoe stared wide-eyed at the sleek contours of the private jet at the small airport just outside of Boston. She tried calling her father a few more times until Noah asked her to put away her phone. She'd be there soon enough, and each unanswered call only made her more anxious.

Noah prepared himself for the worst. If Jason wanted them over there, something must have happened. He said a quick prayer that it didn't involve any harm to her father. She didn't deserve any more disasters happening to her. When the flight attendant offered them each champagne, he turned her away. Neither of them needed weakened reflexes both physically or mentally. The flight attendant returned with water for each of them and turkey sandwiches.

As the engines roared to life, Noah settled into his seat across from Zoe, who remained peering out the window, her gaze unfocused. Her tension eased slightly with the ascent, perhaps the physical distance from her problems on the ground lending a temporary reprieve. A very temporary reprieve. Before they were halfway through their sandwiches, the aircraft was preparing to land.

Noah allowed himself a moment to simply watch her, appreciating the resilience she'd shown throughout this ordeal. The soft light filtering through the window gave her beauty an ethereal quality. He took a moment to appreciate the smooth contours of her cheeks and the way her eyes gave a glimpse into her thoughts. He imagined a world where they could live a simple life, but he didn't live a simple life. He wanted to make a difference. His work targeted ways to help the people who weren't able to help themselves. People like Zoe. He didn't want to give that up.

"Once we're on Nantucket," he said, breaking the silence, "we'll head straight to your house to check on your father."

Zoe turned from the window, offering him a small, grateful smile. Her eyes, though shadowed with worry, shone with a trust that made his heart ache. "Thanks, Noah. I can't tell you how much this means to me."

The words were simple, but the sincerity behind them struck a chord in Noah. He tried to keep his feelings locked behind his character, a person who had more confidence and bravado than Noah, the former analyst, but helping her had become more than just a means to boost him back into fieldwork. He cared about Zoe, deeply, and the lines between duty and affection were becoming increasingly blurred.

The late afternoon light cast a subtle glow over the clouds, bathing the sky in gold and orange hues that reflected on the ocean below. As the plane descended toward their destination, Noah forced his mind to focus on the positive. The constant pressure, the weight of responsibility lifted, if only briefly. This was more than just a flight to ensure Zoe's peace of mind; it was his way of demonstrating to her the lengths he would go to protect her, to prove that he was looking out for her no matter what.

"I've always liked flying," Noah found himself saying, his voice reflective. "There's something about being above it all that puts things into perspective. Makes the problems on the ground seem...smaller, somehow." He hadn't traveled by private jet since his father had left. Once he'd decided to stop being a parent to Elise and him, he held back all but the minimal support the court had ordered him to pay. In the blink of an eye, they lost access to their private school, the golf and tennis lessons, and lavish vacations to the most beautiful places in the world.

Zoe turned to Noah. The thoughtful expression on her face made him forget his bad memories. "Flying like this is beautiful in a way I didn't expect. I've only flown once on a school trip. We were all so exhausted, none of us stayed awake for the final descent. Except Allison. She had a collection of pictures she'd taken as the plane landed. She was always one step ahead of everyone. In intelligence, personality, and strength."

Zoe had truly defined her whole life as a comparison to her sister. Allison was the traveler; Zoe was the homebody. Allison wore the best clothes; Zoe dressed comfortably. Allison fought for her dreams; Zoe stayed complacent. Yet Noah didn't believe Zoe's own analysis of herself and her qualities. Zoe seemed protective of her sister. She nourished her relationships. She supported Allison's dreams, even putting herself at risk to protect her sister. Zoe would push her own needs aside to protect those she loved. And in that, Noah saw a strength and bravery she couldn't see in herself.

When the pilot announced their final descent, Noah felt a twinge of regret that the peaceful interlude had to end. Jason had a reason for letting Zoe visit her father as he wouldn't spend such a huge portion of their travel budget out of the sheer goodness of his heart. As the plane touched down, he reached over and took her hand in his, giving it a reassuring squeeze. "We'll get through this, Zoe. Together."

Her fingers tightened around his, the silent bond between them growing at the speed of an out-of-control freight train. "Thanks for doing this and everything for me," she whispered, her voice filled with gratitude and something deeper. "I don't know what I'd do without you."

His heart filled with something he didn't want, but craved all the same. As the plane came to a stop, he vowed silently that he would do everything in his power to keep her safe.

Not knowing what they'd find at her home, Noah braced himself for the worst, so he could stand with Zoe and support her no matter what they discovered on the island.

Chapter Fourteen

The wheels of the private jet touched down on the tarmac of Nantucket's quaint airport. Zoe had never experienced such a luxurious flight. For most of her life, the ferry had been her main mode of transportation back and forth to the mainland. As the plane slowed, her tension returned. Enjoying the trip even the slightest bit sent waves of guilt through her. She called her father again, hoping he answered even if she'd feel foolish if he did after all the arrangements Fresh Pond Security had put in place for her. He didn't answer. After losing her mother to cancer, her father meant everything to her. Both her father and Allison did, although her father had been the far more supportive of the two. Allison had always found a way to compete over everything from the size of her waist to their relative incomes. Their father had done the opposite, supporting each of them for their own successes and not once pitting them against each other.

As they made their way through the tiny terminal, the salty breeze of Nantucket greeted them, a familiar scent that brought a fleeting smile to Zoe's lips. It was good to be home.

Noah was on his phone next to her. He glanced over and gave her a subtle smile and a wink as they made their way to a waiting car. A black Jeep Rubicon. A man exited the car and handed Noah the keys. Noah acted as though this was no big deal, like anyone could snap their fingers and have a jet gassed up and waiting for them and then a car standing by when they arrived. She couldn't begin to calculate the cost of such extravagances. She wouldn't complain, however, because they'd offered. What she could feel guilty about was her decision to remain behind when the flight returned to Boston. She hadn't mentioned this to Noah, but if her father had any need for her, she would remain at his side. There was no way to be able to handle the complicated task she'd been given if her thoughts remained on her father's safety.

She still worried over Allison's safety as well but had faith in Meaghan's ability to protect her. Even though she had committed herself to stepping away from this charade, it was not because of Noah. She trusted he could keep her safe, although she wasn't prepared to mention that to him yet, in case he became overconfident. She wanted him crossing all his *t*'s and dotting all his *i*'s. The only person she didn't have any faith in was herself. In the past week, she'd been knocked out by someone in her sister's apartment and had pretty much failed her training despite Fiona's irrational confidence in her. She'd had all the excitement she could handle for a lifetime. Curling up for a good night's sleep in her bedroom as her father played the news on full volume in the living room would be a comfortable way to spend the evening and release the stress that had built up in her bones over the past few days. The only difficulty would be convincing Noah that their assignment was better off without her as the unknown variable. She had no desire to be the weak link in this plan to bring down some of the most dangerous men in Boston.

"Let's not waste any time." He guided Zoe toward the waiting car with a gentle hand at her back. His touch both comforting and something more, something she didn't want to think about, because what she was feeling for him couldn't be reciprocated. Her heart had stumbled right into him, and they had no future together. She lived on an island, he lived across the bay. Perhaps she was falling for him because he'd been her hero. A common affliction in romance novels. "Need help?" He held out a hand to help her climb into the passenger seat.

"I've got it." She smiled at him, appreciating his offer, but grabbed the handle and pulled herself up. A much taller ride than her MINI Cooper.

As Noah drove the Jeep, he surveyed everything around him except her. There was a seriousness to him, as though primed for a fight. His demeanor, combined with her father's lack of communication, made the trip excruciating. Fifteen minutes later they pulled into her neighborhood. Not the richest area on the island, not by any means, but it was charming and most of her neighbors lived on the island year round, forming a tight-knit community.

As they turned onto her street, a scene straight out of Zoe's nightmares unfolded. Her home, a white cozy cottage nestled among several beds of flowers and greenery, was besieged by police cars, their lights vandalizing the scene with their harsh, blue flashing.

Zoe's peace shattered, replaced by a rising tide of panic. "What's going on?" she said, her voice barely a whisper over the thudding of her heart. The garden, once a vibrant tribute to her mother's love for horticulture, was now a crime scene.

Before Noah could respond, she was out of the car and running toward the chaos, driven by her biggest fear—losing her father. Noah followed close behind, his footsteps staying close, but not overpowering her.

Her heart raced as that fear had come straight to her doorstep and threatened the person she loved the most. She scanned the officers, searching for someone in charge, someone who could give her answers.

The officers stomping over the pachysandra border carrying an empty body bag stopped Zoe in her tracks. Noah reached her side just in time to catch her as her knees buckled, her ability to hold herself together weakening by the second. His presence anchored her as a rush of emotions barreled over her.

"If he's hurt in any way, or worse—" Her voice faltered over the words.

"One step at a time. Let's see what's going on," Noah said, his voice steady and calm, grounding her amid the chaos.

She braced against him and looked around. Her confusion

eased as most of the faces came into focus. This had been her father's world, her father's officers. One of her father's most accomplished mentees, Lieutenant Talia Coleman, seemed to be overseeing the scene. Talia's family had been on the island longer than most of the houses. Her dedication and service to her job earned her the respect of locals and high profile visitors. When she noticed Zoe, she ran over to her. "Zoe? Where have you been?"

"It's a long story. What…who?" She could barely get the words out. Her eyes locked on the body bag. It represented an answer she wasn't sure she could bear. "Who is it? Please, tell me it's not…" Zoe couldn't finish. Tears released as she anticipated the very worst.

The overwhelming trauma of the past week struck her like a bat to the head. Without Noah still holding her, she would have hit the ground. Her whole family was at risk, and she didn't have enough people in her life to ever be prepared to let any of them go.

Talia hesitated, then sighed. "It's not your father."

Zoe looked over the garden once more, the scene etched into her memory. Half the police force was there, she knew most of them. They didn't meet her gaze. Since they weren't talking to her, she became determined to find out the truth on her own. She rushed past Talia and ran into the garden. As she approached, the other officers turned, their faces a mask of professional detachment, yet their eyes betrayed a hint of sympathy. And then she saw the spot where someone in jeans lay, covered in blood. It wasn't her father, but someone she cared about nearly as much.

Mr. Noonan, Zoe's father's lifelong friend and neighbor, lay motionless, his body bloodied and limp. The vibrant life that had once sparkled in the elderly man's eyes had been extinguished, leaving behind a haunting emptiness. This wasn't a random act of violence, it couldn't be. The timing, the brutality of the act, spoke of a message, a warning. Could Allison's actions really have come across the bay and affected Nantucket, Zoe's home, and family?

She gasped at this fresh horror washing over her. "Mr.

Noonan," she whispered, her hand flying to her mouth. "But…
why? Where's my father?"

Noah's arm came around her again, not holding her up as
much as backing her up. A stone wall blocking out a tsunami
of loneliness and fear. She'd only known him a few short days,
but his presence made everything easier somehow.

Talia arrived a moment later. "Let's step away. You don't
need to see this. Mr. Noonan was a lovely man and this
shouldn't be your last memory of him."

Zoe turned away, closing her eyes and trying to imagine the
last time she'd seen him, only a few days before, before she'd
been pulled into her sister's mess of a life. They'd been on the
porch playing poker. Mr. Noonan, her father, Chief Bishop,
and herself. She always lost, but this time, she'd turned over
the queen of hearts to the shock of all the men at the table. As
she pulled the chips she'd won with her flush toward her, Mr.
Noonan said, "It's about time you took us all down. I knew
you had it in you." That faith in her had supported her through
the death of her mother, applying to college, and applying to
work at the local elementary school. He'd been more than a
neighbor. He'd been family.

"Do you have any suspects?" Noah asked Talia, pulling Zoe
out of the past.

One of the drawbacks of living her entire life in the same
small town was the constant surveillance of her life by everyone, and the assumption that they knew every part of her
personal life. As visual proof of that, Talia eyed Noah up and
down as though he was far too bougie to be Zoe's boyfriend,
as everyone assumed she'd settle for some low-maintenance
local guy, like her mother had.

"This is Noah Montgomery," Zoe said. "He works for Fresh
Pond Security and is sort of my bodyguard."

Talia's gaze returned to Zoe, as though it all made sense
why the preppy guy was standing with her. "Why do you have
a bodyguard?"

"Long story, but it might have to do with Mr. Noonan's murder."

Noah did not appear too pleased that she'd said anything about
him. Perhaps he'd wanted them to stay undercover even here.

Talia didn't seem to notice and answered his question. "We're still piecing it together. It seems Mr. Noonan was tending the garden."

Zoe placed a hand over her chest. He always tended their garden, because neither Zoe nor her father had a green thumb and what did he get for his kindness? She bent over, losing the contents of her stomach.

Noah wrapped an arm around her, offering her his strength to keep her upright. "Go ahead, let everything out," he murmured.

She turned into his embrace, burying her face into the crook of his shoulder. Her sobs echoed across the area, the overwhelming feeling that she was losing everyone she loved. Noah never let go, he continued to hold her, rubbing her back and easing her into the present.

"Who did this?" she managed to utter through slowing waves of sobs.

Talia placed a hand on her arm. "So far, we have no witnesses and no motive. I promise, we'll get the bastard who did this."

Zoe's mind held a tempest of emotions. Relief mingled with pain, fear mixed with terror. Mr. Noonan's murder wasn't a random act. It was a direct consequence of Allison's investigation bleeding over from the mainland. Nantucket, once the most peaceful place on earth, had pools of blood that Zoe might never wash away.

"Do you have a time of death?" Noah asked, leaving one arm around her. He was in investigation mode. Zoe appreciated it. Fresh Pond Security had been hired to figure out who had targeted Allison and find a way to stop them.

"A jogger found Noonan about five hours ago. The Crime Scene Unit just finished, so they're now moving his body to the morgue."

"Oh my God. Where's my father?" Zoe said, her anger rising. This was a crime at her home. Her father was missing. Someone was dead.

"To be honest, we don't know. His boat was out since early this morning, but we've had no radio contact. Someone had seen you on the ferry a few days ago, and no one saw you since then. We assumed you were safe with Allison." Before Talia added to what she'd said, the lieutenant's phone rang. She stepped aside to take the call.

"Let's get you somewhere safe," Noah said to Zoe, guiding her back to the car. "I'm so sorry."

Zoe didn't want platitudes, she wanted her father. After retiring from the police force about five years earlier, he'd bought a boat and would spend hours out fishing with friends or occasionally by himself. The vibrant blue hull of her father's boat caught people's attention, but what really made the boat stand out was the image of a large sperm whale on each side, seemingly cresting out of the water. The boat's absence from the marina was always noticed.

Talia strolled back to them. "Where are you going?"

"To find my father." She also wanted to go into the house, but with police swarming all over the yard, she thought a visit to the marina would be the most useful thing to do.

"No need."

"You have him?" Zoe asked.

"His boat came in fifteen minutes ago. Seems he lost his radar and had no way to contact anyone. He's at the police station speaking with Chief Bishop. The chief wants to speak to you as well."

Zoe didn't care about the circumstances, she only cared that he was alive and well. She clenched her fists together, feeling a twinge of guilt for being so relieved about her father's safety while Mr. Noonan was being taken to the morgue.

"Perfect timing. Let's go see your dad," Noah said, holding the Jeep door open for her.

Talia shook her head. "Give it about an hour. He still needs to speak to the Chief."

"Why? He was gone all day."

"You know the drill. Everyone has to be questioned. You'll be next." Talia sighed. "Why don't you grab yourself some coffee and maybe even a sandwich. It might be a long night."

Unlike most places, they wouldn't have to keep tabs on her here. She couldn't go through the airport or the ferry lines without someone minding her business and tattling. And by now, the movements of the black Jeep would grab residents' attention as well.

As they drove away from her home, Zoe sat in stunned silence, her thoughts focused on seeing her father. Noah reached out and took her hand, a gesture that made her feel less alone.

Chapter Fifteen

Neither Zoe nor Noah were hungry, so they went straight to the police station, a colonial-looking brick building that could easily have passed for the town hall. Noah observed every person around him while Zoe greeted half the building, not with any enthusiasm, but more subdued as though they'd all seen each other only a few days ago and making a dramatic greeting was overkill. Most everyone she spoke to had little focus on him, except to size up whether he deserved to be standing with her. Overall, he felt most of them didn't approve, especially the men. He could imagine Zoe breaking the hearts of half the island, not that she'd even notice. Her self-esteem was rock-bottom, she couldn't see her own sparkle.

Growing up in a large city, he'd never known the claustrophobia of life in a very, very small area. In ways, it seemed comforting and in other ways, smothering. He walked beside Zoe, but kept his hands to himself. No use giving any more gossip to her neighbors. If she needed him, she just had to say the word. Otherwise, his job was to observe and make sure she was safe.

After chatting with the woman at the reception desk, Zoe was asked to wait on a set of benches. "Do you need anything? I could run out for some coffee or something?"

"No thank you, Helen. We'll be fine."

The woman waved her arm at Noah. "Can you show some identification before going back into the offices?"

He looked at Zoe, who gave him a half smile. "Protocol," she said.

He provided his license and put his name on a sign-in sheet, then stepped away for a moment to call Jason. The second he answered, Noah grilled him. "You could have warned me."

"I gave you a heads-up. I didn't specify what, but I had Calvin monitoring police scanners for the locations where we have people of interest on the ground. This came up a few hours ago. I wanted you there to find out what you can. You can also look Zoe in the eye and tell her you had no idea."

"I'd prefer to have all the details instead of a sliver of an understanding. And I will be bringing that up at the next team meeting," he replied, his annoyance so high, he didn't care that he'd just chewed out his boss. What he did wasn't fair to Zoe or him.

"Point taken." Jason said, his voice not perturbed in the least. "Let's get her father back here so Zoe doesn't have to worry about him while she's working tomorrow morning."

Noah forgot all about the early setup time. This was going to be a disaster. They'd both be off after a long night of travel and stress. Perhaps he could call it off or at least delay by a day. "What if she waits to go in, so she has more time to prepare and rest?"

"No." Jason's response did not leave an opening for a debate.

"But…"

"The threats are ramping up, and I do not want any more deaths while we're on the case. It could jeopardize our standing with our client. I have a whole team narrowing down the source of the bribe to Quinn. Now I need the insider at the news station willing to take down his own reporter. My guess is on the producer, but we need to be sure." Their client was an organization in charge of a large segment of U.S. intelligence. They used Fresh Pond Security like a small splinter group, except Noah wouldn't receive a lucrative government pension when he retired. He did, however, have a higher salary than anything on a government pay scale.

He bit back his reply and told Jason he'd have them both back on the plane tonight. When he returned to Zoe, she was being escorted into the back offices. Noah followed. Helen gave Zoe a look that told her Noah would be stopped if she said the word, but Zoe didn't say a word. So he followed her.

In the chief of police's office, two men sat at a table on one side of the office, both with mugs of coffee in front of them. The men seemed of an age, but one was in a uniform and the other wore jeans and an old flannel shirt. The chief seemed to be sharing memories with Zoe's father more than he was interrogating him. When Zoe caught sight of her father, a formidable figure with a heavy-set frame and a gruff expression that seemed to have been etched from years on the police force, she rushed forward. Despite his imposing stature, his overall demeanor exuded warmth, especially when he saw Zoe and enveloped her in his arms.

"Dad!" she exclaimed, her voice mixing relief and excitement. She clung to him and he hugged her back in a grip no person would be able to break.

"I'm so glad you're safe. I worried so much about you after they told me what happened at the house. I still can't imagine life without George." Her father was most likely talking about Mr. Noonan. His relief in seeing Zoe faded as they held each other, knowing someone they cared about had died on their property. He gently stroked her hair.

"Why didn't you call me? I couldn't get in touch with you since last night."

"I left my phone at home when I went out on the boat, then had a mishap with the satellite radio. I will never be on the water again without a backup."

Zoe nodded, her head resting on his shoulder as he rubbed her back. "I may put a tracking device on you."

"I probably deserve that." His expression turned serious. "Were you at the house?"

She nodded. "It's a mess. And Mr. Noonan. I can't believe it." She held her tongue on all that had happened to her and Allison, not knowing what was able to be discussed openly and what should remain confidential to protect Allison.

Noah, however, had a different agenda. After several minutes of discussion about what happened at their home, Noah broke the news of the threats on Allison's life and that Zoe was under their protection and now Mr. Goodwyn, her father, should be under their protection as well.

"Allison is chasing a story that hasn't broken and she's being threatened?" her father asked.

"Yes. Her apartment was broken into and her neighbor killed."

Chief Bishop looked over at Zoe. "Is this true?"

"I was there. They almost killed me too," Zoe said, holding herself together under the most stressful of circumstances.

"Who are the suspects?"

"We don't have any leads yet, but it's most likely tied to one of the bigger criminal organizations in the city," Noah replied.

He gave them as much information as possible without revealing which groups they suspected. He'd started to narrow down his own list of suspects, one group linked to the Russian mob, and another with deep ties to the Irish mafia, but these organizations worked through secret trusts and corporate entities, making it hard to pinpoint the people controlling it all. He also kept out the part where Zoe was bait in this dangerous investigation. If her father learned about that, there was no way he'd let her go with Noah. "I don't want to cut this gathering short, but we need to catch our flight back."

Zoe visibly stiffened at his pronouncement. "I don't think I can go back. It's safer here. Besides, someone needs to watch my father."

Noah stood his ground. "He should come with us. He'll be safer off the island."

Her father did not acquiesce. "Not happening. I have everything I need here to remain safe."

"I have to agree," added his ally, Chief Bishop. "I have more than enough resources to protect both of them."

The argument heated up when the chief's phone rang, cutting through the escalating voices. He answered with a curt, "Chief Bishop speaking."

The room fell into a tense silence, everyone's attention now on Bishop as his expression turned from annoyance to surprise, and then to reluctant acceptance.

He ended the call. "You're not going to believe this," he said to Mr. Goodwyn. "That was Homeland Security. They've just taken jurisdiction over this...situation. And according to them—" he paused, his eyes narrowed, as he looked at Noah "—we need to listen to Mr. Montgomery."

Zoe's eyes widened in disbelief, and her father leaned forward, his interest piqued.

Noah, for his part, remained calm, feeling a rush of vindication, although he didn't want to overstep because he had no official law enforcement role. He wasn't going to fake it either and risk arrest for impersonating an officer. "I work for Fresh Pond Security, as a consultant to Homeland Security. I'm not going to force anyone to do anything they don't want—" he stared directly at Zoe "—but the people who want to stop this story from being published will not rest until the story and everyone associated with it are buried. I recommend coming with me. As the call indicates, I'm not making any of this up. The danger is real, and staying here puts everyone at risk. We need to leave."

Chief Bishop sighed, rubbing the bridge of his nose. "All right. Homeland Security trumps local police. But—" he pointed a stern finger at Noah "—you better make sure nothing happens to them. We'll be coordinating with the federal authorities, but if one hair on the head of anyone in the Goodwyn family is knocked out of place, I will gladly resign my position and hunt you down." He pointed a chubby finger directly in Noah's face.

Noah knew when to accept a gift when he received one, so he merely nodded and stood. Zoe remained seated, as though about to stage a strike, despite what the chief said.

Her father reached over to her, squeezing her hand, offering silent support. "I need to stop at the house and pick up an overnight bag."

"No, we should stay here," she insisted. Noah could see all the anxiety over doubling for her sister rushing back into her thoughts.

"This might take a few days. Once we know the players, we should be able to take them out one at a time. If we don't find them all, this situation could put everyone in danger." Noah's words shot out at Zoe, trying to make it clear that she was a necessary piece in all of this.

She didn't appear too happy about it but did stand and head to the door.

Noah nodded, the tension in his back releasing a bit. "Thank you for your assistance," he said to the chief. "I'll arrange everything and keep them safe." He stopped short of promising, because this situation could go sideways at any moment, and he didn't want to promise anything he didn't have control over.

Chapter Sixteen

After a whirlwind of packing their things and heading out to the airport, Zoe fell asleep on the flight back across Nantucket Sound. When she woke, her father and Noah were speaking together in hushed voices. Noah using his hands to highlight something he was saying, while her father had his undivided attention. She didn't know how Noah did it, but he'd effectively neutralized two of the most hardheaded individuals she knew. Her father and Chief Bishop.

Her father sat up when he saw she was awake. "How are you feeling?"

"Tired."

"Nervous?" he asked.

"About?"

"Noah told me about where you're headed tomorrow. I have to say, I'm proud of you."

She looked over at Noah, who was wearing a neutral expression, though it was evident that something he said to her father resonated. But his response was not what she expected. "Proud? I'm going to be a disaster. I can't carry myself as Allison."

He placed his hand over hers, the familiar contact more soothing that a bottle of wine. "You aren't Allison, but you make a pretty amazing Zoe. And Zoe can handle anything that she puts her mind to. She's pretty similar to her sister, except for the high heels. You never could walk in anything higher than sneakers."

It was the same thing Noah had told her, that she didn't have to be Allison exactly and that some of her own qualities would be more than enough to complete this task. Her father had supported everything she did, but this was beyond her usual risk level. He'd never pushed her to be more or to take chances, even when encouraging Allison to try for bigger and better everything. "Why now? Why do you want me to do this dangerous thing when you've never even encouraged my surfing lessons, telling me that fishing is more than enough of a thrill?"

"Because you can do it and help stop some really bad characters. I believe in you and I think you'd regret it if you didn't make an effort."

She didn't know how to respond, so she just nodded. "I love you, Dad."

"Ditto, darling."

After they touched down, Noah drove them to headquarters. He'd decided they should sleep there for simplicity's sake. It was late and moving to a new location would take too much effort. Zoe glanced at her phone. It was 2:00 a.m. and they wanted her at the studio by ten, coiffed, made up, and dressed to kill. It was going to be a very difficult morning.

She anticipated an argument from her father about where they were going, but he went along with everything, although he took in every bit of their surroundings, and she wouldn't be surprised if he had a handgun packed away with him. Old habits die hard.

They each went to different rooms and Zoe made sure her dad had his cell phone and a charger so she could reach him if needed. Noah was more of a shadow around her. He never stepped between her and her father. A nice gesture. Her father had always watched her back and it was an old habit to rely on him, but she also liked having Noah close by. He seemed to believe in her as much as her father, which felt like a first for someone outside of their family.

She woke at eight to Fiona knocking on her door. "Ready?"

"Ready? For a shower, yes. To leave? Not even close."

Fiona opened the door and carried in two cups of coffee. "For coffee. It's important to fuel up."

Zoe sat up and took the steaming mug. "You're an angel."

"Some days I am. How are you feeling after yesterday?"

"Scared." She needed more time and more preparation, but she also realized her family would be at risk if they didn't take down whoever wanted to stop the investigation.

Fiona nodded. "That makes sense. After years of training and experience in this field, I thought I was prepared for anything. Seeing my house attacked and my family at risk, however, nearly knocked me to the ground."

"Really?"

"Well. I'm not a fall-to-the-ground-in-a-panic type of person, but I was upset."

Zoe couldn't see Fiona falling apart over anything. She'd probably just become really pissed off and transform into someone even more deadly.

She showered and then followed Fiona to a conference room, which had transformed into a beauty salon and pop-up designer store.

Upon entering, she was greeted by Eleni, the stylist, and more coffee. "Hurry in. We only have about an hour to fix you up." She gestured toward three suits hanging on a clothes rack. "I found several outfits that should be perfect for today's undertaking. Pick the one you feel most confident in."

Every suit appeared exactly like the style Allison had curated during her news career. Brighter colors, and the high heels made more for Allison than Zoe.

Zoe, feeling out of her element but intrigued, replied, "Can I try them all on?"

The stylist chuckled, "Absolutely. After we get your hair done."

As the stylist turned on the blow-dryer, warmth spread around Zoe. Dressed in the sweatpants and T-shirt she'd slept in, she sipped on coffee as Eleni worked her magic brushing out Zoe's long hair, section by section. It was a soothing process. By the time her hair was done, she was down to fifteen minutes. At least she'd received a mani-pedi the day before to save time.

Fiona helped her change into a red suit with a skirt, then a bright blue dress, and then a navy pantsuit.

Slipping into the navy suit, Zoe couldn't help but feel transformed. The fabric became a second skin, molding her into a version of herself she barely recognized. "I… I look like someone who knows what they're doing," Zoe admitted, examining her reflection.

"That's the point," the stylist replied, continuing to fix Zoe's hair. "You're not just dressing for today. You're preparing yourself for every challenge that comes your way."

"Do you think I'll look the part?" she asked, loving how she felt, but doubting herself again.

Fiona clapped her hands together. "You look amazing. How do you feel?"

"Honestly? Pretty unstoppable."

"Then my job is done," Eleni said. "The right outfit is more than just fabric. It's armor for today's battle. Elegant, commanding, and absolutely you."

Dressed meticulously and with her hair styled to perfection, Zoe faced the stylist, "Thank you. I feel like an imposter in my own skin, but strangely, it's a good thing today."

The stylist smiled knowingly.

Stepping out to meet Noah, Zoe was a carefully curated version of herself. She was ready. Until she saw Noah. He had transformed into someone else. His posture, upright and relaxed, revealed a sense of authority and control that seemed to come naturally to him. His normally tousled hair had been neatly styled. He stood with assurance clad in a meticulously tailored blue button-down shirt and tan khakis. A portrait of success. He didn't appear to be acting a part. Unlike Zoe.

He smiled when he saw her—his expression glowed with admiration, making her feel wanted, truly wanted. "You look amazing."

"Thanks, so do you." She waved her hand up and down in front of him, emphasizing his fashion choices. An overwhelming urge to hug him nearly got the best of her, but she held back, trying to maintain an air of professionalism.

"It's just an outfit from my life a long, long time ago." His answer had her thinking about his past, and his family, and what he saw as a successful life. She found herself wanting to know more, to peel back the layers he'd hidden from everyone. So far, she'd seen him outsmart most of the people around him, and try to please Jason as though he were the father he'd never had. In addition, he had the utmost respect for women. An intriguing combination.

For a moment, the world faded away. The air crackled with unspoken words and possibilities. Her heart fluttered as though she were falling in love, but that was impossible. They were a team for an assignment. He was paid to look after her. That was all this could be.

He stepped closer, his eyes searching hers. "You really do look incredible, Zoe. It's…different, but in a good way. It suits you."

She felt a flush rise to her cheeks, and looked away for a moment to gather her composure. "I feel like I'm playing a part," she admitted. "But seeing you like this… I'm glad to have you as my partner."

When they arrived out front, Noah pointed to a white BMW. "Jason thought your boyfriend should look well-off but not too ostentatious."

"My boyfriend?"

"We're partners. And I want access to you at all times. Being your boyfriend will draw much less scrutiny than having your manager, agent, or lawyer shadowing your movements. They don't want you bringing in people who want to negotiate a higher salary or a promotion without a heads-up. Boyfriends are generally harmless." He reached out, gently lifting her chin with his fingers, forcing her to meet his gaze. "Generally."

As they drove into the city, she imagined a life where her boyfriend drove a fancy car and had ambition. The daydreaming gave her a reprieve from obsessing over her next few hours acting as Allison. In reality, however, she couldn't imagine having a boyfriend like Noah. He was too polished, too self-assured, too everything. Her former boyfriends had all been down-to-earth guys who wanted a down-to-earth girlfriend who would eventually become a wife and then mother. None of them had ambition or any desire to give her anything but their bare minimum. The way Noah cared for her, although it was his job, made her want something more. She wasn't able to articulate it exactly, but it was definitely more than she'd received in the past.

Before they left the car, he handed her Allison's name badge and her phone. "These are the final pieces. If you are unsure of something, give me a hug and whisper your thoughts in my ear, as quietly as possible. I can help."

His proximity encouraged her and made her want to curl up in his arms and remain hidden for the rest of the day. Everything was so real now.

As they approached the towering glass facade of the news station, Zoe's heart pounded against her chest, adding to her indecisiveness. Noah offered her a reassuring wink. His confidence never wavered, as hers plummeted by the second.

"You look great, Allison," he whispered as they entered the lobby, his breath warm against her ear. The way he looked at her, with such unwavering trust and subtle affection, made her wonder if he felt the same pull she did. She dared to glance up at him and received a lightning bolt of connection between them. The boyfriend ruse certainly felt real.

At the security desk, the familiar face of the guard Allison had often spoken of offered a semblance of normalcy. "Morning, Allison. How's Marlowe? Still chasing his tail?" he joked, his casual demeanor a balm to Zoe's frayed nerves.

"He's doing well, thanks. Keeps life interesting," Zoe replied while Noah signed in and received a guest pass. The small victory bolstered her confidence.

Once in the elevator, she tried to keep her eyes on the door. Noah stood beside her rambling on about the Red Sox. She nodded and smiled, but wasn't listening at all.

When the doors slid open, they both focused on the newsroom and everyone there. Zoe's entrance didn't go unnoticed, with a few of Allison's colleagues offering friendly waves and smiles. She returned their greetings, her smile tight, her mind scrambling to remember any details Allison had shared about them.

"Morning, Allison," Dominique called out as they passed each other. That woman was Zoe's idol and Allison's biggest competitor. The sight of her rendered Zoe starstruck.

After an uncomfortable silence, she managed to say, "Good morning," a bit too enthusiastically. Noah's slight nudge reminded her to temper her responses. She straightened up, acted a bit colder toward the world as she assumed Allison would do, and led Noah to her office.

Once inside, she closed the door and took a deep breath. A Boston University coffee mug waited on the desk for Allison's return while three news reporting awards lined up like military guards to interrogate anyone questioning her abilities.

"So far, so good?" she asked Noah.

He sat down on the wooden chair in front of her desk. "Take your time and breathe, you'll feel more in your body."

Someone knocked. When Zoe opened the door, a woman, dressed head to toe in black with her long dark hair pulled back in an elegant twist of braids, rushed up to her and gave her a hug. Zoe hugged her back and tried to but failed to remember this woman's name.

"Hi, what's up?" Something Allison would never say, but Zoe's nerves blocked out her two days of practice.

"You're on the air in ten. We need you ready pronto." She stood back and stared at her. "Your hair looks great, so let's just touch up your face."

So this was the makeup artist, except her name became lost in the hundreds of other names they'd tried to force down her throat. She made a face at Noah, begging for him to help.

Noah, leaning against the wall, his hands in his pockets stepped toward the woman as a response. Zoe hoped he knew what he was doing, because this would be humiliating if they didn't know the makeup artist. Then he took the woman's hand, clasping it between his hands. "Tansy?" When the woman nodded, he added, "Allison has spoken so highly of you. No one holds a candle to the magic you create."

Zoe wanted to hug him for remembering the name, but bit her lip and tried to appear as though she had known Tansy a long time.

"Thank you," Tansy said to Noah. "Allison is one of my favorites, because it's easy making that girl gorgeous. And who are you?"

"I'm Noah. Don't let me bother you. I'm going to stand back and enjoy."

"You can bother me anytime." Tansy placed a hand on his arm and something twisted in Zoe's gut. She couldn't be jealous. She'd only just met Noah, but she liked that he'd dedicated all of his time and attention to her. He gave her more attention than her past three boyfriends combined had provided, which said a lot about her dating life.

He stepped back, his hands in the air. "Don't get me in trouble. Allison is as possessive of me as I am of her."

His words didn't make Tansy mad, instead she let out a laugh. "Smart woman. Okay, Allison, let's get you ready." She pointed to a chair in front of the mirror.

Only then did Zoe realize what Tansy had said.

You're on the air in ten.

"I think there's a mistake. I came in today to look over a few things and meet with Glenn."

"And Glenn is the person who wants you on the air. You have a new story, something about the baby lion at the zoo. So cute. Now, sit yourself down so I can keep my job."

"No. No. No. I am not ready."

Noah walked over to her and placed his hands on her shoulders to ease her anxiety. It didn't work. "This is perfect. I always wanted to see the news as it happens." He turned to Tansy. "Does she read cue cards, or just speak from the top of her head?"

"There's a teleprompter. It's pretty cool to watch."

"Fantastic," he said, squeezing her shoulders in a sign of encouragement.

She glared at him in the mirror. He responded with a mouth-watering grin, the jerk. So she did what she assumed Allison would do, and allowed Tansy to prepare her for the camera.

Over the next eight minutes, Tansy transformed Allison from what she'd assumed was a working professional into a television star. Zoe stared at herself in the mirror. The woman had amazing skills, polishing Zoe's skin until not a pore could be found.

The door banged again, this time with some heft behind it.

"Come in," Zoe called out as Tansy brushed highlighter over Zoe's cheekbones.

Glenn, a person Zoe had never met, came at her with a smile that the vice principal at her school often used with parents who had demands that would never be met, but he had to keep them on his good side. Except Zoe had assumed Glenn had always been on Allison's side, until he nearly sent Allison to her death.

"Ready?" he asked.

"Let me fix her lipstick and then she's good to go," Tansy responded and then left.

"I thought I should talk about my investigation so far."

"No. We discussed this. You need a complete story to break something like that or we'll be sued for every penny. I handed you the lion cub story. You can head to the zoo tomorrow for some up close and personal time."

"What about my investigation?"

"Dominique is on it."

"Isn't she busy enough?" Zoe said, trying to reflect her sister's opinion.

"Jealousy isn't a good look on you," he said with an oily patronizing tone that made Zoe want to slam down on his foot with her stiletto. "You have the makings of a great reporter, but you need to follow orders and know when you're in over your head. You disappear for a few days and come back with nothing. I shouldn't have sent someone so inexperienced to do a professional's job. When she has the time, she'll continue where you left off." The pitting of one reporter against another and the insulting way he spoke to her provided a whole new look at Allison's job. She'd always said positive things about her work, minus her desire to move up and past other colleagues, but she'd never spoken about the demoralizing treatment she'd had to endure. And now he was effectively cutting her out of a story that she'd discovered herself. "You have two minutes." And then he was gone.

Allison would be furious, not that Zoe had any way of getting her sister's leg healed in under two days. Yet, here she was, trying to protect Allison and drowning in the process. She turned to Noah. This whole charade was his fault. "Now what?"

"You go on camera, and I sneak around. If he's taking Allison off the case, perhaps it's for the best. She'll be safer for the time being until we find evidence linking Glenn to Councilman Brendan Quinn and to some other player, someone with a lot of money and muscle on their side."

"Did I ever tell you I have stage fright? I stand in front of a group of my peers and I freeze. What if I stare blankly into the camera the second the green light goes on, if I can even find the green light. Is it on the camera? Is it just a thing people say on newsroom dramas? I can't do this, Noah," she said. She looked the part, but in this situation didn't have even the slightest bit of experience.

"You have more experience speaking in front of a captive audience than anyone in this studio," he responded. "Third graders are people too. You're beautiful, you're poised, and you have something to say. You're going to tell a story to the audience that you don't even have to memorize because you'll have the teleprompter, and you'll do it with a smile. The same smile you have on your face when some snotty kid forgets his lunch and wants to go home. Nothing to worry about. I'll be right with you every step of the way."

"Except you won't be on camera."

"I like my anonymity. If you don't do it for the good of the city, do it for your family."

His words did little to ease her stress. Yet, she thought of her father, hidden away for his safety, and of Allison, recuperating from an attack meant to silence her. Their courage and sacrifices made Zoe appreciate how much she could help if only by allowing Noah time to search Glenn's office.

"Fine, I'll do it, but do not offer any judgment or positive or negative comments on my performance. I don't want to hear a word of praise or criticism from you from the moment I step away from the camera," Zoe said.

Noah nodded his agreement, so she straightened her spine and left her sister's small office and proceeded to wobble on her heels and nearly fall to the ground. She saved herself and merely shook her head as though she'd just tripped over something. She tried to remember Fiona's advice and strode forward again with a more solid step.

The walk to the studio was a blur, every step added another reason for her to run as far away as possible. When she entered the hustle of the space, no one noticed her presence. Camera crews, lighting crews, and a whole slew of other people rushed around pointing to the two anchors at the desk. Zoe took a deep breath. She was not Zoe Goodwyn, elementary school teacher from Nantucket; she was Allison Goodwyn, investigative reporter. And she would be speaking about a lion cub. She then smiled to herself. Noah was right. That story would be something she could tell her students. And they'd give her their full attention.

During a commercial break, Fred Scott, one of the anchors left. Someone pulled Zoe to his spot at the main desk, next to Natalie Johnson, the longtime anchor, who didn't so much as look up to acknowledge her. Zoe sat up straight and forced a smile as she waited, her stomach wrapped up in knots. There was a countdown down with fingers, not spoken words. Three, two, one... The camera operator pointed at her. The red light on the camera lit up. Everyone went silent.

Natalie's face went from frowning to hyperenthusiastic. The change was incredible, as though she were an actor and the camera shifted her personality immediately into her role.

"In today's Afternoon Smile Segment, we're taking you to the best place in the city, the zoo." Natalie read off her lines with polished perfection. "Take it away, Allison."

Chapter Seventeen

The studio lights blazed down on Zoe, casting her in the spotlight. The red recording light telling her anything she did was being beamed to the whole city. She should have frozen, terrified of the attention, but she remained in her seat, poised and ready to go. With Noah's words whispering in her mind, she found herself not channeling her sister, but rather herself. She was standing before her classroom of eager third graders rather than an entire television viewing audience.

"Good afternoon," Zoe began, her voice steady and infused with a warmth she hoped was convincing. "In today's segment, I'm so excited to announce that Dakari, the beautiful African lioness gave birth this morning to a female cub. Mom and her baby are doing great. Dakari's pregnancy has captured the hearts of everyone as this will be the first birth of a lion at the zoo in twenty years. From what the zookeeper has told us, the cub is very healthy and will be introduced to the public in six weeks. But we have a treat for you. We'll be sneaking back into the veterinary center for a peek at the newest member of the zoo family. When mother and baby are comfortable, a webcam will allow the public to watch mother and baby bond.

"A team of sixteen veterinarians and veterinary technicians helped to deliver the cub. Although they were hoping Dakari would carry three to five cubs, they discovered that she carried only one when they gave her an ultrasound, which is a very tricky thing to do with a full grown lion." Zoe's confidence grew as she described the birth, the details flowing easily since they were typed in front of her.

"Dakari, and now her daughter, will be able to educate people about the importance of wildlife conservation as lions are classified as vulnerable in the wild. With habitat loss, poaching, and conflicts with humans, they face many threats.

"So stay tuned tomorrow to meet our newest resident. Back to you, Natalie."

Natalie asked Allison something quippy, and Zoe responded with a hand to her heart and the look of someone caught up in an adorable lovefest. "I'm looking forward to tomorrow."

As the segment wrapped up and the cameras turned away, Zoe let out a breath she didn't realize she'd been holding. She'd presented a report on live TV without faltering. And then she was literally pulled from her seat, the microphone unclipped and yanked from under her shirt and she was sent on her way while the next segment began.

As she walked off the set, Noah was there to meet her, a huge smile on his face. "You were fantastic," he whispered, guiding her away.

Zoe felt a mix of relief and exhilaration at what she'd done. She'd stepped into Allison's shoes and, for a brief moment, lived her sister's life. It was an experience she would never forget, and in some ways, although she'd never admit it to Allison, she really enjoyed it. She had to thank Noah for that. He'd reminded her of her own set of strengths and, stepping back to her classroom, she could see the skill set required to educate and entertain children for hours at a time.

As they left the studio behind, Zoe walked with a bit more steadiness in the heels. She'd always thought she would be incapable of handling Allison's job because Allison had so much more poise and confidence, and that had been the barrier for Zoe. But it wasn't a barrier. She possessed her own poise and confidence, her own voice, her own personality. No, she didn't want to permanently change lives with her sister, but she could now appreciate the benefits and drawbacks of each of their careers.

Chapter Eighteen

While Zoe was speaking on camera, Noah had seized the moment to sneak into the producer's office. Glenn was caught up in a heated argument with one of the camera operators, which left Noah a few minutes, he hoped. Remembering the map of the building, provided by Allison, he left the studio, turned back to the hallway, and found the third door to the right of the elevator. Noah slipped through the partially open door and returned it to its previous position, about three inches from closing. Three large screens adorned the walls. One had the news show on it with Zoe looking every bit the professional in front of a screen showing a lioness at the zoo. He almost paused to watch her, but refocused on his task. Any delay could get both of them in trouble.

Noah's movements were swift, his senses heightened for any sign of Glenn's return. The desk was a mix of organized chaos, awards mingling with stacks of scripts and production notes. But Noah's target was the computer sitting on the mahogany desk. Regrettably, he couldn't outright steal it, so he had to do the next best thing. Allow Calvin, back at Fresh Pond Security, to scan and store the contents.

"Calvin, you there?" he whispered into his earpiece.

"Ready when you are," Calvin's voice crackled back. "I just need remote access, and I can start digging."

Noah slid the thumb drive into the computer, a way to minimize their fingerprints, both physically and digitally on the target computer. "We're in. Tell me when you've downloaded everything." As Calvin worked his magic, Noah skimmed through the producer's drawers and files, looking for any physical evidence to complement their digital haul. The tension in the air was palpable, a silent countdown ticking away in Noah's mind.

The seconds stretched into eternity as Noah kept one eye on the door, the other on the screen, watching as folders and files flitted across it. He flipped through a few stacks of papers, and located a note for Glenn to contact POR Development. He wasn't sure if it had relevance, but he snapped a photo anyway and waited for Calvin. "You good? Because we don't have much more time."

"One more minute," Calvin said, his voice tense.

"We don't have the time. I need to get back." Noah glanced up at the screen and saw the anchor speaking to Zoe. Not good. "Gotta go." Noah disconnected the thumb drive and reset the computer, erasing any trace of their intrusion. His heart pounded, not just from the thrill of the covert operation, but from the realization that he wasn't sure if he'd be back in the studio before Zoe got off the air.

"I don't know if we have everything," Calvin replied.

"Not my problem. It's enough for now. We'll analyze it when I get back and if we need more, maybe I can make a return," Noah replied, aware that each moment spent in the lion's den increased their risk of discovery.

"We have about 80 percent," Calvin confirmed, a sigh of relief audible even through the digital connection. "It should be enough."

Exiting the office, Noah strolled back to the studio, his expression neutral. Zoe was being manhandled by a hyper sound tech and if his hand slipped any closer to her more sensitive areas, Noah would wrap the cord around the guy's neck.

When she was free, she turned to him. Her excitement beamed across her face. From what he'd seen, she had been brilliant.

"You were amazing out there," Noah said as she walked up to him.

She nodded and then gave him a huge hug, squeezing him tight with a sense of accomplishment and a sense of relief. To play the part, he kissed her cheek and nearly went to her lips but that would be overkill for the assignment.

"I can't believe I did that," she whispered to him.

"Let's get you back to your office." He kept an arm around her and led her inside. His own excitement for successfully getting in and out of the producer's office had him on cloud nine as well.

Zoe slumped into her chair, the tension slowly leaving her shoulders. "That was the most exhilarating thing I've ever done in my life," she admitted, a tired laugh escaping her. "What did you think?"

"You were amazing. And I think we should celebrate by heading out for lunch." He wanted to lean over and give her a hug, but they had to stay focused. The longer they remained in the area, the higher the chance they could be discovered or Allison could be dragged on air again. Either way, they had to leave.

She grabbed the stack of notes on the back of Allison's book-case and placed them in a tote bag from under her desk. Then she held on to Noah's arm with all the strength she had left.

In the car, Zoe leaned her head back and shut her eyes for a moment. "I can't believe I took over Allison's life and actually handled it."

"Don't tell your sister, she'll be furious."

"She probably would be, but I give her a lot of credit. She not only has to look amazing and sound great, but she also puts in hours and hours into researching her assignments on her own. She's not a reader at a desk, she's an on-the-ground hard-core investigator. I wouldn't choose that for my life, and I have a new respect for all she does."

"I agree. Although to be fair, would she be able to manage your classroom for more than a few hours?"

"Not at all. She can barely handle Marlowe. Although they do love each other. I'm not sure Allison would be able to function if she didn't have her little buddy there every night to keep her company." Zoe would never badmouth her sister or anyone she'd met so far, except of course any person who threatened her family. Noah loved this quality about her. A whole mountain of positivity, like his mother, a stark contrast to the competitiveness, materialism, and jealousy he'd seen consume his father.

Perhaps that was why he and his sister had always preferred helping others like their mother rather than focusing their whole lives on bettering themselves. His father's focus had never been on their well-being, it had been on them being more attractive, educated, athletic, and talented than the rest of the community. Parenthood as a means to boost his own ego.

"So where is lunch?" she asked.

"Headquarters. We downloaded Glenn's computer and while you get a refresher course in self-defense, Calvin and I are going fishing."

From the frown on her face, she had probably envisioned something with a better menu. "Can we stop at Allison's apartment? I was hoping to get something more comfortable to wear, like her sweatpants and sneakers." Zoe looked fantastic, but more comfortable clothes would make the rest of the day easier.

"Let me call in to Jason and get permission." Noah pushed the button to have the call go through the car system.

"How did it go?" Jason asked with no preamble.

"Zoe took the folder from Allison's office and Calvin has the download from Glenn's office."

"Fantastic. And great job on the news today, Zoe. Not many people could step into such a public role so easily."

Zoe looked up at Noah, trying to bite back her smile. "Thank you."

"We're stopping at Allison's apartment, unless you've seen anything unusual there," Noah said.

"It's been quiet all day, so go ahead, but get in and out quickly in case you have a tail."

Noah placed a hand over Zoe's, feeling utterly invincible. "We will."

"And don't let your guard down. You're both running off a high. That's the most dangerous time of an assignment." With that, Jason hung up.

Chapter Nineteen

The journey to Allison's apartment in Beacon Hill felt like traveling years back in time, but Zoe had been there only a few days ago. It was a memory Zoe would prefer to forget. The memory of the neighbor's tragic death and her own brush with danger within these walls followed her inside. Although she needed to gather a few of her sister's things to wear, she regretted her impulsive request as they opened the door.

Exhaustion had caught up to her and created all kinds of worst-case scenarios running through her head. Maybe someone was hiding out in the apartment. She paused before entering.

"Are you okay?" Noah waited for her, with no pressure to enter.

"I'm not sure."

"I understand. I'll check the place first. Wait here," he said, disappearing inside.

Zoe took a few deep breaths while waiting in the hallway. Her heart pounded against her rib cage—perhaps she didn't have to enter the place at all. Noah could grab a few things and then they could leave. Before she turned and left the apartment building altogether, Noah reappeared, his posture relaxed, a reassuring smile on his face.

"It's safe," he said, holding the door open for her.

Stepping inside, Zoe had an immediate visceral reaction. One of her sister's vases was smashed on the floor, a chair overturned, and the peonies she'd brought to give her sister sat wilted on the counter, having never made their way to a vase. That Noah had observed the peonies in the middle of the chaotic scene and had decided to bring her some to cheer up her room comforted her. His focus on details helped him to excel in his job and impress the women in his life.

"No one cleaned up the mess?" she asked.

"The police came in and investigated, taking photos and video, but it's the responsibility of the resident to clean up."

"That's unacceptable. Allison's broken apart and when she finally gets home, she does not need to walk into this." She headed to the pantry and grabbed the broom and dustpan from the door.

"What are you doing?"

"I'm cleaning."

Noah walked over to her as she started to sweep. "We can send a service over."

"No one knows where everything in her house goes. I do. I can do it." She swept up the broken vase and threw the pieces into the trash. She also tossed the flowers. They had no chance of recovery at this point.

She cleaned up the countertop and turned on the dishwasher as it had started to smell with the dirty dishes inside. The floor still had tiny shards of glass, so she walked into the back room to grab the vacuum and ran right into yellow police tape and a large bloodstain. The visual of Mrs. Peterson came rushing back to her. Her ignorant assumption that the woman had fallen, when in reality someone had murdered her and then gone after Zoe.

She turned and rushed into the bathroom, retching. Noah appeared immediately, his hand supporting her. She ignored him as she bent over the toilet and sobbed.

"Come on. Let's get you cleaned up." He led her to the sink and then into the living room and sat her on the couch. "I'll be right back."

Returning with two glasses and a bottle of some amber liquid that appeared stronger than anything she normally drank, he poured two generous portions. "This might help," he offered, handing her a glass.

She accepted it, allowing the sting of the alcohol to warm her from the inside out. They sat in silence. She wiped a few more tears from her cheek. "This whole situation is embarrassing. I trained to protect myself, and I fall apart at the sight of blood."

"That's not embarrassing at all. You give a damn. It means you're human. And training for two days doesn't inoculate you from your humanity. People who have no reaction either have lived in such trauma they have no more emotion to give, or they have a psychological disorder that doesn't allow them to feel. Contrary to everything you see on social media, there aren't many people like that." He sat next to her. "We're going to get through this."

Zoe looked at him, really looked. He didn't seem upset over the blood on the floor. It seemed like nothing fractured his composure. She wasn't like him. "I'm scared. After someone tried to kill Allison, attacked me, and went after our dad, I'm terrified that one of us is going to be killed before the end of this," she confessed, her voice barely above a whisper.

Noah reached out, his hand finding hers. "I understand. But you're not alone in this. You have the team. We're stronger together. And I'm not leaving your side."

His support made her feel better. She leaned into him, resting her head on his shoulder. The moment stretched, some calm in the storm, until a deafening crash destroyed the aura of safety. An explosion of sound and glass had Zoe diving to the floor. Noah dropped to the floor over her, a human shield, as another bullet embedded into the wall just inches above where they'd sat.

"Stay down!" he ordered, his body covering hers as he scanned the room.

The silence that followed was deafening, broken only by the sound of their ragged breathing. Her heart raced, and her whole body shivered as she tried to stay as small as possible on the floor. Noah had crawled over to the window and was peering through a corner, a gun in his hand.

"We have to leave. Now," Noah said, as he returned to her side. His arm wrapped around her was the only thing that anchored her to reality.

Zoe struggled to escape. She relied one hundred percent on Noah to help her scramble onto her feet and lead her out of the room. His body protected her from the debris coming from the window. He picked a few of the larger pieces of glass off her back and shoulders. One near her elbow had caused a small laceration. She didn't care—that small cut wasn't as dangerous as the bullets flying at them.

"The police should be here soon," Noah said. "That sound echoed through five other buildings at least. Someone is going to notice the shattered window if they haven't already. Having the whole neighborhood looking at us as we leave will not provide more security, it will create a social media moment and could possibly place a spotlight on your location."

He glanced around the apartment. "I need a view of the back alley. The location of the dumpsters."

She thought about it for a moment and pointed to the back rooms. He grabbed his drink, a paper bag from the counter, and some matches next to a candle on a side table.

"Come on." He waved at her to follow him. One of the back rooms was an office with a huge built-in bookcase and windows overlooking another building, parking, and three dumpsters. With a bit of effort, he opened the window as wide as it would go, a whole five inches, while hiding himself behind the heavy brocade curtains.

Placing the glass and alcohol in the paper bag, he lit a match and set the bag on fire. And then, to Zoe's shock, he sent the flaming package into the dumpster. His throw was perfectly aimed as it sank down between plastic trash bags and cardboard boxes. There was no explosion or other dramatic event. Instead, smoke rose up and then a small flame and then…the contents of the dumpster were burning. With little wind in the area, the fire stayed contained inside the large metal container. As smoke billowed up, people came running.

He pulled Zoe away from the spectacle behind the building and into her sister's bedroom. "Take off the suit and put on some jeans and a T-shirt. Quickly. And cover as much of your figure as possible, then tuck your hair all the way up into that Red Sox hat on your sister's dresser." As he spoke, he unbuttoned and took off his own shirt.

"But you can't go out shirtless." He'd draw too much attention with his abs alone.

"I'll be fine." He went into her sister's closet and rummaged through a drawer of lingerie and pajamas. From the third drawer, in a sea of primary colors, he pulled out a black cotton tank top, two sizes too small. After wetting down his hair in the bathroom, he appeared completely different from the person who had walked into the building only fifteen minutes before.

"Okay, let's go. Keep an eye out for anything." His calm helped Zoe refocus and not panic, although she was a gunshot away from completely falling apart. There was no way out of the apartment except the way they'd entered. If one of the bad guys came inside, he could take out both Zoe and himself before they had a chance to save themselves. The thought scared Zoe to her core.

"We're going out the door?" she asked.

"Unless you want to jump out the window." Taking the gun back out of the concealed holster, he led her to the foyer and turned back to her. "Stay right behind me. If someone's shooting, put me between the bullet and yourself."

"You're not serious," she said, as the continued threat of violence had not yet punctured her everyday reality.

He stared at her, gun in hand, until she nodded. He was very serious.

Pushing open the door with a cautious hand, he paused, allowing it to swing forward until it met the wall with a muted thud. The hallway contained a stillness that made the turmoil churning within her intensify. With a measured breath, he stepped out, leading Zoe. Together, they moved toward the stairway, his gun tucked into his side away from her. They descended the stairs with as much speed as possible. She listened for the presence of anyone else near them, but silence surrounded them.

As they turned at the landing, she caught a glimpse of a man positioned on the first floor. Jeans and work boots were his only identification. He lifted his hand up and pointed a gun at them.

"Over there." She pointed toward him, but Noah had already aimed his weapon over her shoulder and shot him. The man appeared as though he'd been struck in the chest with a two-by-four. Blood splattered on the back wall as he slumped to the ground. Zoe's scream echoed up the stairwell, a sound that shuddered through the walls around them. Then she froze, staring at the blood. More blood. She was not made for this.

"Shhhhh," Noah said, his voice a low, urgent whisper. "We can't risk the extra exposure." She turned to run back upstairs, but Noah's free arm circled around her waist and held her with him as he continued to descend the stairs. His body now blocking anyone in front of them.

"Can we escape by the fire escape?" she asked.

"Not unless you want to be dangling over the back parking lot like a tin can ready for target practice."

"Where are we going?"

"The front door is no longer an option, not with the risk of drawing more attention. We need to go in a different direction."

Several people had opened their doors, and she could hear their footsteps on the floors above them. Noah veered away from the front entrance, dragging her with him, toward an alternative escape, heading to the back of the building, where tenants typically brought their trash.

"How do you know where you're going?" She had been in this building a hundred times and had only gone out the front door.

"It's how I carried you out a few days ago."

The reminder that he'd already saved her life and now he'd done it again added a whole mountain of conflicting feelings that swirled inside of her. His hand tightened on her waist and she trusted him enough to let him lead her through the back exit.

"When we get outside, stare at the fire as though you're a tenant who is concerned for the building. Don't look at anyone directly in case they think you're your sister. Trust me to guide you to the right place." He handed her his sunglasses as they stepped outside.

She nodded in reply, put the glasses on, and accepted the arm he draped over her shoulder, shielding her from too much attention. They joined a group of residents lingering outside and Noah pushed his way around the mob until they blended in. She had her doubts that they'd make it, convinced she'd be recognized as Allison, but so far so good. He edged them closer to the back of the crowd and then swerved her away from everyone by walking with another couple and making it appear that they were together.

When they got to the corner, an old Jetta pulled up next to them. The window was down and Fiona sat in the driver's seat.

"Get in," she ordered.

Zoe didn't question her, she slid into the back seat with Noah as though they'd called an Uber.

Chapter Twenty

The adrenaline surging through Noah's veins was not a familiar sensation for a guy who had spent years at a desk job at the NSA in Washington. The bullets that had shattered the window back at Allison's apartment were a stark reminder of the danger Zoe and her entire family faced, a danger he'd sworn to protect her from. And that didn't include the collateral damage like neighbors in the wrong place at the wrong time. As they drove away from the chaos, his mind raced. How well could he actually protect her against an unknown opponent who seemingly had unlimited resources? If Allison's investigation was important enough, wouldn't the FBI step in and assist? Or was she one small piece of a larger investigation?

"Nice timing," he said to Fiona, who appeared perfectly calm and collected as the fire raged behind them.

"Calvin had alerts for any 911 calls coming in from that area. He sent a call out and I was nearby. Your text giving us a pickup location helped."

Zoe stared at him. "You had time to text her?"

"Alexa contacted Jason while I was in the bathroom wetting down my hair." He'd always been better at strategy and logistics than most people. When the window smashed, his order of thinking became: protect Zoe, secure area, locate source, pull attention from building, contact headquarters, escape in disguise, make sure no one kills either of them while getting to the meeting point. A lot of luck helped his plan succeed.

Fiona focused on the road, but called back to Noah. "Very impressive, Montgomery. I don't know anyone who would have turned everyone's focus toward a controlled fire instead of gunshots. Your plan worked beautifully." He accepted the praise from a veteran of an unknown number of difficult situations.

"It wasn't as successful in keeping the idiot in the hallway from dying," he admitted.

"He pointed a gun at us. I can't even count how many times you've saved my life." Zoe didn't sound as though she were fawning, she appeared exhausted.

All the confidence she'd gained by going on the air as her sister had been wiped away by their visit to Allison's apartment. Jason had warned him to get in and get out. Instead, Noah decided to comfort her with a shot of whiskey. They could have been killed. He had to get his head more on his job and less on his crush on Zoe.

Zoe stared out the window as they drove on a highway to the north of Boston. "Is Allison okay?"

"She's good. Fairly demanding and driving Meaghan crazy, but her leg is healing," Fiona said from the driver's seat.

"And my dad?"

"He's been questioning Jason about his credentials and those of Meaghan and Noah."

"Oh no. I'm sorry. He's very protective of Allison and me."

"Don't apologize for a dad being a dad," Fiona responded. "Jason is confident enough in his team's abilities. At this point, he's probably brought out news articles about our more recent public projects."

"Dad's not easily impressed, but I appreciate your efforts to keep him not only safe, but comfortable as well." Then her expression tensed. "Where are we going?"

Noah was fairly curious too, but when Fiona made a decision, he just followed it to the end, not bothering to argue.

"Noah's place," Fiona said with such definitiveness that Noah hadn't realized she'd said *his* place.

"My place?" He glanced out the window, and sure enough

they were headed to Cape Ann, located about forty miles north of Boston. His small two-bedroom apartment in the town of Rockport had been his sanctuary when he moved to New England. The rocky shoreline, the quaint village that had accepted him as a local after mere months, the smell of the ocean waking him up in the morning, and the sparkling stars sending him to sleep combined to make this place home.

Rockport, with its serene ocean views and the charm of his small place looking over the pier, seemed worlds away from the violence they had just escaped. Here, amidst the calming sound of the waves crashing against the shore, Noah thought Zoe could find a moment's peace. Fiona definitely knew what she was doing.

"No one will look for her there. You rarely crash there yourself."

"How do you know?" Noah knew Fiona had amazing instincts, but did she also have someone following him?

"Because you spend more time sleeping on the couch in your office than you do having a social life. You need more balance in your life. Believe it or not, that balance will actually make you better at your job."

Okay, she didn't exactly have to spy on him to know that. For the past few months, he'd been trying to make up for his inability to be in the field by adding some type of value to every case assigned to him, whether a more detailed analysis than requested or finding and monitoring live stream cameras in areas they were curious about. His extra work paid off a few times when he located information that assisted the people in the field. Yet, his hyper work ethic had led to fatigue and some weaker judgment calls. But there was no balance with Zoe as he tried to watch over her. If he thought too much about his feelings for her, he'd put her at risk, and he wasn't willing to do that.

"You'll be safe here," Fiona assured Zoe as they entered his modest apartment, a stark contrast to the opulence of Allison's place in Beacon Hill, but rich in warmth and security. Sandy Bay appeared like a huge blue watercolor through the window, an endless expanse that made one feel powerful and powerless at the same time.

Zoe, still shaken from the threat against them, managed a weak smile. "Thank you, Fiona. For everything. I... I don't know how to repay you."

All five feet of Fiona walked over to Zoe and gave her a hug. "Take the night off and we'll meet in the morning at headquarters to discuss if you're headed to the zoo."

"Um, the zoo?" Her face paled as she spoke.

Fiona nodded, without a hint of apology for making Zoe uncomfortable. "You said you were reporting from the zoo tomorrow."

"Yes, but that was what the teleprompter told me to say."

"The audience doesn't know that. You should go. It's supposed to be a beautiful day. Noah will be beside you, although he has a thing for giraffes, so don't let him wander off." She winked at them and said goodbye.

After she was gone, Noah and Zoe headed to his kitchen. The room embodied cheerfulness with pale yellow walls, large windows, and white cabinets. He tended to keep the gray granite counters as clean as possible, preferring a more minimal appearance.

"Giraffes?" Zoe asked.

He laughed. "Have you ever seen a giraffe run? It's a thing of beauty. Seriously, one of the coolest animals on earth, but I've already seen them at least three times this year. I'll be able to control myself. Tea?" he asked to change the subject.

She nodded. "Let me help. I need something to do to keep my mind from stress overload."

"The tea is there." He pointed to a cabinet next to the window. "And the mugs are on the opposite side." He realized she'd had a muffin for breakfast and nothing except a sip of whiskey for lunch—no wonder she was feeling off.

"You heat the water and I'll prepare us some lunch. Grilled cheese okay?"

"Perfect. Thanks."

As Zoe moved around his kitchen, Noah stepped away to

contact Jason. The weight of their situation, the news station's desire for her to be outside in public, pressed heavily on him.

"Jason, it's Noah. Zoe's safe, for now. Has Fiona spoken to you?"

"She has. Thinks an evening away from this place will help Zoe get her head back in the game."

"That's the problem. She isn't in the game, she never was. She's a teacher and although she did a damn good job today, she was almost scalped by a projectile through her sister's window. We can't keep putting her in danger. It's too risky," Noah began, his voice tense with barely contained frustration.

Jason's reply was immediate. "I understand your concern, but we need her. She has to head back to the television studio so we can access more of Glenn's data. The information you sent in from Glenn's office that listed POR Development? It was exactly what we needed to get us a focus. Patrick O'Reilly. He runs a real estate development firm in the city, but has many other shadier dealings. He's applied for a few permits in Brendan Quinn's district. All of them turned down. Without the permits, the residential property lots are worth only a fraction of what they would be with commercial rights for much larger buildings. A relatively new LLC purchased the development rights from a title holding trust. Layer upon layer of bureaucracy covering up the actual owner, but Calvin found a way to follow some money and sure enough, they're linked to O'Reilly. The LLC has applied for new permits on the same sites."

"Then you have what you need." The more he thought about sending Zoe into harm's way, the more he wanted her as far away from Boston as possible.

"Not even close. We need more to implicate him directly, and Zoe's our best shot."

Noah clenched his jaw, the protective instinct that had surged to the forefront clashing with his assignment. "I am one person. I need backup if she has a target on her back. We can't afford any mistakes. Not with her life on the line."

"I understand more than you know. You may have a handle on the back workings of criminal organizations, but the actual structures are like spiderwebs. Unless you get rid of the spider, the web will be rebuilt in a day. We're doing this to protect her, to protect all of them," Jason reasoned. "At least we know our enemy now. That keeps things more focused."

Jason told him to report to headquarters in the morning and they'd walk through the logistics of the day. The conversation ended with no resolution. They were fighting an enemy that had massive resources and no morals.

Noah returned to the kitchen, his mind going over everything that could go wrong. Zoe was leaning against the counter in front of the sink with a steaming mug in her hands. The warmth of the room, the sound of the ocean, the sight of Zoe finally relaxing took some of the strain from Noah.

She looked up at him, her eyes searching his. "Any updates?" she asked with a vulnerability in her voice that tugged at his heart.

Noah took a deep breath, choosing his words carefully. "Based on what you and I did this morning, we found a connection between Patrick O'Reilly, who has his fingers in many criminal activities, and Brendan Quinn. It's not 100 percent linked, but all the evidence points to O'Reilly being the person who bribed Quinn. He has a hundred million reasons to make sure certain permits are granted in a timely manner."

She stared at him, her lips pursed. "How is Allison's producer, Glenn, involved in all of this?"

"That's something we don't know. But he did send her out to a highly dangerous situation with no protection, which is not any industry standard I know of, as well as pulling her off the investigation with no regard for what she found." He pulled the frying pan out from under the counter and gathered the ingredients for the grilled cheese. He lifted a large tomato out of the refrigerator. "Tomato?"

"That would be great, thanks." She sat at the island and continued to sip her tea.

"Maybe he put her on the zoo story because he already knew the answers to the bribery investigation and wanted to bury it. She was getting closer to an answer."

Zoe paused, her fingers tracing the rim of her mug. "Or

maybe he was trying to protect her by pulling her from the investigation and putting her on something less risky."

Her optimism and seeing the best in others changed the charge in the air from negative to positive. Noah made the decision to leave it there, a hopeful outlook instead of considering the malice and evil that people could carry with them and use to lash out at anyone in their way. He doubted Glenn had any redeeming qualities, he seemed more dirtbag than do-gooder. As they shared a quiet moment, he found himself relaxing in Zoe's presence, something that rarely happened to him. Granted, he hadn't put a priority on dating these last years, because he'd struggled to feel comfortable enough to open himself up to people around him. Those types of connections left him feeling even more alone than if he'd never made an effort to meet someone. Zoe seemed different. They kind of skipped over the awkward and superficial stage of getting to know each other and ended up in something that had more depth. But in reality they weren't a match. Zoe was a woman from another world, a small island, spending her days teaching and caring for children and her nights keeping her father company. No future existed for them, and why he'd even circled around to those thoughts was a mystery.

He stared at the woman who appeared almost exactly like Allison Montgomery, except she didn't have that cutting-edge reporter instinct to ask two hundred questions and grab a laptop and work all night. She had only one question that she repeated over and over again—would her family be okay?

She returned to the electric kettle with her mug. "Do you want anything to drink?" Her hand shook as she poured the hot water.

"Something a bit stronger than tea. Maybe some scotch." He pointed to a liquor cabinet close to the dining room table. He then buttered the bread and placed a slice of tomato between two slices of cheese and put it on the pan. "I can get it."

"It's not a problem, it's good for me to move a bit." As a new tea bag steeped in the hot water, she poured him a tall glass of Macallan as though she were pouring soda.

"I think that's more than enough," he said in mock alarm. About four times too much.

After he finished cooking, they sat across from each other at the table and devoured their sandwiches.

"Want another or should we move to ice cream?" he asked.

"What kind?" The question added a lightness to her mood and the hint of a smile looked good on her.

"Chocolate Fudge Brownie, Cherry Garcia, or Phish Food."

"Hmm. I'm kind of a chocoholic," she confessed.

"So Chocolate Fudge Brownie it is." He scooped them both the same flavor and filled two large mugs of ice cream to the brim. She'd moved to the couch and he so wanted to sit next to her, but starting something would be a disaster.

"For you." He handed her a mug with a spoon.

He sat across from her on a love seat.

She leaned back and moaned as she took a bite of brownie. "It's funny. If a guy invited me on a first date and fed me this meal, I'd be inclined to marry him."

He laughed, forcing back a completely inappropriate desire for a chance to take her on a real date. "I'll remember that."

His chest filled with a warm, romantic longing for Zoe, and he sensed the same from her. As she curled her legs beneath her on the couch, he thought he saw a similar yearning in her eyes. Was it bittersweet longing, the same feeling that kept him from crossing the boundaries that he wanted to cross more than anything? He couldn't deny the intense pull he had toward her. Yet, the trauma of the past few days made her vulnerable, and although she wasn't a paying client, she was as much a part of the team as anyone in Fresh Pond Security, willing to place herself on the line for the greater good.

He'd walled off his feelings for her, thinking it would keep their relationship easier, but tonight felt different. Maybe the quiet intimacy of the moment or the way her eyes held his convinced him that it would be okay to cross the boundary just for tonight. After all, life was unpredictable and Fiona insisted he needed balance in his life. This would certainly balance it.

"Why did you choose to be a teacher?" he asked, curious about everything to do with her.

She tilted her head slightly, the swirl of her thoughts almost perceptible. "My mother taught at my elementary school. She loved all of her students and they seemed to love her as well. Yet, the second she arrived home, she poured all her attention toward Dad, Allison, and me. I wanted that. A career that changed lives and a schedule that would permit me to have time with my family. How about you? Did you follow your dad's footstep's into security?"

The question cast a shadow over him. Noah hoped he bore no resemblance to a man who had discarded his original family for an upgrade. "I wanted to change the world. My father prefers sucking everything good out of the things and people around him for his benefit. I think I'm more like my mother, who protected my sister, Elise, and me, after our father took off for greener pastures. She went back to school and became a social worker and truly saved lives. I hope I can do even a small bit of the good she's done for world." But so far, he'd had only minimal impact on any assignment.

She listened with undivided attention and never gave him pity. "You saved my life. Your mother would be so proud of the man you are." Her warmth and understanding struck him in the solar plexus, leaving him breathless.

It was too early for bed, but they couldn't just stare at each other with longing, at least longing on his side. "What kind of movies do you like?" he asked.

"I don't care. You pick."

He clicked on the television and turned on the one movie that always made him smile. *"The Princess Bride."* He hoped for the same reaction from Zoe.

"Good choice, Montgomery."

"Last names? Are we teammates now, Goodwyn?" Perhaps that was her way of keeping him at an arm's length. He stopped himself from stretching out next to her, allowing her some space.

"Maybe. I'll let you know in the morning. I can't think straight right now."

"Good enough." Picking up the cream-colored fleece blanket from the back of the love seat, he approached her with far too much contentment for a man who had to watch over a woman who had a price on her head. "Here," he said, draping the blanket over her shoulders, "it gets cold at night." His fingers brushed against her shoulder, a brief touch that mattered far too much and sent him rushing back to the love seat.

She looked up at him, a soft smile gracing her lips. "And Noah?"

"Yeah?"

"Thanks."

"Anytime, Zoe."

The sound of the waves was a constant reminder of the world beyond. Tomorrow was coming far too quickly. As he watched Zoe, her face lit by the soft glow from the television, he vowed to shield her from the darkness she'd willingly stepped into, no matter what it required.

Chapter Twenty-One

The relentless sound of the ocean waves crashing against the shore provided a soothing backdrop to an evening that had unfolded with unexpected intimacy. At the end of the movie, Noah brought her more tea. She shifted over so he could sit next to her. She wanted to sleep, but the idea of closing her eyes only scared her. Too much blood in her memories to promote anything less than a nightmare. Noah pulled the blanket over their laps. She leaned into his embrace.

"I always thought I'd miss the sunny days and cool nights of California," Noah said, his voice a whisper in the now dark room. "But the East Coast suits me. I traded the Pacific for the Atlantic, and warm weather for miserably cold winters, but it's home here now. A view of the ocean helps."

She turned her face toward him, her fascination with everything about him eased the strain of the day. "Do you visit your family at all?"

"My father blotted out his old life for an aspiring actress and a new family with her. My sister and I were casualties. I see my sister when I can, but my mother died a few years ago of a head injury in a car accident," he revealed, the weight of her passing pressing down in each word.

"That's horrible."

He nodded. "She'd been hospitalized. I didn't think there

was a rush to see her, so I delayed. And she died a week later when I was on a plane home." Regret laced through his tone as he explained how he'd been too busy at work to justify an earlier flight to see her.

"That wasn't your fault. How could you know?"

"I'd been so focused on my work, and not on my family. I'll have to live with the regret for the rest of my life."

"This job seems all-consuming." Her fingers brushed over his, offering him comfort without pity.

"Depending on my assignment, it can be near impossible to leave, but I wasn't in this position when she'd died. I was at a cubicle farm in Washington, DC. I guess that was the point where I decided if I was going to work to the detriment of everything else in my life, I might as well be in a field that brings me satisfaction." He caught her fingers in his hand and held on, as though she were a lifeline preventing him from drowning.

She didn't ask any questions about that one memory he'd probably played over and over again in his mind. Instead, she brought them back to the present. "It seems you landed in a good place. The way everyone at Fresh Pond Security knows each other, looks out for each other. There's a sense of belonging there that's hard to find anywhere else." Her gaze drifted to the window and the moonlight dancing on the water's surface. There was something incredibly peaceful about his apartment. The turmoil of the day felt miles away, replaced by the quiet comfort she found in his presence.

Noah nodded, understanding. "I've never really had that. DC is a place where everyone fights to gain power and money. The friends made there were all looking for a leg up, some advantage to move them into a place. When I moved here, I found a sort of family, although there's a schism right now that has taken some of the enjoyment out of the job."

"Would you ever leave and find another firm to work for?"

He shook his head. "Not right now. I like what I do, and I'm hoping the team becomes a cohesive group again. We all have each other's backs and I trust them with my life, but there are a few missing pieces. One of my friends left the team last year. If he came back, my adopted family would be less fragmented."

"What are the chances?" Her voice was soft but curious.

He shook his head. "He and Jason need to have a heart-to-heart, but they're both stubborn."

She turned to look at him. The reflection of the moon shimmered in his eyes. "Your job must be lonely at times. I can see how the team becomes your support group, your friend group, and your family," she said, her heart aching at the thought. "Do you feel isolated living out here?"

"It can be. But it's also peaceful. After being hyperaware of everything and everyone around me all day, it's nice to have solitude at the end of the day. It's where I come to think, to reset. It's my own form of community, I suppose. I can say hi to Debbie at the coffee bar, and Bob at the fish market. They welcome me by name but don't ask anything of me." Noah's smile was wistful. Zoe could see a whole wall of emotions churning inside of him, but also a steadiness, a centeredness that allowed him to be intense and yet grounded at the same time.

Their conversation drifted then, from lighthearted tales of Zoe's childhood in Nantucket to Noah's travels around the world. Each story, each shared memory wove them closer together. The world outside faded away, leaving two hurt souls in the tranquil atmosphere of his apartment.

"Are you ready to sleep?" he asked her at a lull in their conversation.

Zoe, wrapped in a soft blanket, relaxed with her head resting on Noah, shook her head. "I don't want to close my eyes. I know I need sleep, but I'm scared."

He nodded, not once suggesting that she had to sleep to make it through tomorrow. "How about *Amélie*? It's a happy movie."

"I don't want happy. It seems artificial to me right now." Zoe wanted something to punch at her nerves and keep the queasy, heavy feeling that had lodged in her stomach occupied. She'd actually craved a different kind of escape, a physical one, where her body could rock against his, channeling the tensions of the day into sexual gratification. But she didn't want to overstep their current relationship, not that she had any idea what type of relationship it had become. So she said the only movie she could think of. *"John Wick?"* While Westley and Buttercup had eased her back into the present after having survived a series of bullets, John Wick, through his relentless need for revenge, might numb the vision of their attacker's death in the stairwell.

"A bit different from the French heartwarming and whimsical film I suggested, but I can compromise. It'll be the perfect distraction."

So *John Wick* it was. He could kick and shoot and fight the bad guys and would find some resolution before the final credits. When the men came after the dog, Zoe turned into Noah and hid her face. "Maybe this was a bad idea."

He lifted her face to his and kissed her. "Let me keep your mind off everything bad in the world," he said, in a low murmur that rumbled through her heart.

His lips kissed the tip of her nose, then touched her closed eyelids before returning to her mouth and parting her lips. She couldn't help but moan and grip his arms. Her reaction seemed to spur him on, and he deepened their kiss with something urgent, something on fire, something burning down the memories of the day. There was gunfire in the background and instead of making her pull back, it pushed her closer to him. Her hands gripped his shirt, pulling it over his head. He gathered her into him, and somehow they were skin to skin, her shirt tossed to the floor next to his.

His embrace drew her closer, the heat of his body both burning and comforting. They kissed as though they'd never have another night together.

"I don't think…"

"Jason would…"

"…against the rules…" Noah struggled to speak because every time he opened his mouth, she kissed him into silence.

This was so wrong and so amazing. She didn't care if they were breaking rules because she was neither colleague nor client. She was a woman stuck in a crazy situation and as far as she was concerned, she had to earn something for all the trauma she'd been through. His attention was more than enough payment.

"To hell with it," he whispered to her, taking her mouth as fiercely as she'd just taken his.

For this moment in time, she felt in control and completely adored. His strength protected, but never hurt her, making her feel as though she were the most precious thing in the world. Her heart grabbed hold of a piece of him, cherishing every moment they had without regard to the future. The roar of gunfire made her yank away from him, staring at the flashes of light on the screen and the sound of bullets echoing across the room. Fear took over, and tears arrived. Instead of pushing her away, he hugged her into him, kissing her tears and murmuring that it would be okay, that tonight there was nothing to fear. She wrapped herself into his words, his arms, and stared up into eyes that told her everything would be okay, even though they both knew that guns would be out there, pointed on her again in the morning.

The movie ended, their feverish movements slowed, their breath labored, and neither of them moved. She didn't want to leave the safety of his arm wrapped around her or the touch of his cheek against the top of her head. Her head rested against his shoulder as her eyelids grew heavy. The warmth of his body, the steady rhythm of his heartbeat, lulled her into a sense of security she hadn't felt since she'd arrived to watch over Marlowe.

Still on the couch, she awoke as the first light of dawn burst through the window. The soft orange glow gave the room a magical appearance. Curled up against Noah with his arm around her and their bodies entangled in a comfortable but fairly awkward position. With the exhaustion of the day gone, their closeness brought a flush to her cheeks.

The growing daylight seemed to wake Noah as well. He curved his back in a stretch, his arm tightening for a moment across her arm and then loosening. As she met his gaze, any embarrassment dissolved into a warmth that spread through her chest.

"Good morning," he said, his voice deep and groggy.

"Morning. Did you get any sleep with me keeping you in such a strained position?" She sat up.

"I slept just fine." He straightened up as well and pulled his arm from over her shoulder to stretch it. "How about you?"

"I slept, so that's something. I might have a kinked neck all day though."

He rubbed his fingers into her neck and shoulder muscles. "I can help with that. Just tell me if it hurts."

"It feels amazing." She dropped her head back against the couch and allowed his fingers to press into her muscles and soothe away the ache from leaning into him in one position all night. If he never stopped, she'd be stuck there forever, because her whole body woke up with the massage.

They had so much to do, starting with her turning back into Allison. The idea of wearing another suit and more high heels, then acting like Allison, instantly shook the magic out of the morning.

His hands slowed and he looked at her. "I can feel you overthinking everything we're doing today. But you don't have to do anything. This is risky and it's not your job. Stepping back into Allison's life is your decision. Why don't you go take a shower and I'll make us some breakfast? Something more substantial than the muffin you had yesterday."

She didn't want to leave his side, but the day had commenced. She stood, letting the blanket fall onto his lap. "What should I wear to headquarters?"

"I have some sweatpants and a sweatshirt here. No one will see you until we get to headquarters if you're self-conscious."

"That will be great, thanks. If we decide to cancel the whole plan, I have some jeans there I can I wear." She looked over at him, nodding to her statement. He wasn't pressuring her to go and she appreciated it. She appreciated everything about him. Before she disappeared into the bathroom, she wanted to tell him, "I've never felt this amazing waking up in someone's arms." Instead, she chickened out and said, "I haven't woken up next to someone in a long time." Which was probably the more awkward thing to say, but telling him how wonderful she felt with him would also be awkward.

Noah's response was a gentle squeeze of her hand, a silent acknowledgment of the shared sentiment. "Neither have I," he admitted, his honesty yet another lasso around her heart.

Chapter Twenty-Two

When they arrived at headquarters, they headed straight to Jason's office. Jason was already there, coffee in hand, on the phone. He waved them in.

Noah pointed to a chair for Zoe, and he sat next to her. He hadn't asked her what she'd decided. The danger had come too close to hurting her, so he was on board with her stepping back. His own perspective had split between wanting to take down Patrick O'Reilly and his thugs and keeping Zoe safe. After the night before, he wanted her safe more than anything.

When Jason finished his call, he faced Zoe. "Rough night?"

"Noah made it easier." She glanced at Noah and a tenderness there tugged at his heart.

"In what way?" His question hinted at violations of every rule Fresh Pond had on fraternizing with clients.

Zoe didn't seem to pick up the warning coming from Jason toward Noah. "We watched *The Princess Bride*."

"Did you?" Jason's lips wavered on a laugh.

"We watched *John Wick* too," Noah said as though he needed to prove that they hadn't crossed any lines, although they most certainly had, and he didn't regret it one bit.

"I needed something with a bit of a punch," Zoe added.

"I've had many nights like that while I was in the military. I'm impressed how you're handling yourself without any experience and the most minimal training. I understand how dangerous it was at your sister's place yesterday. And it's my decision to pull you out," Jason said.

"What do you mean?" She looked between both men, her expression tensing.

"I mean that I'm sending you and your father to a safe location for the next few weeks as we complete the task we've been given."

Noah felt a weight off his chest. Zoe would be safe. He glanced over at her reaction, and saw a whole lot of apprehension. The exact opposite of how he'd expect her to react.

"No." She stood. "I want to do this."

Jason stood as well. "O'Reilly is not going to let anyone who has any connection with the bribery story live. I will not have blood on my hands when we can finish the job without you."

"I don't care. I'm ready to risk things. What will it look like if Allison doesn't show up for work today? I said on the air that we were going to the zoo. I don't want anything bad to happen to her, and if I'm on the camera, and that will protect her, I'm willing to do that."

Noah stared at her, as if she were someone he didn't recognize. "I understand what you want, but we can keep Allison and you and your father safe." Did she realize that any harm that came to her would hurt her family just as much as something happening to Allison would? Probably not. Zoe tended to see herself as the fixer, the person who made everybody else's life easier. She never seemed to value herself.

"Do you need access to the studio today?" she asked.

"Maybe. We've figured out the link between O'Reilly and Quinn, but we still don't know Glenn Morrow's connection to either of them." Jason frowned. "While it would be nice to walk in with a personnel pass, I can find work-arounds."

"That's easily rectified. I can sneak in at night. That would give me far more time to locate something. If I don't find anything helpful through that, I can head to his house. Even easier, maybe I can swipe his phone, and Calvin can work his usual magic on it."

"Breaking and entering?" Jason had a thing about breaking the law. He tended to be against it unless it was necessary to save a life. "Barbara has a murder trial this month. I don't think she's going to want to bail you out of jail and handle an arraignment."

"Who is Barbara?" Zoe asked.

"Barbara Singer is our attorney. We spent far too much of our budget on legal fees this past year. She's not too pleased about our former actions, and I promised her that we would try to do everything by the book."

"Is sneaking into the newsroom and shuffling through Glenn's desk considered legal?" she asked, looking like she knew the answer.

"If Allison brings a guest into the newsroom, she has no control over what that guest does, and if he happens to sneak into Glenn's office, and no one finds out about it, all the better."

She looked over at Noah, her expression earnest. "So my presence would help protect you."

Jason stopped his standoff with her and sat down. "It would make our lives easier if you took her place for one more day, but I hesitate because it's dangerous and I do not want you to feel any pressure."

Zoe sat again too. She ignored Noah and focused on Jason. "I think I can do it. I want to see this through."

Jason turned his attention to Noah. "What do you think?"

Noah didn't know how to answer. So many things could go wrong. So many things almost went wrong the day before. Yet, taking down the scum of the city might make it worth it. "If she's willing, I've got her back."

"Are you certain?" Jason asked Zoe. "Because you can back out now or at any time."

She nodded without hesitation. "I want to do this."

"Well then, Goodwyn, the stylist is waiting in conference room three."

She nodded again, as though a good soldier responding to her superior officer. The image of her as a soldier didn't make Noah more certain about this, but he'd respect her decision.

Two hours later, they arrived at the news station. He'd always taken pride in his ability to remain unattached, to be more professional than the person next to him, regardless of the situation. Yet, as he stood on the edge of a bustling newsroom, he focused on Zoe and his detachment slipped away bit by bit.

Zoe, on the other hand, had transformed from a nervous imposter the day before to a confident, professional reporter. Dressed in black with a green blazer, she spoke to everyone around her with poise. She stood in heels as though she'd been walking in them for years. When someone asked her to return to camera, she agreed. She stood in front of the camera with grace and determination, and read a short preview of her visit to the zoo.

Glenn, arguing with half the staff around him, had become occupied with the position of a light on the green screen. That distraction was all Noah needed. He slipped back into Glenn's office on a more limited search without the worry of needing access to the computer. Calvin had pulled everything Noah had downloaded the day before. Nothing in his notes would tie him to Brendan Quinn. He spent a good three minutes riffling through any papers that weren't news related. And then paused.

On the credenza by the window stood a family portrait that included someone who looked exactly like O'Reilly's ex-wife. The O'Reilly divorce had been a headline in the news. One of the nastiest legal battles the city had seen in a long time. O'Reilly took custody of their daughter after proving neglect by the wife. Noah remembered shots of the wife breaking down on the steps of the courthouse when the decision had been handed down. He glanced around a bit further, saw two more photos of the woman, took a few shots on his camera, and then stepped back into the newsroom studio. As he walked, he texted the pictures to Calvin and asked for any connection between the two. Since they'd only tied Patrick O'Reilly to the bribes the day before, they hadn't looked in the right directions for Glenn's involvement. Now, however, they had a line from one man to the other.

Luckily, Zoe was still by the cameras when he returned. Glenn, finished with his inspection of the lighting, walked over to him. "Noah, isn't it? I see you're spending quite a bit of time with one of our reporters," he said his tone casual, but his eyes assessing.

"I'd like to think we have something special. I'm here to support her and hopefully take her to lunch."

"No time for that. The van is waiting to take her to the zoo." Glenn paused before walking away. "Whatever you're doing for her, keep it up. She seems more focused on what her actual job is and isn't out running around and making more work for herself."

After he left, Noah went to meet Zoe in her office.

When she spotted him, her face lit up with genuine happiness. She rushed over and hugged him, her excitement visible. "Did you see me? I think I handled it well."

"You were amazing." He held her in his arms until she was ready to let go. Logically, he did that to make them appear more like a couple. Emotionally, her hug gave him an overwhelming sense of joy. When she stepped back, still smiling, he asked, "Are you ready to leave? The van is waiting. I'll follow in my car."

Her smile slipped. "You're not going with me?"

He'd debated staying at her side, but the logistics would be difficult. He'd been told that only employees were permitted to ride in the van. "I'll be right behind you. Not to worry." He would have pushed for her to drive in his car, but too much conflict might make Glenn suspicious and make her more of a target.

It turned out that it wasn't difficult following them. The bright blue and white van had an enormous satellite dish attached to the roof. When they arrived at the zoo, the news van parked up front in a space reserved for buses. Before Noah could park, he saw her exit the van. She only had a cameraman with her, some young guy in his midtwenties jabbering nonstop.

He couldn't afford to drive around the parking area looking for a decent spot, so he parked illegally in order to catch up to them. If Jason's car received a ticket, Jason would probably deduct the cost as a job expense. At the entrance, Zoe and the cameraman walked past the front gate, but Noah was caught up at a ticket booth. No ticket, no entrance. If he'd been with her, he would have gone in as part of the news team.

The line for tickets had ten to fifteen people at each booth. He rushed over to the membership desk, bought an all access VIP pass for a few hundred dollars and hustled past an explosion of children, teachers, parents, and strollers. He saw her up ahead. A few of the visitors waved at her, no doubt recognizing her as Allison, in black pants, a black top, and a bright green blazer with perfectly styled hair. He had almost caught up to them when they disappeared behind a door into the birthing den behind the main big cat exhibit.

He attempted to navigate through the locked entrance, but a formidable barrier in the form of a stern-faced security guard halted his progress.

Noah tried to charm his way past the woman. "Hi, I'm part of the news crew that just went through. They seem to have gotten a bit ahead of me in the crowds." He smiled for good measure.

"May I see your pass?" The guard's gaze swept over him with a calculated assessment.

Noah didn't want to reveal that he was there to protect her, because in this case, it might put her more at risk, but he paused too long.

"I'll need some form of ID or a confirmation from your team to grant you access," she said.

Being her boyfriend wouldn't get him past the guard, and neither would his nonexistent press pass. He decided to play his only card. "Listen, I'm Noah Montgomery, assigned to ensure Allison Goodwyn's security. For her safety, we don't advertise our presence with her generally, but in this case, I need to be with her. She's inside, reporting on the cub," he explained, trying to keep the desperation from seeping into his voice.

Her expression softened marginally, yet her stance remained unwavering. "We've had numerous attempts to breach this point today. It happens all the time when babies are born," she admitted, her voice laced with a hint of regret. "Without proof of what you're saying, I can't let you pass."

"I understand your protocol, but this is critical."

His attempts to contact Zoe failed. She could be focused on the story and would have the phone turned off. "Could you please contact a superior? It's important I reconnect with her."

With a sigh, the guard keyed her radio, engaging in a brief, static-filled exchange with someone named Roy. After a tense wait, she finally motioned for Noah to provide some form of identification.

He presented a laminated card, a makeshift credential Jason had prepared for such predicaments. It was simple—no elaborate designs or security features—just his name, the emblem of Fresh Pond Security, and a photo.

The guard relayed the details to Roy, and after a moment that stretched into eternity, she received the go-ahead. She stepped aside and allowed Noah to enter. He darted through the door, his heart pounding with a mix of relief and annoyance.

He navigated the long hallway, his footsteps echoing off the walls, until he stumbled upon Zoe. There she was, radiant and poised in front of the camera. Behind her, the clear divider protecting her from the lioness sprawled out on a bed of hay with her new cub. Noah felt a surge of pride. Zoe appeared poised, calm, and professional on camera without any visible signs of the threats closing in on them.

While he could have felt foolish for demanding he accompany her, he didn't. If anything happened to her on his watch… no, he was only thinking of his job and her safety. He remained nearby, monitoring everyone in the area and assuring himself that he could keep her safe. One thing for certain, he wasn't leaving her side again.

Chapter Twenty-Three

After the hell she'd gone through the day before, Zoe relaxed into the playful atmosphere of the zoo. Even though she'd been away from her bodyguard for a bit longer than she'd wanted, the zoo had a warm, welcoming atmosphere from the colorful banners to the friendly staff. And now that she'd already been on camera once, she thought she could handle this assignment. Allison's job always looked glamorous, but Zoe never thought it would be so much fun. She'd always pictured her job, down on a colorful rug with a bunch of children reading stories and playing with art and music and LEGO more fun. Yet, the glamor of dressing up and interviewing a zookeeper about a lion cub ranked right up there with the privilege of telling a parent just how wonderful their child was. She held the microphone in her hand and interviewed the zookeeper, who appeared a mere five feet tall, but ran the entire big cat area of the zoo. The woman loved her job and helped make the segment as entertaining and educational as Zoe would try to make each lesson in her class. Not that Zoe had been perfect. She'd never actually interviewed anyone, so she bobbled over some questions, but overall, it seemed successful enough to make anyone think it was Allison in front of the camera. She glanced over at Noah. He was leaning against the wall, one hand in his pocket, the embodiment of classy casual. And the warmth in his gaze sent a lightning bolt straight through her heart. It was fun to be in the presence of somebody who didn't hide his appreciation for her. In the past, the men in her life treated her as a potential wife and mother, or a potential fun Friday night—granted, she was the one who chose poorly. None of them actually spent the time to really look at her as an individual. They seemed far more interested in what she would do for them.

When she finished the interview, she walked over to Noah with a smile. "What did you think?"

He pushed off the wall and stepped toward her. "It's like you were made for this job, or at least some of your DNA was."

"It's been really fun. Have you met Tom?" She called over the cameraman who had been putting away his equipment in a backpack. He'd just graduated film school and was the backup cameraman but was allowed to film the zoo interview when the senior cameraperson called out sick.

"Nice to meet you." Tom shook Noah's hand. "How did you get past security? They're pretty strict when it comes to VIP access."

"It wasn't that hard—I said you forgot your battery pack in the van and I forgot my ID."

"Nice, man." Tom fist-bumped Noah.

When they walked out to the parking lot, Noah swore under his breath.

"What's wrong?" Zoe asked.

Noah pointed to Jason's car being towed away.

"There goes my yearly bonus," he said, although he didn't sound as stressed about it as Zoe would have been. "Do you mind if I grab a ride back to the station with you?" he asked Tom.

Tom waved his arm toward the van. "Sure, if you don't mind sitting in the back with all the equipment?"

"No problem. Feel free to treat me like any assistant."

Tom laughed. "Perfect, assistants are in charge of buying coffee on the way back to the studio."

Zoe enjoyed Noah and Tom's banter back and forth. They argued about the newest Red Sox pitcher and the best place in town for seafood. She sat in the front with Tom but glanced back at Noah. As he spoke to Tom, he scanned out the back window and when he could, through the front windshield.

As Tom turned right onto the highway on-ramp and Noah suggested a specific Dunkin' for coffee, Zoe thought over all she'd accomplished while helping her sister remain safe. It had been quite the adventure, one she never wanted to relive, but it had provided a perspective on her sister she'd never had before. Tom asked Zoe what she wanted in her coffee. Cream and sugar forever.

There was a lightness to the moment, as though she were in the middle of a romantic comedy, until blood sprayed across her face. A bullet had gone through the windshield and straight through Tom's forehead. His head slammed back and then slumped forward. Zoe swallowed her scream, terrified. She ducked to protect herself. Noah, on the other hand, jumped up next to her, taking control of the steering wheel as the van veered off the road.

"Stay down." He slid onto Tom's lap and slammed his leg toward the brake. The van came to a rough stop feet from a huge metal light pole.

Noah, as serious as he'd been casual only a minute before, secured the van, unbuckled Zoe, and made sure she was okay. She wasn't. Blood was everywhere. On her, on parts of Noah, and Tom, he was a mess.

"Is anything hurt?" Noah asked her.

She took a breath, but nearly vomited, and barely indicated she was fine. As she pulled on the door handle to get out, a police officer was already at her side. Another stood at the driver's seat, looking in the window.

"Ma'am, are you okay?" the officer closest to her asked. He took her by the arm and helped her out of the van, escorting her straight into the back of their police car.

"I'm fine." She turned back to see if Noah had followed, but she couldn't see him or the van from where she was sitting. When the second officer returned to the police car, they drove away.

"Wait. What about Noah?" she shouted.

Neither man answered.

Zoe stared out the back window of the police car as they moved away from the accident scene. No, it wasn't an accident scene. It was a murder scene. The blood had seared itself into her mind, an unwanted memory branded onto her soul. The police car with lights flashing cruised onto the highway and away from Noah. For a woman who had been dropped off at school in her father's police car, this car seemed uncomfortably silent, with no siren wailing nor the chatter of a police radio. The two men stared straight ahead, with not the slightest interest in Zoe's health and well-being in the back seat.

The driver, the police officer who had asked her to sit in the car in what she had felt was a protective move, turned his head slightly, his features hard, his expression jagged. "Just relax, we'll be there shortly," he said, his voice lacking empathy.

"Where are we going? We can't leave everyone back there." Tom, that young man who got his big break today, was now dead. Her whole body waved back and forth, trying to relieve the intensity of what she'd seen, to understand what it all meant.

Neither of the men answered. They had zero interest in anything she'd said. The most unprofessional police officers she'd ever met. They hadn't asked her one question about the accident, not one question about who she was, not one question about what she'd seen.

Something was unnervingly precise in the way the driver kept the car just about the speed limit on the highway. Taking her away from the protection Fresh Pond Security had offered to her. Her body understood the situation before her brain registered that her worst possible fear had occurred without her putting up even the slightest fight. She'd been kidnapped.

Her hands fumbled for her seat belt, her fingers trembled. A stupid gesture. She couldn't jump out at sixty miles an hour even if the door would open. Then the car turned off into a secluded area where buildings were sparse and no one would find her. Her mind raced.

They pulled into an abandoned lot and yanked her out of the car. One of the men held her and the other ripped off her necklace, stripped her out of her shoes, her jacket, and her watch. The watch had been given to her from the team as a way to locate her at all times. Without it, no one would be able to come to her rescue.

In no time, they'd stripped her bare and manipulated every part of her clothing. She stood exposed and terrified. Neither one of them, however, gave her a second glance. It was as though she had a force field around her body. She was thankful for that, even as her body shook from the breeze and the fear. When they had accomplished their task, they opened the back door and allowed her to get inside. They tossed her dress and panties inside with her, but nothing else.

As she sat in the back seat, she glanced onto the floor. Hidden by the front armrest was her cell phone. She put her clothes back on and, in the process, picked up her phone, turned the ringer off, and slipped it into her underwear. The car drove around in what felt like circles. Each lap adding another knot to her stomach, turning her insides into a tangled ball.

They stopped outside a large nondescript warehouse. One that could be anywhere. As they opened the door, she couldn't smell the tang of the sea or the lingering diesel of airplane fuel. Inside, the air tasted thick with the smell of oil and rust, a tangy scent that clung to her nostrils and made her stomach churn. As she was dragged deeper into the bowels of the building, past rows of pickup trucks, Honda Accords, and nothing as glamorous as a Ferrari or Lamborghini, she searched for any chance of escape.

The two men who had acted as saviors turned her over to a man she'd never cross. He had to be seven feet tall with hands that could squeeze the life out of her without much effort. He seemed maybe thirty, maybe forty, with his hair in a buzz cut, and his chin coated in stubble.

The man who had pulled her from the van pushed her toward him. "She's yours. Have fun."

The police pretenders laughed, her new captor merely grinned, but didn't put out his hand to grab her as she stumbled forward. He remained focused on the men behind her. "See Bobby for your fee minus the hassle for cleanup in the van. You're getting sloppy."

Zoe straightened herself out and looked around. She'd seen enough of *The Fast and the Furious* movies to recognize this as a chop shop. Her heart hammered in her chest, fear coursing through her veins. The sight of a gun in a holster at her captor's waist warned her just how dangerous a situation she'd found herself in. And how utterly powerless she was. The self-defense training she'd undergone, those futile few days she'd pretended to learn what she'd need to handle this, seemed laughable when faced with this reality.

Alone, without Noah or any hope of immediate rescue, Zoe was acutely aware of her vulnerability. She found some comfort in the knowledge that her father and sister had adequate protection and were in hiding. Despite knowing Allison's behavior was often immature and spoiled, Zoe found it impossible to imagine her life without her.

Zoe's thoughts circled back over and over again to Noah. Her final image of him buckled over in pain as they drove away from the area. With the violent deaths of Mrs. Peterson, Mr. Noonan, and Tom, Noah had to be okay. She refused to entertain even the slightest thought of any harm coming to him. The fear of never seeing him again, of leaving so many words unsaid, even if they'd been inspired by their close proximity to death, brought an ache to her heart almost as painful as the physical threat she faced.

Chapter Twenty-Four

Noah felt he was reliving a nightmare. He had one main task, and that was to keep Zoe safe. In the ten minutes he'd been in the van with her, the driver suffered a bullet through his forehead, and the van transporting them came far too close to slamming into a pole with a four-foot tall, several feet thick concrete base. That they both survived with minimal injury had been a miracle. The psychological damage to Zoe, Noah couldn't calculate, but she'd need some severe trauma therapy after this.

As she had been pulled toward an unmarked police car with one of the police officers who appeared out of nowhere, she'd turned back to Noah in distress.

Another cop knocked on his window. "Stay where you are. We need to ask you a few questions."

"Can it wait? I should check on my girlfriend. She's been through a lot." He'd tried to get out from the passenger seat Zoe had just vacated, but the second officer blocked his exit from the van, asking him to be patient and wait.

That's when the realization hit him like a concrete truck. These officers arrived with an impossible quickness in an unmarked car with blue lights added. They were parked ahead of the van, which meant they either drove backward down the on-ramp, or they were already there...waiting.

He couldn't take a chance that he was right, he had to protect Zoe.

"Stay where you are." The statement promised an arrest if Noah made a move past him, but that was what Barbara was for. Bailing him out.

No police officer would keep an injured man in a van with a murder victim literally under him. He'd help him from the vehicle.

He turned to escape out the opposite door.

"Stay where you are," The officer grabbed Noah's shirt and pulled him back. When Noah saw a gun in his hand, he knew. They were tangled up together, so Noah headbutted the asshole, but received a punch to the nose in the process. Everything blurred in pain, but he managed to grab at the barrel, punching the whole weapon back into his attacker's face and hopefully breaking his jaw.

He pushed through the officer and dived behind some bushes by the side of the road. There were sirens coming closer. The fake or corrupt cop took off toward Zoe.

Noah tried to rush toward them, but the car drove off before he could get closer. As blood dripped from his nose, he was somehow able to pull out his phone and dial Jason.

"Montgomery?" Jason asked.

"They got her. Corrupt cops, if they really were cops," he tried to wheeze out the words while holding back the nausea. O'Reilly had people everywhere.

"Are you okay?"

"I'll be fine." A broken nose wouldn't kill him, just make him miserable for a bit. "Zoe was okay when I last saw her, but I don't know." If anything happened to her, Noah would never forgive himself.

"Focus on the details. I'm putting you on speaker so Calvin and Fiona can hear."

He took a breath and coughed, spitting up the taste of the blood. "The driver's dead, shot by something long-range. Two men arrived, dressed as police, and pulled her to their car before I could stop them." He coughed again and spit out blood.

He could hear Calvin say "shit" in the background. There was definite comfort in knowing that the team had his back.

"I'm on the way. Get yourself into hiding. Do not stay at the scene," Jason commanded.

"What about Zoe?"

"Calvin's already started trying to track her down. Now go. We'll talk when I have you." He hung up.

Since every one of Jason's employees wore tracking devices when on the clock, Jason would track him down quickly. A thought hit him. Everyone wore one, including Zoe. The relief was short-lived as he struggled to push the door open and flee down the embankment into the woods, stumbling over downed trees. He continued moving until he was about a mile from the accident.

He remained hidden in the shadows behind a set of triple-decker houses. For the second time in a year, he'd lost someone he'd been entrusted to protect. The first time was with Jason's son. After Noah's failure, the team made a daring rescue mission to save him, but not Noah. He'd been in the hospital with a gunshot wound. This time, he'd lost Zoe. Frustration gnawed at his insides, a physical manifestation of failure. That Zoe had been placed in such a dangerous situation and could be hurt or worse added unbearable shame and guilt to his turmoil.

A black Explorer arrived on the road where Noah had hidden. He moved between the two houses, alerting a dog from one of the apartments. To his relief, Jason was at the wheel. Through the fading pain in his face, Noah could see the fury in Jason's expression. He climbed into the passenger seat and remained silent for most of the ride as Jason blasted orders to the team through his phone.

When they returned to headquarters, Jason took off to his office while Noah was given enough medical intervention to make him functional again. But he didn't care much about his own health. All he could think about was Zoe. Not only had she seen the brutal murder of a man that she'd been laughing with only minutes before, but then she was kidnapped by the very people that she'd trusted.

When he arrived at Jason's office, he stalled at the door.

Jason was talking to someone on the phone, his hand clenched in a fist as though about to punch some imaginary demon. When he saw Noah, he told the person on the line to get their shit together before slamming the phone on his desk.

"How are you holding up?" Jason asked, his voice filled with genuine concern.

"What's going on? Have you located her yet?" Noah demanded, ignoring any worry about his own well-being.

Jason fixed Noah with a look that was hard to read. "I thought we had her location, but they found our tracker. Calvin tracked it to an empty lot in South Boston. Fiona drove there to investigate and possibly rescue Zoe, but she found the watch and several other articles of her clothing and shoes with no sign of anyone else in the area," Jason explained, his voice revealing his growing frustration.

The realization that they'd lost the lifeline to Zoe's location sent a wave of cold dread through Noah.

Her tracker had been a silver watch with a black onyx face. Elegant and more like jewelry than a technical gadget so she could wear it on the air. Without it, it would be almost impossible to locate her. That terrifying thought felt like a boulder pulling Noah down.

She'd become a needle in a haystack. At this moment, Noah's nausea surpassed anything he'd felt after being hit in the nose. He was usually someone who could come up with a dozen different scenarios with corresponding plans. Being stuck on the sidelines, powerless, ate him alive. Doubt crept in on this assignment, on his abilities, and his place at Fresh Pond Security. Two people he'd been assigned to protect, two people taken. Perhaps he was not only not qualified for this job, but his arrogance in thinking he was placed Zoe directly in danger.

He paced back and forth, frustrated and furious. Jason led him to Calvin's office. Before they entered, Jason pulled him aside.

"Noah, I need you to hold it together." Jason's voice was firm.

He couldn't hold it together, not with Zoe out there without any protection at all. Calvin had three assistants, all of whom were manically tapping away at their keyboards. Noah could see a map of Boston on one and a few live streams on another. Jason stood with his arms crossed, standing over Calvin, looking at one of his computer screens. Noah turned and began pacing again.

"Anything?" he asked.

Calvin remained fixated on the screens, which irritated the hell out of Noah. He nearly pulled Calvin back to demand an answer when he felt a hand on his shoulder. Jason. The gesture stopped Noah from pushing. He stepped back from Calvin's desk.

Calvin glanced over his shoulder at them without the slightest indication that he was aware of Noah's anxious behavior. "So far, no. Zoe has no footprint and the police car you described, unmarked dark sedan with lights in the back windshield could describe a thousand cars in the city."

Calvin's focus on finding Zoe forced Noah to place his attention back on the important details and not his own failures. "But the police are only tracking their cars, so if there's a car that's acting a bit erratic and it's not on any police scanner, etc. it may give us something to focus on."

Jason shook his head. "What are the chances?"

Calvin shrugged. "Ten percent? Maybe less?"

That was not what Noah needed to hear. His rage built inside of him and he struggled to keep it under control.

"We can check traffic cam live web feeds from various parts of the city," Calvin added. "If she's in Boston, we'll find her."

"And if she isn't?" Noah replied, his voice hostile.

Jason, stepped toward him, as though he were going to give him some fatherly advice or comfort. That was not happening. He didn't need to be calmed down like some super hormonal teenage boy. Not in front of other members of the team. He had to get a grip and act like a field team member. He had years of experience tracking criminal organizations at the NSA, both domestic and international. He sat in a chair next to Calvin and shut his eyes to refocus on the situation and get his head back in the game.

After several minutes, he remembered something everyone else seemed to have forgotten. "What about her cell phone?"

"Cell phone?" Jason asked. "She didn't have one. We took it into custody so no one could track it."

"You took Allison's phone, not Zoe's. We've been in touch all day on it. Can we triangulate her phone's last known signal? It was on when we left the zoo. I'm pretty sure most of her location tracking was turned off to protect her."

Jason appeared at once furious and relieved. "We should have confiscated it and replaced it with a burner, but at this moment, I'm glad we didn't."

Calvin started typing something on his keyboard, "Let me see what I can do. If she and her sister share locations, we might be able to go directly into her GPS. That would be the most accurate way to go."

"Her sister's phone is in the trunk of my car, in a Faraday bag to block any tracking," Jason said.

"That's going to be a problem." He'd forgotten to tell Jason about his car being towed with everything happening.

"Where's my car?" Jason rubbed his temples.

"I don't know. Last time I saw it, it was hitched to a tow truck and driving away from the zoo."

The room filled with a desperate energy as Jason and Noah waited for Calvin's analysis. Noah leaned in closer to read the data pouring onto Calvin's monitor.

"Guys, it's going to take longer than five minutes." Calvin glared at Noah. "Go get some coffee or check back in with everyone else, then come back. There has to be something else for you to do."

Jason pulled on Noah's arm. "Let's go."

Once in the hallway, Jason strode away in silence. He never liked when things went wrong on an assignment and he probably hated that this current disaster was directly related to Noah's second chance in the field. Noah followed a few steps back. They both needed some breathing room.

As they entered the kitchen, Fiona arrived.

Jason poured everyone coffee, while Fiona leaned against the counter. She rubbed Jason's arm and then stepped over to Noah.

"First," she said to him, "you need to examine this incident with complete impartiality. It wasn't your fault. There's no one on the team that would've been able to stop a bullet going into the head of the driver. Second, that spot was chosen by those butchers because of a lack of cameras in the vicinity as well as being a decent place for a shooter to hide, which is why the so-called police arrived so quickly. I went to the site before the coroner arrived while Jason went out to pick you up. The fact that you were able to stop that van from slamming into the light pole saved Zoe's life."

"How did you know it was me?"

"Dead men don't brake up an incline as steep as that on-ramp, and Zoe was in the passenger seat. I doubt her instincts would have been to hop into the lap of a man she'd only just met to stop the bus. Grabbing the steering wheel maybe, but not braking."

He didn't want compliments, he wanted Zoe back. "We can run a whole crime scene reconstruction after we get Zoe back. We don't even know if she's alive."

"Focus on the what is, not the what-ifs. We know she was alive when taken. If they only wanted her dead, they could have added a bullet to her head as well and been done with it. They didn't." Fiona had never been one to beat around the bush. She was as direct and deadly as a missile. "Third, and most important," she added, "I found something. I put a call into a friend at the real estate tax office at City Hall after you told me about Patrick O'Reilly. He emailed me a list of every property under O'Reilly's name in Boston in the vicinity, including those obscured by an LLC or trust." She waved her iPad in the air.

Jason brows lifted. "How many?"

"Over two hundred."

The volume was overwhelming, but with the right program, Noah could scan it quickly for the most likely locations. "Can you forward that to my email?" he asked. At least it would give him something to concentrate on. Doing nothing was not an option.

"Absolutely." Fiona picked up the cup of coffee Jason had

made her and headed to the door. She turned around before she left. "We can both look over the addresses. Let's do this separately and then we can compare lists. Once Calvin narrows down the cell location, we can reduce the possible locations even further, although cell phone pings are notoriously difficult to trace to an exact point, especially in a city."

It didn't matter how difficult the task. Noah would not stop until he located Zoe and put an end to O'Reilly's hold on the city.

Chapter Twenty-Five

Zoe followed the beast of a man through a few more rows of cars, her bare feet cold on the concrete floor, until she reached a row of offices and what looked like an employee lounge from the 1970s with harvest yellow vinyl chairs and gray linoleum worn through in places. He pointed for her to sit in one of the chairs. The cold metal of his gun caught a piece of the sun, menacing her by sight alone. She forced herself to breathe, to think. Panic would not help her out of this situation. She had to use her brain more than her self-defense-for-beginner tactics if she had any hope of surviving this.

"Noah," she whispered under her breath, more of a prayer than a request. She wondered if he knew where she was, if he was plotting her rescue. She thought of the rest of the team as well, but not once did she allow herself to think about Noah's fate at the van. The idea of Fresh Pond Security focused on her provided a bit more courage, a reminder that she was not entirely alone in this fight.

But as the seconds ticked by, each one stretching into an eternity, hope faded. She thought of her sister and all she'd done to protect Allison only to find herself caught up in the same web. She'd worked so hard to become her sister and to learn whatever it took to save her. Instead, she'd ended up in a place where her neck could be snapped, her body violated, and her mind twisted. Regret mingled with fear. She'd failed.

Her only positive had been that it was her and not Allison in this mess. She'd handle whatever obstacles were thrown at her. She might be terrified, staring at the gun, a weapon that had ripped a hole in Tom's head, but she wouldn't give up yet. The fire that had driven her to take on this mission, to protect her family, still burned within her. Even more so after seeing the level of violence these people were capable of.

"Wait here." He left her alone with the door open and she didn't dare stand from the chair to which he'd specifically sent her. When he returned, he tossed a greasy set of overalls toward her. She looked up at him with no idea what he wanted. She cataloged his appearance, burly guy in jeans and work boots. His brown hair a wavy mess stuffed under a baseball hat, but his hands weren't as calloused as the mechanics she'd known on Nantucket.

"Go ahead and put it on over your dress. It gets cold in here." Then he left, shutting the door this time.

The gray outfit was huge, made for a much larger person than herself, but she liked the idea of covering up, so she put it on, rolling up the legs and the sleeves to fit her better. While fixing the overalls, she shifted her phone to an inner pocket by her hip. There was no time to look at it, since the door opened without a knock.

She looked up to see not the beast, but an Adonis in a tailored suit stroll in, completely out of place in the grimy surroundings. His entrance commanded her attention as his eyes took in every aspect of her appearance. He scanned over her outfit and seemed to scrutinize her in a cold and calculating manner as if assessing her worth—or lack thereof. Her intuition told her exactly who she was looking at—Patrick O'Reilly.

"Sit." He pointed at her with a dismissive flick of his wrist, his voice smooth but holding an icy detachment. "Miss Goodwyn, nice to meet you." He did not attempt to shake her hand. This was a show and she was the only audience.

"What's going on? Why am I here?"

"Because I told you to stand down and you didn't."

"Stand down? I was doing a story at the zoo," she countered.

"That was convenient, but your blog says differently."

Zoe bit back her response because she had nothing to say. A blog? If Allison had recently written something about the bribes, she'd not only undercut all the preparation and risk Zoe had gone through to protect her, but she'd sent her into a deadly situation. Worse, Zoe couldn't exactly ask about the blog or risk exposing herself as a fraud.

"Who assigned you to the lion cub story?" he asked her.

"Glenn did," she replied, an easy answer after a bunch of impossible ones.

O'Reilly stepped up to her, his piercing blue eyes appearing more glacier than sky. "Did he?"

Zoe nodded.

"And yet even with something to occupy your time, you couldn't let up on the other investigation. Are your life and the lives of those you love worth so much less than this story?"

"No. I don't care about the other story." She honestly didn't. "I can promise you that I dropped that story."

"Promises are convenient words, but words mean nothing to me. Actions do and so far, you have proved to be far more stubborn than everyone around you." He shook his head as though Zoe had disappointed him in some way. He stepped toward her, something about his expression made Zoe pull back from him.

The door creaked open. The beast entered, his bulk eclipsing O'Reilly. His mere presence stilled the air in the small space, bringing the tension down. A sigh of relief escaped Zoe, more terrified of the tailored suit than the blue jeans.

"Did you get your questions answered?" He looked from O'Reilly to Zoe. His emotions remained hidden beneath surliness.

O'Reilly took a moment to consider Zoe and then frowned. "I have enough to be satisfied for now, but I'm afraid she'll need to remain here for a bit longer. There are still questions she needs to answer."

She hadn't thought he'd open the door and let her get away, not when her sister's knowledge could subject him to criminal prosecution.

"Where do you want her?"

"Put her with Maisie," O'Reilly said with wave of dismissal. "She could use a babysitter. And frankly, we've relied too much on you for such services. I'd prefer if you increase security here."

"I'm here to help in any way I can." For such a large intimidating man, he certainly kowtowed to O'Reilly.

"And I appreciate that. Monitor the warehouse and keep the facility free from visitors until tomorrow. I'll send O'Donnell to pick the kid up before bedtime."

"I understand. Anything she should eat for dinner?"

O'Reilly made a face. "I really don't give a shit."

Before Zoe had time to process anything, the beast lifted her by the arm. His grip never slipped as he dragged her further into the warehouse. She fought to get onto her own feet.

"This would be easier on both of us if I could walk," she said.

He dropped her and she fell hard onto the floor without him saying a word. The humiliation hurt more than any other part of her. She scurried up and followed him, not willing to risk an escape while the floor had a dozen men working on the cars around her. He opened an office door.

"Through here," he said, pointing.

As she stepped inside, he closed the door behind her. Although dimly lit, she could make out a wooden desk in front of her, scarred from scratches and coffee stains. The desktop contained a chaotic array of papers and Post-it notes. The vinyl of the office chair had split open long ago, its padding pushing through the broken material.

She froze and contemplated her first minute alone without someone threatening her. A soft whimper caught her attention. In the shadows of the room, a little girl sat curled up on an old sofa, dressed in a parochial school uniform, her red curly hair pulled into a ponytail, her blue eyes wide with fear. Zoe's heart clenched at the sight, her own fear forgotten.

"Hi," Zoe said softly, moving closer to the girl, her voice instinctively adopting the soothing tone she used with her students. "What's your name?"

The girl hesitated, then whispered, "Maisie. Maisie O'Reilly."

The name sent a shock through her. O'Reilly. The asshole in a thousand-dollar-plus suit who didn't give a damn about what some girl ate—this was his daughter. The realization added a layer of complexity to her situation even more intricate than she'd imagined.

Maisie watched her warily, but the kindness in Zoe's voice seemed to offer some comfort. "Are you my new babysitter?" Maisie asked, a tremble in her voice betraying her attempt at bravery.

Zoe's heart not only ached for the girl, but burned in anger. They were both prisoners, but Zoe would never allow a child to be hurt in any way if she could do something about it. She had to be the fierce one, not a woman cowering in the corner. "I think I am your babysitter. For now, anyway. I'm Miss Goodwyn," she said, which wasn't a lie. She and Allison were both Miss Goodwyns. "Have you been here all day?"

Maisie nodded. "Daddy has to work, so I stay here after school."

So he left her in a place where thugs roamed freely and the police could arrive at any moment, armed and able to use deadly force? Her anger at O'Reilly grew. That lazy jerk. There had to be a thousand other options he could afford for his daughter. This was negligent.

"When do you go home?" Zoe asked, her mind racing to formulate a plan.

"Before I go to bed."

If Zoe were a super spy, she could use Maisie as a human shield to escape, but she'd rather sacrifice her own life before ever risking the life a child.

Instead, Zoe took the opportunity to pull her phone out to call for help. She stared at the black screen. The battery was dead.

Chapter Twenty-Six

While Noah waited for Calvin to get a location on Zoe's phone, he listed out the twenty places out of two hundred where O'Reilly might hide someone. His analysis wasn't perfect, but after years in the NSA analyzing the empires of high-level criminals, he had an excellent understanding of kingpin portfolios. He searched real estate in somewhat isolated locations, preferably not listed under O'Reilly's legal name, probably held under a trust, partnership, or LLC. After he finished, he handed his list to Fiona to compare to her own.

Each minute that passed put Zoe further at risk. He had managed to keep his tension under control, channeling his focus on the facts and figures Fiona had him analyze. Now, however, as he mulled over the potential locations where he might find her, his patience frayed at the edges. He headed to Calvin's space, but the tech guru ignored him, as he listed out tasks for his team to handle. Noah didn't want to disturb them, but he had to know if Calvin had triangulated her location, or even better, found her through GPS. Instead, he went to see Jason.

The atmosphere in Jason's office simmered with the strain of a ticking clock and an entire city to search. The harsh lighting cast long shadows across the room that mirrored the stormy mood that seemed to be emanating from Jason. The tight furrow of Jason's brows made Noah anxious to talk to him yet nervous over what he'd found. His boss was engrossed in a sea of maps, printouts and the glow of his computer screen. As Jason lifted his attention toward Noah, a silence stretched out between them as taut as a rubber band.

Jason finally broke the silence, his voice a controlled fury that Noah had rarely heard directed at him. "How are you feeling?"

"How do you think? I had one job. Keep Zoe safe. And now? We have no idea where she is." Noah's jaw tightened, his guilt and frustration warring within him. "I was sitting right next to her."

"How would you have known someone would assassinate the driver? That's another level of violence and intimidation."

Noah understood Jason's reasoning, but Noah hadn't been as cautious as he should have been. He'd let her be driven to the zoo without him, leaving her even more vulnerable until he'd finally caught up to her as she handled the interview. Overall, he'd made some stupid mistakes, and in reality, she should have been in the back seat in the van with him. Instead, he'd allowed her to sit up front, where a bullet might have killed her instead of Tom.

Jason leaned forward, his hands clenched on the desk. "You should have anticipated anything and everything. I gave you a second chance after Matt. You are in the field because you belong there. I would never place anyone who didn't have the skill set to handle their assignment."

The more Noah thought about it, the more he realized that Jason hadn't second-guessed his abilities, Noah had done it to himself.

Fiona burst into the room, her entrance like a gust of wind.

"Jason, listen to me." Her glare at Jason was sharp, a clear indication that she wasn't an ordinary subordinate but a force to be reckoned with. "Noah did nothing wrong. If anything, you should have had a backup following them. That was your blunder. Fresh Pond Security has taken on too many assignments, and we've all been pressed into more dangerous work with less coordination and backup."

Noah, momentarily taken aback by her assertiveness, felt a

surge of gratitude for her intervention, although she had it all wrong. It was Jason providing the support.

"This isn't just Noah's responsibility," Fiona continued, her stance beside Noah a literal and figurative support. "Just like Matt's kidnapping wasn't his fault. You, Meaghan, and I were all in the same house when Matt was taken. We all failed. We win together, we lose together."

Jason lifted his brows at his wife's arguments. He sighed, the rigid lines of his body relaxed slightly. "Are you done berating me in front of my team?"

"Our job right now is finding Zoe. We don't have time to dwell on what should have been done. We'll go over all of that in the postmortem."

Jason nodded. "If you actually listened in on our conversation you'll know I agree with you. I was trying to give Noah a pep talk."

"Oh… Good." Then without a speck of embarrassment, she turned to Noah. "I went over your analysis. We had five locations in common. Your criteria fit the general workings of a criminal enterprise. My choices reflected something similar, but also integrated the area Calvin plotted as the most likely area where the phone last pinged."

"We have a spot?"

"Yes, but there are multiple factors that affect the accuracy of that spot. In the city, there's a ton of signal interference, and her cell phone was an older model, so it isn't connected to the fastest cellular network. There's a bunch of other factors that could diminish accuracy. I think we should look at these five places," she said.

The news gave him more hope than he'd felt all day. The isolation and the weight of responsibility that had threatened to crush him now seemed more bearable.

"Let me see the list," Jason said, taking over his position as leader again. "Noah, Fiona, you're both coming with me. We'll start with the closest location and work from there. Have Calvin contact the Bureau after he gets confirmation that we've located her and are going into a location." He stood and approached Fiona. "Thanks."

"I've always got your back," she said to her husband, but her glance at Noah conveyed that her commitment extended to him as well.

As they prepared to leave Jason's office, Noah felt the dynamics of their team shift, solidifying into something stronger, more cohesive. He had a renewed sense of purpose, bolstered by his continued inclusion on the team and Jason's and Fiona's unwavering support for him. "I'll tell Calvin," he replied.

When he pulled Calvin aside to tell him the plan, Calvin stepped out of the room with him. "Listen, with the location narrowed down, our plan makes sense and I think we have a real shot at finding her." He clapped a hand on Noah's shoulder. "And Noah, you're better out in the field than you think you are. Keep your focus on the present, not on what-ifs or what happened. Your instincts were right about sneaking into the producer's office. Not only were you not caught, but you gave us more information than you realize. Without your work, we'd still be trying to figure out who was going after Allison. And those photos you downloaded from his desk provided us the connection between Glenn Morrow and O'Reilly."

"What is it?"

"O'Reilly's ex-wife is Glenn Morrow's first cousin. They're family."

Noah shook his head. "I still don't get it, why would he put Allison in harm's way?"

"When you find out, tell me."

Ten minutes later, Noah was dressed for a fight in black cargo pants, a black T-shirt and armed like an Army Ranger. He followed Jason and Fiona in his own car.

The first location was an old retail site, abandoned about three years before. He hoped she was there, safe, and mentally okay. The area was known for its crumbling infrastructure and had become a haven for unsavory characters, making it a dangerous place to search and a perilous place to be held for hours. Noah raged with a fierce and unrelenting determination. He would find her safe or he would burn the whole place to the ground.

Chapter Twenty-Seven

The dimly lit back office of the warehouse, with its dusty piles of folders and the distant sound of muffled voices, seemed a place where Patrick O'Reilly discarded everything he didn't care about, including his daughter. The thought broke Zoe's heart. She'd read about the fierce custody battle where he had witness after witness disparage his ex-wife. Yet, he wasn't the caring person he'd pretended to be. Without regard for the well-being of Maisie, he struck out to hurt her mother and in the process was destroying Maisie as well.

Zoe sat cross-legged across from Maisie on a small couch in the back room of the warehouse. Some extra clothes for the little girl were left on a dusty file cabinet, and a pink-and-blue comforter and a very loved stuffed puppy were on the couch. Someone had placed a pile of worn books between them, some chapter books, some a bit more advanced. An iPad offered some one-way companionship for her.

"Is this where you live?" Zoe asked.

Maisie shook her head. "I only stay here when Daddy is away or busy." A tear rolled down her cheek, and Zoe shifted over next to her, holding her in her arms as more tears fell. "He's away right now."

Zoe couldn't think what kind of monster would be fifty feet away from his daughter and not even check in on her. She absorbed some of Maisie's unhappiness. "Who watches you when your dad is away?"

"Johnny and David and Freddy."

"Do they work here?" Any and all information related to her captors would be a benefit.

Maisie nodded. "They help Daddy."

"Why aren't you at your home?"

"Mrs. Gallagher had to visit her sister." She looked up at Zoe. "She'll be dead soon."

"Mrs. Gallagher or her sister?" The words slipped out before she realized it, the strain of being manhandled and then thrown into limbo added to the stress twisting her thoughts.

"Her sister. She has cancer."

"Cancer stinks." It had murdered Zoe's mother.

"Yeah." Maisie hesitated, then began to recount her story in halting sentences. As Zoe listened, she pieced together a narrative that was heartbreaking and illuminating. The details Maisie provided could be the key to understanding the motives of her father, to finding a way out.

As they talked, Zoe's resolve hardened. She was no longer just fighting for her own life and her sister's safety; she was fighting for Maisie, for this innocent child caught in the crossfire of a conflict she couldn't comprehend.

In the dim light of the back room, Zoe Goodwyn found a new sense of purpose. With Maisie by her side, she was no longer just a teacher or a sister; she was a protector.

Maisie picked up a book, her small fingers tracing the illustrations with evident delight. "I like the pictures," she said, her voice a whisper of enthusiasm. Perhaps she'd learned that loud noises were not acceptable here.

Despite her fear, Zoe smiled, encouraged by Maisie's interest. "Do you want to try reading some of it together?" she suggested.

Maisie hesitated, her excitement dimming. "I... I'm not good at reading." Her gaze dropped to the book in her lap.

"I can help. I teach kids to read. Sometimes, it's not easy, but they all get there on their own schedule."

Maisie did not appear convinced.

As they attempted the words together, Zoe noticed the way Maisie struggled with the letters, her frustration mounting with every stumbled pronunciation. The struggle culminated in Maisie throwing the book across the room.

It hit the door, and O'Reilly's giant minion, who had locked her inside, opened the door. "Maisie? You okay?"

She nodded, but didn't say anything. He must have noticed her tears, because he rushed inside and lifted her up. "Come on. Let's get you something to eat." He glared at Zoe and then slammed the door shut, the lock clicking before they walked away.

The way he cared for Maisie made Zoe feel a bit better. Someone gave a damn about her. Not in a normal adult-child relationship, but he minded her and cared about her feelings. That show of empathy toward her wouldn't get Zoe out of this situation, but it did give her an opportunity to help her own circumstances.

She grabbed the iPad from the table and found it was protected by a password. While she couldn't get into the programs, she saw that it had an internet connection. If she could convince Maisie to log on, she could contact Noah or Allison. She placed it back on the table and sat on the couch again as Maisie returned, carrying a can of Coke and a handful of Oreo cookies. The man never came back, instead, he opened the door enough for Maisie to return and then locked the door behind her.

"Thank you, Freddy," she called out through the door before sitting on the couch beside Zoe.

Freddy.

"Feeling better?" Zoe asked Maisie, as the little girl sat in one of the two chairs at the desk.

She smiled between sips of soda. "Do you want a cookie?" Maisie held out an Oreo.

Zoe wasn't sure when or if they'd feed her, so she accepted the gift and thanked her. "Do you want to read some more?" she asked, trying to build up their trust.

"No." She glanced down at the book, a frown forming all over again.

"Hey, it's okay," Zoe replied, her heart aching for her. "Letters can be tricky. A *C* can be like four different sounds, and it takes a while to figure out which is which. They don't always look the way they sound. Words can be trickier. English is a very difficult language to learn. Many adults have trouble too."

Maisie looked up, her eyes searching Zoe's. "I thought... I thought I was just dumb," she confessed.

Zoe's heart clenched at Maisie's words, a fierce protectiveness rising within her. "No, Maisie, you're definitely not dumb. I've worked with lots of kids who see words in a different way from other kids. Have you ever heard of dyslexia?"

Maisie shook her head. Zoe explained it in the simplest terms that would hopefully encourage Maisie and not crush her under a label. "Dyslexia means your brain has a different way of looking at words than other people. It doesn't mean someone can't read or learn, they just need some different strategies to help. I bet if you speak to your teacher, they can get you tested to find out if you see the words differently too."

"Maybe I can go home if I'm better. Mom said I have to study really hard and maybe we can be together again."

Her words broke Zoe's heart. How could a man be so cruel to the woman he'd married and his child? Then again, he thought nothing of murdering Mrs. Peterson. "Anything is possible." And she meant it.

"So, I'm not stupid?" she asked, a glimmer of hope breaking through her uncertainty.

Zoe held her small hand. The connection, the human touch, fortified Zoe and reminded her of what was at stake. She needed to protect Maisie, to get them both out of this nightmare.

"Absolutely not," Zoe replied, her voice firm. "You're incredibly smart, Maisie. And I think you are brave too. Being here, away from your mom and dad. That takes a lot of courage."

Their conversation meandered then, from ballet classes to the yellow curtains in her bedroom.

Zoe reached across the couch and picked up the stuffed dog. "Who is this?"

"That's Buttons. He's my puppy." She put her arms out and

Zoe brought him to her. She squeezed him close when he was in her arms. "He's very naughty sometimes."

"Naughty dogs are sometimes very smart and feel bored."

"I think he's very bored. He bites people too."

"Does he? He doesn't bite you and he didn't bite me."

"He liked you."

That was exactly the type of statement Zoe wanted to hear. It meant Maisie was building trust in her. Even though they'd only known each other an hour or so. So perhaps she could convince Maisie to let her use the iPad. One step at a time. Not too much pressure, but she couldn't wait too long either in case Maisie was summoned back to her father's house.

Zoe flopped down on the couch. She made a dramatically loud sigh. "I'm bored too. Do you have any games on the iPad?"

Before answering, Maisie jumped up and ran over to the table as though she'd forgotten that she had it. She carried it back to the couch, but by the time she arrived, she'd already put in the password. They played Minecraft, Maisie focused on building a zoo, while Zoe cheered her on. When she asked if she could try, she purposely hit the off button.

"Oh no. I think I messed it up." She stared at the screen acting as confused as possible.

"I can fix it," Maisie offered. She took the iPad back and plugged in the password—1235. Not too hard to remember. After a few minutes, Maisie banged on the door to go to the bathroom. Although Zoe felt the need for a bathroom break as well, she let Freddy lead Maisie from the room, locking Zoe inside with the iPad.

She unlocked the iPad and logged on in order to Direct Message Noah. Only she didn't know Noah's information. So she contacted Allison instead. She found a way to drop her location into the map and sent a screenshot of it to her. Her only message was "hurry, with Maisie."

Just as she finished logging out and cleaning the account, Maisie returned.

Zoe returned to Minecraft. "I think I figured out how to get a camel."

But Maisie wasn't listening. She was occupied with what

sounded like a dog. Zoe tossed the iPad aside and watched in confusion as Maisie led Marlowe in on a leash. He wagged his tail and became excited at the sight of her.

"I think he likes you," Maisie squeaked. "My dad sent him to me. He said I could keep him."

Freddy stood in the door with a slight smile on his face, as though Maisie having this dog was a good thing.

If Marlowe was in the warehouse, that meant they'd found Allison and Meaghan. Zoe nearly buckled at the thought of more harm coming to her sister.

"Where did you get him?" Zoe asked Freddy, who ignored her. "WHERE DID YOU GET HIM?" she screamed out, panic filling her.

He replied by slamming the door shut again.

Maisie stared at her, her demeanor now walled off toward Zoe. Marlowe continued to wag his tail, only he rushed to Zoe's side and licked her face. Zoe rubbed Marlowe's ears and placed her forehead to his. The comfort she received helped her get her emotions under control again.

"This is Marlowe," Zoe explained as calmly as possible to avoid bursting into tears. "He's an old friend of mine." She didn't want to lie to the little girl, but she didn't want to spill the truth either. The truth being that Maisie's father was the devil incarnate. As Zoe blamed herself for how bad her charade had gone, she made a weak attempt to be happy so as not to scare Maisie any further.

"Hi, Marlowe." Maisie sat on the floor and Marlowe rushed to her, wagging and licking and hopping onto her lap. She laughed. "He's so silly."

Zoe sniffled. "He is." Never the best guard dog, but always the best companion.

Zoe held on to the hope that Noah and the others were searching for them, that they'd soon be rescued. But she wouldn't rely on that. There were no guarantees. As she played with Maisie and Marlowe, she began to make a plan.

When the door creaked open, Freddy walked in with a box of pizza and two sodas. Maisie's eyes lit up at the sight of the pizza. Zoe's stomach growled.

"How's your dog?" her jailer asked.

Maisie grabbed Marlowe and gave him a hug before saying, "He's hungry. Can he have a slice of pizza?"

"Sure." He winked at her, ignored Zoe, and then slammed the door shut, leaving them once again in isolation.

"Dad always orders pizza to eat on Friday nights. Maybe he's coming back to get me soon."

"Maybe. Let's eat," Zoe said, forcing a smile as she opened the box. Melted cheese and tomato sauce masked the smell of oil and dust.

They ate in silence, the pizza taking up the focus of everyone's attention, including Marlowe. Zoe took a huge bite and tried to figure out a way to escape with Maisie and now Marlowe too. She couldn't focus on what had happened to her sister, so she ignored the raw ache lingering in her chest. There was no proof of any foul play, besides Marlowe's presence with them. The truth was that Marlowe's presence was a glaring sign that Allison had been found and harmed, but Zoe had to believe that Allison was safe. If she didn't, she'd completely fall apart and would be no use in getting herself and Maisie out of there.

As darkness enveloped the warehouse, Maisie began to cry.

Zoe pulled her onto her lap on the couch. "What's the matter?"

"I want to go home."

"I know. Maybe your dad is just late. He works long hours."

Maisie nodded and leaned her head on Zoe's shoulder. It would be impossible to understand everything this child felt in this situation. Abandoned by her father, taken from her mother, and left to be raised with men who thought nothing of kidnapping and murder.

No light came under the door. It appeared they'd closed up shop and left Maisie and Zoe in the warehouse alone for the night. Zoe set Maisie up with Minecraft on her iPad. She acted as though she'd never played before, although she'd made it a habit to try out whatever the most popular games were in order to understand the other worlds her students visited. Maisie was more than happy to explain everything. They remained next to each other, with Marlowe curled up beside Maisie. When

Maisie stopped talking, becoming more absorbed by the technology, Zoe made her move. Compelled by curiosity, Zoe rose, her movements casual as she approached the file cabinets. She didn't want to alert Maisie to what she was doing. She opened each drawer, finding files and information that perhaps they hadn't meant to leave with her.

Maisie looked up, her expression a question.

Zoe thought fast. "Do you know if there are any blank pages in the drawers? I'd love to draw something." She picked up a few files and glanced through them, making a disappointed face when she read the front pages. In reality, those first pages told her a few things that might help put O'Reilly behind bars. They had inventories of various stores throughout Boston. One of them also contained a map with some random symbols on it.

She took out the map and drew on it with a golf pencil she found under some of the files. While Maisie remained engrossed in the game, Zoe flipped the map over and examined it more closely. From the information she'd acquired from Noah and Fiona, this was a map of the properties that O'Reilly had tried to get permitting for in Brendan Quinn's district.

Maisie was still playing her game. Zoe went back to the file cabinet and flipped through a few more files. Permitting issues, zoning requirements, and other building issues had been listed out for a variety of properties. All of the addresses were located on the map.

Finally, Maisie fell asleep, the iPad dropping onto the couch bedside her. Zoe ignored Marlowe's thumping tail as she picked up the iPad and used it to take a picture of the map and some of the other documents. Then she sent them to her sister and hoped someone on the other side would receive them.

"Don't let the mobs escape," a tired voice warned Zoe.

Not quite sure what a mob was, Zoe pulled up the Minecraft screen again and handed it back to Maisie. "I wasn't playing, just enjoying your work. You did a great job."

"Thanks." Maisie put the iPad down next to her, curled into Marlowe and fell asleep again. There was nothing else to do, so Zoe sat on the other side of the couch and grabbed some sleep too.

Chapter Twenty-Eight

The search of the old retail site proved fruitless. The storefront had large windows boarded up and a few cameras set up around the periphery. Fiona and Noah walked around, giving a wide berth to the cameras while Jason remained in the car. They both stopped at a faint buzzing sound headed toward them. As Fiona stepped toward a dumpster, Noah dropped to the ground. He landed in a puddle that smelled like something had died there. The buzzing disappeared and Noah stood up.

"That was dramatic," Fiona said, holding back a smile.

"What was that?" He'd been attacked in the most unexpected ways in the past twenty-four hours and his body reacted to every anomaly.

"A microdrone. Jason prefers using them for surveillance when we don't know what we'll encounter. People can set booby traps in abandoned property to keep out trespassers. It's too much of a risk to go in and potentially trip a wire. Their protection systems may even *accidentally* burn the place to the ground, which would provide them with a lucrative amount of insurance funds. A win-win for them, a potential lost limb for us." She waved him back to Jason's car.

Jason's laptop, sitting next to him, showed an infrared video from the drone flying through the second floor of the building. Despite focused attention on every corner of the building, they saw nothing but abandoned clothing racks and a few mannequins.

By the time the drone returned to the parking area, Jason wore a tight frown on his face. "Cross this building off the list. Where are we headed next?" he asked, attaching the drone battery to a charger and putting the drone in a hard case.

Fiona looked at her list. "A three-building complex, former housing project, about a half mile from here. The police had been called a few times in the past few weeks for trespassers, but overall, it's pretty quiet."

Noah wanted to have some hope, but he was a pragmatist. If the next group of buildings had trespassers, then O'Reilly wasn't protecting it enough. So the chances of Zoe being there seemed low.

A sharp ring cut through their conversation, silencing them. The name "Meaghan" flashed in bold font on his phone screen. He answered her over the speaker of the car, allowing Meaghan's voice to fill the space of his Explorer.

"Meaghan, I have Noah and Fiona on the line." He gave her a heads-up of the audience.

"Good. We had a breach. Two armed men," she reported as though she'd just escaped a war zone.

The words hit Noah like a freight train. "Damn. Are you and Allison okay?"

"You should be asking about the two men. One is at the hospital under police guard with a significant bullet wound in his stomach and the other might have a broken leg, but he took off with Marlowe. Allison is upset, understandably, but physically fine."

"And you?" Jason asked, his voice tight with concern.

"I may have a bruise on my jaw, but otherwise, I'm good." She sounded a bit winded, but completely professional. "I'm in the process of finding a new location. It will be low-tech except for my phone."

"How did they find you?" Noah asked. His need to understand the entire situation was imperative to find and then protect Zoe going forward.

"Allison had logged into one of the nurse's phones that she'd stolen at the hospital. They tracked her. It also explains why they went after Zoe. Allison had agreed to stay off the investigation, but she was blogging details in order to keep herself in the story. She could have been killed. *A stupid thing to do*," she said, her voice chastising Allison, who had probably already endured a verbal backhand from Meaghan laced with annoyance and anger. She hated when clients placed others in danger.

"What about Marlowe?" Allison said from Meaghan's end. She sounded exhausted, but alert.

"Marlowe will probably be fine. If they didn't kill him in front of you, he has a decent chance of just being let go. Are you as concerned about Zoe?" Fiona's normally even-tempered voice was edged with irritation. "Your sister was out there protecting you, and you carelessly made her the target. If they saw that you're still on the investigation, and you then had announced that you'd be at the zoo for an interview, where the hell do you think a second team would be headed?"

Allison's reckless actions killed Tom and almost killed Zoe. That thought left a bitter taste in Noah's mouth. If something he did could put Elise in harm's way, he would never even think of doing it. His sister's life was worth more than anything he'd ever gain from a career.

"Meaghan, we have to go," Jason interrupted Noah's thoughts and Fiona's lecture. "We have another building to clear. Keep in touch with Calvin."

"Copy." And the phone went silent.

Noah wanted to wring Allison's neck. How selfish could a person be to put her sister at risk to get ahead in her job? That was the same BS his father would do to his own family. Everyone had to sacrifice their own needs for him to get ahead.

An hour later, they were no closer to finding Zoe. The three abandoned buildings had a few squatters living in them, but otherwise, were clear.

"Where are we going?" Jason asked as he put away his drone again.

Fiona punched up her list. "A warehouse by Andrew Station, up closer to Dorchester."

Noah already had the directions. "I'll see you there."

The drive to the third location would take twenty minutes, thirty if the lights and traffic worked against him. He could feel the clock counting down. Zoe would be exhausted and scared by now. They had to move through these next locations quicker. If she wasn't found soon, it would be more and more difficult to find her.

They drove from some bustling streets to areas where streetlights needed replacing and people seemed forgotten. The warehouse looked as large as an Amazon shipping facility, as though an entire town could be packaged up and delivered from the warehouse to anywhere in the world.

Noah slipped into the back seat of the Explorer when they parked. "What do you think?" he asked Jason and Fiona.

Fiona pointed to the cameras at each of the corners of the warehouse and over entrances, all fairly new technology. "We need to clear through that mess. But there's a light on in that small window to the right. There are also about three expensive cars parked at the building that no one would leave in view without a certainty that there was adequate protection."

Jason nodded. "I agree. Let me send the drone once around to look for anything you missed, and then we head in." He pulled out the microdrone and it circled the building just above the height of the cameras.

While he was looking for problems, Noah prepared to enter. He slipped on a pair of thin gloves that had enough of a grip to help him climb, if necessary. A utility belt held his handgun, a knife, and a small set of binoculars. By the time Jason had finished his task, they were ready to head toward the door. Jason wore asphalt gray and slid through a partially open loading dock. Fiona slipped into the darkness like a shadow, her movements more cat than human. Noah took a path that required him to navigate the unseen margins of the warehouse.

A car accident on the street in front of the building that sounded as if it crashed into a dumpster shattered the quiet of the area. Noah took advantage of the noise and sneaked through the back entrance and straight past the camera. Hopefully, if someone were watching the cameras, the accident would draw their attention just enough so he could get inside.

The interior was a maze of rows of cars and abandoned rooms. Almost no light penetrated the grimy windows. Cars in various stages of disassembly created an obstacle course. If Zoe was in the building, she wouldn't be lingering with the skeletal remains of an Acura. She'd be hidden in a side room.

Noah paused, ducking behind a half-stripped sedan, as the faint sound of voices reached his ears. He focused his attention on the movement around him. The steps and voices grew louder. He peered over his shoulder and saw shadows a few rows over.

"Check on the accident outside. Make sure the police keep their attention on it and nothing on our property," said a man with a deep voice and a body size to match.

The two men split. Noah had crouched low and remained silent as their steps faded in different directions. He waited for a few minutes to ensure that he was alone and continued toward the back wall. Lined with drywall, unlike the concrete of the main area, it would have offices and other rooms. On one end, he could see several video monitors through a small glass window in the door. The rooms next to that one had no light coming from under them, so he ignored them and continued down the line. A commotion from further inside had Noah on alert. He could rush there and risk missing Zoe, or he could leave the sound and keep moving door to door.

Chapter Twenty-Nine

Zoe wasn't able to sleep. She listened to the creaking joints of the old building. The door opened, and she tensed. Marlowe barked and hopped up to check out their visitor. Instead of attacking, he wagged his tail and jumped up on Freddy. Zoe was terrified the huge man would club the dog away from him, but he merely put his hand down and rubbed his head, then shifted him to the side so he could enter.

He walked over to Maisie and pulled her blanket up over her. Then nodded to Zoe. She lifted her head, about to say something, but he didn't feel threatening, so she remained where she was. Before he left the room, he picked up the pizza box and the drinks.

Zoe stayed silent until he was gone. In the silence, she noticed one very important thing. She didn't hear the familiar clip of the lock each time someone came and went into the room. Freddy hadn't locked the door after him. A few minutes after he left, she walked over and slowly tried the doorknob. It turned with ease, and she pulled it enough to peek out the door, and then close it without a sound. She took a deep breath, trying to remain calm. This was her chance to get out.

"Maisie," Zoe said, shaking Maisie's shoulder gently. "We can leave now."

Maisie yawned and stretched, and then looked at Zoe, snuggling her stuffed dog tight. "I have to stay here until I go home."

It was a Friday night. There was no school the next day. Was this jerk going to leave his daughter in a warehouse all weekend?

"And I don't wanna leave Freddy. I like him," she said.

"Freddy wants you to be safe, and that means getting out of here." She tried to reason with her, but this couldn't become a lengthy debate. Zoe felt an urgent need to move now or lose her chance. "What about your mom? Don't you want to see her?"

That seemed to do the trick because Maisie sat up and was more enthusiastic than only a minute ago. "Will you stay with me the whole time?" Maisie's waking voice was barely a whisper.

"Every step of the way," Zoe assured her. Not that she was so certain about this plan either but knew she wasn't going to be safe if she remained.

Maisie finally nodded, slipping her little feet into her sneakers. "Okay."

Zoe breathed a sigh of relief. She pulled the door open with caution and peered into the hall. It was dark and quiet inside the warehouse with none of the rustling of people working on cars or the whirring of drills and other tools.

"Maisie, stay close," she whispered, her heart pounding as she stepped into the dimly lit corridor. The little girl's hand gripped hers.

With each step, Zoe's hope grew, the possibility of escape becoming a tangible reality. Marlowe remained with her, although without a leash, she couldn't guarantee he wouldn't run off.

But as they reached the back exit, one of the men Zoe had seen earlier stood there, his hand on a holster. Marlowe rushed to him, and she almost took that chance to slip around him and run, but when the man kicked the dog, something snapped inside of her. She punched at the man's face, only he caught her fist before it made its mark. Her brief moment of hope shattered as he twisted her arm behind her back, turned her around, and walked her back to the room. Maisie and Marlowe followed, no force needed for either of them.

He pushed her into a chair, and when she tried to stand he grabbed her hair and pulled until she was seated. He tied her hands behind her back, the thin rope biting into her skin. When he left, the lock clicked behind him.

Maisie's cries filled the room, a heartbreaking sound that pierced Zoe's heart. "Daddy's going to be mad at me."

Zoe calmed herself at that statement. Her attempt to flee might have created a dangerous situation for Maisie. She might have been safe if she merely remained quiet in the room, but sneaking out with Zoe meant she could be punished.

She struggled against her bonds, her gaze meeting Maisie's tear-streaked face. "It's going to be okay, Maisie. I promise, I'll tell your father it's my fault."

As they sat in the darkness, the hope of escape became a cruel joke.

But even in her lowest moment, Zoe refused to give in to despair. She had to believe that they would be found, that Noah and the team were out there, searching for them.

Chapter Thirty

Noah remained crouched by one of the cars, staying hidden, but able to see down the long wall of doors. He heard shuffling feet, muffled thumps, and perhaps someone swearing in an angry voice. The sounds drew him to one of the doors toward the end of the building. He paused, frozen, as he saw Zoe pushed through the doorway by one of the guards, a little girl following her, and to his surprise, Marlowe. Allison's dog trotted in after them, his tail between his legs, and he seemed to be limping. The guard pushed Zoe into a chair, and Noah nearly sprinted into the room to destroy him. But patience would keep them safer, so he squeezed his fists and stayed put. The guard, after a quick glance around, locked the door and left.

Waiting until the coast was clear, Noah approached the door. The key was in the doorknob, able to be opened from the outside. He entered.

"Zoe," he whispered. She was a mess, dressed in mechanic overalls, with a strained expression on her face.

She looked up with surprise, then relief. "I'm so glad to see you," she said.

"Who is this?" he asked in a friendly voice about the little girl on the couch as he untied Zoe.

"This is Maisie," Zoe said, her voice tender.

The little girl looked up at Noah with tears in her eyes. He had no idea who she was, but she'd just joined their team. He wasn't leaving this building without Zoe, Maisie, and Marlowe.

"And you've already met Marlowe," Zoe said.

Noah rubbed his fingers behind the dog's ears and touched his sore leg. Marlowe whimpered a bit, but was otherwise okay. "Allison's going to be happy to know he's been found."

"What happened? I was so worried about her."

"She and Meaghan had some unexpected visitors, but Meaghan handled it. They're both safe."

Noah glanced at the rope he'd untied from Zoe's hands, then at Marlowe. In a swift decision, he fashioned a makeshift leash and attached it around Marlowe's neck. "Let's go." He waved them to follow him and Marlowe.

They hadn't gone far when the sound of a gunshot echoed across the warehouse, followed by multiple shots, and then a small explosion. The building shook lightly and smoke began to fill the air.

"Keep close," Noah commanded, leading them through the maze of crates and machinery. The smoke billowed toward them, making it hard to see, but Noah kept moving through the cars toward an exit.

Another explosion rocked the building, sending a wave of heat and smoke in their direction but it didn't slow them down. He froze when they arrived at the exit and saw a wall of flames blocking them. He turned them around and led them to another door.

Chapter Thirty-One

Despite Noah's rescue attempt, Zoe found herself grappling with a terror that threatened to overwhelm her resolve. A tower of fire chasing them down.

Maisie clung to Zoe, her small body trembling with fear. Zoe, ignoring her own distress, wrapped an arm around Maisie, offering what little comfort she could. "We're going to make it out of here," she whispered, more a promise to herself than to the frightened child by her side.

When they turned a corner around a large pickup truck, they were blocked by one of the guards. As the guy reached for a gun, Noah shot him, and continued forward, pulling Marlowe with him. There was a strange sense of relief that the man wasn't Freddy. Maisie definitely acted as though he was a friend to her. Seeing him shot would devastate her.

They ran further and Noah stopped. Between another row of cars, Jason was on the ground, his head bleeding. Zoe nearly tumbled over in panic.

Maisie knocked her out of her paralysis when she asked if he was okay.

"I'm sure he is," Zoe lied.

Noah ran back to her and handed her the leash. "Take them and go."

She wanted to complain, but the fire was moving fast, and

she had to get Maisie to safety. She glanced back at Noah and Jason. Noah had rushed over to him, squatting down by his side. She couldn't do anything for them, so she ran toward the exit.

Zoe tried the door, but it was locked. Panic rose like bile in her throat, she had no idea how close another door was.

Fiona appeared from behind her.

"We can't get out," Zoe told her.

Fiona tried the door as well and it wouldn't budge. She told Zoe and Maisie to move away from the door. "I have a plan."

She climbed into the driver's seat of a forklift that was a few yards away from them. "Cover your ears," she shouted over the roar of the fire and the forklift's engine. With a determined grimace, she maneuvered the vehicle toward the door, the forks lowered like the lance of a charging knight. The impact was deafening as the forklift tore through the door. Fresh air rushed in to fill the void left by the broken door. She backed up and pointed for them to go through.

As they stumbled away from the warehouse, Zoe stopped in panic. Maisie was no longer by her side. She spun around, her eyes frantically searching the darkness for any sign of her.

"Maisie!" she yelled, despite the risk of alerting their whereabouts to their captors. With everything going on, they would not be the top priority to those men. Without a second thought, she released Marlowe's leash and turned back inside the warehouse.

Just in front of her, Noah shouted, as he carried Jason in a fireman hold over his shoulders. "Zoe?"

But Zoe was already moving back to the office, almost straight into the fire. Her lungs burned as the smoke obscured her vision. And then she saw her, coming out of the office—Maisie, coughing and scared, clutching her stuffed puppy to her chest. She'd gone back for her dog.

One of the burning cars, groaned ominously before a shower of sparks fell around them. Zoe wrapped Maisie in a protective embrace, shielding her from the falling debris.

"Zoe?" Noah's voice felt closer now. He appeared through

the smoke, no longer carrying Jason. Zoe handed Maisie over to him, the child's small form curled into his arms.

They made their way back toward the exit. The heat was unbearable, but the sight of the night sky through the broken doorway urged them forward.

As they emerged from the building, the cool air eased the burn in her throat. Behind them, the warehouse groaned as the entire building erupted in flames.

Maisie clung to Noah, shaking with sobs, part relief, part terror. Zoe, her own relief mingled with the aftershocks of fear, watched as the entire area filled with police cars and firetrucks. An ambulance arrived and Fiona stood over the EMTs as they lifted Jason onto a stretcher.

Chapter Thirty-Two

Under the sterile fluorescence of the police station, Zoe tried to relax, but so much had happened, she had a difficult time coming down from it all. They'd been assigned a small conference room to wait between police interviews. Noah sat across from her on the phone with Marlowe on his lap. Maisie rested on the floor with her stuffed puppy and a bag of pretzels.

"I've just spoken with Fiona," Noah said, putting his phone back in his pocket. "She's optimistic about Jason's recovery. Not a bullet, but a smack in the head by something flying through the air, probably in one of the explosions caused by one of O'Reilly's idiots sending a bullet into a generator. She's going to spend the night with him. He didn't need stitches, just a good cleaning and some bandages."

Relief washed over Zoe at his words. She'd been terrified that Jason had been grievously injured or worse. Despite the weariness that clung to her bones, she mustered a smile. "I can't thank you all enough. You came at the perfect time."

He offered her a smile in return, though it held shadows. "I was terrified we wouldn't be able to find you," he said. "If it wasn't for your phone, we'd be all over the city searching for the building."

"My phone?"

"It saved you."

She then remembered something. "I took photos on Maisie's iPad of everything I found in the files."

"Do you have it?"

She nodded and pulled it from her overalls. "Should I hand it over to the police?"

Noah thought about it and shook his head. "I think the person who hired us should have first dibs at that information."

She wouldn't argue. She trusted him completely.

"We should try to rest," he suggested, his voice a calm anchor in the storm that had been their night. "It's been...quite a night. And tomorrow isn't going to be any easier."

Zoe knew he was right. They were all running on fumes, and Maisie, the young girl who had become an unexpected responsibility, needed rest more than any of them. "You're right. Maisie, sweetheart, we're going to get some sleep soon, okay?" Zoe said, turning her attention to the child who had shown remarkable resilience in the face of fear.

Maisie's small voice broke the heavy silence that had resettled. "Did... Freddy make it out?" she asked, her eyes searching Zoe's for reassurance.

She leaned toward her, her voice gentle. "I think everyone made it out of the building, even Freddy." Although she really had no idea. But Maisie had been through enough, and she didn't need another thing to stress her out.

"Okay," Maisie said, and she took another pretzel out of the bag and bit into it. Her arms squeezed her stuffed dog a bit tighter. Someone from Social Services had already determined that Maisie wouldn't be returning to her father's custody, as the probability of him being arrested was high.

The conference room door burst open and a woman with long blond hair tied back in a ponytail rushed in. She scanned the room until she saw Maisie. The recognition was instantaneous, and Maisie's reaction was ecstatic.

"Mommy!" Maisie screamed, her voice echoing through the hallway as she jumped up and ran into her arms.

The reunion was a burst of raw emotion, the mother enveloping Maisie in a tight embrace, tears streaming down her cheeks as she whispered words of love and reassurance into her daughter's hair. Zoe watched, her heart swelling with a bittersweet joy at the sight of their reunion, feeling a sense of loss and relief as Maisie found solace in her mother's arms.

As the initial wave of emotion from their reunion eased, Maisie's mother, her eyes red from crying, turned to Zoe and Noah. "Thank you. I don't know how to ever repay you for bringing her back to me."

"Seeing you two together is more than enough," Zoe said. Then, remembering the discovery she'd made during their captivity, she added, "Do you mind if I ask you something?"

"Sure."

"Have you ever had Maisie diagnosed for reading difficulties?"

Maisie's mother frowned. "I haven't had any say in Maisie's education."

Zoe had seen plenty of parents use custody battles in an attempt to harm their former spouse, end up hurting their child instead. She nodded. "I understand. I'm a teacher, third grade."

"Really? I thought you were in law enforcement?"

"No. I just had a wonderful opportunity to stay with Maisie." She picked the stuffed puppy off the floor and handed it to Maisie as she sat on her mother's lap. There was never an easy way to tell a parent something like this, so she just stated her belief and hoped for the best. "I think Maisie might have dyslexia. It could be why she's been struggling in school."

The revelation seemed to take Maisie's mother by surprise. This often happened when Zoe discussed learning disabilities. "Dyslexia?" she repeated, her gaze shifting to Maisie, who looked back with a mix of apprehension and hope.

Zoe nodded, her voice soft but firm. "Maybe. I wasn't able to truly diagnose her with four books and a few hours, but it's a possibility. If she does have it, it doesn't mean she can't learn or succeed. There are strategies and resources that can help Maisie be a great student. It might be challenging, but she's so smart and brave, she can conquer anything."

A glimmer of hope replaced the fear in the mother's eyes. "Thank you," she said again, her voice steadier. "I'll make sure she gets the help she needs. I... I had no idea."

Glenn Morrow, Allison's producer, stood by the door and watched the reunion. His face seemed pale without the bravado he'd exhibited at the newsroom. He walked up to Zoe and apologized. "Patrick O'Reilly wanted you out of the picture. I had to follow his orders or he threatened to harm Maisie."

Zoe didn't bother explaining she wasn't Allison. Instead, she nodded toward him and then turned back to Maisie, giving her a huge hug. "Be good for your mom."

"I will," she said, wearing a smile that declared that she was finally home,

As Maisie's mother gathered her daughter to leave, Zoe felt a pang of emptiness. The adrenaline that had sustained her was fading, leaving exhaustion in its wake. She wasn't ready to face the solitude of her own home—not yet.

Turning to Noah, who had been a constant presence by her side, she hesitated a moment before speaking. "Noah, I…would it be okay if I crashed at your apartment again tonight? I'm not quite ready to go home and I don't want to stay at Allison's place."

Noah's response was immediate, his warm smile reaching his eyes. "Of course, Zoe. My place is your place, for as long as you need."

Zoe felt a wave of calm at his words. The idea of a quiet space to process everything that had happened, away from the echoing emptiness of Allison's apartment or the guest room at headquarters, and before she boarded the ferry back to Nantucket, offered some comfort she hadn't realized she needed until now.

Chapter Thirty-Three

In the soft glow of his waterfront apartment, Noah found himself sharing a peaceful moment and another grilled cheese with Zoe. They had been through a whirlwind and Zoe had to be exhausted. She'd held herself together and Noah was convinced she'd been strong for the benefit of Maisie. If she'd fallen apart, the little girl would have been far more traumatized after witnessing a death and outrunning a raging fire.

As they settled into the comfort of the living room, the tension that had accompanied their adrenaline-fueled day dissipated.

"I was so incredibly proud of you today," Zoe said, her voice low and sincere. She moved closer, her presence a calming force. "And I... I care about you, more than I thought possible in such a short time," she admitted, her gaze locked with his, vulnerable and searching.

Their fingers intertwined naturally, as if meant to fit together all along. The distance between them on the couch gone.

The softness of her fingers and the sweetness of her breath forced him to acknowledge how bad he wanted her. He felt a shift within him. The barriers of their professional relationship, now gone, left them standing on new, uncharted ground. "We're not working together anymore," he said, the reality of their situation dawning on him, both liberating and daunting. "But, our jobs, they're still...complicated."

"I'm willing to make sacrifices if you are," Zoe whispered.

"Definitely," he replied. "I refuse to let you go. Not without exploring what this is between us." He'd have to speak to Jason, but there must be a way to stay in the field and still be a part of Zoe's life. A significant part.

She traced his lips with her finger until he bit it lightly. "I'm hoping it goes further than *The Princess Bride*," she teased, pulling his shirt over his head.

"And *John Wick*," he replied, doing the same to her shirt. She had on a simple white bra underneath. Despite his urgency, especially after the hell of a day they'd both had, he wanted to respect her pace.

Noah's breath hitched as Zoe stood, her movements deliberate and unhurried. She slipped out of her sweatpants, letting them pool around her feet and, with a soft sigh, unhooked the front of her bra. Her eyes never left his as she approached, the intimacy of the moment making his heart pound.

She straddled his legs and leaned in to kiss him, her lips tender and searching. Noah held her hips gently, his touch reverent as he pulled her closer. The world outside ceased to exist; it was just them, wrapped in a bubble of mutual longing and unspoken feelings.

Zoe let her head fall back, her body instinctively moving against his. Her vulnerability touched him deeply. He had intended to take things slow, to savor every moment and focus on her pleasure first. But the urgency in her movements spoke volumes about her needs, and he found himself matching her pace, his own desire heightened by the depth of their connection.

"I've been wanting this since the first time I stayed over here," she whispered, her voice trembling slightly. "I need to feel close to you tonight."

Noah cupped her face in his hands, his thumbs gently brushing her cheeks. "Whatever you want, Zoe. I'm here."

Their kisses deepened, growing more passionate, as they shed the last of their clothing. Every touch, every caress, a silent promise of love and devotion. Noah took his time exploring her, memorizing every curve. Zoe responded in kind, her hands roaming over his skin with a tenderness that made his heart ache.

When they finally came together, it was a culmination of all their unspoken emotions, the love, the fear, the relief of having survived. Their movements were slow and synchronized, a dance of two souls finding solace in each other. He held her gaze as he whispered her name like a prayer.

Zoe's breath caught, her fingers digging into his shoulders. "I love you, Noah." The words hung in the air, wrapping around them like a warm embrace.

"I love you too, Zoe," he replied, his voice thick with emotion.

They moved together, their lovemaking a gentle exploration of their connection. It was more than physical; it was a merging of hearts, a silent conversation of love and trust. They took their time, savoring each moment until they both found release, their cries mingling in the quiet room.

Afterward, they lay entwined in the delicate shimmer of the moonlight filtering through the curtains. Noah held her close, his fingers tracing idle patterns on her back, while she nestled against him.

As he drifted toward sleep, a sense of peace settled over him. They had found each other in the most unlikely of circumstances, and now he couldn't imagine a life apart. The night was still, the only sound the gentle thrumming of the waves on the rocks below.

Zoe broke the silence. "What happens next?" she asked.

He kissed the top of her head, a smile playing on his lips. "Something wonderful."

"Can we talk about the elephant in the room?" she said, her fingers caressing his arm.

He turned to face her, noting the seriousness in her eyes. He nodded. "What would that be?"

"The fact that your job has you jet-setting to who knows where and dodging fists and bullets, while I'm teaching third graders how to spell *Mississippi* on an island that barely gets cell service."

Noah smiled, appreciating her attempt to inject humor into their dilemma. "Sounds like the plot of a bad romantic comedy, doesn't it? *The Spy Who Taught Me*."

Zoe swatted his arm. "Be serious for a minute. I admire what you do, Noah. I saw you in action, saving us, being the hero. And I want you to thrive in your career, but I'm scared. Scared of the danger you face and scared of being left behind."

Noah took her hand, the gravity of her words settling over him. "I think you're the bravest person I know. You faced danger without any training, saved Maisie, and you still managed to locate enough evidence to put O'Reilly away for a long, long time. You're my hero."

"But that's just it, Noah. I don't want to be a hero, I just want to be with you. And I'm terrified of what your job means for *us*," Zoe confessed, her gaze locked with his. "Which is ridiculous, because you can't have an *us* after a week."

He squeezed her hand, his mind racing for the right words. "I won't lie and say my job isn't dangerous, not after you had bullets flying over your head, but the question of whether you and I can be an *us* is determined by...us. We can label this whatever we want."

Zoe sighed. "So, what do we do? I teach by day, you dismantle criminal organizations by night, and we meet in the middle for the occasional heart-stopping make-out session?"

Noah laughed, the tension between them easing. "I like the sound of that."

Their eyes met, a silent understanding passing between them. They were navigating uncharted waters.

"So, we take it one day at a time?" Zoe suggested, her voice steady.

"One day at a time," Noah agreed, pulling her into his arms.

In the quiet of the night, with Zoe's steady breathing as his only comfort, the reality of their choices settled around Noah like a heavy fog. He understood that for them to continue their journey together, they'd have to endure a mountain of challenges, but the thought of facing the world without Zoe by his side was unimaginable.

Chapter Thirty-Four

Zoe lingered in the doorway of Allison's apartment and smiled. Allison, her leg encased in a cast and elevated on a pile of cushions, had a makeup artist dabbling blush over her cheeks. Despite the constraints of her injury, Allison had transformed her living space into a makeshift newsroom, her commitment to journalism undeterred by physical limitations.

"Allison, you're a force of nature," Zoe remarked with a mixture of admiration and concern as she stepped inside, closing the door behind her before a hyper Marlowe escaped for a run down the hallway.

Allison's face brightened at Zoe's presence and she waved away the makeup artist to speak to Zoe alone for a minute. "Now that I don't have threats hanging over my head, I've got a story to tell, and a broken leg isn't going to stop me." She was still determined to complete her story about the city councilman being bribed by the Irish crime boss. O'Reilly didn't care about Allison's investigation anymore. He had far bigger problems. The documents Zoe had taken pictures of provided a crucial link in his illegal financial dealings. And there had been an undercover mole inside of his group. Zoe was convinced it was Freddy, a gentle giant, who had been a guardian angel to Maisie. In addition, their investigation helped get the mole in the FBI field office as well, one of O'Reilly's own men. The only negative for Allison had been when two other news stations broke the story. Allison, refusing to give up a scoop, had decided to make her own ordeal into a story. Zoe thought that was a brilliant way to get some credit for it, but warned her to not reveal Zoe's part. Allison promised, not that Zoe held her breath. She'd never trust her sister the way she had in the past, and in a way, that freed her from her complex over Allison's purported perfection. When push came to shove, Zoe wanted to be Zoe, not her sister.

She moved closer to Allison, sitting on the arm of the couch. "I know you'd do anything to get your story out. But remember, to think about collateral damage," she said, reaching out to gently squeeze her sister's hand.

"I will. And I'm sorry for everything." She seemed remorseful enough.

Their conversation was interrupted by a knock, followed by an assistant peeking in. "Allison, the crew is ready for you whenever you are."

"All right, give us a few minutes, please," she replied, turning her attention back to Zoe as the assistant disappeared.

A quiet resolve settle within Zoe. She'd decided to remain in Boston for a few days to assist her sister and spend her nights out with Noah. They could enjoy some time together before they had a separation. Summer camp began in a week and soon she'd be on the ferry home. Noah had to find out his next assignment, which could take him anywhere. But they had committed to merging whatever time they had free.

Their father had also moved in to help Allison for a few days, although he wanted to return to his boat and heal after the death of his best friend, Mr. Noonan. Living in a close community would provide him with support and take some of that burden off Zoe. They both had healing to do, and being surrounded by friends and neighbors who cared would make a huge difference. She couldn't wait to get back to their house and felt better with her dad living with her. Allison took their imminent departure well. Her college roommate would move in to help until she got the cast off.

"It won't be quiet when Dad and I leave."

"I prefer pandemonium. It relaxes me," Allison said with a smile. Then her expression softened, the gratitude in her eyes clear. "Zoe, thank you. I don't know what I'd have done without you."

Zoe smiled, warmth spreading through her at the thought of being able to give back to her sister. "I can't say placing my life in danger was fun, but I did enjoy being on camera for two days. It was so much fun. And I also had fun being your courier when you came back to your apartment. And your stylist, chef...whatever you needed."

Allison stared at Zoe's sweatpants and tank top. "Stylist?"

"Okay, maybe not that."

The mood in the room lightened. Their relationship wasn't perfect, but maybe it could be strengthened over time.

When the crew finally entered to film Allison's segment from her makeshift home studio, Zoe watched from the sidelines, pride swelling in her chest. Allison was a natural. Zoe, however, was done with her broadcast work. She wanted to return to her classroom full of children. Her only regret would be leaving Noah behind.

A few hours later, Noah arrived with their father. They'd bonded over their worry for Zoe, a very annoying thing for them to bond over in Zoe's opinion.

"I'm going to miss you, John," Noah said to her father.

"It's only a short ride over to the island. When you come, I'll take you out on the boat." He slapped Noah's arm, and while Noah smiled, there was something in his expression that told Zoe he might not be around enough to ever get out to the island. He had a meeting with Jason about his next assignment in the morning. For all Zoe knew, he could be flying off to Asia for three months. The thought made her stomach ache. The problem was that neither of them belonged in the other person's world.

"Sounds great," Noah answered in a noncommittal way.

She walked him to the front entrance so they had a moment alone. They chose to take a quick walk up to the State House and back, hand in hand. The black sky had a glitter of stars and probably satellites overhead. The hustle of the city had slowed a bit as people drifted back home and headed to sleep. They strolled along, step by step. Zoe couldn't think of any words to say to him that wouldn't make her overly emotional.

He spoke instead. "Have fun in summer camp next week."

She laughed. "It will be fun. Four weeks and then I'm preparing to be back in my classroom. You could quit your job and be one of my assistants."

"Sounds great, is the pay good?"

She shrugged. "Minimum wage."

"I'm ready. I'll tell Jason tomorrow." He squeezed her hand and her heart broke.

He turned to face her, pulling her into his arms. "I plan on coming by after my next assignment. I might not be able to travel there by private jet, but I'm sure I could catch a ferry easy enough."

"I'd like that, but promise me you'll stay more focused on your job than on me, because I know how important and dangerous it is." And the idea of anything happening to him…it scared her.

He drew her close, their breath mingling in the chill of the night air. The city stood still for a moment, the weight of the goodbye, even if temporary, drowning out their surroundings. His hands framed her face, as though he could imprint this moment into his memory forever. She closed her eyes and absorbed his touch. And then he kissed her, a whisper of love, a tenderness of care, a restrained passion. Perhaps in a year or two or three, they could find a way to make it work with less time apart and more time side-by-side.

He paused and rested his head against hers. The connection giving her a false sense of security. He'd been in her life for such a short time and yet she considered him home. His thumb brushed away a tear from her cheek.

He studied her face, tracing all of the contours with such a soft and gentle touch. "It's all going to work out."

"How?"

"It just will. As far as I'm concerned, we belong together, so we will be."

"That's profound."

"It's the truth." He kissed her again, his lips pressing softly against hers until she parted her lips. The gentle caress of his tongue against hers made her crave far more for the night and her entire life. She leaned into him as his hands held her close and refused to let go.

When they finally separated, Zoe tried to pull herself together but feared time and distance would keep them apart. She stood outside for several minutes after he drove away and let the tears fall.

Chapter Thirty-Five

Noah found himself staring at Jason on a computer screen. Jason's injury didn't allow him to get back into the office yet, but he insisted on running everything until his partner, Steve, got back in two days. He was in a sweatshirt in bed, with his wound covered and his whole face swollen. The air between them was charged with an unspoken understanding of everything they'd endured together and Noah's stepped-up belief in his own value on the team. Jason, looking as worn as any man who had been hit hard in the head, leaned forward, locking eyes with him.

"I haven't always supported you as a full-fledged member of the team. Perhaps it was your lack of on-the-ground training and experience. Ironically, Fiona, whose opinion I respect more than anyone, believed in you from the moment she met you. You not only put your life on the line for Matt, but you acted as both field agent and analyst in finding Zoe. Not many on our team could handle both roles simultaneously. You did a great job. Brendan Quinn is under arrest, as is the entire top tier of the O'Reilly crime family. Not only did we get them on conspiracy and bribing a government official, but the DA is also holding O'Reilly on kidnapping, murder, and assault charges. A lot of this is due to your vigilance. I should never have faulted you in Matt's kidnapping," Jason began, his voice tinged with regret. "It was my fault for leaving the team unprepared, and you...you took a bullet on top of it. I owe you for that and for this..." He gestured vaguely, encompassing the recent ordeal with Allison and Zoe Goodwyn. "You handled yourself on this case exactly as I'd hoped you would when I hired you years ago."

Noah absorbed Jason's words, a mix of surprise and appreciation warming him. "Thanks," he said. "I appreciated the opportunity to prove myself."

Jason didn't hand out compliments easily. That alone was enough to keep Noah happy in his work. Not one hundred percent happy though. He was missing something in his life... love. The job, however, wouldn't make having a relationship easy. He had to travel often and might work round the clock for days, weeks, and even months at a time, only then earning enough free time to have a normal life for a week or two. The unpredictability of it made for a difficult dating life. He'd seen both Sam and Meaghan experience the downside of their random hours on their relationships. Noah had never tried to fit someone into his life, but now that he'd met Zoe, it was all he wanted.

Since Jason spoke so highly of him, perhaps this was the best time to broach the subject of a different work schedule. No matter what happened between him and Zoe, the decision for more of life than he'd had before had solidified in the wake of recent events. Their conversation was abruptly interrupted by the sound of a door swinging open. Fiona, a woman with no understanding of hierarchy, barged into their meeting, her presence filling Jason's room with her intense energy.

"Sorry to interrupt, but I wanted to add to any praise Jason should have given to you." She practically pushed her injured husband out of the computer screen to speak to Noah. "Your analytical skills are near perfect, but your fieldwork, is topnotch. I'd have you as my partner anytime."

"I appreciate that."

"She's right. You're one of the best people we have in the field." Jason leaned back in bed. "I hope you're ready for something international, because we have a CEO of an AI company that could use some backup when he flies to Southern France."

"For how long?"

"About three months."

Three months was a lifetime when the woman he loved only had the summer free. "I'm glad you see my value because I've been thinking," Noah said, ignoring Fiona and focusing on his boss. "I'd like to step back a bit to have some more free time." His voice stayed steady despite the uncertainty of how his request would be received.

Jason's expression tightened. "Your timing is poor. We have more and more government contracts every month. We need all hands on deck."

"I work part-time, why can't he?" Fiona interjected, her tone challenging and playful, a smirk playing at the corners of her mouth.

Jason sighed, running a hand through his hair in exasperation. "That's different, Fiona, and you know it."

Fiona, unfazed, leaned against the wall, her gaze shifting between Jason and Noah. "Maybe it's time to think outside the box. If Noah needs the space, we should find a way to make it work. He's too valuable to lose."

Jason looked at Noah, his mouth open to say something, but nothing came out. It was good to see him struggling, because it meant he wanted Noah at Fresh Pond Security and Noah certainly wanted to stay.

"I have no plans on leaving, to be clear," Noah said to fill in the space left by Jason. "But I do require a different schedule."

Jason shook his head. "We're down to a skeleton crew as it is."

"Why don't we reach out to Finn? He left because you hid information from the team, Jason. But maybe it's time to beg and bring him back into the fold." Fiona's suggestion nearly knocked Noah over. It had been his wish for Finn to return, but it wasn't his decision, and every time they spoke, Finn didn't sound as though he'd ever come back. Being a good friend, Noah refused to broach the subject, but the prospect of Finn rejoining their ranks made him second-guess his own request to step back. Finn had been one of the most valuable assets on the team, his departure a loss that diminished Noah's work satisfaction. Yes, Noah loved his job, but he loved it more when his best friend had been with him. But would he be willing to forgive Jason for lying to him?

Jason seemed to consider Fiona's suggestion, the gears clearly turning in his head. "Finn, huh? That might just work," he conceded, the hint of a plan forming behind his eyes. "I suppose I'm the person who needs to reach out to him. Although I can't guarantee I'll have any luck with it."

"Until you grovel to him, which is precisely what needs to happen, you won't know what his decision is," Fiona said.

Noah remained silent. Perhaps he could put in a good word for Jason to Finn, or he could stay out of it. He didn't know which path would help Finn return.

"Is there a way I could have some time off this summer before we learn about Finn's potential return?" Noah asked.

"Anything's possible," Fiona replied.

Jason closed his eyes for a second then nodded. "Okay. I'll ask Meaghan to head to France," he pointed at Noah, "and you can look after one of the Kennedys on Martha's Vineyard for a week. Then you can take a few weeks off before Zoe's classes begin."

"How do you know I…"

Jason lifted a brow. Noah stopped his question because Jason knew everything. Besides, it wasn't as if he'd done a great job hiding his attraction for Zoe.

"Can you handle that?" Jason asked.

"I definitely can. Thank you." One week and then he could breathe.

Whatever the future held for him professionally, he knew that the connection he had forged with Zoe was something he wanted to pursue.

As the meeting drew to a close, Noah left with a sense of cautious optimism. Only time would tell if Finn would be willing to return to the team. Even more important, he had a schedule that just might turn his relationship with Zoe into something much, much more.

Chapter Thirty-Six

Nantucket had always been home for Zoe, but now she felt a strain on the island since the death of Mr. Noonan. She'd spent the past few weeks getting back into her old life, although the sleeves no longer fit and the waist was too tight. Her father had melted back into his day-to-day activities as though he hadn't lost his best friend and almost lost his daughters, although the retired cop had always faced adversity, such as the death of his wife, by working harder. He replanted some of the flowers trampled by first responders, polished his boat, and hung around at the police station offering wisdom for the price of a cup of coffee and some company.

Zoe buried her own trauma by surrounding herself in the laughter and energy of summer camp. She loved working with children outside and away from the rigidness of books and testing.

As sun filtered through the trees bordering the local park, casting shadows on the play fields, she organized a game of soccer among a group of enthusiastic children. Her laughter mingled with theirs, a sound of pure joy that felt worlds away from the tension and danger that had nearly killed her.

She paused to catch her breath, and a familiar figure caught her eye. Noah Montgomery, casual and relaxed, strolled up to the edge of the play area, watching her with an affectionate smile that made her heart skip a beat. His board shorts and Salt Life T-shirt had him blending in to the summer island crowd.

She turned to one of the camp assistants, a young woman helping some of the campers paint small rocks into ladybugs and spiders. "Hey Lori, can you take over on the field for a minute?" she asked, receiving a nod and a smile in response.

As Lori stepped in to continue the game, Zoe led Noah away from the laughter and toward a quieter spot under the shade of a large oak tree. He placed a wicker picnic basket on the ground. The coolness of the shade was a welcome respite from the summer heat, a secluded enclave where they could speak freely.

"I came to tell you in person that I've told Jason I need a break from security work," he said.

His announcement confused her. She'd been sure that he'd finally felt as though he had become part of a valuable team at Fresh Pond Security. Leaving now didn't make sense. "I don't understand. You're quitting your job?"

"No. I do love my work, but after everything that's happened, I think it's time I stepped back and found some balance. I'm working on an assignment by assignment basis. I figured I could up my workload when September comes and you return to the classroom."

Zoe's eyes widened. She'd expected to see him for a few days in the next few months. Instead, she'd have him for the whole summer. "Really? That's awesome. I can't think of anyone who deserves a break more than you do." She'd never thought they would be able to work out a situation where they'd be an actual part of each other's lives.

"I don't see myself at the beach for days at a time. I'd rather spend my time wisely," he said, his gaze locked on hers. A ball rolled over to them, and he kicked it back to the children.

"Are you looking for assistants?" he said, his voice carrying over playful shouts.

"Only if they can pass a rigorous background check," she teased.

Noah chuckled. "I don't think that'll be a problem," he said, his confidence evident in his easy stance.

"Are you sure being a camp counselor would be a break?"

"I can't think of anything better than being right here… with you."

The intensity of his words, the promise they held, filled Zoe with an overwhelming sense of happiness. She stepped closer, wrapping her arms around him in a hug that felt like a coming home.

"I'd like that," she whispered against his shoulder. The simple admission lifted the heavy weight she'd carried on her shoulders since the last time she'd seen him.

As they pulled back, their eyes met, and in a moment of mutual understanding, they leaned in for a kiss, simple and sincere. It was a kiss of new beginnings, of summers filled with possibility, and the promise of countless tomorrows.

When they finally broke apart, the world around them—the laughter of children, the rustle of leaves in the gentle breeze—seemed brighter.

Zoe pointed to the basket he brought. "What's in the basket? Is it a gift?"

"It depends? Can we consider this our first date?"

She glanced over at the children and the other counselors. She was on the clock, but everything for the moment seemed under control. "A quick first date."

"That's doable." He opened the lid, and pulled out two wrapped grilled cheese sandwiches and a tub of Chocolate Fudge Brownie ice cream.

"This is a pretty serious first date," she said, her voice light with laughter.

"I'm told it's the perfect lunch to capture the heart of a potential bride."

She nearly blushed at his remembering her statement about this meal on a first date would make her seriously consider marrying the man. She reached past the sandwiches for the pint of ice cream and then wrapped her arms around him again. "It sure is."

* * * * *

Romantic Suspense

Danger. Passion. Drama.

Available Next Month

Colton At Risk Kacy Cross
Renegade Reunion Addison Fox

....

Canine Refuge Linda O. Johnston
A Dangerous Secret Sandra Owens

....

LOVE INSPIRED
Searching For Justice Connie Queen
Trained To Protect Terri Reed

....

LOVE INSPIRED
Wyoming Ranch Sabotage Kellie VanHorn
Hiding The Witness Deena Alexander

....

LOVE INSPIRED
Lethal Reunion Lacey Baker
A Dangerous Past Susan Gee Heino

AVAILABLE NEXT MONTH!

THE McCORDS

LOGAN & RICO

Every cowboy has a wild side — all it takes is the right woman to unleash it...

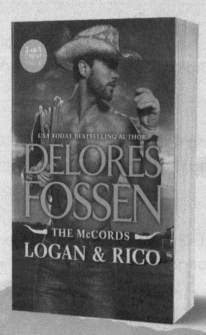

In-store and online February 2025